More Than
~Fire~

Tor books by Philip José Farmer

More Than
~Fire~

Philip José Farmer

A WORLD OF TIERS NOVEL

TOR®

A Tom Doherty Associates Book
New York

To Lynn and Julia Carl,
Gary Wolfe, and Dede Weil

This is a work of fiction. All the characters and events portrayed in this book are fictitious, and any resemblance to real people or events is purely coincidental.

Edited by David G. Hartwell

A Tor Book
Published by Tom Doherty Associates, Inc.
175 Fifth Avenue
New York, N.Y. 10010

Tor® is a registered trademark of Tom Doherty Associates, Inc.

ISBN 0-312-85280-0

Printed in the United States of America

1

*T*his'll be it!" Kickaha said. "I know it, know it! I can feel the forces shaping themselves into a big funnel pouring us onto the goal! It's just ahead! We've finally made it!"

He wiped the sweat from his forehead. Though breathing heavily, he increased his pace.

Anana was a few steps behind and below him on the steep mountain trail. She spoke to herself in a low voice. He never paid any attention to her discouraging—that is, realistic—words, anyway.

"I'll believe it when I see it."

Kickaha the Trickster and Anana the Bright had been tramping up and down the planet of the Tripeds for fifteen years. Their quest was not for the Holy Grail but for something even better: a way to get out of this backwater universe. It had to exist. But where was it?

Kickaha usually looked on the cheerful side of events. If they had none, he lit the darkness with his optimism. Once, he had said to Anana, "If your jail's an entire planet, being a yardbird isn't so bad."

Anana had replied, "A prison is a prison."

Kickaha had been carrying the key to unlock the gate leading to other worlds and to the mainstream of life. That key was Shambarimem's Horn, the ancient musical instrument he carried in a deerskin pouch hanging from his belt. During their wanderings on this planet, he had blown the Horn thousands of times. Each time, he had hoped that an invisible "weak" place in the fabric of the "walls" separating two universes would open in response to the seven notes from the Horn and make itself visible. There were thousands of such flaws in the walls.

But, so far, he had not been in an area where these existed. He knew that, every time he blew the Horn, a flaw, a way out of their vast prison, might be a hundred yards away, just out of the activating range of the Horn. As he had said, knowing that made him feel as if he owned a ticket in the Irish Sweepstakes. The chances of his winning that would be very, very low.

If he could find a gate, an exit deliberately made by a Lord and often evident as such, he would have won the lottery. The natives of this planet had heard rumors of gates or what could be gates, countless rumors. Kickaha and Anana had followed these, sometimes for hundreds of miles, to their sources. So far, they had found only disappointment and more rumors to set them off on another long trail. But today, Kickaha was sure that their efforts would pay off.

The trail was leading them upward through a forest. Many of the giant trees smelled to Kickaha like sauerkraut juice mixed with pear juice. The odor meant that the leaves at the tips of the branches would soon be mutating into a butterflylike, but vegetable, creature. The brightly colored organisms would tear themselves away from the rotting twigs. They would flutter off, unable to eat, unable to do anything but soar far away before they died. Then, if they were not eaten by birds on the way, if they landed on a hospitable spot, the very tiny seeds within their bodies would sprout into saplings a month later.

The many marvels on this planet made it easier to endure their forced stay on it, Kickaha thought. But the longer they were here, the more time it gave their archenemy, Red Orc, to track them down. And Kickaha also thought often of his friends, Wolff and

Chryseis, who had been imprisoned by Red Orc. Had they been killed by Red Orc, or had they managed to escape?

Kickaha, who on Earth had been named Paul Janus Finnegan, was tall, broad-shouldered, and muscular. The exceptional thickness of his powerfully muscled legs made him look shorter. He was deeply sun-browned; his shoulder-length and slightly curly hair was red-bronze; his face was craggy, long-lipped, and usually merry. His large wide-set eyes were as green as spring leaves.

Though he looked as if he were twenty-five years old, he had been born on Earth seventy-four years ago.

Buckskin moccasins and a belt were his only clothing. His belt held a steel knife and a tomahawk. On his back was a small pack and a quiver full of arrows. One hand held a long bow.

Behind him came Anana the Bright, tall, black-haired, blue-eyed, and also sun-browned. She came from a people who thought of themselves as deities, and she did look like a goddess. But she was no Venus. A classical scholar seeing her slim and exceptionally long legs and greyhound body would think of the hunting goddess, Artemis. However, goddesses did not perspire, and Anana's sweat ran from her.

She, too, wore only moccasins and a belt. Her weapons were the same as Kickaha's except for the long spear in one hand, and she bore a knapsack on her back.

Kickaha was thinking about the natives who had directed them up this path. They had seemed certain that the Door to the Sleeper's Tomb was on top of the mountain. He hoped that the Door was a gate. The natives he had questioned had never been to the mountaintop because they did not have the goods to give the Guardian of the Door for answers to their questions. But they knew somebody who knew somebody who knew somebody who had visited the Guardian.

This was probably another disappointing journey. But they could not afford to ignore any rumor or tale about anything that could be a Lord's gate. Anyway, what else did they have to do?

A little more than a decade and a half ago, he and Anana had escaped from the Lavalite World into the World of Tiers. Then, he had been very confident that they would soon be able to do what must be done.

Their adventures on the Lavalite World, that planet of insecurity, instability, and constantly shifting shape, had been harrowing. Kickaha and Anana had rested for several weeks after escaping from it to the World of Tiers. Then, having renewed themselves with rest and fun, they had sought out and found a gate that teleported them to Wolff's palace, now uninhabited. This was on top of the monolith on top of the World of Tiers.

They had armed themselves in the palace with some of the weapons of the Lords, weapons superior to anything on Earth. Then they had activated a gate that had previously passed them to a cave in a Southern California mountain. This was the cave through which Kickaha had first come back to Earth after many years of absence.

But when he and Anana had stepped through the gate, they had found themselves on a planet in this artificial universe, the Whaziss world. The gate had been a one-way trap, and Kickaha did not know who had set it up.

Kickaha had boasted more than once that no prison or trap could hold him long. Now, if those words could be given substance, he would have to eat them. They would taste like buzzard dung sprinkled with wood ashes.

Yesterday, he and Anana had stopped two-thirds of the way up the mountain and camped for the night. They had continued their climb at dawn and thus should, by now, be close to the top.

Five minutes later, he heard the voices of children drifting down the path. Within two minutes, they stepped over the edge of the small plateau.

The village in the middle of the plateau was much like others in this area. A circular wall of upright and pointed logs enclosed approximately forty log houses with conical roofs. In the center of the village was a temple, a two-story log building with a round tower on top and many carved-wood idols in and around it.

If the natives' stories were true, the temple could contain a gate. According to these, the building contained a vertical structure of "divine" metal. Its thin beams formed a six-sided opening into the world of the gods. Or, as some stories said, a door to the world of the demons.

The natives also said that the hexagon had been on the top of the hill before the natives were created by the gods. The gods—or the demons—had used the opening long before the natives came into being and would use it long after the natives had become extinct.

The first one to tell Kickaha this story was Tsash. He was a priest of a deity that had once been very minor but was now up and coming and perhaps destined to be number one on this island the size of Earth's Greenland.

Tsash had said, "The Door to the Otherworld is open. Anyone may step through it. But he will only find himself on the other side of the six-angled door and still in our world unless he can utter the magical word. And there is no assurance that he who does know the word will like what he finds on the other side."

"And just where is this door?" Kickaha had said.

Tsash had waved his hand westward. The gesture took in a lot of territory, since he was standing in a temple on a cliff on the shore of the Eastern Sea.

"Out there. It is said that the Door is in a temple—dedicated to what god, I do not know—which is on a hilltop. But then, all temples are on the tops of high hills or mountains."

"How many temples are there in this land?" Kickaha had said.

"Only the gods could count them, they are so numerous!"

He had lifted both four-fingered hands above his head, and he had cried, "Do not use the Door even if you find the magical word to open the Door! You may awake the Sleeper! Do not do that! You will die the Undying Death!"

"Which is what?" Kickaha had said.

"I do not know, and I do not wish to know!" Tsash had shouted.

Kickaha had asked more questions, but Tsash seemed to have submerged himself in prayers. His huge eyes were closed, and the mouth under the green hair growing all over his face was murmuring something rhythmic and repetitive.

Kickaha and Anana had left the temple and set out westward. Fifteen years later, after going up and down and around but always working toward the Western Sea, they were on another mountaintop with a temple on it.

Kickaha was excited. He believed that the long-sought gate was inside the building. Despite the many failures and consequent disappointments, he allowed himself to believe that their quest was at an an end. Perhaps "allowed" was not the correct word. He had no control over his enthusiasms. They came and went as they pleased; he was the conduit.

If Anana was delighted or expectant, she did not show it. Many thousands of years of life had rubbed away much of her zest. Being in love with Kickaha and sharing his adventures had restored some of this—far more, in fact, than she had expected. Time was a chisel that had reshaped the original substance of her spirit. Yet it had taken that relentless dimension a long, long time to do it.

"This has to be it!" Kickaha said. "I feel it in the bones of my bones!"

She patted his right cheek. "Every time we get to a temple, our chances to succeed increase. Provided, of course, that there is any gate on this planet."

The children playing outside the wall ran screaming toward them. Kickaha figured that they must have been forewarned. Otherwise, they would have run screaming away from them. The children surrounded the two and milled around, touching them, chattering away, marveling at the two-legged beings. A moment later, a band of armed males chased the youngsters away. Immediately afterward, the priest appeared in the village gate and waved a long wooden shaft at them. The outer end of this sported a scarlet propellor spun by the wind. Halfway down the shaft was a yellow disc bearing on its surface several sacred symbols.

Behind the priest came two minor priests, each whirling above his head a bull-roarer.

All the natives were naked. They were, however, adorned with bracelets and with ear-, nose-, and lip-rings. Their heads and faces were covered with a short greenish fur except for the chin region.

And they were three-legged.

Ololothon, the Lord who had long ago made their ancestors in his biology factory, had been very cruel. He had made the tripeds as an experiment. Then, having determined that they were functional though slow and awkward, Ololothon had let them loose to breed and to spread over this planet. They had no generic name for themselves, but Kickaha called them the Whazisses. They looked so much like the illustrations of a creature called a Whaziss in a fantasy, Johnny Gruelle's *Johnny Mouse and the Wishing Stick*, which Kickaha had read when very young.

Kickaha called out in the dialect of the locals, "Greetings, Krazb, Guardian of the Door and holiest priest of the deity Afresst! I am Kickaha, and my mate is Anana!"

Word of mouth had carried the news of the funny-looking bipeds and their quest to Krazb many months ago. Despite this, protocol forced him to pretend ignorance and to ask many questions. It also required that the council of elders and shamans invite the two strangers into the council house for the drinking of a local brew, for much talking, for a slow working up to the reason why the strangers were here (as if the Whazisses did not know), and for dancing and singing by various groups.

After three hours of this, the priest asked Kickaha and Anana what brought them here.

Kickaha told him. But that caused much more explaining. Even then, Krazb did not understand. Like all the natives, he knew nothing of the Lords or artificial pocket universes. Apparently, the long-ago dead Lord had never revealed himself to the natives. They had been forced to make up their own religion.

Though Kickaha did not succeed in making everything clear in Krazb's mind, he did make him understand that Kickaha was looking for a Door.

Kickaha said, "Is there one in your temple or is there not? Anana and I have entered more than five hundred temples since we started our search fifteen years ago. We are desperate and about to give up the search unless your temple does indeed contain a Door."

Krazb gracefully got to his feet from his sitting position on the ground, no easy movement for a triped.

He said, "Two-legged strangers! Your long quest is over! The Door you seek is indeed in the temple, and it's unfortunate that you did not come here straightaway fifteen years ago! You would have saved yourself much time and worry!"

Kickaha opened his mouth to protest the injustice of the remark. Anana put a hand on his arm. "Easy!" she said in Thoan. "We have to butter him up. No matter what he says, smile and agree."

The Whaziss's lips tightened and the place where his eyebrows should be under the green fur was drawn down.

"Truly, there is a Door here," he said. "Otherwise, why should I be called the Guardian?"

Kickaha did not tell him that he had met twenty priests, each of whom titled himself "Guardian of the Door." Yet, all of their Doors had been fakes.

"We had no doubt that your words were true," Kickaha said. "May we be allowed, O Guardian, to see the Door?"

"Indeed you may," the priest said. "But you surely are tired, sweaty, dirty, and hungry after your journey up the mountain, though you should no longer be thirsty. The gods would be angry with us if we did not treat you as hospitably as our poor means permit us. You will be bathed and fed and, if you are tired, you will sleep until you are no longer fatigued."

"Your hospitality has already overwhelmed us with its largesse," Kickaha said.

"Nevertheless," Krazb said, "it has not been enough. We would be ashamed if you left us and went to other villages and complained about our meanness of spirit and of material generosity."

Night came. The festivities continued under the light of torches. The humans fought their desire to vent their frustration and boredom. At last, long past midnight, Krazb, slurring his words, announced that it was time for all to go to bed. The drums and the horns ceased their "music," and the merrymakers who had not passed out staggered off to their huts. A minor official, Wigshab, led the humans to a hut, told them that they were to spend the night there on a pile of blankets, and wobbled off.

Having made sure that Wigshab was out of sight, Kickaha stepped outside the hut to check out the situation. Highly looped Krazb must have forgotten to post guards. Except for the drunken sleepers on the ground, not a Whaziss was to be seen.

Kickaha breathed in deeply. The breeze was cool enough to be pleasant. Most of the torches had been taken away, but four bright brands on the temple wall made enough light in this moonless night to guide them.

Anana stepped out from the hut. Like Kickaha, she had drunk very lightly.

"Did you hear Krazb when he said something about the price for admission to the Door?" she said. "That sounds ominous."

2

*I*t was too noisy. What did he say about the price?"

"That we'd talk about it in the morning. That there were two prices. One was just for looking at the Door. Another, the much higher price, for using the Door."

The price, Kickaha knew, would not be in money. The Whaziss economy was based only on the trading of goods or services. The only item of any value Kickaha could offer was the Horn of Shambarimem. Krazb wouldn't know what it could do. He would desire it just because there was nothing like it anywhere on his world.

Thus, he and Anana were not going to get through the Door unless they gave up the Horn. If they did not surrender it, they would have to fight the Whazisses whom Krazb would use when no one was watching.

He told Anana his thoughts while they stood in the doorway of the hut.

"I think we should sneak into the temple right now and find out if there is a gate. If there is, we go through it. Provided we can."

"That's what I expected," she said. "Let's go."

While they were putting on their belts, backpacks, and quivers, Kickaha was thinking, What a woman! No hesitancies, no shilly-shallying for her. She quickly figures out what the situation is—probably had it figured out before I did—and then acts as the situation demands.

On the other hand, he did get irritated sometimes because she knew what his thoughts were before he voiced them. And, lately, she obviously was having the same reactions to him that he was having to her.

For far too long, they had rarely been out of each other's sight, and they had been without the company of other human beings. The Whazisses were unsatisfactory substitutes for "people." They had a very stunted sense of humor and of art, and their technology had not progressed for thousands of years. Though they could lie, they were unable to conceive of the big whoppers that humans told just for the fun of it. Nowhere had Kickaha heard a Whaziss express an unconventional thought, and their cultures differed very little from each other.

Anana, holding her spear in one hand and a torch in the other, led the way. Tomahawk in hand, Kickaha walked a few steps back from her side until they reached the temple. The log building was dark. The guards who should have been here were drunk and snoring in the village square. While Anana followed him and cast the light of the torch around for him, he went around the temple to check for other entrances. But it had only one, the big wooden two-sectioned door in its front.

That had a thick wooden beam across the sections. He pulled it back from one of its slots and then swung a section back. Torch lights burning in wall sockets showed a smaller building in the center of the temple floor. It was a duplicate of the temple.

No Whaziss was here unless he was inside the House of the Door, as the priest had called it.

Kickaha shot back the bar on the small door and swung a section back. Anana got close behind him. He stayed outside the building but leaned far in to look around it. The two torches there lit up a structure flanked by two wooden idols.

Anana said, "At last!"

"I told you that this was it."

"Many times."

Both had seen gates like the one before them. It was an upright six-angled structure composed of arm-thick silver-colored metal beams. It was wide enough to admit two persons abreast.

They walked into the building and stopped a few inches from the hexagonal gate. Kickaha thrust the head of his tomahawk into the space enclosed by the beams. It did not, as he had half-expected, disappear. And, when he went to the other side and stuck the tomahawk in it, it was clearly visible.

"Unactivated," he said. "Okay. We don't need the codeword. We'll try the Horn."

He stuck the tomahawk shaft inside his belt and opened the bag hanging from his belt. He withdrew the Horn of Shambarimen from it. It was of a silvery metal, almost two and a half feet long, and did not quite weigh a fourth of a pound. Its tube was shaped like an African buffalo's horn. The mouthpiece was of some soft golden substance. The other end, flaring out broadly, contained a web or grill of silvery threads a half-inch inside it. The underside of the Horn bore seven small buttons in a row.

When the light struck the Horn at the right angle, it revealed a hieroglyph inscribed on the top and halfway along its length.

This was the highly treasured artifact made by the supreme craftsman and scientist of the ancient Thoan, which meant "Lords." It was unique. No one knew how to reproduce it because its inner mechanism was impenetrable to X-rays, sonic waves, and all the other devices of matter penetration.

Kickaha lifted the Horn and put its mouthpiece to his lips. He blew upon it while his fingers pressed the buttons in the sequence he knew by heart. He saw in his mind seven notes fly out as if they were golden geese with silver wings.

The musical phrase would reveal and activate a hidden gate or "flaw" if one was within sound range of the Horn. The notes would also activate a visible gate. It was the universal key.

He lowered the Horn. Nothing seemed to have happened, but just-activated gates did not often give signs of their changed state. Anana thrust the blade of her spear into the gate. The blade disappeared.

"It's on!" she cried, and she pulled the blade back until it was free of the gate.

Kickaha trembled with excitement. "Fifteen years!" he howled. Anana looked at him and put a finger to her lips.

"They're all passed out," he said. "What you should be worried about is what's on the other side of the gate."

He could stick his head through the gate and see what waited for them in another universe. Or perhaps somewhere in this universe, since this gate could lead to another on this planet. But he knew that doing that might trigger a trap. A blade might sweep down (or up) and cut his head off. Or fire might burn his face off. Sometimes, anything stuck through a gate to probe the other side conducted a fatal electrical charge or a spurt of flaming liquid or guided a shearing laser beam or any of a hundred fatal things.

The best way to probe was to get someone you didn't care for, a slave, for instance, if one was handy. That was the way of the Lords. Kickaha and Anana would not do that unless they had captured an enemy who had tried to kill them.

Her spear had come back from that other world without damage. But a trap could be set for action only if it detected flesh or high-order brainwaves.

Anana said, "You want me to go first?"

"No. Here goes nothing—I hope not."

"I'll go first," Anana said, but he jumped through the empty space in the hexagonal frame before she could finish.

He landed on both feet, knees bent, gripping his tomahawk and trying to see in front of him and on both sides at the same time.

Then he stepped forward to allow Anana to come through without colliding with him.

The place was twilit without any visible source of light. It was an enormous cavern with dim stalagmites sticking up from the ground and stalactites hanging down from above. These stone icicles were formed from carbonate of calcium dissolving from the water seeping down from above. They looked like the teeth in the jaws of a trap.

However, except for the lighting, the cavern seemed to be like any other subterranean hollow.

Anana jumped through then, her spear in one hand, a blazing torch in the other. She crouched, looking swiftly around.

He said, "So far, so good."

"But not very far."

Though they spoke softly, their words were picked up, inflated, and, like frisbees, spun back toward them.

Ahead was the cavern, huge as far as they could see. It also extended into darkness on both left and right. He turned to look behind him. The six-sided gate was there, and beyond it was more vast cave. Air moved slowly over him. It cooled off his sweating body and made him shiver. He wished that he had had more time to prepare for this venture. They should have brought along clothes, food, and extra torches.

The Lord who had set this gate up had probably done it thousands of years ago. It might have been used only once or twice and then been neglected until now. The Lord knew where other gates were and where they led to. But Kickaha and Anana had no way of knowing what to do next to get out of this world. There was one thing he could do that might work.

He lifted the Horn to his lips and blew the silver notes while his fingers pressed on the seven buttons. When he was finished, he lowered the Horn and thrust the tomahawk head through the gate. The head disappeared.

"The gate's activated on this side!" he cried.

Anana kissed him on his cheek. "Maybe we're getting lucky!"

He withdrew the tomahawk, and he said, "Of course . . ."

"Of course?"

"It might admit us back to the world we just left. That'd be the kind of joke a Lord would love."

"Let's have a laugh, too," she said. She leaped through the hexagon and was gone.

Kickaha gave her a few seconds to move out of his way and also to come back through if she had reason to do so. Then he jumped.

He was pleased to find that he was not back in the Whaziss temple. The stone-block platform on which he stood had no visible gate, but it was, of course, there. It was in the center of a round, barn-sized, and stone-walled room with a conical ceiling of some red-painted metal. The floor was smooth stone, and it had no opening for a staircase. There was no furniture. The exits were open arches at each of the four cardinal points of the compass; a strong wind shot through the arch on his left. Through the openings he could see parts of a long, rolling plain and of a forest and of the castlelike building of which this room was a part. The room seemed to be five hundred feet above the ground.

Anana had left the room and was pressed against a waist-high rampart while she looked at the scene. Without turning to look at him, she said, "Kickaha! I don't think we're where we want to be!"

He joined her. The wind lifted up his shoulder-length bronze-red hair and streamed it out to his right. Her long, glossy, and black hair flowed horizontally like octopus ink jets released in a strong sea current. Though the blue but slightly greencast sun was just past the zenith and its rays fell on their bare skin, it was not hot enough to withstand the chill wind. They shivered as they walked around the tower room. Kickaha did not think the shivering was caused only by the wind.

It was not the absence of people. He had seen many deserted

castles and cities. Actually, this castle was so tall and broad that it could be classified as a large town.

"You feel uneasy?" he said. "As if there's something unusually strange about this place?"

"Definitely!"

"Do you feel as if somebody's watching you?"

"No," Anana said. "I feel . . . you'll think I'm being irrational . . . that something is sleeping here and that it'll be best not to wake it."

"You may be irrational, but that doesn't mean you're crazy. You've lived so long and seen so much that you notice subtleties I can't . . ."

He stopped. They had walked far enough that he could see part of the view from the other side. Past the roofs of many structures, up against a hill of rock, was a round, bright blue structure. He resumed walking around the tower until he could see all of it. Then he stopped and gazed a while before speaking.

"That globe must be four or five miles from here. But it still looks huge!"

"There are statues around it, but I can't see the details," Anana said.

They decided that they would walk through the castle-city to the enormous globe. But the room had no staircase. They seemed to be imprisoned on the top room of the tallest tower in the castle. How had the former citizens gotten to this room? They busied themselves intently going over every inch of the inside and outside of the tower room. They could find no concealed door, no suspicious hollow spaces, nor anything to indicate a secret exit or entrance.

"You know what that means?" Kickaha said.

Anana nodded and said, "Test it."

He went to the side of the invisible hexagon opposite that from which they had stepped out. He lifted the Horn and blew the seven notes. Nothing visible happened, but when he thrust his tomahawk through the space where the hexagon must be, the weapon disappeared up to his hand. As they had suspected, each side was a gate.

"It's probably part of a gate maze," she said.

He leaped through the hexagon, landed on both feet, and stepped forward. Two seconds later, Anana followed. They were in a large, doorless, and windowless room made of a greenish, semitransparent, and hard substance. The room could have been carved out of a single huge jewel. The only light came from outside it. It showed unmoving objects too dim to be seen clearly. Against the wall opposite him was the outline of a hexagon in thin black lines. Unless a trick was being played upon them, the lines enclosed a gate.

The air was heavy, thick, stale, and unmoving. Near his feet were two skeletons, one human and one semihuman. In the midst of the bones were two belt buckles, golden rings set with jewels, and one beamer. Kickaha leaned over and picked up the pistollike beamer. That made him breathe deeper than he should have. The lack of oxygen was making his heart beat overfast, and his throat was beginning to tighten.

"I think," Anana said, "that we don't have much time to spend trying to get through the gate. Our predecessors didn't have the code, and so they died quickly."

Theoretically, the two previous occupants of the room should have used up all the oxygen in it. But there was enough here to keep the two from beginning to strangle at once. Obviously, the owner of the gate had brought in some oxygen to replace what the dead intruders had used. Just enough to torture the next occupants with the knowledge of their sure fate.

"We've got maybe a minute!" Kickaha said.

He pressed the button on the beamer that indicated the amount of energy left in the fuel supply. A tiny digital display by the button showed that enough fuel was left for ten half-second full-power bursts. After shoving the barrel of the beamer between his waist and his belt, he put the mouthpiece of the Horn to his lips. It was not necessary to blow hard. The output of the seven notes was at the same noise level, regardless of the input.

As the last silvery note bounced around in the small room, Anana thrust the head of her spear into the area of wall on which the lines were painted. It disappeared. Then she withdrew it. It showed no signs of damage or fire. That did not mean much, as both knew. Nevertheless, by now Kickaha's lungs were sending signals to him, and his throat seemed to be falling in on itself. Anana's face showed that she, too, was feeling panic.

Despite his increasing need for fresh air, he turned around and blew the seven-note sequence again, directing it at the blank wall opposite the inscribed one. It was possible that there was a gate there also, one its maker had hidden there. The gate with the hexagon might be a deadly trap for the uncautious.

He could not see any change in the wall, but Anana drove her spear hard against it at different places to determine if an invisible gate was there. The metal head clanged and bounced off the glassy substance, which boomed as if it were a drum. They would have to take the one way open.

Anana, her spear held out, leaped through the gate. He followed her several seconds later. As usual, he winced a little when it seemed that he would slam into the wall. Though his conscious mind knew that he would not do so, he could not convince his unconscious mind. As he passed through the seeming solid, he glimpsed the hexagonal structure a foot beyond the gate. Then he was through a second gate and had landed by Anana. She looked astonished. This was the first time she had encountered a second gate immediately beyond the first.

Fresh air filled his lungs. He said, "Ah! My God, that's good!"

If they had not had the Horn, they would be dead by now.

"Less than a second in one world and on to the next," Anana said.

They did not have much time to look around. Now, they were in an enormous room. The ceiling was at least a hundred feet high, and it and the walls were covered with paintings of creatures he had never seen before. The bright light came from everywhere.

And then the room was replaced by a sandy plain that stretched unbroken to a horizon much more distant than that on Earth, an orange sun, and a purple sky. The air was heavy, and Kickaha suddenly felt as if gravity had increased.

Before he could say anything, he and Anana were on the top of a peak, a flat area so small that they had to cling to each other to keep from falling off. For as far as they could see, mountains extended all around them. The wind blew strong and cold. Kickaha estimated it must be producing a chill factor of zero or lower. The sun was sinking below the peaks, and the sky was greenish-blue.

There was nothing to indicate that a gate was nearby. It was probably buried in the rock on which they were standing.

A few seconds later, they were on a beach that seemed to be tropical. It could have been on Earth. The palm trees waved behind them in the sea breeze. The yellow sun was near its zenith. The black sand under their bare feet was hot. They would have had to run for the trees if they had not built up such thick calluses on the bottom of their feet.

"I think we're caught in a resonant gate circuit," Kickaha said.

But hours passed, and they were not moved on. Tired of waiting for something to happen, they walked along the beach until they came to the place where they had started.

"We're on an island—actually, an islet," Kickaha said. "About half a mile in circumference. Now what?"

The horizon was unbroken. There could be a land mass or another island just beyond the horizon, or the sea could go for thousands of miles before its waves dashed against a beach.

Kickaha studied the trees, which had seemed at first glance to be palm trees. But they bore clusters of fruit that looked like giant grapes. If they were not poisonous, they could sustain life for some time. Maybe. The trees could be cut down and trimmed to make a raft with the beamer. However, there were no vines to bind the logs together.

The Lord who had arranged for his victims to stop here had meant for them to starve to death eventually.

Kickaha walked along the beach again while he blew the Horn. Then he walked in decreasing circles until the range of the notes had covered every bit of ground. There were no flaws or unactivated gates here. That the Horn could not reactivate the gate that had admitted them here meant one thing. It was a one-way gate. The Lord who had set this up had put a "lock" on it, a deactivating device. It was seldom used because it required much energy to maintain it. Also, not many Lords had this ancient device.

"Eventually, the lock will dissolve," Anana said, "and the circuit will be open again. But I think we'll have died before then. Unless we can get away from here to a large landmass."

"And then we won't know where we are unless we've been to this universe before."

He used the beamer to cut a cluster of the baseball-sized fruits from a branch. The impact of the fall split some open. Though he was forty feet from the cluster, its odor reached him immediately. It wasn't pleasant.

"Phew! But the stink doesn't mean they're not edible."

Nevertheless, neither offered to bite into the fruit. When they became hungry enough, they would try it. Meanwhile, they subsisted on the rations in their backpacks.

On the evening of the third day, they lay down on the beach to sleep. This area was where they had entered the universe, and they stayed within it as much as possible. If the gate was reactivated, they would be within its sphere of influence.

"The Lord has not only made us prisoner on this islet," Kickaha said. "He has also confined us to a cell of sorts. I'm really getting tired of being in a prison."

"Go to sleep," Anana said.

The night sky was replaced by bright sunlight. They scrambled up from their sand beds as Kickaha said, "This is it!" He and Anana grabbed their backpacks and weapons. Three seconds later, they were standing on a narrow platform and looking down into an abyss.

Then they were in a cave, bright sunlight coming from its opening. He lifted the Horn to his lips. Before he could blow it, they were on a tiny rock elevated a few feet above a sea. He gasped, cutting off his blowing of the Horn, and Anana cried out. A gigantic wave was charging toward them. Within seconds, it would carry them off the rock.

Just before the base of the wave reached the rock, they were in one of the small rooms so numerous in this circuit. Again, Kickaha tried to blow the Horn and activate a gate that would shuttle them off from this circuit. But he did not have time. Nor did he have during the next twelve stations they whizzed through.

Like it or not—and they did not—they were caught in the dizzying circle. Then, when they were again in the room at the top of the tower set in the deserted city, he had just enough time to complete the seven notes. And they were transmitted to the most amazing and unexpected place they had ever encountered.

"I think we've broken the circuit!" Kickaha said. "Have you ever heard of a place like this?"

Anana shook her head. She seemed to be awed. After living so many thousands of years, she was not easily impressed.

3

*T*he scaly man was the centerpiece of the enormous room.

Whether he was a corpse or in suspended animation, he had perhaps been born one or two hundred thousand years ago. The two intruders in this colorful and vibrant tomb had no way of testing its antiquity. They just felt that the tomb had been built when their own exceedingly remote ancestors had not been born yet. It seemed to sweat eons.

"Have you ever heard of this person?" Kickaha whispered. Then, realizing that he had no need to whisper, he spoke loudly.

"I get this feeling that we're the first to be here since that . . . creature was laid to rest here."

"I'm not so sure that he is permanently resting. And no, I've never heard of this place. Or of him. Not his name, anyway, whatever his name is. But . . ."

Anana paused, then said, "My people had stories about a sapient but nonhuman species who preceded us Thoan. They were said to have created us. Whether the tales were originally part of the prehistoric Thoan cultures or were early fiction, we don't know. But most Thoan insist that we originated naturally, that we were not made by anybody. My ancestors did make the *leblabbiys*, your kind. These, with a multitude of lifeforms, were made in my ancestors' biofactories to populate their artificial pocket universes. But that we Thoan could be artificial beings, never!

"However, the stories did describe the Thokina as somewhat like that creature there. But the Thokina were a different species from us. We were supposed to have invaded their universe and killed all but one. I don't know. There were conflicting legends about them."

In the middle of the room was a short massive pillar on top of which was a large, transparent, and brightly lit cube. The being, its seemingly dead eyes open, was suspended inside the cube.

"One of the early tales was that the one Thokina who survived the war hid somewhere. He placed himself in an impenetrable tomb. Then, he went into a sleep from which he will not be awakened until the worlds are in danger of destruction."

"Why should he care if the worlds are destroyed?"

"I'm just telling you the story as it was handed down for countless generations," she said. "But how do you explain him? Or this place? Part of the legend was that he was keeping an eye on the world. Look at all those images on the wall. They show many universes. Some of them look contemporary."

"How could he keep an eye on the worlds? He's unconscious or, for all we know, dead."

Anana spread her hands out. "How would I know?"

Kickaha did not reply. He was looking around the dome-shaped chamber, which was larger than a zeppelin hangar. In the source-less light filling the room, the intensely blue ceiling dazzled him. Despite this, he could, by squinting his eyes, see that thousands of shifting forms were spaced along the curve of the ceiling. Most of them seemed to be letters of a strange alphabet or mathematical formulae. Sometimes, he glimpsed art forms that seemed to have been originated by an insane brain. But that was because of his own cultural mindset.

Horizontal bands of swiftly varying colors and hues sped around the wall. Set among the bands were seemingly three-dimensional scenes, thousands of them. These flashed on and were replaced by others. Kickaha had walked around the wall and looked at the scenes that were at eye level. Some were of landscapes and peoples of various worlds he had visited. One was a bird's-eye view of Manhattan. But at its lower end was a twin-towered skyscraper higher than the Empire State Building.

The images came and went so swiftly. His eyes ached after watching them for a few minutes. He closed them for a moment. When he opened them, he turned to look at the main attraction. The base of the tomb was round, and vertical bands of colors and hues raced up and down it. The creature inside the cube was naked and obviously male. Its testicles were enclosed in a globular sac of blue cartilage with air holes on its surface. Its penis was a thick cylinder with no glans or foreskin and bore thin, tightly coiled tentacles on each side.

Anana, first seeing these, had grunted and then said, "I wonder . . . ?"

"What?" Kickaha had said.

"Its mate must have had an extra dimension of sex, of sexual pleasure, I mean. True, those tentacles could have just been used for purely reproductive purposes. But they may have titillated the female in some way I can't imagine."

"You'll never know," he had said.

"Maybe I won't. However, the unexpected happens as often as the expected. It certainly does when I'm in your neighborhood."

The creature was about seven feet long. Its body was very similar in structure to a man's, and the four-toed feet and five-fingered hands were humanoid enough. Its massive muscles were gorilloid. The skin was reptilian; the scales were green, red, black, blue, orange, purple, lemon-yellow, and pink.

The spine, ridged like a dinosaur's, curved at its top so that the very thick neck bent forward.

Seven greenish plates that could be of bone or cartilage covered the face. The eyes were dark green and arranged for stereoscopic vision though much more widely apart than on a man's face.

A bony plate just below the jaw made it seem that the creature was chinless. Its lipless, slightly opened mouth was a lizard's. From it hung a tongue looking like a pink worm.

The nose and the rest of the face above it formed a shallow curve. Halfway up the head, short, flat-lying, and reddish fronds began and proceeded down around the back of the head to its columnar neck. If there were bony plates under the mat, they did not show.

The tiny ears were manlike but set very far back on the head.

"You don't suppose," Anana said, "that that thing could actually be the last of the Thokina?"

She answered herself. "Of course not! It's just coincidence!"

They stood silently for a while and stared around. Then Kickaha said, "There's no way we can find answers to our questions here. Not unless we stay a long while, and we don't have the food, water, and instruments needed to do that. Yet, we should spend some time here."

"We have to get out of here," she said, "and we don't know we can do that. I suggest we find out how to do that now!"

"There's no danger. Not any we know about, anyway. I think we should stay here awhile and see what we can find out. It might come in useful someday."

They had enough food and water to last four days if they were conserved. There was no place to get rid of their body wastes, but a corner in this immense chamber could serve. It seemed to Kickaha that doing that desecrated the place, but that was an irrational feeling.

"What if something happens here that makes it imperative we leave at once?" she said.

Kickaha thought for a moment, then said, "Okay. You're right."

He walked to the place near the wall where they had stepped

through the gate, and he blew the Horn of Shambarimen. As it often did, the music evoked in him images of marvelous beasts, wondrous plants, and exotic people. It seldom failed to send shivers along the nerves of those who heard it and to summon up from the depths of their minds things and beings never imagined before.

The last note seemed to hover like a mayfly determined to have several more seconds of its short life. A shimmering area about five feet wide and ten feet high opened before Kickaha. The flashing wall of the chamber behind it disappeared. He was looking at a stone floor and stone walls. He had seen them before and not long ago. From the room they formed he and Anana had gated through to this gigantic tomb. It was an escape avenue, but he preferred to take another gate, if it was available. This one would lock them into the circuit again.

The room faded away after five seconds. The walls of the chamber and the on-off bursts of light were views of parts of other universes.

"Find another gate if you can," Anana said.

"Of course," he said, and he began walking slowly along the wall and blowing the Horn over and over again. Not until he had gotten halfway around the chamber did a gate open. He saw a large boulder twenty feet ahead of him. Around and beyond it was a flat desert and blue sky.

He did not know in what universe this landscape was located. For all he knew, it could be somewhere on the planet on which he now stood. Gates could also transport you only a few feet or halfway around the planet.

The rest of the walk along the wall found no more gates. He then began a circuit twenty feet out from the wall. But Anana, a few feet from him, called.

"Come here! I just saw something very interesting!"

He strode to her side. She was looking up at a spot where

images seemingly shot out of the wall and then shot back into it.

"It showed Red Orc!" she said. "Red Orc!"

"Recognize the background?"

"It could have been on any one of a thousand worlds. A body of water, could have been a large lake or a sea, was behind him. It looked as if he were standing on the edge of a cliff."

"Keep watching it," he said. "I'm going to work my way around the wall again in a smaller circle. But I'll be looking for other views of Orc. Or anything familiar. Oh, I did find another gate. But it led to a desert. We won't take it except as a last resort."

She nodded, her gaze still locked onto the images.

Before he turned to go, he saw a flash of what had to be downtown Los Angeles. There was the Bradbury Building. The next twenty views were of unfamiliar places.

Then he saw briefly a landscape of the Lavalite planet, the world from which he and Anana had escaped. A mountain was slowly rising from the surface, and the river at its base was spreading out as its channel flattened out.

What was the use to anyone of all these monitor views when no one was here to see them?

He felt creepy.

There were too many questions and no answers. The practical thing to do was to quit thinking about them. But being pragmatic did not stop him.

After completing the circuit, he stopped. The Horn had opened no more gates. And he had not seen any more scapes of things familiar. Nor could he see the higher views on the curving wall.

He started when Anana yelled, "I saw Red Orc again!"

Before he could get to her, the view was gone.

"He was about to walk through a gate!" she said. "He was on the same cliff by the sea, but he'd walked over to a gate. An upright hexagon!"

"Maybe he's not doing that right now. The view could be a record of the past."

"Maybe, maybe not."

Kickaha went back to his work with the Horn. When he was done, he had opened no new gates. Anana had not seen their most dangerous enemy again.

He started toward the tomb to examine it when Anana cried out a Thoan oath, "Elyttria!"

He wheeled just in time to see the last two seconds of the view. It showed part of the interior of the great chamber and the nearer half of the tomb and occupant. Very close were himself and Anana staring slightly upwards.

"Us!" he bellowed.

After a few seconds of silence, she said, "That should not surprise us. If so many worlds and places are being monitored, it's only natural that this place should be. For one thing, the monitors should know when this room has been invaded. And we are intruders."

"Nothing has been done about us."

"So far, no."

"Keep an eye on the views," he said. He walked to the tomb and felt around the base but could not detect any protuberances or recesses. The controls, if there were any, were not on the base.

The cube resisted his efforts to raise it from the base.

After that, he toured the wall again. Inside of an hour, he had examined the wall for as far as he could see up. He even pressed his hand against the displays to find out if this disclosed any means of control. He also hoped that the pressure would swing open a part of the wall and offer access to somewhere else. As he expected, it did not happen. It was not logical that it would, but he had to try. If there was any central control area, it was not visible. And it was not available.

Meanwhile, the hidden monitors in this chamber would be recording his actions.

That thought led to another. Just how did these monitors record so many places in so many worlds? They certainly would not do it by the machines Earthpeople or the Lords used. The "cameras" on these worlds would be of an indetectible nature. Permanent magnetic fields of some sort? And these transmitted the pictures through gates of some sort to this place?

If they were stored as recordings, they would have to be in an immense area. Inside this planet?

He just did not know.

There had to be some purpose to all this.

"Kickaha!" Anana called.

He ran to her. "What?"

"That man who was wearing the clothes of Western Earthpeople of the late eighteenth or early nineteenth century," she said, looking excited. "The man we saw inside that floating palace on the Lavalite planet. I just saw him!"

"Know where he was?"

She shook her head but said, "He wasn't in the house. He was walking through a forest. The trees could have been on Earth or the World of Tiers or any of hundreds of worlds. I didn't see any animals or birds."

"Curiouser and curiouser," he said in English.

He looked around again, then said, "I don't think we can do anything more here. We can't just wait around hoping to see flashes of Red Orc or the stranger or, I wish to God we would, Wolff and Chryseis."

"But we might be able to retrace our gate routes back to here someday."

"We'll do it. Meanwhile, let's go. I don't like to re-enter the tower room, but we have no choice."

They walked to the wall area enclosing the gate through which they had entered the chamber. He raised the Horn to his lips and blew into the mouthpiece. The air shimmered, and they could see the room in the tower they had left a short time ago. Anana stepped through with Kickaha on her heels. But he turned around for a last view of the chamber.

He saw that the cube was being filled with many beams of many colors and hues. They flashed and died and were replaced within a blink of an eye by other beams. An orange light surrounded the corpse, which was sinking slowly toward the floor of the cube.

"Wait!" he cried out.

But the view faded swiftly. Not, however, before he saw the lid of the cube beginning to raise up.

He did not explain to Anana why he was blowing the Horn again. This time, the gate to the gigantic room did not open. Instead, they were in another place.

He was in despair. It seemed impossible that they could ever retrace their route to the tomb.

Nevertheless, he automatically blew the Horn again and again as they were shot through a circuit. And then they were on a plain on which two-foot-high grass flourished. Far beyond that was a thick forest and, beyond that, a wall of rock towering so high that he could not see its top. It ran unbroken to his right and his left. The sky was bright green, and the sun was yellow and as bright as Earth's.

They had time to run out of the area of influence of the gate before it shuttled them onwards. They leaped like two jackrabbits startled by a coyote, and they ran. They had known instantly where they were.

They were in the universe of the planet called Alofmethbin. In English, the World of Tiers. This was his most beloved planet of all the universes. The vast wall of rock many miles in front of them was one of the five truly colossal monoliths forming the vertical parts of the Tower-of-Babylon-shaped planet. And they were standing on top of one of them, though they did not as yet know which.

After they had stopped running, Anana said, "Didn't it seem to you that the gate lasted suspiciously long? We had plenty of time to get away from it, and we never did in any of the others."

"I thought of that," he said, "but we can't be sure of it. However, it did seem like we were on a nonstop train that slowed down long enough for us to jump off."

She nodded. Her face was grim.

"I think someone set it up so we'd get off here."

"Red Orc!"

4

*T*hat seems most probable," Anana said. "However, he might've set up the circuit and the trap for one of his numerous enemies. And done so long before you and I appeared on the scene. Or it might've been his emergency escape route."

"Nothing is certain until it happens. To quote your Thoan philosopher, Manathu Vorcyon, 'Order is composed of disorder, and disorder has its own order.' Whatever that means. In any case, I'm mighty suspicious."

"Whenever were you not?"

"When I was still living on Earth, though even there I was what you might call wary. The things that happened after I came here have made me trust very few people. And they've made me consider what might happen in every situation before it could happen. You look at all the angles or you don't live long. It's not paranoia. Paranoia is a state of mind in which you suspect or are certain about things that really don't exist. The dangers I've been suspicious of have existed or could exist."

"Almost every Lord is paranoiac. It's a deeply embedded part of our culture, such as it is. Most of them don't trust anybody, including themselves."

Kickaha laughed, and he said, "Well, let's go on into Paranoia Land."

They began walking across the plain. They were as constantly watchful as birds, glancing up often at the sky, at the grass just ahead of them, and at the vista beyond their feet. The grass could conceal snakes or large crouching predators. Something dangerous could suddenly appear in the sky. But for the first hour, they saw only insects in the grass and herds of large four-tusked elephantlike and four-horned antelopelike beasts in the distance.

Then a black speck emerged from the green sky. It was behind them, but Anana saw it during one of her frequent glances behind her. After a few minutes, it came low enough for them to see a bird with a ravenlike silhouette. It got no lower then but continued in the same direction as they. When they saw it circle now and then before resuming the same path, they suspected that it was following them.

"It could be one those giant language-using ravens that Vannax made in his laboratory for spying and message-carrying when he was Lord of this world," Kickaha said.

He added, "Looks more and more like Red Orc is watching us."

"Or somebody is."

"My money's on Orc."

He and Anana stopped to rest awhile in the knee-high, blue-stalked, and crimson-tipped grass.

"I suppose it could be a machine disguised as a bird," he said. "But if it's a machine, it's being controlled by a Lord. That doesn't seem likely."

"When did we ever come across anything but the unlikely?"

"Seems like it. But it's not always so by any means."

He was on his back, his hands behind his head, looking at the dark enigma in the sky. Anana was half lying down, leaning on one hand, her head tilted back to watch the bird or whatever it was.

"That figure-eight the bird's now making in the sky," Kickaha said, "looks from here like it's on its side. That reminds me of the symbol for infinity, the flattened figure-eight on its side. One of the few things I remember from my freshman mathematics class in college. Which I never finished. College, I mean."

"The Thoan symbol is a straight line with arrowheads at each end pointing outwards," she said. "If the line has a corkscrew shape, it's the symbol for time."

"I know."

Visions of Earth slipped past in his mind like ghosts in coats of many colors. In 1946, he had been twenty-eight years old, a World War II veteran going to college on the G. I. Bill. Then he had been hurled into another universe, though not unwillingly. This was the Lord-created artificial universe that contained only the tiered planet, Alofmethbin.

This was, he had found, only one among thousands of universes made by the ancient Thoan, the humans who denied that they were human. Here was where he, Paul Janus Finnegan, the adventure-loving Hoosier, had become Kickaha the Trickster.

And, since coming to the World of Tiers, he had seldom not been fleeing his enemies or attacking them, always on the move except for some rare periods of R&R. During these relatively infrequent times, he had usually gotten married to the daughters of a tribal chief on his favorite level, the second, which he called the Amerindian level.

Or he had become involved with the wife or daughter of a baron on the third level, which he called the Dracheland level.

He had left a trail of women who grieved for him for a while before inevitably falling in love with another man. He had also left a trail of corpses. The debris, you might say, of Finnegan's wake.

Not until 1970 did he return to Earth, and that was briefly. He had been born in A.D. 1918, which made him fifty-two or fifty-three Terrestrial years old now. But he was, thank whatever gods there be, only twenty-five in physiological age. If he'd stayed on Earth, what would he be there? Maybe he would have gotten a Ph.D. in anthropology and specialized in American Indian languages. But he would have had to be a teacher, too. Could he have endured the grind of study, the need to publish, the academic backbiting and throat-slitting, the innumerable weary conferences, the troubles with administrators who regarded teachers as a separate and definitely inferior species?

He might've gone to Alaska, where there was, in 1946, a sort of frontier, and he might have been a bush pilot. But that life would eventually have become tedious.

Perhaps by now he would own a motorcycle sales and repair shop in Terre Haute or Indianapolis. No, he couldn't have stood the day-to-day routine, the worrying about paying bills, and the drabness.

Whatever he would have been on Earth, he would not have had the adventurous and exotic life, albeit hectic, he had experienced in the Thoan worlds.

The beautiful woman by his side—no, not a woman, a goddess, poetically speaking—was many thousands of years old. But the chemical "elixirs" of the Lords kept her at the physiological age of twenty-five.

She said, "We're assuming that the raven is on an evil mission, bad for us. Perhaps it's been sent to keep an eye on us, but by Wolff. He and Chryseis might have escaped from Red Orc's prison and gotten to this world and now be in the palace. And they may have ordered the Eye to watch over us."

"I know."

She said, "It seems to me that we've been saying a lot of 'I knows.' "

"Maybe it's time we took a long vacation from each other."

"It wouldn't do any good," she said. Then, looking slyly sidewise at him, "I know."

She burst into laughter, fell on him, and kissed him passionately.

Kickaha kissed her back as enthusiastically. But he was thinking that they might have been isolated from other human beings too long. They needed lots of company, not all the time, but often enough so that they did not rub against each other, as it were.

Her comments about "knowing" probably indicated a sadness born out of expectation based on hindsight. Because she had lived for many millennia, she had had far more experience than he. She had lived with hundreds of male Lords and had had a few children. Her longest time with a man had been about fifty years.

"That's about the limit for a faithful couple, if you don't age at all," she had said. "The Lords don't have the patience of you *leblabbiy,* a word I don't mean in a derogatory sense. But we are different in some respects."

"But many couples have lived together for thousands of years," he had said.

"Not continuously."

He was not tired or bored with her. Nor did she seem to be so with him. But being able to look backward on so many experiences, she was unable to keep from looking forward. She knew that a time would come when they must part. For a while, a long while, anyway.

He was not going to worry about that. When the time came to deal with it, he would. Just how, he did not know.

He rose, drank water from his deerskin canteen, and said, "If Wolff had sent that Eye, he would have told it to tell us that it was watching for us. And he would have told the Eye to give us directions to get to wherever he is. So it definitely was not sent by Wolff."

He paused, then said, "Do you want to go now?" He knew better than to order her to leave with him. She resented any hint of bossiness by others. After all, though more empathetic and compassionate than most of her kind, she was a Lord.

"It's time."

They put their knapsacks and quivers on their backs and started walking again. He thought, On top of the many thousands of feet high monolith ahead of us is, probably, the level called Atlantis. And on top of that is the monolith, much more narrow and less lofty than the others, on top of which is the palace Wolff built.

Three hours passed while they strode toward the forest. By now, they could see that another hour would bring them to its edge. Kickaha stepped up his pace. She did not ask why he was in such a hurry now. She knew that he did not like being on the plain for very long. It made him feel too exposed and vulnerable.

After about ten minutes, Kickaha broke the silence between them.

"I suspect that no one had come through that gate in the tomb until we did. There were no signs of previous entry. And, surely, the thing in the tomb or whoever put him there had set up many safeguards. Why, then, were we able to use the gate?"

"What do you think?"

He said, "There was some reason we and only we were allowed in. Emphasis on the 'allowed.' But why were we?"

"You don't know that we were the first there. You don't know that we were 'allowed' in."

"True. But if someone else did get in, he or she didn't trigger the raising of the cube, and, I bet, the resurrection of the scaly man."

"You don't know that for sure."

"Yes, but I think that only someone with the Horn of Shambarimem could have penetrated that tomb."

She smiled and said, "Perhaps. But the scaly man must've put himself in that tomb eons before the Horn was made. He couldn't have known that the Horn would be made or that its frequencies would open the way to the tomb."

"How do you know that he didn't know it would be made? In his time, a device similar to the Horn could have been available."

She laughed and said, "No one can predict the future. Besides, what significance did our entering there have?"

"It started a chain of events that's only begun. As for predicting, maybe it's not a matter of predeterminism or predicting. Maybe it's a matter of probabilities. Don't forget that that chamber contains devices surveying many universes. I think that, when certain events are observed, the scaly man is raised from the tomb. After that, I don't know."

"You don't know. That's it."

"Okay, you're probably right!" he said. "But if I'm right, I expect you to apologize and kiss my foot, among other things, and be humble and obedient thereafter to the end of eternity, amen."

"Your face is red! You're angry!"

"You're too skeptical, too blasé, too jaded. And too almighty sure of yourself."

"We'll see. But if you're wrong, you can do to me what I was supposed to do to you."

They did not speak for some time afterwards. While crossing the last few miles to the edge of the forest, detouring once to avoid a herd of giant bison, they looked back twice. The raven was still following them but was much lower.

"Definitely an Eye of the Lord," Kickaha said.

She said, "I know," laughed, and then said, "I've got to quit saying that."

They entered the shade of the thousand-foot-high sequoialike trees. The forest floor was thick with dead leaves. That was strange, since there was no change of season on this planet. But when he saw a few leaves flutter down from the trees, he realized that it shed old leaves and replaced them with new ones. A few other plants on Alofmethbin did that.

The undergrowth was sparse, though here and there thorny bushes forced the two to go around them. Many small, blue-eyed creatures that looked like furry and wingless owls watched them from the safety of the brambles.

Monkeys, birds, and flying and gliding mammals screamed,

hooted, and chittered in the branches. But in the immediate area of the humans, silence fell, only to be broken after they had passed.

Once, a weasel the size of a Rocky Mountain lion looked around the side of a treetrunk at them but did not charge them. The two humans knew that a predator was there before the weasel revealed itself. The clamor in the area ahead of them had ceased.

Kickaha and Anana had already strung their bows. There was no predicting what dangerous man or beast dwelt in this twilit but noisy place. They had also loosened the straps of their knife scabbards.

They had gone a mile when they came to a clearing about sixty feet wide. This had been made by two sequoias, which had fallen together. That had been a long time ago, judging by the rottenness of the wood. Kickaha looked up in time to see the raven just before it settled down on a branch halfway down a tree next to the open ground. The big leaves of a parasitic plant hid it then.

"Okay," Kickaha muttered. "No doubt of it now. It's ahead of us but may not know it is. It may be waiting for us to come by here since we were walking in a more or less straight line. I don't know how it's kept its eye on us so far."

Since the raven was the size of a bald eagle, it could not flit from branch to branch.

"Maybe it knows where we're going," Kickaha said.

"How could that be? We don't know ourselves where we're going except in a general direction. And the woods are thick here. It couldn't have followed us. Oh, I see! It followed the silences falling around us."

They withdrew a few feet into the shade. Then he whispered, "Let's watch from here."

Presently, just as he had expected, he saw the big, black bird spiral down and land on a branch projecting from one of the fallen and decaying behemoths. Then it glided to the ground, its wings half-outspread, and walked toward them. Kickaha thought that it had come to the ground to find out where they were. It would hide and listen for the two humans.

But it could, at the moment, neither see them nor, in the still air, smell them. Kickaha and Anana were lucky that they had spotted it before it saw them.

Kickaha placed a finger to his lips, then whispered very softly in Anana's ear.

"It can see like a hawk and hear almost as well as a dog. Let's move on. We won't be quiet. It can follow us until we're ready to catch it."

"If it's sent by a Lord, that might mean that a Lord is in Wolff's palace."

"If there is, we'll be lucky to elude the traps there."

"Lots of ifs."

Kickaha pointed a finger at the huge, black bird and then touched his lips. Deliberately, he stepped on a dry branch. The loud crack made the raven whirl around and waddle swiftly to a hiding place behind a low-growing bush on the side of the clearing across from the two. No doubt, after they had passed it, it would return to the clearing and use it as a runway so it could take to the air again. But if it saw that the humans were walking slowly, it might just follow them on foot. Ravens, however, did not like to walk far.

Thinking that it had located them without being detected, it would be as smug as a raven could be. In this universe, as on most, smugness often caused a tumble into the dust.

"We must take it alive," Kickaha said.

"I know."

"For God's sake!" he said in English. Then, seeing her smile slightly, he knew that she was just having fun with him.

They crossed the clearing slowly, looking left and right and, now and then, behind them. If they did not behave cautiously, the raven would know that they were pretending carelessness to deceive an observer.

Nor did they swing wide of the bush. Silently, they passed within a few feet of it. Kickaha looked at the bush but could not see the bird. Now, if he were so inclined, would be the time for him to break suddenly into a run. Anana would do so a half-second behind him, but she would head for the side of the bush opposite the one he would be racing for. The raven would flee, but it would not have time to take to its wings nor to hide again.

Anana said nothing. She was waiting to see what Kickaha would do. He walked on by the bush and into the forest. He did not have to tell her that they were going to pretend they were not aware of the bird. Let the raven follow them. Eventually, they would find out why it was stalking them.

And then he almost halted. He grunted.

Anana noticed the break in stride and heard his suppressed exclamation. Instead of looking around and thus notifying whatever had startled him that she was aware of its presence, she looked straight ahead. She said quietly, "What is it?"

"I wish I knew," he said. "I saw . . . off to the right . . . just a flash . . . a something like a man but not human. Not quite, anyway. Maybe my mind's playing tricks. But he, if it was male, looked like he was human. He was very big and very hairy for a human being. Only . . ."

She waited several seconds, then said, "Well?"

"His face, I don't know. It was not quite human. There was something, uh, bearlike about it. I've been all over this planet and have never seen nor heard of anything like it. On the other hand, this planet has more land area than Earth. So, I just never knew anybody who knew about it."

She looked to the left, then to the right.

"I see nothing."

He half stepped out from behind a tree, then stepped back. "Angle casually over toward the tree."

She went in the direction he had indicated by bending his head. She must have noticed that the arboreal animals in the branches five hundred feet above her had fallen silent. But, like him, she must have thought that it was their approach that had caused this.

They went approximately a hundred feet before he spoke.

"The one just ahead."

It was one of the gigantic sequoialike plants. Its bark was as shiny as if thousands of pieces of mica were embedded in it.

"I hope there's only one of him," he said.

He fitted his bow with an arrow and started to go around on the left side of the enormous trunk. She headed toward the right side. Anybody still on the back side of the tree would be caught between them.

When they came around the trunk, they saw only each other. Though the thing Kickaha had glimpsed did not look as if it had claws, he looked upwards along the bole. No creature clung to it, and not even a squirrel could have gotten to the branches this fast. Anana had stepped back so she could see more of the other side of the trunk. The tree was so huge, however, that a section of it was invisible to both of them. After telling Anana to stay where she was but keep looking upward, he ran around the tree. At the same time, he kept his gaze on the upper reaches of the bole. But he saw no living creature.

When he returned to Anana, he said, "It was too heavy to climb up the trunk even if it'd had claws a foot long. I had to make sure, though."

She pointed at the thick piles of dead leaves on the ground. He was already looking at them. They were scattered in so many directions that he could not tell if the creature had been coming to or going from the tree.

He sniffed. There was a faint musky odor in the still air.

"I smell it, too," she said. "Maybe we should capture the raven. It might know what the thing is. In fact, it could be working for it."

She paused, then said, "Or it could be working for the raven."

"Why don't we wait a while before we grab the bird?"

They pushed on at a faster pace. Now and then, they looked behind them but saw neither the bird nor the bear-thing. After a few minutes, they smelled a whiff of woodsmoke. Silently, they walked toward the odor, guided by its increasing strength. They waded through a narrow creek to the other side. When they heard voices, they slowed their pace and made sure they did not step on dry sticks. The voices became louder. They were women's, and it seemed to Kickaha that he heard only two speakers. He made a few signs to Anana, who crept away to circle around the place. She would be his unseen backup if he got into trouble. Or vice versa.

He got down on the ground and wriggled forward very slowly to keep from rustling the dead leaves. He stopped when he was behind a thick bush between two massive treetrunks. He peered through the lower part of the bush and saw a small clearing. In its center was a small fire with a small iron pot suspended by its handle from a horizontal wooden stick set between two forked wooden uprights. Kickaha smelled boiling meat.

A blonde who was beautiful despite her disarrayed hair and dirtied face stood near the fire. She was speaking Thoan. Crouching down on the other side of the fire was a red-haired woman. She was as good-looking as the blonde and equally disheveled and dirty.

Both wore ankle-length robes reminding Kickaha of illustrations of the type of dress worn by ancient Greek females. The material was thin, clinging, and far from opaque. At one time, the robes had been white, but brambles and thorns clung to them, and dirt and blood smeared them.

On the far side of the clearing were two knapsacks and a pile of Thoan blankets, paper-thin but very heat-keeping. Three light axes, three heavy knives, and three beamers, which looked like pistols with bulbs on the muzzles, were on top of the blankets.

A butchered fawn was lying on the far side of the clearing. No flies buzzed around it; the planet Alofmethbin lacked flies. But crawling and scavenging insects were beginning to swarm on the carcass.

Kickaha shook his head. The women were not very cautious, hence not very bright, if they had not kept the weapons close at hand. Or, perhaps, this was a trap.

He turned and looked behind him and up into the tree branches but neither saw nor heard anything to alarm him. Of course, the raven could be hidden among the leaves overhead. After he had turned around toward the women, he lay for a while watching and listening.

Though the two looked to be no more than twenty-five, they had to be thousands of years old. They spoke in the same archaic Thoan Anana fell into sometimes when she was excited. Except for a few words and phrases, Kickaha understood it.

The blonde said, "We can't survive long in this horrible place. We must find a gate."

"You've said that a thousand times, Eleth," the auburn-haired woman said. "I'm getting sick of hearing it."

"And I'm sick of hearing nothing practical from you, Ona," the blonde snarled. "Why don't you figure a way out for us, suggest just how we can find a gate?"

Ona said, "And I'm about to vomit from your childish bickering and screaming."

"So, throw up," Eleth said. "At least you'd be doing something instead of sitting on your ass and whining. And vomiting certainly wouldn't make this place stink more than it does even if your puke stinks more than anybody else's."

Ona got up and looked into the pot. "It seems to be done, but I still don't know how to cook."

"Who does?" Eleth said. "That's slave work. Why should we know anything about it?"

"For Shambarimem's sake!" Ona said, and she shook her head so violently that her long auburn hair swirled like a cloak around her shoulders. "Can't we do anything but talk about things that don't matter? A fine pair of sisters we are. Lords one day, and the next, we're no better than slaves."

"Well, at least we don't have to worry about putting on weight," Eleth said, and she grinned.

The redhead looked hard at her.

"I'm trying be as light-hearted as possible," Eleth said. "We have to keep our spirits up or they'll be so heavy they'll sink down to our toes and ooze out onto the ground. And we'll die or become *leblabbiys*. We'll get eaten by some beast or, worse, be captured and raped by *leblabbiys* and spend the next hundred years or more as wives of some stupid, ignorant, dirty, smelly, snot-wiping-on-their-hands, wife-beating savages. They'll be our Lords."

"You really know how to make me feel good," Ona said. "I'd kill myself before I'd submit to a *leblabbiy*."

"It wouldn't be hopeless. We could escape and find a gate and then find Red Orc and get revenge by killing him. After some suitable tortures, of course. I'm thinking about eating Red Orc's balls just as he ate his father's. Well cooked, though, and with a suitable garnish, not eaten raw as Red Orc did."

"Speaking of cannibalism," Ona said, "we may have to resort to that before we find a way out of this mess. Now, who should be the eaters and who the eaten?"

"Stop that!"

But both burst out laughing.

Kickaha knew the Lords well enough to doubt that Ona was

jesting. If they did starve, one of them would kill and eat her companion.

He listened several minutes to their bickering but did not learn much. The only thing he knew for sure was that their predicament was caused by Red Orc and that they had escaped from him with the few possessions in the clearing.

The two women fell silent while they were looking into the pot. By now, they were getting ready to dip out deer stew with rough spoons made of bark.

Suddenly, Anana stepped out from the bushes into the clearing. She held her bow and an arrow at the ready.

"Hail, iron-hearted daughters of Urizen and Ahania!" she called. "Your cousin Anana greets you in peace! What brings you here?"

5

*T*he two women shrieked and jumped as if they had stepped on biting ants. The redhead, however, flashed out of her paralysis and darted toward the beamers near the edge of the clearing. After a few steps, she halted, then walked slowly back to Eleth. She had realized that she could not get to the weapons before Anana's arrow drove through her.

"Ona the Baker!" Anana called to the redhead. "You were always the quickest witted, the coolest, and the most dangerous in physical combat. But how could you be so stupid as to leave your arms out of reach?"

Ona scowled and said, "I am very tired."

Anana addressed the blonde. "Eleth the Grinder, also known as Eleth the Worrier! You were the planner, the thinker, and so in many ways the most dangerous!"

The blonde was not so pale now. She smiled, and she bowed. "Not as dangerous as you, Anana the Bright, Anana the Hunter!"

Anana said, "Ona, you and your sisters, Eleth the Grinder, and Uveth the Kneader, now dead, were known as the kind-hearted daughters of Ahania. Now you are called iron-hearted! But you have always been the kindliest and sweetest of the three!"

"That was long ago, Anana," Ona said.

"Your father, Urizen the Cold, changed you three from kittens to ravening tigers," Anana said. "Your hatred for him is well known."

She paused, then said, "Do you know that he is dead?"

Eleth said stonily, "We had heard that he was. But we were not sure that it was true."

Ona said, "Nor are we sure now. That you say our father is dead does not make it true. But, if your news is true, we're glad."

"Except that we would be sad that we were not the ones who killed him," Eleth said.

During this talking, Kickaha had been moving stealthily around the clearing to make sure that no one else was watching the scene. Though he looked for the raven and the bearish creature, he did not see them. Nor was there any sign of anyone lying in ambush.

When the two women saw him step into the clearing, they started only slightly. Evidently, they had suspected that Anana was not alone. Eleth said, "Who is this, Anana?"

"Surely you have heard of Kickaha? Kickaha the Trickster, the killer of so many Lords, the man who slew the last of the Black Bellers? You have also heard of ancient Shambarimen's prophecy that a *leblabbiy* will destroy the Lords. Some say that Kickaha is the man of whom Shambarimen prophesied."

Eleth bit her lower lip. "Yes, we have heard of the *leblabbiy* who has been so lucky so far. We have also heard that he is your lover."

"He is a *leblabbiy*," Anana said cheerily, "and he is such a lover as you should wish you had."

"Thanks," Kickaha said, and he grinned broadly.

"You killed our father?" Eleth said to Kickaha. Her tone indicated that she did not believe Anana.

"No," Kickaha said. "I wish I had. But it was Jadawin, the Lord also known as Wolff, who killed him."

"You saw Jadawin kill him?"

"No. But Jadawin told me that he did, and Jadawin does not lie. Not, at least, to me."

Anana herded the sisters to the end of the clearing most distant from the pile of weapons. Then she ordered them to sit down. She did not frisk them. Their filmy robes made it evident that they were not carrying concealed weapons.

"We're starving," Eleth said. "We were just about to eat the soup. Such as it is."

Kickaha looked inside the pot. "Nothing but meat. Very unhealthy. Why didn't you put some vegetables in?"

"We don't know what plants are good to eat and what're poisonous," Eleth said.

"But all Thoan, male or female, are given survival courses," he said. "You should know that . . ."

Ona said, "We don't know this planet."

"You can get up now and eat," Anana said. "By suppertime, we'll have much better food for you. If, that is, we stay with you. That depends upon how open and truthful you are with us. Now, I heard enough while you were talking to believe that Red Orc is responsible for your being here. Tell me . . ."

"Red Orc!" Eleth said viciously, and she spat on the ground. "There's a man who needs killing!"

"After suitable torture," Ona said. "He killed Uveth years ago and came close recently to killing us. It's because of him that we're stranded in this wretched wilderness."

Anana let them rave and rant for a while about what they would do to Orc when they captured him. Then she said, "Tell us just how you came to be here."

They stood by the pot, and Eleth was the first to speak. Ona ate while her sister talked, then Ona talked while Eleth ate. After fleeing Red Orc, not for the first time, they had managed to "take over" Nitharm, the universe in which they had taken refuge. "Take over" was a euphemism for slaying the Lord of Nitharm and his family. Since there were no male Thoan in that world, they had taken *leblabbiys* for lovers. This practice was acceptable by Thoan standards because their lovers were their slaves, not their equals, and were often replaced by others.

They had been happy there, they said. The only thing lacking to make their happiness complete was that they had not yet been able to find and kill their father. Then Red Orc had somehow evaded the traps they had set at the two gates into their world. He had taken them by surprise despite their security systems.

At this point in the story, Eleth had interrupted Ona.

"I told them many times that we should just close all gates and stay there forever. That would have kept any Lord from invading our world."

"Yes, you fearful trembling sniveling little bitch!" Ona had said. "And just how then would we be able to go to other worlds and make sure that our father was dead!"

"Don't call me names, assface!" Eleth fired back.

The rest of the story was longer than Kickaha wished to hear. But he and Anana let them ramble on since they might reveal something about themselves that could later be used against them.

Red Orc would have killed them if they had not happened to be very close to a gate to another world. They had been able to grab some weapons before they fled. After passing through a circuit of gates, they had come out on this level of the World of Tiers. Since then, they had been trying to survive while searching for another gate. This, they hoped, would not take them to another world but to the palace on top of the topmost monolith of the World of Tiers. There, they knew, was the structure that had been Jadawin's, then Vannax's, and, once again, Jadawin's stronghold. They had heard that no Lord now lived there. Thus, they planned to become the new Lords.

Their story could be true, but, if so, certainly showed them as inept. Kickaha did not believe that they really were, though he knew that Red Orc was ingenious enough to defeat even the most competent.

Anana said, "Then you'll be willing to join us in the fight against Red Orc?"

They agreed enthusiastically.

"What good will they be to us?" Kickaha said loudly. "We don't need them! In fact, they'll be a big liability!"

"You are wrong," Ona said. "You need information, and we know many things about Red Orc that you don't."

Anana, who was aware of what Kickaha was doing, spoke. "That's right, Kickaha. They must know about gates and his activities and strongholds we don't know. Isn't that right, daughters of Urizen?"

They spoke as one. "That is correct."

"Very well," he said. "We're a band, and I'm the leader. What I order must be obeyed immediately and without question. If, that is, the situation calls for action at once. If it's not pressing, I'm open to suggestions."

Eleth, the blonde, looked hard at Anana. "He's a *leblabbiy*."

Anana shrugged and said, "He and I spun a flat stone marked on one side up into the air, and he called out the right side that fell uppermost on the ground. We had agreed beforehand that the one who did this would be the leader. In times of emergency, he is not to be questioned or disobeyed.

"As for his being a *leblabbiy*, what of it? He's a better man than any Thoan I've ever met. You two should try to get over your absurd opinion of *leblabbiys* as inherently inferior to the Lords. It's nonsense! Dangerous nonsense because it makes Lords underestimate them. By the time the Lord gets killed, he finds out how wrong he was. About Kickaha, anyway."

Eleth and Ona said nothing, but their expressions showed disbelief.

"You'll learn the hard way," Anana said.

The sisters protested when Anana took their beamers.

"How can we protect ourselves?"

"You'll be given them when we think you're one hundred percent trustworthy," he said. "Meantime, you can carry your axes, spears, and bows. We'll camp here tonight. Come morning, we start that way."

He pointed west.

"Why that way?" Eleth said. "Are you sure that's the right direction? What if . . . ?"

"I have my reasons," Kickaha said, interrupting her. "You'll know why when we get there."

They would be heading toward a gate on this level that would transmit them to the palace. It would take them days to get there and, perhaps, days to find the gate after they got there. The area in which it was placed was immense, and he was not sure of its exact location. By the time the party reached it, he and Anana would know if the two women could be trusted. Or the sisters would be dead. Possibly, he and Anana would have been slain by them, though he much doubted that.

That night, around a small fire, they all lay down to sleep. The sisters had eaten well or, at least, much better than they had been eating. Kickaha had foraged in the woods and brought back various edible plants. He had also shot a large monkey, which had been roasted on a spit.

The sisters had washed their robes in the nearby creek and scrubbed off their body dirt, though they complained about the coldness of the water. The robes quickly dried on sticks thrust into the ground near the fire. When time for bedding down came, Kickaha took the first watch. The sisters slept near the fire in their thin but warm blankets. Anana, wrapped in her blanket, her head pillowed on her knapsack, lay close to the edge of the clearing. Kickaha stationed himself for a while on the opposite side of the clearing. After a while, he stepped into the forest and prowled around the clearing. He carried two beamers in his belt and another in his hand.

He looked out for big predators, of which one could be that huge, hairy creature he had glimpsed. He also kept an eye on the sisters. If they were going to attack their captors, they might try tonight. However, none of them stirred during his and Anana's watches.

In the morning, when Urizen's daughters wanted to leave the campsite together to empty their bowels in the forest, he insisted that they go one at a time. It was impossible to watch all of them at the same time unless they all went together. But he wanted them alone out among the trees. If a confederate was hanging out around there, he, she, or it might make contact with one of the two. Kickaha watched each of them, but he was hidden behind bushes.

No one approached Eleth while she was in the forest. While Ona was squatting, a raven waddled out from behind a big tree. No, not *a* raven, Kickaha thought. It's *the* raven, the one who's been following us. He watched as the big bird silently came from behind Ona and stood in front of her. She did not look surprised.

They spoke to each other briefly and in low tones. Kickaha was too far away to make out the words. He did not need to do so. A conspiracy was flourishing. But who besides the sisters and the raven was involved?

After the bird had gone back into the woods and Ona started back to camp, Kickaha followed the raven. The bird led him for less than a mile before it came to a clearing large enough for it to wing away. Kickaha plunged into the woods then to gather more plants and to catch several large insects that he knew were delicious eating. He got a perverse pleasure out of insisting that the sisters eat them.

"They contain several vital ingredients lacking in the other plants," he said. "Believe me, I know."

"You're not trying to poison us, are you?" Eleth said.

"Stupid, he doesn't have to do that if he wants to kill us," her sister said.

"I wouldn't say that," Kickaha said, grinning.

"You demon!" Eleth said. "Just knowing that you might do it makes me want to throw up."

"It'll be good for you if you do," Kickaha replied cheerfully. "Your stomach needs emptying after all that heavy meat-eating you've been doing."

Ona giggled and said, "Don't vomit in the pot. I'm really hungry."

Kickaha did not trust Ona at all, but he liked her spirit.

On the way westward that day, Kickaha asked Eleth where the sisters had been heading after they had come through the gate.

"Nowhere in particular," she said. "Of course, we got away from the area of the gate as swiftly as possible because Red Orc might be following us. Then we traveled in the direction of the monolith. If we didn't find a gate on this level, we were going to climb the monolith, though we were not happy about having to do that. It looks formidable."

"It is and then some," he said. "It has the jawbreaking name of Doozvillnavava. It soars sixty thousand feet high or more. But it's climbable. I've done it several times. Its face, which looks so smooth from a long distance, is full of caves and has innumerable ledges. Trees and other plants grow on its face, which also has stretches of rotten rock that crumbles underfoot. Predators live in its caves and holes and on its ledges. There thrive the many-footed snakes, the rock-gripping wolves, the boulder apes, the giant axe-beak birds, and the poison-dripping downdroppers.

"There are others I won't mention. Even if you could climb to the plateau on top, you would then have to travel about five hundred miles through a vast forest teeming with many perils and, after that, a plain with no less dangerous creatures and humans. And then you'd come to the final monolith, atop which is Jadawin-Wolff's palace. The climb is hard, and the chances that you'd evade the traps set there are very low."

"We didn't know the details," Eleth said, "but we supposed that climbing the mountain would not be enjoyable. That's why we were looking for a gate, though we knew we probably wouldn't recognize one if we saw it. Most of them must be disguised as boulders and so forth. But some might be undisguised. You never know."

During their journey so far, Kickaha had not taken the Horn of Shambarimen from its deerskin bag. If the sisters knew that he had it, they would not hesitate to murder him and Anana to get it. However, the time would soon come when he would have to use it.

Once a day, while the others rested, he or Anana climbed to the top of a high tree and scanned the country around them. Most of this consisted of the waving tops of trees. But, far away and toward the monolith, was a three-peaked mountain. This was his destination. At its foot was a huge boulder shaped like a heart, its point deep in the ground. This contained a gate to a gate that transmitted its occupant to the palace of the Lord of Alofmethbin. Though Kickaha had forgotten the codeword activating it, he had the Horn, the universal key.

If the raven was following them, it was keeping well hidden. And there had been no sign of the bearish creature. His brief encounter with it might have been accidental, though that did not seem probable.

Next day, during the noonday halt, he went out into the woods for a pit call but stayed there to watch. Presently, Eleth left the campsite, seemingly for the same reason he had left it. Instead of selecting a tree behind which to squat, she went deeper into the forest. He followed her at a distance. When he saw her stop in a small clearing, he hid behind a bush.

Eleth stood for a while haloed in a sunbeam shooting through a straight space among the branches overhead. She looked transfigured, as if she were indeed the goddess she thought she was.

After a while, the raven waddled out from behind a bush. Kickaha began crawling slowly so that he could get within hearing distance. After a few minutes of very cautious progress in a semicircle, he stopped behind the enormous flying-buttress root of a giant tree.

". . . repeats that you are not to kill them, no matter what the temptation, until he has found the gate," the raven said.

"Which will be when?" Eleth said.

"He did not tell me, but he said that it will probably not be long."

"What does he mean by 'not long'?" she said. She looked exasperated. "A day? Two days? A week? This is a hard life. My sister and I long for a high roof, warmth, clean clothes, a shower, good things to eat, much time to sleep, and plenty of virile *leblabbiy* men."

"I don't know what he means by 'not long,'" the raven said. "You'll just have to do what he says. Otherwise . . ."

"Yes, I know. We will, of course, continue to obey his orders. You may tell him that—if you're in communication with him."

The raven did not reply. She said, "What about the oromoth?"

Kickaha did not know what an oromoth was. He would have to ask Anana about it.

"It is trailing you for your protection. It won't interfere unless it sees that you're in grave danger from those two."

"If that happens," Eleth said, "it may be too slow. Or it might be off taking a piss somewhere at that time."

The raven sounded as if it were trying to imitate human laughter. When it stopped that, it said, "That's the chance you have to take. That's better than what will surely happen if you fail. I wouldn't even think about betraying him by telling Kickaha and Anana what's going on and throwing in your lot with theirs."

"I wouldn't dream of it!" Eleth said.

The raven laughed again and said, "Of course not! Unless you thought you'd have a better chance to come out on top! Just remember what he will do to you if you turn traitor!"

Eleth said, stonily, "Is there anything else you have to tell me? If not, get out of my sight, you stinking mess of black feathers!"

"Nothing else. But don't think I'll forget your insult! I'll get my revenge!"

"You stupid snakebrain! We won't even be in this world! Now, get the hell away from me!"

"You Thoan don't smell so nice yourselves," the raven said.

It turned and disappeared into the forest. Eleth looked as if she were about to follow it. But she turned and walked into the woods. As soon as Kickaha was sure that she could not see him, he rose, and he ran bent over along the edge of the clearing. Then he went more slowly and in a straight line. Presently, he saw the raven. It had entered a large clearing and was heading for a fallen tree lying half within the other trees and half into the clearing. The raven hopped up onto the trunk, clawed its way to the upper part, and began ascending that. Obviously, it planned on leaping off the end, which was about thirty feet above the ground, and flapping in a circle around the big clearing until it could get high enough to fly above the treetops.

Kickaha took the beamer from its holster. The weapon was already set on half-power. Just as the raven leaped from the end of the fallen tree, Kickaha aimed at the bird and pressed the trigger. A faintly scarlet narrow beam shot part of the raven's right wing off. It squawked, and it fell.

Kickaha ran around the tree. The bird was flopping on the ground and crying out. He grabbed it from from behind by its neck and choked it. When its struggles had become feeble, he released it. It lay on the ground gasping for air, its legs upraised, its huge black eyes staring at him. If ravens could turn pale, it would have been as white as a snowbird.

He waved the beamer at the raven.

"What is your name, croaker?" he said harshly.

The bird struggled up onto its two feet.

"How do you like Stamun?"

"A good enough name. But what is yours?" Kickaha said. He stepped closer and shoved the end of the beamer close to the raven's head. "Now is not the time for wisecracking. I don't have much patience."

While he spoke, he kept glancing around. You never knew what might be creeping up on you.

"Wayskam," the raven said.

"Who sent that message to Eleth?"

"Awrk!"

Kickaha translated that as an expression of surprise mingled with dismay.

"You heard us?"

"Yes, dummy. Of course I did."

"If I tell you, will you let me live? And not torture me?"

"I'll let you go," Kickaha said, "and I won't touch you."

"You could not touch me and still could torture me," it said.

"I won't give you any pain," Kickaha said. "Unlike the Lords, I take no pleasure in doing that. But that doesn't mean I won't make you talk if I have to. So, talk!"

The raven was doomed to be killed or to die of starvation. It could never fly with half of its right wing sheared off. But the bird was still in shock and had not thought of that.

Or could it, like Lords, regenerate amputated limbs?

It did not matter. It would not survive long enough in the forest to grow back the severed part.

"I'll talk if you'll take me back to your camp and nurse me until I can fly again. And then release me. Not that my life will be worth much if Red Orc finds out I betrayed him."

The raven was thinking more clearly than Kickaha had expected it would. Also, its remark that it could, if given time, fly again showed that Eye of the Lord ravens could grow new parts.

"I promise I'll take good care of you," he said, "if you tell me the truth."

"And will you protect me from the iron-hearted daughters of Urizen? Those bitches will try to kill me."

"I'll do my best," Kickaha said.

"That's all I can ask for. You have a reputation for being a trickster, but it is said that your word is as solid as Kethkith's Skull."

Kickaha did not know that reference, but its meaning was obvious.

"Talk! But keep to the point!"

Wayskam opened its beak. A squawk grated from it. Out of the corner of his eye, Kickaha saw something dim and moving. He jumped to one side and at the same time started to whirl. His beamer shot its scarlet ray, but it did not hit his attacker. Something—it looked like a paw moving so fast it was almost a blur—struck his right shoulder. He was slammed down onto the ground; pain shot through his shoulder. For a second, he was not fully conscious.

However, his unconscious mind had taken over, and he automatically rolled away. The thing growled like the birth of thunder. Kickaha kept on rolling for several yards, then started to get up on a knee. The thing moved very swiftly toward him. Kickaha raised the beamer. A paw knocked it loose from his grip and numbed his hand. Then the creature was on him.

Its sharp teeth closed on his shoulder, but it did not sink them deeply into his flesh. Its breath was hot, though it did not have the stink of a meat-eater. It quickly released the bite as a paw hooked itself under his crotch and lifted him up and away.

Kickaha was vaguely aware that he was soaring through the air and that his groin was hurting worse than his shoulder. When he struck the ground, he blacked out.

Through the slowly evaporating mists, Anana's face passed from a dark blurry object into lovely features and bright black hair. Her face was twisted with concern, and she was crying, "Kickaha! Kickaha!"

He said, "Here I am. Down but not out, I think."

He tried to get up. His knees could not keep their lock. He sank back onto his buttocks and gazed around. The creature was lying face up and unmoving on the ground. The raven was not in sight.

"You got here barely in time," he said. "What were you doing? Following me?"

She looked relieved but did not smile.

"You were gone too long just to be urinating. And I smelled trouble. That's nonsense, I suppose, but I have developed a feeling for the not-quite-right. Anyway, I did go after you, and I got here just in time to see that thing throw you away as if you were a piece of trash paper. So, I beamed it."

Kickaha did not reproach her for killing a source of possibly very important information. She must have had to do it.

"The bird?"

"I never saw a bird. You mean the raven?"

He nodded slightly. "The one I told you about. As we suspected, the sisters are working for Red Orc. Willingly or unwillingly, I don't know which."

"Then Red Orc must know we're here!"

6

*N*ot necessarily the exact spot," he said. "We can't assume he's keeping close tabs on us."

He told her how he had spied on Eleth and the raven and how noiselessly and swiftly the bearlike thing had attacked him.

"I'm glad you got here in the proverbial nick of time. But I think I would've gotten away from it and managed to kill it with the beamer."

"Your lack of confidence is pathetic," she said, smiling. "You stay here and get your strength back. I'll go after the raven. If I catch it, we'll get the rest of its story out of it."

"Don't look for it more than twenty minutes. If you haven't caught it by then, you'll never find it."

Before leaving, however, she ran to a small creek nearby and returned with her deerskin canteen full of fresh water. She poured water over his wounds, held the container to his lips so that he could drink deeply, then stood up.

"There! That'll hold you for a while."

She touched her lips with her thumb and forefinger together, forming an oval, and snapped the fingers of her other hand, a Thoan gesture symbolizing a kiss. Then she disappeared among the trees. He lay staring up into the bright green sky. After a while, he slowly and painfully got to his feet. Everything seemed to whirl around him, though he did not fall. His shoulder hurt more than his crotch did. His lower back was stiff and would be worse soon. He was bleeding from the shoulder, though not heavily, and from less deep claw marks on his belly and testicles.

When he got to the corpse, he studied it—her—in detail. The first thing he noted, though, was that Anana had shot the beam through the forehead just above the eyes. Though she had had to take swift aim, she had coolly decided to pierce its brain and had done so.

The creature was at least seven feet long and formed like a hybrid of woman and bear. The face lacked the ursine snout, but its jaws bulged out as if they would have liked to have become a bear's. That forehead indicated that she was highly intelligent. The structure of her mouth and the teeth, however, showed that she might have had much trouble pronouncing human words. Whether or not she could speak well, she must have understood Thoan speech.

It was then that Kickaha remembered some stories told by the Bear People, an Amerindian tribe on the second level. These were narratives he had thought were tribal myths until now. They spoke of creatures descended from a union between the original Great Bear and the daughter of the original human couple. Indeed, the Bear People claimed that they, like the Man-Bear, were descended from this couple. But this creature's first ancestors must have been made in some Lord's laboratory. Probably, the Thoan was Jadawin, he who became Wolff on Earth I.

By now, the scavenging beetles and ants, attracted by the odor of decaying flesh, were scuttling across the clearing. Kickaha walked woozily into the forest and sat down near the edge of the clearing, his back against a giant aboveground root. He watched from there. Presently, Anana walked into the clearing for a few feet and looked around. Her stance showed that she was ready to dive back into the woods if she saw or heard anything suspicious.

He hooted softly, imitating the call of a small tree-dwelling lemuroid. She hooted back. He got up stiffly and approached her.

"The raven was already dead when I found it," she said. "One of those giant weasels was eating it."

They talked for a few minutes. Having decided on their course of action, they started back to the camp. Kickaha's plan to shock the sisters into confessing their part in Red Orc's plan had been discarded. He had wanted to cut the head off the Man-Bear and to throw it down at the women's feet. But he agreed with her that it was best to keep them in the dark. For a while, anyway.

By the time they reached the camp, they had concocted a story to explain his wounds. Though a big cat had attacked him, he said, he had gotten away from it. Anana had supported him while he limped into camp. That needed no acting by him, nor did his lying on the ground and groaning with pain.

"We'll have to stay here until I've recovered enough to resume walking," he said.

Whether or not Eleth and Ona accepted his story, he had no way of determining. That they were Thoan made them suspicious of even the most simple and straightforward statement.

Two days later, he was ready to go. Like all humans in the Thoan universes, except for the two Earths, he had remarkable powers of physical recovery. Except for faint scars, which would disappear entirely, his gashes were healed over. However, he had to take in far more food and water than he would have normally eaten. A faster healing required more fuel.

During this time, Anana trailed the sisters into the woods whenever they went there for privacy.

"It's obvious they're trying to get into contact with the raven, and they're upset because it isn't showing up."

"Let them seethe in their sweat," he said.

"Their bickering and quarreling is getting on my nerves."

"On mine, too. They're ten-thousand-year-old infants. They

hate each other, yet they feel as if they have to stay together. Maybe it's because each is afraid that the other will be happy if she isn't around to make her life miserable."

She said, "Most Thoan couples are like that. Are Earth mates the same way?"

"Too many."

He paused, then said, "I suppose you know both asked me to roll in the leaves with them."

She laughed, and she said, "They've asked me, too."

On the early morning of the third day, they broke camp and set out toward the target mountain. Two days afterwards, they left the great forest. About two days' journey across a vast plain was before them. They crossed it without harm, though they were attacked twice by the sabertooths, which dined chiefly on mammoths, and once by six of the moalike birds called axebeaks. And then they came to the foothills of the mountain named Rigsoorth.

"Here we make camp for the night," Kickaha said. He pointed to an area halfway up the steep three-peaked mass. "By late noon tomorrow, if we push hard, we'll be there."

Only he and Anana knew that he was not indicating the place where the gate was located. He seldom revealed to strangers what he truly intended to do. Misdirection, sleight of hand, and deviousness were traits stamped with the label: KICKAHA.

Eleth said, "The gate is in a large heart-shaped boulder?"

"That's what I said," Kickaha replied.

Just before they got under their blankets that night in the entrance of a small cave, Anana said, "If they think they're that close to the gate, they might try to murder us tonight."

"I doubt it. I think Red Orc has other plans for us. On the other hand, maybe they might try it. I'll take the first watch." He kissed her lips. "Sleep well."

After fifteen minutes, he slipped out from the blankets and crossed by the seemingly sleeping sisters. He crawled up the rocky slope to a boulder and climbed onto its top. After wrapping himself in a blanket, he sat and watched the small fire in the cave opening and the three women around it. Now and then, he looked in all directions. And he listened intently. Once, a huge dark body snuffled around fifty feet below the cave, kicked a few rocks, and sent them sliding noisily down the slope. Then it disappeared. Once, a long-winged bird—or was it a flying mammal?—swooped down and seized a small animal that squeaked once, and then predator and prey were gulped by the darkness.

Night thoughts covered Kickaha as if a black parachute were collapsing over him.

Foremost and most often recurring of the images that questioned him was Red Orc's.

Kickaha was certain that the Lord was nudging him and Anana toward a trap. Even if he had not overheard the raven and Eleth, he would have been sure. So far, he had gone along with with the Lord's plot, whatever it was. That Red Orc had not tried to have them killed proved to Kickaha that the Lord wanted him and Anana alive. He was planning something special for them. Such as intense physical torture or a long imprisonment involving mental pain, or both.

Kickaha thought back to when he and Anana had been in Los Angeles and Orc and his men had been trying to catch them. Now that he considered the events, it seemed to him that Orc's men had been rather inept. And Orc's organizing had not been of the best.

Was that because Orc was playing with him?

It seemed likely. One of the rules of the games Lords played with each other was that the opponent was always given a slight chance to escape a trap. If, that is, the enemy was quick and ingenious enough. And also had a certain amount of luck.

The opening was always so slight that many Lords had been killed trying to get through their foes' trapped gates into those foes' private universes. Thus far, Kickaha and Anana had been fortunate. Their enemies, not they, had died or been forced to flee their strongholds.

But it seemed to Kickaha that Red Orc had not tried hard enough, up to now, to capture or kill them.

However, Red Orc might have gotten tired of the game and determined to get rid forever of his archenemies.

Kickaha did not intend to allow that to happen.

But Red Orc did, and he was not one to be ignored. Of all the Lords, he was the most dangerous and the most successful. No other Thoan had invaded so many universes or killed so many of their owners. No one else was so dreaded. Yet, it was said, according to what Anana and others had told Kickaha, that he had been a somewhat compassionate and loving youth. That is, by Thoan standards.

But the unjust and harsh treatment by his father, Los, had metamorphosed Orc into a brutal and vindictive man. That was some people's theory. But Kickaha believed that the change was caused by the genetic viciousness of the Lords. Whatever the reason, Orc had rebelled against his father. After a long struggle with him, during which several planets in several universes had been ruined, he killed Los. He had then taken his mother, Enitharmon—and his aunt, Vala—as his mates. This was not against Thoan morality, nor was it uncommon.

Much later, Enitharmon had been killed by a raiding Lord. Red Orc had tracked the killer down, captured her, and tortured her so hideously that the Lords, though proficient and merciless torturers, were shocked.

"It was shortly after this, only a thousand or so years afterwards, but at least fifteen thousand Terrestrial years ago," Anana had said, "that Red Orc became the secret Lord of both Earths. But you know that."

"Yes, I know," Kickaha had said. "And Red Orc made the universes of the two Earths about then."

"That's what I told you," she had said. "When I told you that, I thought Red Orc had made them and that it was he who populated both planets with artificial human beings. But I believe now that I was mistaken. You see, there is also a story that the two Earths were made by a Lord named Orc. Not our Red Orc. He was one of the very first to make pocket universes. He was born many millennia before Red Orc. But he was killed by another Lord. The two Earths had no Lord for a long time. Then, one called Thrassa took over. But Red Orc, who was born long after the original Orc, killed Thrassa and became the Lord of the two Earths."

Kickaha, his mind leaping ahead to form a conclusion, had said, "The original Orc became confused with Red Orc."

She had nodded. "That's it. Or something like it. During all those thousands of years and with the Lords' failure to keep records and the infrequent communication among the Lords of the many universes, Red Orc became identified with the original Orc. Red Orc, he's my uncle, you know, my mother's brother, and Los and Enitharmon are my grandparents. Jadawin, who is also Wolff, is my half-brother . . ."

"Don't confuse me," Kickaha had said. "Stick to the story."

"Sorry. Red Orc now sincerely believes that he did make the last of the universes to be made, the universes of Earth I and Earth II. He is not sane, though he functions extremely well. Very few Lords are, in fact, entirely sane. Living so long seems to unbalance the mind of all but the most stable."

"Such as yourself," he had said, grinning.

"Yes. Let me tell you how I arrived at this conclusion."

"That too long a life makes it hard for the brain to continue accepting reality and thus slips into unreality?"

She had smiled and had said, "I wasn't referring to that, though what you say is close to the truth. One night, some time ago when we were on the planet of the Tripeds, while you were sleeping soundly but I could not sleep at all, I got to thinking about Orc and Red Orc. And I saw what the true story has to be."

"Why didn't you didn't tell me about it in the morning?"

"Because that was the night we were attacked by the Shlook tribe. Remember? We fought our way out but had to run for two days before we shook off the last of those three-legged cannibals. That made me forget about it until now. In fact, I was lucky to be able to recall it. After thousands of years, my brain, like all of the long-lived Thoan, stores only certain significant memories. It seems there's only room enough . . ."

"A struldbrugian's lot is not a 'appy one," Kickaha had said in English.

"What?"

"Never mind. The true story, as you call it."

"You have these two stories about who made the two Earths. The one about the original Orc doing it is not now widespread. Most people now accept the story that Red Orc did it, and his claim that he did so has reinforced that belief. But he could not have done it."

She had paused so long that Kickaha had said, "Well!"

"There's the tale I've heard from several unhostile Lords; not many of those, I'll admit. It's supposed to have come from Red Orc's boasting to his various mistresses, though he has a reputation for being close-mouthed about his personal life.

"It concerns the time when he was stranded by his father on Anthema, the Unwanted World. Los thought his son would die there, though he did have a very slight chance to survive and a lesser chance to find the gate out of that world. But, if he did find it, it would only lead him to Zazel's World, also called the Caverned World. And there was no way out of that. Or so thought Los.

"Red Orc did find the gate, and he went into Zazel's World.

This, according to Red Orc's story, was a single vast computer but with countless caves and tunnels inhabited by plants and animals. Zazel had died long ago, but an artificial being was still the caretaker of it. This thing eventually let Red Orc talk it into sending him out through a gate Los knew nothing about. But Red Orc intended to re-enter that world if he could—after he'd killed his father. That took several thousands of years, an epic in itself.

"The reason my uncle wanted to get back into the Caverned World was that its memory contained the data for making a Creation-Destruction engine."

"Ah!"

"You know what I'm talking about?"

"Sure," Kickaha had said. "The ancient Lords used such engines to make their artificial universes. But as time went by and then during the millennia-long and very destructive war of the Lords against the Black Bellers, the engines were destroyed or lost. And the data for making them were lost, too. Am I right?"

"Right! But Red Orc found out that the data were still in the Caverned World's circuits. He was in no position to get it then, but he was determined to come back someday and do so. Unfortunately for him, fortunately for us, he could not get back in. The creature that ruled the world must have sealed up the gate. Red Orc's been trying to find a way to penetrate that world, though he hasn't tried continuously. Other things, such as warring against the Lords, have kept him busy. But I think that he's almost given up the effort. He's been frustrated too often."

"From what I know of him, I doubt that," Kickaha had said.

One of the recent things occupying Red Orc would have been trying to find Kickaha and Anana. The Thoan's pride would be deeply wounded because the two had eluded him so successfully and for such a long time. He would be in one of his well-known rages. God help the people around him; God help the men he had sent to track down and catch Kickaha and Anana. However, these people were no innocents. Anything bad that happened to them, they deserved.

He might know by now that his greatest two enemies were on—had been on—the Whaziss planet. But he did not know exactly where they were. Or did he?

Though Orc might never have completely lost the trail on Earth of Kickaha and Anana, he must have lost it when they escaped to the Lavalite planet. He must have been trying to find them during the fifteen years they were on the Whaziss planet.

Just what else had the Thoan been up to during that decade and a half? How many Lords had he killed, and how many of the pocket universes were now his?

Who was the mysterious Englishman costumed in early nine-teenth-century clothes who had been in that aerial mansion on the Lavalite planet?

Where were Wolff and Chryseis now?

Then the ancient sleeper with the insectile face swam into Kickaha's mental sea. He was an enigmaed enigma. Why had he awakened just as the intruders from a much later time had left that curious chamber? Just how and why had they blundered into that room, which must surely be heavily guarded by whatever guarded it?

Kickaha did not believe that they had "blundered" into it or that the awakening was a coincidence. Coincidences might happen, but even these, he believed, if dug into deeply enough, would reveal the connections.

Anana came to take over her watch. They talked in whispers for about ten minutes. When they were clear on what to do the next day, Kickaha went to the cave to sleep, though not deeply. Thus, the night passed with each taking turns on the boulder. He was on it when a brief gray light announced that the sun was just around the curve of the planet.

The sisters had not once gotten up, though they had shifted around a lot trying to find a comfortable position on the hard rock.

After they had spattered some water on their faces and eaten their simple breakfast, they scattered to various boulders and rocky projections behind which to evacuate. After returning to the camp, they loaded up their gear and set out, Kickaha leading. Before they had put a half-mile behind them, Eleth called a halt.

"This is not the way you told us we'd be going!"

Kickaha said, "I pointed out the spot we'd travel to. But we don't take a direct route. This way will be much easier."

After two hours, the sisters complained that they were taking a hell of a long way roundabout.

Kickaha stopped in front of an eighty-foot-high monolith of reddish granite. Its base was within a few feet of the edge of the cliff on which the group stood. Ten feet up from the base, a half-sphere of glossy black rock extruded from the granite. It looked like a cannonball that had been shot at close range into the monolith.

"Is that the gate?" Eleth said, pointing at the stone pillar.

"No," Kickaha said.

"Then where is it? Are we anywhere near it?"

"It's not the gate, but the gate site is in it."

He opened the deerskin bag attached to his belt and pulled out the silvery trumpet.

Eleth, eyes wide, sucked in air noisily. "The Horn of Shambari-men!"

Ona was too awed at first to make any sound. Then she and Eleth broke into high-pitched chatter. Kickaha let them go on for about a minute before calling for silence.

He raised the Horn to his lips and blew. As soon as the last note had faded away, an arch-shaped area seven feet high and five feet wide formed at the base of the rock. It shimmered as if made of heat waves. Kickaha thought that he could almost see through the ripplings to the other side and that something huge and dark was there. But that was, of course, an illusion.

"We have ten seconds before it closes!" he said loudly. He waved the Horn. "Everybody into it! Now!"

Anana and he pulled out their beamers and shoved the sisters toward the gate. Eleth was shouting, "No! No! How do we know it's not a trap you've set for us!"

She tried to run away. Anana tripped her with an extended leg and then kicked her in the buttocks as she struggled to get up on her feet.

Looking terrified, Ona stumbled toward the entrance, then darted to one side and tried to get past Anana. Anana knocked Ona down with the side of her hand against her neck.

Eleth also ran, holding up the hem of her robe, then she stumbled and fell flat on the ground. She refused to get up, though Kickaha shouted that he would cut her in half.

The shimmering on the face of the rock was gone.

He and Anana stepped back so that they could cover the sisters with their beamers.

"It's plain as the nose on a camel that you two don't want to go through that gate," Kickaha said. "Yet, a moment ago, you seemed quite willing to go with us. Why're you so reluctant all of a sudden?"

Eleth got onto her feet and tried to rub the dirt from the front of her white robe. She said, "We really don't trust you."

"A very weak excuse!" Anana said loudly. "What is the real reason you tried to get away? You know something's waiting for us there? Were you hoping to lead us into a trap?"

"We panicked!"

"Yes," Ona said, faking a snuffling, "we got scared."

"Of what?" Anana asked.

Kickaha bellowed, "You were afraid that Red Orc would catch you along with us, betray you, and kill you, too? Is that right?"

Whatever surprise Eleth felt, she did not reveal it. But Ona winced as if he had struck her with a fly swatter.

"Red Orc?" she screeched. "What does he have to do with that?" She half turned and waved at where the gate had been.

Kickaha walked up to her until his nose almost touched hers. He spoke even more loudly. "I overheard your raven, Wayskam, talking to Eleth! So I know all! All!"

He thought, I don't by any means know all. But I'll scare them into confessing everything. If I can't, I'll let Anana loose on them. Her heart isn't as soft as mine. I hope I can stand the screaming.

The sisters said nothing. That he knew the name of the raven showed them that he was on to them.

"Your protector, the bear-woman," he said, "is dead. Anana killed it."

Eleth smiled slightly and said, "Ah! It wasn't a big cat that clawed you! It was . . ."

"I didn't catch her name," Kickaha said. "Yes, she did tear me up a little. Anana shot her before I could do it."

Eleth still kept silence, but Ona said, "We couldn't help ourselves! We . . ."

Eleth screamed, "Shut up! They don't know anything! They're just trying to get you to talk!"

"Tell you what, Ona," Anana said. "You tell us everything—I mean everything, nothing left out—and I'll spare your life. As for Eleth . . ."

She stabbed the beamer at Ona.

"Spill it all!"

Eleth spoke with a diamond-hard voice. No quaverings in her. "If we talk, we'll die. If we don't talk, we'll die. It's better not to talk. Ona, I absolutely forbid you to say another word about it!"

"You think Red Orc'll save us now?" her sister said, sneering. "He'll pop up just in time to save us? How could he? Besides, what does he care about us? I think . . ."

"That's enough!" Anana said. "You've both said enough to damn yourselves. Not that we needed a word from you to know that. Eleth, you talk first. If you hold anything back, and Ona then reveals that you have been holding back, you die! Immediately!"

Eleth looked around as if she expected Red Orc to come riding down from the mountains to rescue her. No savior was in sight, and Eleth was realist enough to know that none was coming. She began talking.

It was much as Kickaha had expected it to be. The sisters had not, as they had claimed, escaped from Orc when he invaded their palace. They had been caught before they could get to a gate. Instead of killing them, Red Orc had forced them to be tools to catch Kickaha and Anana.

At this point, Anana snorted and said, "Forced? You, the iron-hearted daughters of Urizen, had to be forced to become our enemy?"

"We never claimed to be friends of yours," Eleth said. "But we would never have gone out after you."

"You're too lazy," Anana said.

"He did not tell us why he thought you were there," Eleth said. "We were not in a position to ask him questions about his methods and results."

The Lord had not been able to determine just where the two were on Whazzis. But he did find the only gate existing, the one that Kickaha and Anana eventually came to. The hexagon in the Tripeds' temple had long been there. Orc had rechanneled it, making it a resonant circuit, and then gone elsewhere.

"He did say that it would lead to a certain area on the World of Tiers. When the alarm was set off—where, I do not know—Red Orc would know that the circuit had been entered. Of course, he could not be sure that some other Lord had not activated it. But he said that he was approximately ninety percent sure that you two would do it."

"How could he be sure that we could survive all the traps?" Kickaha said.

"He apparently had great faith that you two would. He did pay you both a compliment. He said that if anybody could get through the circuit, you could."

"I had Shambarimem's Horn."

"He never mentioned that."

"He wouldn't. If you'd known that, you would've been tempted to betray him and risk everything for this great treasure."

"You're right," Eleth said.

The Lord or, perhaps, a servant of his, had gotten them somehow to the middle of the forest where Kickaha and Anana had found them. The sisters had been unconscious during the entire journey from their world to this.

"I can assure you that there is no gate in that forest," Kickaha said. "I know. I've seen the diagram of the gates, in Wolff's palace. You must have been sent through another gate somewhere on this world and then transported by air to the forest."

"There couldn't be gates of which you have no knowledge? Red Orc could not have opened a new gate?"

Kickaha shrugged.

The women had awakened among the trees. For fifty-five days, they had had to struggle to survive there. Orc had given them only a few necessities, the stuff they might have taken with them during a very hasty departure.

"We had almost given up on your getting here," Eleth said. "It wasn't certain that you would survive the circuit or that you would find us. But Red Orc, may he suffer the tortures of Inthiman, did not care if we starved to death or were killed by predators! We had decided we'd stay there five days more. If you hadn't shown up by then, we'd set out for Jadawin's palace."

"A noble ambition," Anana said. "But you had little chance to make it up the two monoliths."

Eleth did not have much to add to her story. She only said that she and her sister did not know why Red Orc wanted them to lead the two to this gate. Ona said that that was true.

Kickaha and Anana withdrew from the women to talk softly.

"They probably don't know why," he said. "Red Orc wouldn't tell them. What I'd like to know is how he knew about this gate."

"I'm not sure that he did or does know," she said. "He may be following us now to see where we go. When he sees us open the gate, he'll pounce."

She looked up the mountain slope and then down it and across the great plain.

"Or, if not he, then someone in his service," Kickaha said.

"He or whoever may be a hundred miles away. Across the plain or up there in an aircraft. One missile would wipe us out."

"He wouldn't blow us apart," Kickaha said. "He wants us alive. We're in a Hamletish situation. There're so many ifs and buts to consider, we're being paralyzed. Let's do something now, and ride out the consequences."

He blew the Horn again. Anana herded the sisters, who protested strongly but vainly, through the shimmering curtain in the rock. She stepped in on their heels. He dropped the Horn into the bag and leaped through the shimmering. On its other side was a hemispherical chamber. The floor was as covered with the opaque brightness as the walls. He could, however, feel bare and level rock under his feet.

Ona screamed and darted by Kickaha. He thrust out an arm to catch her. She ducked it and leaped back through the curtain. The upper part of her body had disappeared when the shimmering snapped off. Only part of her robe, her buttocks, her long legs, and some blood remained. Eleth shrieked and then began sobbing loudly.

Without warning, they were in another place, some sort of pit cut out of rock. Crouching, he spun around, his beamer ready, taking in all that was his new environment. There did not seem to be anything that demanded immediate defense or attack. A man whom Kickaha recognized stood at one end of the pit, but his open hands were held high above his head in a sign of peace.

Kickaha's gaze passed from him to examine the prison they were in. It was a hole twelve feet square and approximately ten feet deep. Straight above was a bright blue sky. The sun was out of sight, and the shadows of the vast cliff on one side were moving swiftly toward the opening of the hole.

They were in a pit at the bottom or up on one side of an immense abyss. Both sides went up at a thirty-degree angle from the horizontal, though they had many ledges and holes. Here and there on the walls, some puny trees grew, extending at forty-five-degree angles from the steep slopes. Great patches of some green mosslike stuff covered parts of the walls.

The heat was a vicious magical wand that tapped him and brought forth from his skin a spring of water. He estimated that the temperature was approximately 101°F.

He did not waste time. He took the Horn from its bag and blew it. The seven notes died, but no gate appeared on the walls of the pit. Red Orc had trapped them, no doubt of that.

He put the Horn back in the bag and turned to face the man at the end of the pit. He was tall and handsome and looked twenty-five years old, though he must have lived at least a century and a half ago, possibly more. His long hair was brown and pulled tightly back into a ponytail. His suit of clothes was of a style in fashion among the Lords a long time ago. But he must have had them made in some Thoan universe. The threads of the jacket pulsed with green, red, white, blue, and yellow as if they were colored tubes. His once-white shirt was ruffed and open at the neck. His trousers were a bottle-green velvety material ending at the calves in a tight band. A scarlet triangular patch covered his groin.

On the middle finger of his left hand was a heavy ring of silver. It wound around the finger three times. Though Kickaha had glimpsed the ring when he had entered the pit, he now saw it in detail. He was startled. It was in the form of the scaly man. That insectile head on the ring looked exactly like the head of the being in the chamber of the dead.

"We meet again," the man said in English, smiling. His pronunciation, though, was not like any English Kickaha had ever heard.

"I am Eric Clifton. At your service. Like you, I am the prisoner of Red Orc. At least, I assume that that loathsome Lord brought you here against your will."

7

*E*leth was now wailing loudly. Kickaha shouted, "Stop that caterwauling! You hated your sister, yet you're carrying on something awful as if she was very dear to you!"

Eleth stared with red eyes at him while she choked back her grief. Sniffling, she said, "But I did love Ona! Just because we disagreed now and then . . ."

"Disagreed? Now and then?" He laughed. "You and your sister were bound in a ring of loathing and spite! The only reason you didn't kill each other was because you'd lose somebody you could hate!"

"That's not true," Ona said. She sobbed once, then said, "You wouldn't understand."

"No, I wouldn't."

He turned back to Eric Clifton.

"I'm Kickaha. You may have heard of me. This is Anana the Bright. She was born at the beginning of the war with the Black Bellers, so that gives you an idea of how long she's lived. This wailer is Eleth, one of the hard-hearted daughters of Urizen, once known as the gentle-hearted daughters of Ahania, Urizen's wife. You may have heard of them."

He paused, then said, "Anana and I saw you briefly when you were in the floating palace of Urthona, Lord of the Shapeshifting

World. Anana and I had a hard time with Urthona and Red Orc when we were passing through Urthona's World. But we killed him. Red Orc was also a prisoner on the palace, but he escaped."

"I wondered what happened to you," Clifton said.

"Details later. You can explain to us just how you got into the Thoan universes from Earth and how you happen to be here. And how in hell did you get that ring?"

While he was talking, he was looking at the sides of the pit. An oily substance filmed them.

"It's a long story," Eric Clifton said. "Shouldn't we be thinking just now about how to get out of here before Red Orc shows up?"

"I'm doing that," Kickaha said. "But that won't interfere with my hearing your story. Keep to the highlights, though."

Clifton said that he was born somewhere around 1780 of very poor parents in London, England. His father had managed to work his way up from a day laborer to owner of a bakery shop. When that failed, he and his wife and six children had been put in debtor's prison. There his father and three children had died of malnutrition and fever. His mother had gone insane and was sent to Bedlam. Not long after he and his siblings had been released, his fourteen-year-old brother was caught and hanged for having stolen a pair of shoes. His younger sister became a whore at the age of twelve and died at eighteen of syphilis and gonorrhea.

At this point, Clifton sucked in a deep breath, and tears filmed his eyes.

"That was a very long time ago, but, as you see, I am still affected by the memory of . . . Never mind . . . Anyway . . ."

He had been very fortunate in being adopted, though not legally, by a childless couple. That had saved him from being deported to Australia.

"Though that could have been my great chance to be a free man and, perhaps, a rich man," Clifton said.

The man who raised him was Richard Dally. "A bookseller and

publisher. He and his wife taught me to read and write. I became acquainted with Mr. William Blake, the poet, engraver, and painter, when my stepfather charged me with delivering a book to him. Mr. Blake . . ."

"Does this have anything to do with the main story?" Kickaha said.

"Very much so. I cannot leave it out. Do you know Blake's poetry?"

"I read some of his poems when I was in high school."

Blake had been born, if he remembered correctly, in 1757 and had died in 1827. He was an eccentric who was Christian, but his ideas about religion differed much from the views of his time. Or from any other views then and in Kickaha's time. That much he had learned from his English teacher.

Clifton said, "Did you know that Blake wrote poetic works in which he made up his own mythology?"

"No."

"He mixed them with Christian elements."

"So?"

"His didactic and symbolical works were apocalyptic poems in which the characters were gods and goddesses he invented, or said he invented. He conceived his own mythology, and the deities in them had names such as Los, Enitharmon, Red Orc, Vala, and Ahania."

"What? You must be . . . no, you're not kidding!" Kickaha said. He turned to Anana. "Did you know this?"

Her eyes widened. "Yes, I did, but don't get angry with me. The subject just didn't come up, though I've met Blake."

"You met Blake?"

Kickaha was so flabbergasted that he spluttered. Yet he knew that she must be telling the truth. This Blake matter had meant little to her, and she would have recalled it if he had mentioned the poet's name.

He said, "All right. It's okay. I was just surprised." He turned to Clifton. "Tell me how this happened."

"Mr. Blake was a mystic visionary and exceedingly eccentric. His eyes were the wildest, the brightest, and the piercingest I've ever seen. His face was like an elf's, one of the dangerous elves. Mr. Dally said that Blake claimed that, when he was a child, he saw angels in a tree and the prophet Ezekiel in a field. It was also said that he had seen the face of God at his bedroom window. If you saw him and heard him talk, you'd believe that these stories were true.

"A few times, Mr. Blake visited Mr. Dally to buy a book on credit. He was very poor, you know. Twice, I overheard him and Mr. Dally in conversation, though Mr. Blake did most of the talking. Mr. Dally was fascinated by Mr. Blake, though Mr. Dally felt uneasy when Mr. Blake was indulging in his wild talk. I did too. He seemed possessed by something strange, something not quite of this world. You'd have to talk to him to know exactly what I mean.

"Anyway, one afternoon, Mr. Blake, his eyes looking more wild than I'd ever seen them, more spiritual or more visioning, I should say, told Mr. Dally that he had seen the ghost of a flea. I don't know what he meant by a flea since the ghost, as he described it, had very little of the flea in it. It looked just like the figure on this ring, except that its hand did not hold a cup for drinking blood."

Clifton held up the hand with the ring on its finger.

"The flea was just one of what he called his 'visitations.' That is, the figures of beings and things from the supernatural. Though, sometimes, he spoke of them as visitors from other worlds."

Anana said, "Sometimes, he called them emanations from the unknown worlds."

"From whom did you hear this?" Kickaha said.

"I heard it directly from Blake. As you know, after Red Orc made the universe of Earth and the universe of Earth's twin, he forbade any Lords to visit them. But some did go there, and I was one of them. I've told you that I've been on Earth I several times, though I didn't mention all the times and places I've been there. When I was living in London, a fascinating though disgusting place, I was disguised as a wealthy French noblewoman. Since I collected some of the best of the primitive art of Earthmen, I went to see Blake. I purchased some engravings and tempera sketches from him but asked him not to tell anyone I'd done so. There didn't seem to be the slightest chance that Red Orc would hear about it, but I wasn't taking any risks."

"And you didn't tell me about this?" Kickaha said.

"You know how it happened that I didn't. Let's hear no more of that."

"All right," he said. "But how could Blake have known anything of the Thoan worlds?"

Clifton opened his mouth to say something, but she spoke first.

"We Thoan who know about Blake have wondered that, too. Our theory is that Blake was a mystic who somehow tuned in, you might say, to a knowledge of the people inhabiting the other universes. He had a sensitivity, perhaps neural, perhaps from a seventh sense we know nothing about. No other Earthperson has ever had it. At least, we haven't heard of his like, though there is a theory that some Earth mystics and perhaps some insane Earthpeople . . ."

"No theories unless they're absolutely relevant," Kickaha said.

Anana said, "We just don't know. But, somehow, Blake received some—what should I call them? visions? intimations?—of the artificial pocket universes. Perhaps of the original Thoan universe or of that universe that some say preceded the Thoan's. In any event, it couldn't have been coincidence that he knew the exact names of many Lords and some of the situations and events in which they played their parts.

"But his, ah, psychic receptions of them were distorted and

fragmentary. And he used them as part of his personal mythology and mingled Christian mythology with them. The mixture was Blakean, highly imaginative and shaped by his own beliefs. Blake was a freak, though of a high order."

Kickaha said, "Very well. Anyway, what he saw as the flea's ghost was the scaly man we saw in that curious tomb. No Thoan knew about the scaly man, yet Blake saw him."

"Obviously."

"Remarkable!"

"All universes and everything in them are remarkable," Anana said.

"Some more than others," Kickaha replied.

He pointed at the ring. "What about that, Clifton? How'd you get it?"

"And how did you get into the Thoan worlds?" she said.

Clifton shook his head. "That is the strangest thing that's ever happened to an Earthman."

"I doubt it's any stranger than how I happened to get to the World of Tiers," Kickaha said.

"I have some ability at drawing," Clifton said. "Mr. Blake's description of the flea's ghost so intrigued me that I drew a sketch of it. I showed it to a friend, George Pew. Like me, he had been a child of the streets, a cutpurse who also was a catchfart for a jeweler named Robert Scarborough."

Kickaha said, "Catchfart?"

"A footboy," Anana said. "A footboy was a servant who closely followed his master when he was out on the street."

Clifton said, "Pew showed the sketch to his employer, Mr. Scarborough, though he did not mention its source. Mr. Scarborough was so taken up with the sketch that he told a customer, a wealthy Scots nobleman, Lord Riven, about it. Lord Riven was very intrigued and ordered that a ring based on the sketch be made for him. It was done, but it was never delivered because it was stolen."

Clifton paused to hold up the ring to look at it. Then he said, "My friend Pew was one of the gang that stole it. He gave it to me to hide because his employer suspected him. I didn't really want to have anything to do with it, though, to be truthful, I did consider plans to obtain permanent possession of it. I was at that time not as honest as the rich people would wish me to be, and you might not be if you had been me."

"We're not judges," Kickaha said.

"Pew had told me that only he knew he'd given me the ring for safekeeping. But Pew was killed while fleeing the constables. Thus, I considered the ring to be my property. But I did not plan to sell it until much time had passed. The constabulary had a good description of it; it was dangerous to try to sell it.

"And then, one fine summer day, that event happened that resulted in my being propelled willy-nilly into these other worlds and resulted in my being confined in this pit. Though just what Red Orc plans for me, for us, I don't know."

Thunder, amplified by the deep chasm, rumbled in the distance. With the suddenness of a Panzer attack, dark clouds were speeding from the west. In a few seconds, they had covered the bright sky, and a wind whistled over the top of the pit. The air that reached down into the pit blew away the sweltering heat and chilled Kickaha's naked body.

He said, "We'll hear the rest of your story later, Clifton. We've got to get out of this hole."

Anana did not have to ask him why they had to vacate the pit. She knew what a big downpour in this chasm would do.

Kickaha had considered using the beamers to make a forty-five-degree channel from the bottom of the hole to the surface. They might be able to escape from the pit that way. But there was no time to use the beamers.

Kickaha gave his orders. The two men stood side by side, their faces close to the north side of the pit. Anana, who was very strong and agile, climbed up onto them and stood with one foot on Kickaha's right shoulder and one foot on Clifton's left shoulder. By now, Eleth had recovered enough to join them in their effort. The lightest in the group and very athletic, she had no difficulty climbing up until she was on Anana's shoulders. The thin rope taken from Kickaha's backpack was coiled around Eleth's waist. A few seconds later, she called down.

"The edge is just too slippery for me to get a hold."

"What do you see?" he said. "Anything that might hold a grappling hook?"

"Nothing at all!" Eleth sounded desperate. A bellow of thunder and the cannon blast of nearby lightning tore her next words to shreds. She shrieked and fell backward off Anana. But she twisted around and landed, knees bent, on her feet.

After Anana had come down, she said, "What were you going to say?"

Eleth's reply was again shattered by thunder and lightning. A few raindrops fell on them. Then she shouted "I saw a torrent of water pouring down the mountainsides! We're all going to drown!"

"Maybe," Kickaha said, grinning. "But we might be able to swim out of this pit."

He sounded more hopeful than he felt.

"Red Orc wouldn't put us here just so we could drown!" Eleth shrilled.

"Why not?" Anana said.

"Besides," Kickaha said, "he may have overlooked the possibility of flash floods. He may have picked this place out but not been around when it rained."

By then, a darkness not as black as midnight but blacker than the last gasp of dusk filled the pit. The wind was stronger and colder, though it was not in its full rage. Suddenly, a heavy rain fell upon them. Whips of lightning exploded near them. A few minutes later, water spilled over the edges of the pit. The water rose to Kickaha's ankles.

Eleth cried, "Elyttria of the Silver Arrows, save us!"

A wave of cold water crashed into the pit and knocked all of them down. Before they could struggle to their feet, a second and larger one fell on them. And then a third wave, the edge of the flood, cataracted into the pit.

Kickaha was rammed against the wall. He almost became unconscious but struggled to swim upward, though he did not know where upward was. When his hand struck stone, he knew that he had been swimming downward. Or had he gone horizontally and felt the side of the pit?

Somebody bumped into him. He grabbed for him or her but missed. Then he was sliding and bumping against stone for an indeterminable time. Just as he thought that he had to suck air into his lungs or die, his head rose above water. He gulped air before he was again drawn down. But he had seen a mass to his right, a mass darker than the darkness around him.

It must be a mountainside, he thought. Which means that I've been carried out of the pit.

He swam again in the blackness. If he had not been turned upside down, he was going for the surface. His chances for surviving were few, since he could, at any moment, slam into a mountainside. He kept struggling, and his head was suddenly out of the water, though a wave at once slapped his mouth and filled it. Choking and spitting, he got rid of the water.

It was no use to call out. The lightning and thunder were still cursing the earth. No one could hear him, and what if they did?

Now he was also in danger of being electrocuted. Lightning was plunging into the flood. But he could see in their flashes that he was being sped past solid rock that soared almost straight up into a darkness not even the lightning could scatter.

A roaring louder than the thunder's was now ahead of him. A waterfall? And he was swept over the edge and fell he knew not how far. When he struck the bottom of the raging river and was scraped along it, he was again half out of his wits. By the time he had recovered them, he was on top of a maelstrom. It whirled him around and around, and then, once again, he slammed into something hard.

When he awoke, he was lying on rock, his upper body out of the stream. It tugged feebly at him. Lightning still blazed through the darkness, though it was not near him.

He lay choking and coughing for a while. After he had gotten back his wind, he crawled painfully up the sloping rock. His face, feet, knees, ribs, hands, elbows, buttocks, and genitals felt as if they had been skinned with a knife. He hurt too much to crawl far. He rolled over; the scene was briefly lit by the lightning. He was on a triangular shelf of stone that dipped its apex into the storming river. Across it was a straight-up God-knows-where-its-top-is wall.

He turned, grunting with pain, sat up, and looked upward. Another flash showed him the wall that towered there. It was only about fifty feet from him. When the rain first came down its side, it must have been a torrent. But now it was a shallow brook.

Kickaha's luck, he thought. One of these days, though . . .

He got up and staggered through a thin waterfall and under a wide shelf of stone. He sat down. After a while, the thunder and lightning retreated far down the canyon. Somehow, despite the cold and wetness, he fell asleep. When he woke, he saw daylight. Hours passed, and then the sun had come over the edge of the seemingly sky-high mouth of the chasm. It seemed to him that he was even deeper in it than when he had been in the pit.

He said, "Anana!"

His equipment and most of his weapons had been torn from him. He still had his belt and the beamer in its holster. Somehow, the bag containing the Horn of Shambarimem had not been torn from the loop on his belt . . . He grinned then because he would have given up even the knife and the beamer in exchange for the Horn.

By the time that the sun was directly overhead, he rose stiffly. The storm had cooled the air, but tomorrow the heat would be stifling. He had to get to the top of the chasm. He went back and forth as far as he could along the base of the cliff. When he found cracks and fissures and plants to hold on to—even at this depth little treelike plants projected at angles from the wall—he began to climb. His hands ached and some skin had been ground off from four of his fingers. Gritting his teeth and groaning, he got to an estimated eighty feet above the river. By then, the water had ceased falling down the wall. And he saw, fifty feet above him, the side of a large nest sticking out from a small ledge.

Maybe the nest contained eggs that he could eat.

When, shaking with fatigue and hunger, he got to the nest, he found that it was made of sticks and twigs and a gluey substance that had dried out. Inside the nest were four mauve eggs, each twice as large as a hen's. He looked around to make sure that the mother was not in sight. After piercing the eggs with the point of his knife, he sucked some yolk from each. Then he broke them open to disclose embryonic chicks. He ate these raw except for the heads and the legs.

Having rested a while, he rose to climb again. It was then that he heard a scream. He whirled. Mama Bird was home, and she was so angry she had dropped the rabbit-sized animal she had been bringing home. It fell, and he did not see it strike the river because he was busy defending himself. The sky-blue bird, somewhat larger than a bald eagle, slammed into him. He gutted it with a slash of his knife, though not before its beak had slashed open an arm and its talons had sunk deep into his chest.

He had thought he could not hurt more than he had. He was wrong.

After defeathering the bird, he butchered it and ate part of it. Then he spent the rest of the day and all of the night on the ledge. At least the night air was warm.

Twelve days later, he got to the top of the chasm. He had eaten on the way, though not much. Despite the regenerative powers of his body, it still had many abrasions and bruises. But these had been acquired recently.

He pulled himself over the edge after he had looked to make sure that nothing dangerous was there. Then he lay on his side, panting. After several minutes, he rose.

It was as if the vessel had appeared out of the air, and perhaps it had. It was a silvery and shiny craft, a cylinder with a cone at each end. Under the transparent canopy at the end nearest Kickaha was a cockpit that ran half of the length of the cylinder. From two sides of the craft, four struts extended to the ground to stabilize the vessel while it was on the ground.

The airboat landed, and the fore part of the canopy rose. The man sitting in the front seat climbed out and strode toward Kickaha, who by then had risen shakily to his feet.

The pilot was tall and muscular; his face was handsome; his flowing hair was shoulder-length and red-bronze. He was clad in a black-and-white striped robe that came down to his calves. A belt set with many jewels held a holster. It was empty because the beamer it had held was in the man's hand.

The man smiled broadly, exposing very white teeth.

He spoke in Thoan. "Kickaha! You are truly a remarkable man to have survived! I respect you greatly, so much that I could almost just salute you and let you go on your way! However . . ."

"You're full of howevers, Red Orc," Kickaha said. "Not to mention other things."

8

*A*t the Thoan's command, Kickaha slowly took his beamer and knife out and threw them ten feet ahead of him. Very reluctantly, he cast the bag containing the Horn to a spot near the weapons. Red Orc, his face glowing with triumph shot with delight, picked up the bag with his right hand.

He gestured with his weapon. "Turn your back to me, reach for the sky, and get down on your knees. Stay in that position until I tell you otherwise."

Kickaha obeyed, but he was considering what his chances were if he leaped up, ran to the chasm's edge, and jumped. He might go out far enough to avoid the projecting parts of the side of the chasm and fall into the river. But would he survive the plunge into the water? Would the Thoan be able to shoot him before he got to the chasm edge?

The answer to the first was no; to the second, yes. Anyway, he was crazy even to think of such a plan. But it might be better to die thus than to get what Red Orc could have in mind for him.

He never heard the man's footsteps. He did hear a slight hissing and feel something against his back. When he awoke, he was in the back seat of the vessel. A long sticky cord bound him around and around and secured him to the seat of the chair and its back. His wrists were tied together, and his feet were also bound. His head ached; his mouth was very dry. When he looked through the canopy, he saw that the boat was at least a thousand feet in the air and was heading northward.

Red Orc, seated before the control panel, was looking at the TV screen to one side and above him. He could see Kickaha in it. He rose, having set the vessel on automatic, and walked back in the narrow aisle between two rows of seats.

The Thoan stood about four feet from his captive. "You've always gotten away before this," he said. "But you've come to the end of the road."

Kickaha spoke huskily. "I'm still living."

"And you may live for quite a while. But you'll be wishing that you were dead. Perhaps. I really haven't decided what I'm going to do with you."

Kickaha glanced through the canopy and saw the chasm he had climbed or, perhaps, another chasm. At this point, it was at least forty miles wide and went down so far that he could not see the dark bottom. He did not think that erosion had caused this. There must have been one hell of a cataclysm at one time on this planet.

Apparently, Red Orc guessed what he was thinking. He said, "This is the planet Wanzord, created by Appyrmazul. My father, Los, and I fought each other here. Los had a weapon of terrifying destructive powers. I don't know where he got it. Probably, he found it buried in some ancient vault. He used it on me and my forces, and I was forced to gate out, leaving my men behind me. That chasm was caused by Los's weapon."

"What happened to it?" Kickaha said. His voice rasped.

"My father won that campaign. Eventually, during an attack on his army, I got hold of the ravener, as it was called. But I had to destroy that ancient weapon. Luck went against me, I was forced to retreat, and I didn't want my father to have it. So, I blew it up.

"However, as you may have heard, the final victory was mine. I captured my father. After I'd tortured him almost enough to satisfy me, I killed him. A long time before that, I had cut off his testicles and eaten them, after I stopped him when he was trying to kill my mother. I should have slain him then. When his testicles regrew, he launched an all-out war against me.

"But, in the end, I won, and I burned his body and mixed the ashes in a glass of wine and drank him down. That was not quite the end of him. The next day, I flushed him down the toilet."

Red Orc laughed maniacally. And maniac he is, Kickaha thought. But he's quite rational and logical in most matters. Very cunning, too.

"That's interesting and informative," Kickaha said. "But what about Anana, Clifton, and Eleth?"

Red Orc smiled as if he was pleased by what he was going to tell his prisoner.

"While you were struggling to get out of the chasm, I was looking for the others. Eleth's body was left on a large rock when the flood subsided. The face was torn off, and one side of her head was caved in and the scalp ripped from it. But enough of her blond hair was left to identify her. Thus ended the last of the iron-hearted daughters of Urizen. No one will mourn them.

"Clifton is probably buried under tons of silt and gravel. End of his story. He was in the pit because he was caught in one of my resonant-circuit traps and directed to the same terminal, the pit, to which you and your party were channeled. That pit and the circuit in which Clifton was caught were made by Ololothon long ago. But I took over ownership. In fact, he arranged it as a sort of catch-as-catch-can for any Lord who came along. But it got the Englishman for me. I had almost forgotten about him after I last saw him in Urthona's floating palace on the Lavalite World. Urthona got away from there with you two. What happened to him?"

"Urthona was killed just after we escaped from the palace and gated through to the World of Tiers. He got caught in his own trap, you might say. Cheated me out of killing him."

Red Orc raised his brows and said, softly, "Ah! One more of the very old Lords is dead. I am unhappy about that, but only because I wanted to be the one who killed him. Since he was my father's ally, I had him down in my books."

Kickaha said, "What about Anana?"

A ghost of a smile hovered over the Thoan's lips. He knew that Kickaha knew that he was delaying his account of her to torment him.

"Anana? Yes, Anana?"

Kickaha leaned forward, preparing himself for very bad news. But Red Orc said, "I had expected Ona to be caught in the pit, too, but I assume that something happened to her while she was with you. Or did she escape from you to wander around on Alofmethbin?"

"She died trying to escape. What about Anana?"

"You must be wondering just how you were trapped. Only I could have done it. The many obstacles and the little time to get the necessary things would have been too much for anyone else. Fortunately, the circuit in which you two were caught, originally set up by Ololothon, had a three-day delay holding you in one gate before you were sent forward again. That gave me the time I needed to bring in the necessary equipment in an airboat through a gate from my base. You have heard of Ololothon?"

"For Christ's sake!" Kickaha said in English. Then, speaking in Thoan, "You are going to drag out the suspense, aren't you? Although you've lived so long, you're juvenile as hell!"

"I am not above taking pleasure in small things," Red Orc said. "If you are almost immortal, you find that there are long intervals between pleasures, and these are short-lived. So, even the smallest pleasures are welcome, especially when they are unexpected."

He paused, meeting Kickaha's glare with his unwavering gaze. Then he said, "Ololothon?"

"We were on his world, the planet of the Tripeds," Kickaha said. "You know that."

"I know it now," the Thoan said. "Before you told me, I had only suspected that you were there. But I could not be sure. What I was sure about was that, if you took the only exit gate on Ololothon's world, you would be caught in the resonant circuit he set up. Long, long ago, after I invaded his palace and slew him, I studied the charts of his gates and recorded them to file in my bases. I might need to use them someday. And I was right: I did. Very few Lords, perhaps none, have such foresight."

Brag, brag, brag, Kickaha thought. However, he was interested in knowing just how the Thoan's plot had been carried out.

"Eleth and Ona were very clever. They managed to escape from my prison on my base while I was elsewhere. I suspected that they had bribed the guards, but I did not have time to torture the truth out of anyone. I killed all of them. However, the corruption might have spread throughout my palace. So, I completely depopulated it. I did not slay their children, of course. I made sure that they were adopted by a native tribe."

Just like that, Kickaha thought. Torture and murder, and then he compliments himself for his mercy.

"It took me some time to track the sisters down to this planet and then locate them. I found them wandering half-starved and totally miserable in the forest where you came across them. Instead of immediately punishing them as I had promised, I decided to use them against you and Anana. They were in such terror, wondering if they would be released without harm as I had promised they would if they cooperated. Or would I break my word? I also arranged for a raven, an Eye of the Lord, and an oromoth to work with them, to keep a watch on you and Anana when you showed up and also make sure the sisters did not betray me. The Eye and the oromoth would get a suitable reward, but I promised them they would die if they tried treachery. I . . ."

"Anana and I know about that," Kickaha said. "We killed both of them."

Red Orc's face crimsoned. Glaring, he shouted, "Do not speak unless I give you permission!"

When he had regained his composure, he said, "I was faced with a problem. You had the Horn or, at least, I assumed you still had it. The Horn changed normal conditions for those in a circuit. With it, you might escape even if caught in one. And then the alarms I had set up in the circuit sounded through the series of gates and registered in my base. I knew then that you and Anana had entered the gate from the planet of the Tripeds.

"The gate-circuit chart I inherited from Ololothon after I killed him so many years ago showed that one of the brief stops would be on Alofmethbin. But it would be for only a few seconds. I gambled that you would recognize Alofmethbin and would run out of the area of influence of the gate before it could send you on. Or that you would be sounding the Horn at that time and that would nullify the action of the gate. And I was right, of course. I would have preferred that you be much closer to the sisters when you exited, but I had to work with what was available. Nor did I know, of course, whether or not there was a flaw near the gate.

"For this reason, I could not erect a cage there to imprison you and Anana when you entered. You would only have to blow your Horn, and you would escape through the flaw, if there was one. The probability that there would be was about fifty-fifty."

Kickaha opened his mouth to ask a question, thought better of it, and closed his lips.

"I knew you would head in a straight line for the nearest gate, the one in the boulder. My usual good fortune held because I knew about the gate. Ololothon was on this planet several times when Wolff was its Lord, found four gates, and charted them. He connected the gate in the boulder to the pit."

Kickaha cleared his throat, then said, "Permission to speak?"

Red Orc waved his hand.

"What happened to Anana?"

"I have a story to tell!" the Thoan said harshly. "It will enlighten you so that you will know whom you are up against! Now, be silent! Ololothon must have dug that pit shortly after the chasm was made by my father's engine of destruction during my campaign against him on Wanzord. I found the pit a long time ago when I went briefly to the planet Wanzord. I like to prowl around universes and gather data that I may use later. You never know when it will be useful. Then, when you two disappeared from the circuit for a few hours, a delay that came too soon for you to be on the islet . . ."

He paused, then said, "You used the Horn to escape the circuit before you got to the islet, of course. But you got caught in it again?"

Kickaha nodded. Though he did not see how the Thoan could use knowledge of the scaly man's existence to his own advantage, it was best to keep him ignorant. Never give anything away; you might regret it.

"Few things make me anxious," the Thoan said, "but I am not above admitting that your disappearance gave me a bad time. But I went ahead with my plan. However, there might be a flaw in the walls of the pit. It was not likely there was, but I could not take the chance. One blast from the Horn, and you might escape through that. So, I placed a generator near the pit—you could not see it from the bottom of the pit—and set it to form a one-way gate completely around the pit and just below the surface of the rock wall. As long as that one-way gate shield was there, even the Horn could not open a flaw."

Red Orc paused.

"Permission?" Kickaha croaked. His throat and mouth were very dry, but he'd be damned if he'd ask the Thoan for a glass of water.

"Go ahead."

"Why didn't you just wait for night while we were on the plains or in the forest, then swoop in in your aircraft and capture us?"

"Because I take no chances unless I am forced to do so. You might have had enough time to use the Horn and escape through a flaw. Once you were in the pit, you could not escape. Your Horn could not get you out of it."

"But you overlooked the flash floods," Kickaha said.

The Thoan's face became red again. He shouted, "I had not been on the planet long enough to know that there were floods caused by rainstorms! That planet is very dry! I never saw a cloud while I was there!"

Kickaha said nothing. He did not want to goad the Thoan into doing something painful, such as burning his eye out with a beamer ray. Or God knew what else.

"So!" Red Orc said. "I got a bonus! That Englishman, Clifton, apparently escaped from the floating palace of Urthona in the Lavalite World. But he fell at last into one of my traps in another world, and I shuttled him into the pit! All my most elusive enemies—except for Wolff and Chryseis—were collected like fish in a net!"

"Wolff? Chryseis?" Kickaha murmured.

"Wolff and Chryseis!" Red Orc howled. His voice was so loud in the narrow area of the boat that Kickaha was startled again.

The Thoan yelled, "They escaped! They escaped! I should have dealt with them as soon as I caught them!"

"You don't know where they are?" Kickaha said softly.

"Somewhere on Earth!" the Thoan said, waving one hand violently. "Or perhaps they managed to gate through to another world! It does not matter! I will catch them again! When I do . . . !"

He stopped, took a deep breath, and then smiled. "You can quit being so happy about them! I did find Anana!"

Kickaha knew that Red Orc wanted him to ask about her. But

he gritted his teeth and clamped his lips. The Thoan was going to tell him anyway.

"Anana's body, what was left of it, was sticking out from under a small boulder! I left her for the scavengers!"

Kickaha shut his eyes while a tremor passed over him, and his chest seemed to have been pierced by a spear. But the Lord could be lying.

When he felt recovered enough to speak in a steady voice, he said, "Did you bring back her head to show me?"

"No!"

"Did you photograph her body? Not that I'd believe a photo."

"Why should I do either?"

"You're lying!"

"You will never know, will you?"

Kickaha did not reply. After waiting for a few moments for his captive to say something, the Thoan returned to the pilot's seat.

Kickaha looked out through the canopy again. Though he saw no more vast chasms, he did see a world the surface of which had been swept clear of soil and vegetation. Yet new growth had managed to get a roothold here and there. Some species of birds, as he well knew, had survived, and he supposed that some animals had escaped the apocalyptic raging. Perhaps, somewhere, were small bands of humans. They must not be eating well, though.

He became more angry than usual at the arrogance and scorn for life of the Lords. They would destroy an entire world and think little of doing it.

It was a miracle that Anana was not like her own kind.

In ten minutes, the vessel began to slow, then hovered in the air for a few seconds before sinking swiftly. It landed by a corrugated monolith of stone that bent halfway up in a thirty-degree angle from the horizontal. At its base was an enormous reddish boulder roughly shaped like a bear's head. The Thoan squeezed several drops of a blue liquid from a container onto a small part of the sticky rope. A moment later, the rope became smooth and was easily loosened by Kickaha's efforts. But the bonds tying his hands before him were still sticky.

He was shepherded out of the vessel. After the Thoan had commanded the craft to close the canopy, he guided Kickaha toward the boulder. Then he spoke a code word, and part of the side of the boulder shimmered with bands of red and violet. Looking steadily at it hurt Kickaha's eyes.

"Go ahead," Red Orc said.

Kickaha entered the gate into a small chamber in the rock. The next second, he was in a large windowless room made of greenish marble and furnished with carpets, drapes, chairs, divans, and statuary. A few seconds later, part of the seemingly solid wall opened, and Red Orc stepped inside the room.

He motioned with the beamer. "Sit in that chair there."

After his captive had obeyed, Red Orc sat down in a chair facing Kickaha's. He smiled, leaned back, and stretched out his legs.

"Here we are in one of my hideaways on Earth II."

"And?"

"Are you hungry? You may eat and drink while I'm discussing a certain matter with you."

Kickaha knew he would be foolish to refuse just because his enemy offered it. He needed the energy to get free, if he was going to do that, and he had no doubt that he would. "When," not "if," was the way it was going to be.

He said, "Yes."

Orc must have given some sort of signal, or he had assumed that his captive would not refuse a meal. A door-sized section of the wall opened. A woman pushed in a cart on which were goblets, covered dishes, and cutlery. She was a black-haired, brown-eyed, and dark-skinned beauty. She wore only some sort of silvery and shimmering hip band from the front of which hung a foot-long fan-shaped band of the same material. A peacock feather was inserted into her hair. She stopped the cart by a table, bowed to Red Orc, transferred the food and drink to the table, and pushed the cart out of the room, her narrow hips swaying. The section swung shut.

"You may not only have the best food and drink this planet offers but her, too," the Thoan said. "And others equally as beautiful and skilled in the bodily arts. If, that is, you accept my proposal."

Kickaha arched his eyebrows. Proposal? Then Red Orc must need his help in some project. Since he was not the man to draw back from danger, he had something near-suicidal in mind.

Afterwards? If there was an afterwards?

Kickaha held up his bound wrists and pointed a finger at the table. Red Orc told him to raise his arms high and to hold them as far apart as he could. Kickaha did so. There was approximately an inch between his wrists.

"Hold steady," the Thoan said, and he drew his beamer so swiftly his arm seemed to be a blur. A yellow ray lanced out; the bond was cut in half; the beamer was holstered. It was done within two eyeblinks.

Very impressive, Kickaha thought. But he was not going to tell Red Orc that. And what kind of beamer projected a yellow ray?

"I'll be back when you've finished eating," the Thoan said. "If you wish to wash first or need a toilet, utter the word 'kentfass,' and a bathroom will extrude from the wall. To make it go back into the wall, say the same word."

A curious arrangement, Kickaha thought. But Red Orc had a curious mind.

The Thoan left the room. Though Kickaha did not have much appetite, he found that the food, which consisted of various vegetables, fruits, and different kinds of fish, was delicious. The wine was too heavy for his palate, but it did have an inviting don't-know-what taste and went down easily. Afterward, he used the bathroom, which was decorated with murals of undersea life. It slid into the wall, and the wall section swung shut. Some of these sections must conceal gates.

A few minutes later, the Thoan entered. Now he wore a longer robe and sandals. With him were three dark men wearing conical helmets topped by peacock feathers, short kilts, and buskins. All were armed with spears, swords, and knives. They took positions behind Red Orc, who had drawn up a chair shaped like a spider and sat down in it facing his captive. He was unarmed.

"You must be very puzzled," he said. "You're asking yourself why I, a Lord, require the assistance of a *leblabbiy?*"

"Because you've got something to do that's too big for you to handle by yourself," Kickaha said.

Red Orc smiled. He said, "I suppose you're wondering what your reward will be if you succeed in carrying out my desires? You also doubt that I'd keep my word to reward you."

"You have an astounding ability to read my mind."

"Sarcasm has no place here. I have never broken my word."

"Did you ever give your word?"

"Several times. And I honored it though my natural inclination is to break it. But there have been situations . . ."

He was silent for a few seconds. Then he said, "Have you heard about Zazel of the Caverned World?"

"Yes," Kickaha said. "Anana . . ."

He choked. Even speaking her name summoned up grief like a thick glutinous wave and burned his heart.

After clearing his throat, he said, "Anana told me something about him. He created a universe that was a ball of stone in which were many tunnels and caves. Which, in my opinion, only a nut would do. According to her, Zazel was a melancholy and gloomy man, and he eventually killed himself."

"Many Lords have committed suicide," Red Orc said. "They are the weaklings. The strong kill each other."

"Not fast enough for me. What does he have to do with us?"

"When I was a youth, I mightily offended my father. Instead of killing me, he gated me through to a world unfamiliar to me and very dangerous. It was called Anthema, the Unwanted World. I wandered around on it, and then I met another Lord, Ijim of the Dark Woods. He had gated through to Anthema while being pursued by a Lord whose world he had tried to invade. For forty-four years he had tried to find a gate through which he could travel to another universe."

The Thoan paused. He looked as if he were recalling his hard times on that planet.

He spoke again. "His long solitude had made him paranoiac. But we teamed up, though, of course, each of us was planning to kill the other if we escaped that very undesirable world. We did finally find a gate, but it had been placed by Los inside a structure built by some fierce predators. Nevertheless, we got inside, found the gate, and jumped through it. It was a shearing gate. That is, Los had set it up so that we had to calculate the few seconds when it was safe to enter. Otherwise, we would be cut in half.

"Ijim was halved like an apple, and I lost some skin and a slice of flesh on the end of my heels and my buttocks. After wandering through tunnels, I came to a very large cavern. There I met Dingsteth, a creature made by Zazel to be his overseer or manager. After Zazel committed suicide, Dingsteth was the only sentient being in that vast ball of stone perforated with tunnels and large caverns.

"Dingsteth was very naive. It did not kill me at once as it should have done. It wasn't loneliness, a desire for companionship, that stopped it. It did not know what loneliness was. At least, I think it does not suffer from that emotion. There were certain signs . . ."

Red Orc again became silent. He looked past Kickaha as if he were viewing a screen displaying images of the Caverned World. Then he spoke.

"I found out from Dingsteth that the whole stone world was a computer, semi-protein and semi-silicon. It held enormous amounts of data put there by Zazel. Much of that data has been lost to the rest of us Lords."

The Thoan paused, licked his lips, and said, "So far, only I have entered Zazel's World. Only I know of the priceless data-treasures contained in it. Only I know about the gate that gives access to it. Only I know about certain data that would give me complete power over the Lords and their universes."

"Which is?" Kickaha said.

Red Orc laughed loudly. Then he said, "You are not only a trickster, you are a jester. It's not necessary that you know what I am specifically looking for, and you know that. I know that, if you should somehow get into Zazel's World, you will make a desperate effort to find out what I so greatly desire. I won't tell you because I won't take the slightest chance that knowledge of it should ever get to other Lords. And I certainly would not trust you with that knowledge."

"How can I tell anybody else about something I'm ignorant of?" Kickaha said.

"You can't. But some Lords might be able to guess what it is."

This reasoning did not seem entirely logical to Kickaha. But he could not expect the Thoan to be completely rational. Hatred and a passion for power had driven Red Orc insane. Or vice versa.

Nor did he expect Red Orc to keep any promise or give any lasting reward. The Thoan knew that Kickaha would not give up revenge for Anana's death. Even if Anana had somehow survived, she had come near death because of Red Orc. That was unforgivable.

He said, "What do you need me for?"

"We know that I am using you as a pawn whom I will sacrifice if the occasion demands it. However, I swear by Shambarimen, Elyttria, and Manathu Vorcyon that if you succeed, you will be set free, and . . ."

"Anana, too, if she didn't die?"

Irritation at the interruption flitted across Red Orc's face. But he spoke evenly.

"Anana, too."

Kickaha asked the Thoan what he wanted him to do.

"Get into Zazel's World. When you've done that, you can communicate with me, and I'll come swiftly."

Kickaha bit a corner of his lip.

"Why can't you do it yourself?"

Red Orc smiled and said, "You know why. It'll be a dangerous project, and your chances of surviving are small. But if you die, I'll know what killed you and avoid it. I can do that because I have the Horn. Besides, I'd like to determine if you are the greatest of tricksters, which some Lords claim you are. My experience with you has impressed me even though you are a *leblabbiy.*"

"You enjoy deadly games?"

"Yes. So do you."

"You did catch me," Kickaha said. "Several times."

"And, up until now, you slipped away from me. When we were chasing you through the city of Los Angeles, I was playing with you. My hired criminals were not very bright, and luck favored you. And then I was caught in the Lavalite World and came too close to being trapped there forever. I suspect you were responsible."

Kickaha did not confirm that. Let him guess.

"In any event," Red Orc said, "I will no longer be playing cat-and-mouse with you."

"I will try to do what you want me to do, and I won't attempt to escape," Kickaha said. Probably, Red Orc did not believe him any more than Kickaha believed Red Orc. But Red Orc described in detail how he had gotten into and out of the Caverned World.

Los, Red Orc's father, had gated his son from the family world to a cave on Anthema. Red Orc still did not know exactly where the Antheman gate was. But Los could have had more than one on that planet.

He and Ijim had found the gate from Anthema to Zazel's World because his father had provided his son with a map. But that had been cryptic and very difficult to figure out, and he might never have been able to read it.

"I was able to leave the Caverned World because Dingsteth showed me the gate out," Red Orc said. "However, it allowed exit but not entrance. The same was true for the gate by which I got from Anthema to Zazel's World. You will have to find a gate that is at present unknown. Or, if you can find it, use the gate Ijim and I used. I've been trying so long to find it again, and I've been so obsessed with it that I'm going around in a circle. I need someone to search for it whose view is fresh. Someone who's also ingenious or, at least, has the reputation for being so. Thus, I'm asking you to volunteer for the venture."

"Give me the Horn," Kickaha said. "That can open any gate, and it reveals weak places in the walls among the universes."

"You can't stop joking, can you?"

Kickaha said, "No. Very well. I must know more about these gates and the worlds in which they're located. And other items, too."

After an hour, Red Orc left the room, though the evil which Kickaha imagined as emanating from him still hung in the air. What the Thoan required was clear. His secret motives were not. For one thing, Red Orc had been in Zazel's World when he was eighteen years old. That was at least twenty thousand Terrestrial years ago. What had he been doing in the meantime? Why hadn't he stormed the fort, so to speak, and invaded the Caverned World to get the data he wanted? Or had he tried again and again and always failed?

If the Thoan had tried many times to do that, then he was indeed desperate. It would be almost impossible to succeed where the Thoan had failed, yet he was turning over the job to a despised *leblabbiy*.

Almost impossible. But Kickaha was convinced that, as long as something was one-thousandth of one-thousandth of one-half percent possible, he could do it. Though he sometimes laughed at his own egotism, he believed that he was capable of everything but the impossible, and he was not so sure that he could not defeat those odds, too.

During the next three days, Kickaha did not see his captor. He exercised as vigorously as possible in this large room, which was not large enough, ate well, and, mostly, chafed and fumed and sometimes cursed. The beautiful servant made it evident through signs that she would bed him if he so desired. He refused her. Not until he was certain that Anana was dead could he even consider another woman.

He indulged in fantasy scenes about how Anana could have lived through the flash flood. And Red Orc, searching in his aircraft up and down the chasm, might have missed her because she was in a cave or under a ledge, or because he just did not see her even if she was in the open.

After a while, he quit imagining these scenarios. He would just have to wait and see.

The afternoon of the third day, Red Orc entered the chamber. His beamer was in his holster, and a sheath hanging from his belt carried a long dagger. In his right hand was a large bag. Behind him came five armed bodyguards, one of them a bowman. He did not greet his captive but said, "Come with me." The men grouped around him. Kickaha was conducted from the room and through a series of exotically decorated halls, all empty of natives. Then he was taken into a vast room blazing with the light of a thousand torches. The ceiling was six or seven stories high. Its gold-plated walls bore many figures of animals and human beings, all outlined in jewels. It had no furniture. At the far end was a gigantic bronze statue of a man with an enormous upright phallus, four arms, and a demon's face. Twenty feet before it was an altar with a block of stone at its base. The block was stained with old blood. A stone platform half its height surrounded it, and stone steps led up to it.

"Am I to be sacrificed?" Kickaha said, grinning.

The Thoan's smile seemed to be carved from granite.

"Not as part of a religious rite."

He spoke in the mellifluous native tongue, and the guards marched out through the main door. One of them shut the door and slammed a huge bolt shut. The bang sounded to Kickaha like a note of doom. But he had met many dooms and defeated them.

Red Orc said, "Go to the block, walk up the steps, and stand by the block."

When Kickaha turned around to face the Thoan, his back almost touching the stone, which still was higher than his head, he saw Red Orc swinging the bag backward. Then the bag soared up and landed with a thump near Kickaha's feet.

"Empty the bag," the Thoan said loudly. His words echoed.

Kickaha removed a beamer, a bundle of batteries, a long knife, a canteen full of water, and a smaller bag. He dumped its contents: a bundle of clothes, a belt holding a holster and a sheath, a pair of shoes, a smaller knife, and a box of compressed rations.

"There is no battery in the beamer," Red Orc said. "After you reach your next destination, you can put the battery in it."

"And after you're out of knife range," Kickaha said. "You're taking no chances."

"I'm not as reckless as you, *leblabbiy*. You have your instructions and as much useful information as I am able to give you. Rebag those items, then climb up on the top of the stone."

When Kickaha was standing up on the top of the block, he looked at the Thoan. He was smiling as if he was deeply enjoying the procedure. He called, "I would really prefer to keep you prisoner, work my pleasure on you, and eventually drink your ashes down as I did my father's. But I am pragmatic. I give you sixty days to complete your mission, and . . ."

"Sixty days?" Kickaha bellowed. "Sixty days to do what you couldn't do in ten thousand years!"

"That's the way it's going to be! By the way, Trickster! Here's an additional incentive for you to return to me! Your traitor bitch, Anana, is in the room next to the one you occupied!"

He paused, then shouted, "Or am I lying?"

Kickaha felt as if a giant icicle had slammed through him. Before he could unfreeze, he heard Red Orc scream out a code word.

The hard stone beneath his feet became air, and he dropped straight down.

9

*H*is right hand shot out to catch the side of the pit that gaped below him. His fingertips scraped along the stone shaft just below the edge. A gate, not a trapdoor, had opened to swallow him. How typical of Red Orc not to warn him that he was going to fall!

Holding the bag in his left hand close to his side, he struggled to maintain his vertical attitude. The light that had come through the gate was cut off. Total darkness was around him as he pierced the air. The shaft down which he hurtled must have narrowed by now. Its circular wall seemed to be an inch away from his body. Then he became aware that it was twisting. The soapy texture of the stone kept the skin of his back from burning—so far.

By then, he had begun counting seconds. Twenty of them passed. He had dropped perhaps five seconds before starting to time his descent. Four more passed before the shaft began curving gently and then became horizontal. The darkness was tinged with a dusklike light. It quickly became brighter.

Oh, oh, he thought. Here it comes!

He cannonballed from the hole. Above him was a wall of stone lit by a strong light. He began twisting around so that he could land on his feet. As he did so, he saw that he was in a chamber of stone about twenty feet wide and thirty feet high. What he had thought was a wall was a ceiling. Below him was a pool of water, and he was about to strike it. Though he tried to go in feet first, he crashed on his side with enough force to plunge him to the bottom. He struggled upright despite his half-daze and shoved upwards toward the light. With the bag still in his hand, he swam to the side of the pool. It was only several inches above the water, and thus it was easy to drag himself onto the rock floor.

"Damn!" he said loudly.

His voice came back hollowly. After sitting up to catch his breath and to look around, he stood up. The light was sourceless—nothing new to him. It showed three tunnel openings in the walls. Kickaha undid the string on the bag and removed most of its contents. Though he was wet, he donned the snug jockey shorts and long-sleeved shirt. After drying his feet with the short kilt, he put that on and then the socks and the shoes. These were much like tennis shoes. It did not take him long to fasten the belt around his waist, sheath the beamer and knife, and attach the bag to the belt.

"It's been fun, so far."

Not much fun was his uncertainty about Anana's fate. The demon son of a bitch Thoan had given him a brief joy when he had said that Anana was still living. Then he had blown out the joy as if it were a candle when he said that he might be lying. That, of course, was said to bedevil Kickaha throughout his mission.

Red Orc was left-handed. Was that a clue that the left tunnel was the right one to take? Or were they all the right ones? It would be like Red Orc to do that.

He entered the tunnel on his left. It was filled with the same sourceless and shadowless light as the room, though the illumination was no stronger than twilight. He walked slowly, wary of any signs of traps, although it seemed to him that Red Orc would have deactivated these. He would not want to stop the mission just after it had begun. Not even Red Orc was that crazy.

After an estimated fifteen minutes, the tunnel turned to the left and then, after ten minutes, to the right. Soon, it straightened out. Presently, he came to a brightly lit chamber. He laughed.

Just as he had anticipated, three tunnels opened into it and only one tunnel led from it. Red Orc had set it up so that the person who had to choose one of three in the room of the pool would torment himself with anxiety. That Red Orc had not given him instructions on choosing the correct tunnels meant that the Thoan was not going to make it too easy for him.

The stone wall seemed to be unbroken, but some part of it could hold a disguised TV receiver. The Thoan might be watching him now. If he were, he would be grinning.

Kickaha gave the invisible watcher the finger.

He walked more swiftly than before down the single tunnel. It, too, was filled with a dusky light. After about a mile, the light began to get brighter. Within forty or so steps, he was in a straight tunnel. Bright daylight was at its end. When he stepped out of its mouth, he was on a ledge on the side of a mountain. It towered straight up, its surface smooth, and below the ledge it was just as straight and smooth. If he cared to jump into the river at the foot of the mountain, he would fall an estimated thousand feet. A wind blew cold up the face of the mountain.

Where was the gate?

Some seconds later, he felt warm air on his naked back. He turned to see a shimmering area ten feet within the tunnel. Beyond it were the vague shapes of chairs and tables.

"Play your little game, Red Orc," Kickaha murmured.

He started to walk toward the shimmering but stopped after a few steps. Another shimmering wall had appeared in front of the first and blanked it out.

This was the first time he had ever experienced that.

"Now what?"

Through this gate, he could dimly see what looked like the trunk of a tree at one side beyond the wavering curtain. He could make out nothing other than that. He shrugged and, beamer in hand, leaped through the gate. He landed in a crouch and looked around him. When he saw nothing threatening, he straightened up.

Trees twice the size of sequoias were around him. A red-and-green striped plant, something like Spanish moss, hung from the branches of many trees. Now and then, a tendril twitched. The ground was covered with a soft, thick, pale yellow moss. Large bushes bearing reddish berries grew here and there. The forest rang with many types of melodious birdcalls. Around him was a soft dappled light and a cool air, which made him quite comfortable.

He waited for a while for someone to appear. When they did not, he walked on into the forest, not knowing or caring if he was going deeper into it or approaching its edge. Since he lacked directions from Red Orc, he would do what seemed best to him or go wherever his whim led him.

He was thinking about the puzzling appearance of the second gate in the tunnel when a man stepped out from behind a giant tree. Kickaha stopped but, not one to be caught easily from behind, glanced to his rear, too. No one was there. The man was as tall as he, had long straight black hair done in a Psyche knot, wore no clothes, and was barefoot. The crimson feather of a large bird stuck out of his hair, and his cheeks were painted with slanting parallel bars: green, white, and black. A long blue band that fell halfway to his knees was tied around his penis. He was unarmed and was holding up his hand, palm outwards, in a peace gesture.

Kickaha advanced toward the man, who smiled. The high cheekbones, the snub nose, and the epicanthic folds were definitely Mongolian. But the eyes were hazel.

The stranger called out in a Thoan that differed from the standard speech but was understandable. "Greetings, Kickaha!"

"Greetings, friend!" Kickaha said. But he was on guard again. How in hell could this man have known his name?

"I am Lingwallan," the man said. "You won't need that weapon, but you may keep it if you prefer to. Please follow me." He turned and started to walk in the same direction Kickaha had been going.

Kickaha, after catching up with him, said, "What is this world? Just where on it are we? Where are we going? Who sent you?"

"If you'll be patient, you'll soon have the answers to your questions."

Kickaha saw no reason to balk. If the man was leading him into an ambush, he had an unconventional way of doing it. But it was effective. His "guest" was too curious to reject the invitation. Besides, he had a hunch that he was in no danger. Not that his hunches had always been right.

During the several-miles-long hike, Kickaha broke the silence once. "Do you know of Red Orc?"

Lingwallan said, "No."

They passed a band of some deerlike animals feeding on the mossy stuff. They raised their heads to look once, then resumed grazing. After a while, the two men passed near a young man and young woman, both nude. These sat with their backs against the trunk of a tree. Between the woman's navel and pubes was a triangle painted in green. The man sported a long orange ribbon tied around his penis. He was playing a primitive kind of flute; she was blowing on a curved wooden instrument that had a much deeper tone. Whatever tune the two were playing, it was a merry one. It also must have been erotic, if the male's erection was an indicator.

Kickaha put the beamer into the holster. Presently, they heard the loud and shrill voices and the laughter of children playing. A moment later, they stepped into a very broad clearing in the center of which was a tree three times as large as a sequoia and swarming with birds and scarlet-faced monkeys. Round houses with cone-shaped roofs made from the branches and leaves of a palmlike plant formed nine concentric circles around the tree. Kickaha looked for the gardens usually found on Earth among preliterate tribes but saw none.

There were also none of the swarming and stinging insects that infested such Terrestrial hamlets.

When he and Lingwallan had stepped out of the forest into the light cast by a sun that had passed beyond the treetops, a silence fell over the place. It lasted only several seconds. Then the children and the adults surged forward, surrounding the two. Many reached out to touch Kickaha. He endured it because they obviously were not hostile.

His guide conducted him through an aisle formed by the wider separation of houses. When they got to the inner circle, the crowd stopped, though its chatter did not. Before then, Kickaha had seen the windows cut into the trunk of the Brobdingnagian tree and the large arched entrances at its base. Except for the arch directly in front of him, all the apertures were crowded with brown faces.

In the arch stood a giantess wearing only a necklace that flashed on and off and a green hipband. A huge red flower was in the hair on one side of her head. She held a long, wooden staff on which carved snakes seemed to crawl upward.

Though almost seven feet tall, her body would make any man's knees turn to jelly. Her face would bring him to his knees. Kickaha felt a warmth in his loins. She seemed to radiate almost visible rays. No man, no matter how insensitive and excited, would dare to try to board her without her permission. Truly, she not only looked like a goddess, she was surrounded by a goddess's invisible aura.

Her leaf-green eyes were bright in the golden-skinned face. Their color is just like mine, Kickaha thought, though my handsomeness is not in the same league as her beauty.

Lingwallan ran ahead of Kickaha and sank to one knee at her feet. She said something, and he rose and ran back to Kickaha.

"Manathu Vorcyon bids you to come to her. She says that she does not expect you to bow to her."

"Manathu Vorcyon!" Kickaha murmured. "I should have known."

Almost all of the Lords he had encountered he considered to be deeply evil. They were really only human beings, as he well knew, despite their insistence that they were a superior breed to Homo sapiens in kind and in degree. They cruelly exploited their human subjects, the *leblabbiys*.

But Manathu Vorcyon, according to the tales he had heard, was an exception. When she had created this universe and peopled it with artificial human beings, she had devoted herself to being a kind and understanding ruler. The *leblabbiys* of her world were said to be the happiest of people anywhere in the thousands of universes. Kickaha had not believed this because all except two of the Lords he had met were intolerably arrogant and egotistic and as bloody-minded as Genghis Khan, Shaka, or Hitler.

Wolff and Anana were two Thoan who had become really "human." But both had been, at one time, as ruthless and murderous as their kin.

He walked up to Manathu Vorcyon. And then, despite his determination never to bow to any man or woman, he dropped to one knee. He could not help himself; he was overwhelmed with the feeling that she did shed the radiance of a goddess. Never mind that his brain knew that she was no more divinely born than he. His knee bent as if he had been conditioned to do so since childhood.

Now that he was closer to her, he saw that her necklace was made of living fireflylike insects tied together.

He started. Lingwallan's voice had sounded loudly behind him.

"Manathu Vorcyon! The Great Mother! Our Lady! The Grandmother of All! I present to you Kickaha!"

"Rise, Kickaha, the many-angled man, the man of countless wiles, the man who is never at a loss!" Manathu Vorcyon said. Her voice was so melodious and powerful that it rippled his skin with cold. "Enter this house as my guest."

There were many things to note when he entered the great room just behind the entrance. The tree, though still flourishing, had been cut into to make rooms and winding staircases. Following just behind Lingwallan, he climbed one of the staircases. The lighting was only from the sun, in the daytime, anyway, but what devices transmitted it, Kickaha did not know. The furniture in the rooms he saw as he passed the doorless entrances was carved from the tree and was not removable. There were thick carpets and paintings and statuary and fountains in every room.

But he was too eager to know why he had been whisked here by Manathu Vorcyon to take time to inspect the artifacts. After being shown into his own room, he showered by standing in a waterfall that ran alongside the outer wall and disappeared down many small holes in the floor. When he stepped out, he was toweled dry by a young woman who could win any Miss America contest on Earth. After drying him off, she handed him a pair of sandals. Thus dressed, making him think that sandals were probably formal wear here, he went down a polished staircase. Lingwallan met him and conducted him into the feasting room. It was large but unfurnished except for a very thick carpet. The ruler of this world sat cross-legged on it with her guest and two large but very good-looking men and two large and beautiful women. Manathu Vorcyon introduced them and then said, "They are my bedmates."

All at one time? Kickaha thought.

She added, "They are also my lovers. There is, as you know or should know, a widely separated difference in meaning between bedmate and lover."

The food was brought by servants, including Lingwallan, who seemed to be a sort of head butler. The dishes held a variety of fruit and vegetables, some unfamiliar to Kickaha, and roasted pig, venison, and wild bird. The buttered bread was thickly coated with a jam that made his eyes roll and his body quiver with ecstasy.

The goblets were formed from some sort of sea shell and held four different kinds of liquors. One contained water; one, a light and delicious wine; one, a watered-down whiskey; one, a liquor that he had never before tasted.

He ate and drank just enough to satisfy his belly, though he went easy on the meat so that he could have another slice of bread with jam. Manathu Vorcyon nodded approvingly at his restraint. The truth was that he would have liked to get a big buzz on, not stuff himself. But this was not the time or place for that.

What would be appropriate, he thought, would be to stop the small talk and get answers to his questions. The Great Mother seemed to be in no hurry, which could be expected from a woman who had lived more than thirty thousand years.

After dinner, they went outside to watch a ceremony in honor of the guest. The dances were colorful and noisy, and the songs were full of references to myths and legends about which Kickaha knew nothing. Lingwallan, standing by his side, tried to explain what these were but gave up because he could not be heard above the din. Kickaha did not care about any of them. He wanted to get the inside information about his predicament from the one who should know, Our Lady, Manathu Vorcyon.

Tired and bored though somewhat agitated, he went to bed in his room. After an hour of sighing, yawning, and turning to both sides on the thickly padded blankets on the floor, he managed to get to sleep. But he was awakened by a vivid dream in which he saw Anana's face, looking very distressed, appear out of gray and menacing clouds.

The next morning, after he had showered and had eaten and done all those things that are necessary but time-consuming, he went down the staircase and out of the tree to breakfast, served near the entrance. The giantess did not show up until after Lingwallan had conducted Kickaha through the hamlet and shown him all the sights and spoken of their history and meaning. Kickaha was disgusted. No matter what the universe, a guest had to go through a visiting fireman's tour.

However, he did learn what kind of Lord the giantess was. She was a benevolent despot. That is, she had determined what kind of environment the *leblabbiys* would live in and also what kind of society they would have. Jungles and forests and many rivers and lakes occupied most of the landmass. There were no deserts, though there were many low mountain ranges.

Through the dense vegetation wandered small families or somewhat larger tribes. Hunting, fishing, and food-gathering occupied a few hours a day. Agriculture was limited to small gardens. Their leisure time was spent in conversation (the *leblabbiys* were very gabby), raising the young, council meetings, arts, athletic contests, and copulation. The latter was sometimes a public game, which was why male winners wore penis-ribbons and female winners had painted deltas on their stomachs. Those sporting blue, green, and orange awards had won first, second, and third places in the very popular competition.

Women and men had equal rights. Instead of warring against other groups, the men and women engaged in intense and sometimes very rough athletic games with neighboring tribes.

If Kickaha was to believe Lingwallan, Manathu Vorcyon's subjects were as happy as human beings could be.

Kickaha, who had lived among many preliterate tribes, knew that the closeness and security of tribal life demanded a rigid conformity. A rebel threatened cultural unity and was usually treated harshly. If he did not submit after harsh censure and then the silent treatment, he was exiled or killed. The rebel usually preferred being slain. Being ousted from the tribe was unendurable to the members.

He asked Lingwallan about this.

"Our Lady has decreed that innovators in the arts and technology are not to be discouraged. But explosive powder and firearms will not be tolerated, nor will engines needing fuels be made. She says that things of iron, except as art objects, breed poisons in the land, air, and water. She has told of us what is happening to your native planet, Earth I."

He paused, shuddered, then said, "We do not want that, and, if we did, She would not permit it."

"But there's no chance for overpopulation here," Kickaha said. "All Thoan maintain a limit on the number of births in every universe except those of Earth I and II. For instance, Jadawin, once Lord of the World of Tiers, reduced the rate of births among his subjects by making sure of an ample supply of an antifertility chemical in the waters."

"I know nothing of him or the other Lords," Lingwallan said. "But Our Lady wisely made our bodies so that we are fertile only after long intervals."

"You don't have murders or theft or hatred of neighbors or sex crimes?"

Lingwallan shrugged and said, "Oh, yes. The Great Mother says that that is unavoidable since we are human beings. But the tribal councils settle arguments, from which there is no appeal except to Manathu Vorcyon. It's very difficult to escape detection if you murder someone. It is rare, anyway. As for sex crime, that too is rare. The punishment for sex with a child under the age of twelve is death. After that age, the couple who mate must do so only by a mutual agreement."

He thought for a moment, then said, "Treating a child brutally, physically, mentally, or emotionally, is punished with death or exile. But I have never heard of such a thing in any tribes I know. Children are our most precious possessions, if, that is, a child can be owned."

Kickaha did not ask him if he resented being dictated to by the

Great Mother. He would have wondered about Kickaha's sanity if the question had been uttered.

"Everybody's happy, in ecstasy?" Kickaha said. "It's all advantage and no disadvantage?"

Lingwallan shrugged, then said, "Where in this world or any others are there not disadvantages?"

Kickaha knew that he would be bored if he stayed long here.

Manathu Vorcyon greeted him at the main entrance to the tree and said, "We will talk now about Red Orc, you, and me. About many things."

She led him up the central staircase to the sixth story and through a doorless entrance into a large room. Against one wall was a twelve-foot-high mirror. On the only table was a silver pitcher and three silver goblets, all with figures of humans and beasts in alto-relief. One of these caught his eye. It was an image of the scaly man.

Manathu Vorcyon told him to sit down on one of the two chairs in the room.

"This place is taboo, except for me and my guests, of course. We won't be interrupted."

After she sat down, she filled two goblets with a greenish liquor. She said, "Among other questions, you want to ask me just why and how you were transported from Red Orc's place to here."

Kickaha nodded and then sipped the liquor. It tasted . . . only one way for him to describe it—like layers of sunlight, moonlight, and starlight liquefied. His heart beat faster; his head seemed to expand slightly; his body became pleasantly warm.

"Don't drink it swiftly," she said.

Kickaha was used to nudity, but those huge, round, and unsagging breasts across the table from him aroused a strange feeling. It was partly sexual and partly . . . what? It evoked an image of himself as an enwombed fetus and the sloshing of the amniotic sea rocking him back and forth while he slept and dreamed dreams without words. No, without any knowledge of words. He just thought. And he thought not only without language. He thought without images. He was without words, and his brain was equally empty of images. He was floating and rocking in pure emotion. He was safe and well-fed and quite cozy and never wanted to leave this place. Here was heaven, and outside it was hell.

Quickly, the feeling slipped away. The amniotic ocean receded with a low roar as if there were a hole in the sac and it was pouring out in a waterfall. Panic shot through him, and then he was again the man he had been a second ago.

He shook his head slightly and swore silently that he would drink no more of the green liquor. Not in this room and not when she was present, anyway.

Manathu Vorcyon smiled as if she knew of his moment of transport. She said, "I have been aware for a very long time of Red Orc and his plans. For a much shorter time, I have also been aware of you. And I know somewhat what has been happening in many of the worlds."

Not looking behind her, she stabbed a backward-pointing thumb at the silvery mirror on the wall. "Through that, I hear and see people and events in other worlds. It's hooked up to gates made by others and to gates that I've made in the weak places in the walls among the universes. The transmission is not always good, and I often have trouble maintaining the frequency lock on the gates. But I can keep watch on certain key places. You could say that I have my finger on the pulsebeat of many worlds. My people believe it's a magic mirror."

Kickaha wanted to ask her if the device was an ancient one she had inherited or if she had made it herself. Anana had told him stories about her. One was that she was the only scientist, with the possible exception of Red Orc, among the Lords. But, true or not, she did have the device, and that was all that mattered now.

"I have heard about you and now and then seen you," she said.

"But, until recently, when you were detected by the glind-glassa"—she indicated the seeming mirror again—"I had set no traps to gate you through to me. I had no strong reason then to do so. As soon as I had a reason, I set up more traps—no easy thing to do by remote control—hoping to catch you someday. I also connected alarms to the gates to sound when you and you alone were in one."

"How did the detectors know me?" Kickaha said.

"The skin of every person has unique patterns in its electric field. The glindglassa detects these and also registers the individual's mass. It employs a visual detector, which I don't use very often because it's so difficult to keep a lock on it. But I had put your physical description, which I got from other sources, into the computer. It stores a display of every person caught in its field. When you were finally detected, it emitted an audio and visual notice along with your image and frequency field.

"From then on, the traps were set to detect you when you were in the range of the glindglassa and to shunt you here. The probability that you would be caught was very low because there are thousands, maybe hundreds of thousands of gates, and I could only lock into a thousand."

"Why don't you also trap Red Orc?"

"I doubt that he knows that I would like to do that. But he probably knows that such a device as the glindglassa exists. I believe that he carries a frequency-emitter canceler."

Kickaha said, "Wouldn't the absence of a frequency field at the same time that a mass is detected identify Red Orc? And what about the visual detector?"

She smiled. "You're not just a tricky but simple killer of Lords. For one thing, the visual detection field often drifts away from the transmission-reception lock. For another, Red Orc has never entered any of my traps—not to my knowledge, anyway. He may have a visual-detector damper and a false-mass emitter. You're not the only wily one."

"Why did you gate me through into the forest instead of directly to your tree?"

"You needed time to adjust and to be peacefully greeted by Lingwallan. Who knows what might have happened if you had appeared among strangers? You're very quick. You might have used your beamer before you understood the situation."

"Not me."

"You don't lack self-confidence. That's beneficial for a person, up to a point."

Kickaha did not believe her explanation. The probable truth was that she was very cautious. She just did not want anyone she had gated through to be close to her when they came through. The gatee might carry a very powerful bomb or some other very destructive weapon. The trees around him when he came through doubtless held hidden detectors. They would notify her if he carried any such weapons.

She said, "This is not the time for minor questions. But I will answer one you must have. Why did I not shunt to here all persons in my traps? One of them might have been Red Orc. I did try that method for a long time, five hundred years to be exact. I quit doing that when I learned that he was somehow able to avoid being caught.

"Now. Hold your tongue until I tell you that you may loose it."

=== 10 ===

Manathu Vorcyon had long ago known about Red Orc, his wars against his father, Los, and against other Lords after he had slain his father.

"I also have heard about you, Kickaha. Many Lords fear you. They identify you with the *leblabbiy* who an ancient prophecy says will destroy all Lords. Prophecies are nonsense, of course, unless they're self-fulfilling. Despite their mighty powers, the Lords are not only decadent but are superstitious."

So far, Red Orc had not tried to invade her universe. She had too many weapons of the ancients for him to attack her even if he brought about the deaths of all other Lords.

"That is," she said, "I thought so until recently. But he now has the Horn of Shambarimem. That may give him the courage to try to invade my world. And I have heard through my spies that he is again striving to get into Zazel's World though he had ceased doing that several millennia ago. The Horn may enable him to enter it. It is said that he knows that the last of the ancient creation-destruction machines is buried in there. My spies have told me that Red Orc has often said that he would destroy all universes except one if he could get his hands on the creation-destruction engine."

Ah! Kickaha thought. So, that's it! Red Orc would tell me only that he wanted "certain data" in the Caverned World. That data was this creation-destruction engine, whatever that is.

"Your pardon for interrupting, Great Mother," Kickaha said. "Hearing you say that, I just can't keep quiet. That is not accurate information. The machine is not there. However, the data to build it is. I know because Red Orc himself told me so. I mean, he might just as well have told me that he wanted to find the data, plans, schematics, I don't know. But from what you said, I'm sure the engine itself isn't there."

She raised her thick and glossy black eyebrows. "That is so? He is the lord of all liars and may not have told you the truth."

"He thought I was unable to escape him and that I was certain to return to him. Thus, he revealed much that he would not otherwise have told. He is indeed a great liar. I don't hold that against him since I've indulged in a few untruths myself. In this case, however, he had no reason to lie."

Manathu Vorcyon was silent for a half-minute. Then she said, "It may be best that you do speak now. First, tell me how you, an Earthman, came to the World of Tiers. I have heard parts of your story. These may or may not be true. Tell me your story from the beginning until now but do not make an epic of it. I need now only a swiftly told outline."

Kickaha did as she commanded. But when he described the scaly man, he heard her gasp.

Her eyes opened very wide, and she cried, "The Thokina!"

"What's the matter?"

"Just go on. I'll tell you later. What happened after you first saw him?"

Kickaha told her how the scaly man, whom they had thought dead, had begun to move just as he and Anana gated out of the tomb.

She got to her feet and began pacing back and forth while vigorously swinging her arms. She looked disturbed.

He thought, Even goddesses can lose their composure.

"The Thokina! The Thokina!" she muttered. "It can't be!"

"Why not?"

She swung around to face him. "Because they are only creatures of folklore and legend born of primitive fears and imagination! When I was a child, my parents and the house slaves told me stories about them. In some of these, the Thokina were a nonhuman species who were the predecessors of the Thoan. In other tales, they made the first Thoan and enslaved them. Then the Thoan revolted and killed all but one. That sole survivor fled to some unknown universe, according to the story, and put himself into a sort of suspended animation. But the tale, which was a very spooky one for a child, told how he would rise one day when the time was ripe and would join the greatest enemy of the Thoan and help him slay all of them. That greatest enemy would be a *leblabbiy*.

"The tale also described how he would then kill the last Thoan and become the Lord of all the worlds.

"But another story said that he would join the *leblabbiy* and help them overthrow the Lords. The tales made enjoyable hair-raising stories for the children. But that the Thokina could actually be . . . that . . . that . . ."

"I am not lying," he said. "And I was wondering about the image of the scaly man I saw on a goblet during the feast."

"If a Thokina has risen from his sleep and is somewhere out there, what does he intend to do?"

"All you know now is that they did and do exist. You really don't know if he'll be hostile or friendly."

He wondered if some of that fright she'd felt as a child when hearing the tale was still living in her.

She sat down, leaned toward him, and clamped her hand around his wrist. He winced as his wristbones seemed to bend in toward each other. Her grip was as strong as he imagined a gorilla's would be. He certainly did not want to tangle with her, not in a fight, anyway.

"This scaly man is an unknown factor. Therefore, until we know better, he's a danger. Tell me. Did you tell Red Orc about him?"

"I did not. I wouldn't tell him anything that he might use."

She loosed her grip. Kickaha felt like rubbing his wrist, but he was not going to let anyone, not even a goddess, know that her grip was so powerful that she had hurt him.

She said, "Good. We have that advantage. Another is that Red Orc does not know where you are. Now, when you resume your journey to the Caverned World, you . . ."

One does not twice interrupt a goddess, but he did it anyway. "Resume my journey?"

"Of course. I took it for granted that you would. You did give your word to him that you would, didn't you?"

"It doesn't matter if I did or not. He knew I'd return to him because he said that Anana might be alive and his prisoner. I doubt very much that she did survive the flash flood. But I can't chance it that she didn't."

"You didn't get to tell the rest of your story."

He ended his narration at the point where he had jumped into the trap she had placed before the Thoan's gate.

She said, "You're an extraordinary man, though you've had more luck than most would have had. It may run out soon. Then, again . . ."

They talked of other things. Kickaha sipped on the liquor. Near the end of their conversation, he felt even more hopeful than he usually did, and he was almost always high on optimism.

The goddess stood up and looked down at him. Her expression seemed to show fondness for him. He felt more than fondness for her.

"It's agreed that you will go on looking for Zazel's World. You'll have an advantage doing that because I know a gateway that I doubt anyone else knows. My powers are not small, though this is a mammoth project. I will try to keep you within detection range of the glindglassa, though I am not at all sure that I can do that. You will spend several more days here resting and exercising and discussing with me the details of our plan. You look tired. You will go to bed, and you may rise when you feel like it."

"I sometimes rise when I don't feel like it."

She smiled and said, "Unless I'm wrong, you are implying more than appears on the surface of your words."

"I usually do."

"For a *leblabbiy*, you are very brash."

"There's some doubt that I am a *leblabbiy*, completely *leblabbiy*, that is. I may be half-Thoan, but I'm not eager to find out if I am. What is is, and I am what I am."

"We'll talk about that some other time. You are dismissed."

She's really putting me in my place, he thought. Oh, well, it was the liquor talking. Or was it?

Anana's bright face arced across his mind. For a moment, he felt as if he were going to weep.

She patted him on the shoulder and said, "Grief is a price paid for admission to life."

She paused, then said, "Bromides help few people in times of sorrow. But there are some things I know that could ease the grief."

She said nothing more. He went up to his room and prepared for bed. When he got into it, he had some trouble getting to sleep. But only fifteen or so minutes passed before he was gone from the waking world. He awoke with a start and reached for the beamer under his pillow. A noise? A soft voice? Something had awakened him. By then, the beamer, which he kept under his pillow, was in his hand. Then he saw, silhouetted in the doorless entrance against the dusk-light of the hallway, a woman's figure. She was so tall that she had to be Manathu Vorcyon. He smelled a faint odor. This might have brought him up out of sleep; the nose was also sentinel against danger. The odor was musky but not perfume from a bottle. It hinted at fluids flowing and fevers floating hot and steamy from a swamp, a strange image but appropriate. The odor was that of the flesh of a woman in heat, though stronger than any he had ever smelled.

She walked slowly toward him.

"Put the beamer down, Kickaha."

He placed it on the floor and waited, his heart thudding as if it were a stallion's hooves kicking against a stall door. She eased herself down on her knees and then on her side against Kickaha. Her body heat was like a wave from a just-opened furnace door.

"It has been eighty years since I have had a child," she whispered. "Since then, I have met no man whose baby I cared to bear, though I have bedded many splendid lovers. But you, Kickaha, the man of many wiles, the man who is never at a loss, the hero of many adventures, you will give me a child to love and to raise. And I know that I have stirred in you a mighty passion. Moreover, you are one of the very few men not afraid of me."

Kickaha was not sure of that. But he had overcome fear most of his life, and he would ride over this fear, which was not a big one, anyway.

He thought of Anana, though the withdrawal of blood from his brain for nonmental uses paled the thought. If she were dead, she would be no barrier for him to other women. But he did not know if she had died, and he and Anana had sworn faithfulness to each other. They would honor the vow unless they were separated for a long time or were forced by circumstances to suspend it for a while. What they did in such situations was left to each to justify to himself or herself.

Her mouth met his, and the right breast of Mother Earth, in itself a planet, rested on his belly.

He thought, I am in her power. I depend upon her to help me

in the battle with Red Orc. The fate of whole universes is on the scales. If I say no to her, I might weigh the balance in favor of Red Orc. No, that's nonsense, but she might not be so enthusiastic in helping me. Also, a guest does not offend a hostess. It's not good manners.

Mainly, though, I want to do this.

He sighed, and he said, "I am indeed deeply sorry, Great Mother. But Anana and I swore absolute fidelity to each other. Much as I desire you, and I've desired only Anana more than you, I will not do this."

She stiffened, then got up. Looking down at him, she said, "I honor your vow, Kickaha. Even though I can see plainly in this dim light that you are not at all indifferent to me."

"The body does not always override the dictates of the mind."

She laughed, then said, "You know the Thoan proverbs well. I admire you, Kickaha. Fidelity is a rare trait, especially when I am the temptress."

"That is the truth. Please go before I weaken too much."

Three days later, Kickaha and Manathu Vorcyon were standing before the silvery screen of the glindglassa. Kickaha was fully clothed and well armed with various weapons. His backpack contained food, water, and some medical supplies. His head was full of advice from the Great Mother.

She leaned close to the glindglassa and whispered a code word. Its surface instantly shimmered and expanded slightly, then contracted slightly. Kickaha looked into it but could see nothing beyond.

Manathu Vorcyon turned, enfolded him in her arms, pressed him close to her breasts, and kissed his forehead.

"I shall miss you, Kickaha," she murmured. "May you succeed in your mission. I will be attempting to keep you under surveillance as much as possible, but even that will not be much."

"It's been more than fun," he said. "It's been very educational. And you have highly honored me."

She released him. He stepped toward the gate. She lightly touched the back of his neck and ran the tip of her finger down his spine. A shiver ran through him. It felt as if a goddess had blessed him.

She said, "If anyone can stop Red Orc, you'll be the one."

He wondered if she really meant it. It did not matter. He agreed wholeheartedly with her. However, his best might not be enough.

He stepped through the wavering and shimmering curtain.

11

*T*hough Kickaha had been told by the giantess that he would find nothing dangerous during his first transit, he was ready for the unexpected. He was crouching, beamer in hand, when he was suddenly surrounded by darkness. Per Manathu Vorcyon's instructions, he walked forward three steps. Bright sunlight dazzled him. Before him was an open plain—no surprise, since the Great Mother had told him what to expect. He straightened up, looked around, and reholstered the weapon.

The sky seemed to be one vast aurora with shifting and wavering bands of violet, green, blue, yellow, and gray. The plain was covered with tall yellow grasses except for groves of trees here and there. Far away, a large herd of huge black animals was grazing. Behind him was a house-sized and roughly pyramid-shaped boulder of some smooth, greasy, and greenish stone.

He had fifty seconds to get to the other side of the boulder. The Great Mother had arranged this detour to mystify any enemy who might be traveling through the gateways. He ran around the stone and saw a shimmering on its side. But he stopped for several seconds. Here was something not even the Great Mother could have anticipated. Two tiger-sized beasts with long snouts and predators' teeth were standing in front of the gate. They roared but did not charge.

Kickaha, yelling, ran at them, his beamer again in his hand. One beast bounded away; the other held its ground and crouched down to spring at him. His beamer ray drilled through its head. It slumped and was silent. He leaped over the carcass, which stank of burned flesh, and through the gate. A roar filled his ears. The other beast had turned and was, he supposed, charging him. He envisioned the gate disappearing and the animal bouncing off the suddenly hard side of the boulder. But he was rammed forward by its flying body and slammed into a wall. The force of the impact stunned him.

When, after an underterminable time, he regained his senses, his groping hand felt a sticky liquid. An odor like a weasel's filled his nostrils. But he also smelled blood. He felt the device on his wrist and pressed a button. Light sprang from it, momentarily dazzling him. It lit up a small chamber cut out of stone like the first one. But he doubted that he was in the same boulder, if it was a boulder. He got to his feet and noted as he stepped over the big predator that only its front part had gotten through the gate.

He walked toward the wall through which he had just entered. There were shimmerings on each of the other walls. The Great Mother had told him that two were false gates containing devices that would spray poison on the intruder. He jumped through the safe gate while hoping that he had not been delayed too long by the animal. As he emerged on the other side and yelled out the code word, he landed on top of a six-foot square and six-inch-deep metal box. It was poised a thousand feet in the air above a land of bare stone. The sky was blue, and the wind whistling past him was cold. Below were row on row of Brobdingnagian busts carved out of monoliths. They extended to the horizons. Manathu Vorcyon had told him that this was the world of Arathmeem the Strutter. That Lord, long since slain by Red Orc, had made a planet of which a fourth consisted of billions of rock or jewel busts of himself.

He was glad that he had not arrived when an electrical storm was in full rage. Thunder and lightning and a strong wind might have drowned out the code word. In which situation, the metal box would have automatically turned over and dumped him.

On the bottom of the box, near the edge, was a slightly raised metal plate. He got down on his belly, reached over the edge, felt the plate, and pressed it. Then he was, as the Great Mother had said he would be, in darkness and enclosed by a very thick fluid. It pressed on him and flowed up his nostrils and into his ears. He had not been given an oxygen mask because he would not be in this gate-trap very long. But an enemy of Manathu Vorcyon would be unless he knew what Kickaha knew.

He reached out with his right hand and felt up and down the wall until his fingers came to a rounded protuberance. He pushed with the flat of his hand on it, and he was free of the strangest trap he had ever been in. It was inside a massive rock on Wooth's World, a stone that was a living-nonliving thing, analogous to a virus. The slow-moving fluid eventually emerged from fissures in the rock and dripped onto the ground outside the gigantic boulder. From this lava were born—if that word could be used for the bizarre process—small balls flat on the bottom.

The natives on this planet worshiped the "mother," and they would take the "babies" and set them in the center of their villages. These minor gods grew into stones as large as the mother. Moreover, there was a thriving trade in "babies." Those villages that had a monopoly on the supply sold them to those who lacked them. Many wars had been fought to protect or to seize a source of the most precious commodity on this planet.

Dripping with the heavy gray fluid, Kickaha stood motionless until it had oozed away from him and spread in a puddle around him. Then he jumped to the ground beyond the puddle. He began walking toward the east. Manathu Vorcyon, during millennia of the use of spies and eavesdropping via gates she had tapped into, had a rough idea of where the gate to Zazel's World was located

on this planet. It was up to Kickaha to find the exact location, but
he knew the direction he should go from her gate.

Getting there was not easy. He was on the Unwanted World,
a planet so crowded with dangerous beasts, birds, plants, and other
forms of life that it was a wonder they had not killed each other
off long ago. After some days of avoiding or shooting these,
Kickaha had great respect for the survival abilities of Red Orc.
After ten days, four of them spent in hiding from a five-foot-high
and city-block-wide creature that oozed across the ground and
emitted a deadly gas, Kickaha topped a high ridge. Below him was
a plain and a river. Near the river were the remains of the gigantic
square nest built by some kind of creatures. Manathu Vorcyon did
not know what they were. The structure was built with a concrete-
like substance made in the creatures' bellies and spat out to dry.

Los had set up a gate there, the only entrance, as far as anyone
knew, to Zazel's World. When Red Orc had finally returned to this
place, he had slain all of the creatures living in it. Unable to find
the gate, he had destroyed the construction. Believing that the
creatures had broken the gate off at its foundation and buried it
somewhere, he searched the land for a hundred-square-mile area.
He had very sensitive metal detectors that could determine the size
and shape of any metal mass a hundred feet down in the ground.
The first time he looked for the gate, he did not find it, and he did
not succeed during his many other searches.

"The truth," the Great Mother had said, "is that we can't be sure
that those creatures removed and hid the gate. Perhaps a Lord did
it, though that does not seem likely."

Kickaha had refrained from saying that he had already thought
of that. She might, as on previous occasions, be irritated enough
to chew him out and thus put him in his place. Sometimes, the
Great Mother was a Big Mother.

After crossing the plain, spooking a herd of bisonlike animals on
the way, he got to the ruins. There were no pieces left from Red

Orc's beam-blasting. He must have disintegrated these and burned out a huge hole in the ground. The hole was brim-full of water.

Kickaha took the backpack off and placed it on the ground. After opening it, he took out a device shaped like a big cigar, but twice the size of the largest cigar he had ever seen. Attached halfway along its upper part was a monocular cylinder. He pointed it toward where the building had been. He could see crosshairs and the sky through it. He slowly moved it back and forth, working upward. Then he saw a brightness like a short lightning streak.

He murmured, "I'll be damned! There it is!"

Manathu Vorcyon had told him that the instrument was a gate or crack-in-the-wall detector. Kickaha had not known that such a thing existed until she had handed it to him. It was many thousands of years old, and, as far as she knew, the only one.

"Shambarimen is supposed to have made that, too," she had said.

"You must have a hell of a lot of confidence in me," he had said. "What if I lose it or have it taken away from me?"

She had shrugged and had said, "I've been saving it for a truly important time, a serious crisis. This is it."

So, here was the gate or, since the metal hexagram had been removed, the weak spot made by the gate. Red Orc had not known where it was since he did not have the detector.

Kickaha put the detector down. Up there, perhaps fifty feet above the ground, was the crack in the wall between two universes, visible only to his instrument. To reach it, he would have to build a series of platforms and ladders. There was plenty of wood around, and he had the tools he needed.

"Might as well get to work," he muttered.

"Thank you," a voice said loudly behind him.

He whirled, his hand darting at the same time for the holstered beamer.

Red Orc stood forty feet from him. He was smiling, and his

beamer was pointing at Kickaha. On the ground behind him was an airboat, its white needle shape gleaming, its canopy open.

"No!" the Thoan said.

Kickaha stopped his hand. At a gesture from Red Orc, he raised both hands above his head. His heart was beating so hard that it seemed to be close to exploding.

"How . . . ?" Kickaha said, then closed his mouth. The Thoan would certainly explain how clever he had been.

"Now you may move your hand slowly, use two fingers to remove your beamer, and toss it far from you," Red Orc said. "Then throw the finder to me."

Kickaha obeyed, looking at the same time for Thoan backups. The nearest cover for them was a grove of woods a hundred yards away.

"I knew Manathu Vorcyon had gated you away," the Lord said. "I detected her trap long ago, and I deliberately sent you through my gate so that she would bring you to her world. I knew that she would probably give you some device to find the crack—I admit I didn't know why the hexagram was no longer there—and that you would use her gates to get here."

Kickaha had many questions. One was how Red Orc knew that Manathu Vorcyon had been the one to whisk him away to her world. But he would not ask them. What mattered was that he was in as bad a situation as he had ever been.

"I don't intend to kill you just now," Red Orc said. "Rest awhile while I use her device."

Keeping his eyes on Kickaha, he bent down and picked up the finder. Then he pointed the beamer at Kickaha. He must have set it only for stun power, but the ray hit Kickaha in the chest and knocked him backward and down. The effect was as if Kickaha had just opened a door and a team of men running with a big rammer had slammed its end into his chest. The world grew dim around him; his breath was knocked loose from him. He could not get up though he strove to do so.

By the time that he could draw in enough air and raise himself on one elbow, he saw Red Orc looking through the device. A second later, he took it from his eye. He turned with a grin of delight and triumph toward Kickaha.

A bright flash blinded Kickaha, and a roar deafened him.

Pieces of bloody flesh struck his face and chest. Then the smoke surrounding Red Orc was blown away by the wind. His left hand and much of his lower arm gone, his head and torso a red ruin, the Lord lay on the ground.

Kickaha fell back onto the grass and stared at the bright and blue sky. He just could not grasp what had happened. The man of many wiles, the man never at a loss, was bewildered. Not until his heart had slowed down to near a normal rate and his chest pain had eased was he able to think straight.

Anger replaced the pain. Manathu Vorcyon had betrayed him. She had used him as a pawn, not caring that he might be mutilated or killed. Her "detector" was a fake designed to lure Red Orc. The light, the supposed crack in the wall, automatically came on a few minutes after he had turned the instrument on. And something, he did not know what, triggered the explosives when the Thoan came within a certain range. That her decoy also could be killed had not stopped her.

The Great Mother was a great bitch.

"She could at least have warned me," he muttered.

Her reasoning for not doing so would have been that he might act differently if he knew the true intent of the finder. And she would have explained that Red Orc was such a danger to everybody in the universes, to the existence of the universes themselves, that any means to kill him was justified.

Not to me, he thought. Now, I have to kill Manathu Vorcyon.

I won't go after her, but if I should ever happen to run across her, I'll deal her the dead man's hand.

Then he groaned. A thought had inserted itself in the flow of his images of revenge against the Great Mother. Only Red Orc knew whether or not Anana had drowned in the flash flood, and he was dead.

Groaning again, he rolled over on his side to get ready to stand up. He said, "God!" Shock had come after shock. Standing not ten feet from him was Red Orc. He held a beamer pointed at his enemy and was smiling as the slain man had been smiling. Behind him was another airboat, the exact duplicate of the first one.

Kickaha looked at where Red Orc had been—where he still was. He was a corpse. Yet the living man was here. It was too much to understand. But if his mind could not handle the inrush of events, his body was able to struggle to its feet. Weaving back and forth slightly, he spoke hoarsely.

"You have nine lives!"

"Not quite as many as a cat," Red Orc said.

Kickaha waved at the dead man but did not speak.

"Clones, flesh of my flesh, genes of my genes," the Lord said. "I raised them from babies and educated them. Being, in a sense, I, they have my inborn drive toward power, so I have seen to it that they don't have a chance to usurp me. I wouldn't turn my back to any of them. Since they're as intelligent as I am, though not nearly as well educated or experienced, they were reared to be staked-out goats, decoys with highly expendable lives. Four of them have been sacrificed so far, including that man there, but I did avenge the first three."

He paused, smiled, then said, "Of course, you could be talking to one of them now, not the real Red Orc."

"But how did you get here? How did you know when I got here?"

"Manathu Vorcyon is not the only one who has secrets. Tell me what happened here. I assume that the device was not able to detect a crack and that it was a trick to blow my head off. You must also have thought of the high probability that your head could have gone the way of my clone's. However, I take nothing for granted. There wasn't a gate or a crack, was there?"

"No."

Red Orc smiled. "I know there isn't. I tried the Horn here, and nothing happened. If I'd known that when I sent you out, I would've told you not to waste your time or mine."

He gestured with the beamer and said, "Walk ahead of me to the boat."

Kickaha obeyed. He wondered where the Horn was now. Probably it was in the Lord's boat. Then the same thing that had happened when Red Orc caught him at the cliff top occurred again. He felt a slight prick in his back, and he awoke in an unfamiliar room, a twenty-foot cube. He was not bound, and he was naked. There was in the cube no furniture, rugs, door, or window. In one corner was a hole in the floor, apparently for excretion, but it looked and smelled clean. Cool air moved slightly over him, piped in through a nozzle on a wall near the ceiling.

His chest still hurt. When he looked down, he could see the five-inch-wide black and blue bruise across his breast. But his head was clear, and he no longer felt emotional shock. What he did feel was frustration and rage.

To work off the stiffness in his muscles and his emotions, he exercised as vigorously as the chest pain would allow him. Then he began pacing back and forth while waiting for Red Orc to make his next move. Hours must have gone by before a cough behind him startled him. Red Orc or one of his clones stood there, holding a beamer. Kickaha was beginning to think that the weapon had been grafted to the Lord's hand. And the Lord had popped out of a gate or had opened a section of the wall while his captive's back was turned to him.

"Turn around," the Thoan said.

Kickaha did so, and the upper and lower sections of the wall before him parted. The top section slid into the ceiling; the lower, into the floor. At the Lord's command, Kickaha marched down a very wide and high hallway, doorless and windowless, then went around a corner and down a similar corridor. Two men armed with spears stood by the sides of a door twelve feet high. Their square steel helmets and bulging cuirasses were arabesqued in gold, and their short kilts were crimson and embroidered with small green female sphinxes. Kickaha had never seen such armor or dress before. The guards stepped aside, their spears ready to plunge into Kickaha. The door slid to one side into the wall.

The two, followed by the guards, entered an enormous room furnished with laboratory equipment, most of it strange to Kickaha. They walked down a half-mile-long aisle past many tables and big machines. When a wall barred farther progress, Red Orc told Kickaha to stop. The Thoan spoke a code word swiftly, but not too fast for Kickaha to understand it and to store it in his memory.

A huge square area of the wall became transparent. Kickaha could not help crying out. Anana, unclothed, was in the room beyond the wall. She was bound into a chair, her head held in a brace. Her eyes were closed. Above her head was what at first seemed to be a giant hair dryer.

He whirled around and snarled. "What are you doing to her?"

"I would think you'd be overjoyed because she is alive. If I had left her on that ledge just above the floodwaters, she would have died. She had a broken leg and arm, three broken ribs, and a slight concussion. Now she's in excellent physical shape because of my medical skills. You're a hard man to please, Trickster."

"What are you doing to her?"

The Lord waved his free hand. "What you see, *leblabbiy*, is a process I conceived and built and experimented with during those many times I worked to relieve myself of the inevitable boredom that comes to all immortals. The machine there is not an ancient device I inherited. I invented it."

He paused, but Kickaha said nothing. If Red Orc was waiting for another outburst, he was not going to get it.

The Lord spoke sharply. "Look at her, Kickaha! And say good-bye to the Anana you knew!"

Reluctantly, Kickaha turned to the window.

"That machine is removing her memory. It's doing so slowly because a quick process injures the brain, and I do not want a mindless mistress."

Kickaha quivered but did not move or speak.

"The machine requires an hour a day for ten days to remove all memory back to when she was approximately eighteen years old. When the process is completed, she will believe—and in a sense it will be true—that she is on her native planet and her parents and siblings are still living. It will be as if she has journeyed back in time, but without any knowledge of the thousands of years that have passed since she was eighteen."

Kickaha could not speak for a moment, and, when he did, he croaked.

"She won't remember me."

"Not at all. Nor will she remember me. But I will introduce myself and, in time, make her love me. I can make any woman love me."

"What about when she finds out the truth?"

"She won't," Red Orc said, and he laughed. "I'll see to that. Of course, when I get tired of her, if I do . . ."

"Do you plan to do the same thing to me? Or do you have something painful in mind?"

"I could remove your memory up to the time, say, when you were a college student on Earth and went through Vannax's gate to the World of Tiers. Or I could torture you until you scream for death. Any man, no matter how brave, can be made to do that, even I. Or, if you volunteered to kill Manathu Vorcyon and succeeded, you could earn your freedom. First, though, you would have to complete the mission of finding a way into the Caverned World. If you do so, you will get the gift of keeping all your memories. That would indeed cause you great pain because of your memories of Anana."

Kickaha had no trouble choosing one of the options. But he would not tell Red Orc his decision until he was forced to do so. Just now, he could think only of Anana.

If we ever get free and are reunited, Kickaha thought, I'll see that she loves me again. And I'll tell her about our life together in detail.

Red Orc spoke another code word. The window became the wall. All four marched off through three halls and entered a large room ornately furnished in a style that Kickaha assumed was that of the natives. He and the Thoan sat down in comfortable chairs, facing each other across a large table of polished red wood in which were spiral green streaks. The table legs were carved with the figures of mermen and merwomen. Food and drink were brought in by a man and a woman, one of whom stood behind the Lord and the other behind Kickaha.

"You may bathe, eat, and rest after we've finished here," the Lord said. "Now! I assume you've decided that you'll try to carry out the two missions for me and for your own sake. I would certainly do so. While you live . . ."

"While I live, I hope," Kickaha said.

"I know that. Let us eat."

"I am not at all hungry," Kickaha said. "I would choke on the first bite."

"Sometimes the belly overrides everything. Very well. You may eat later in your own quarters."

The Thoan waited until he had chewed and swallowed several bites and drank wine before he spoke again.

"Describe your experiences while with the ogress slut."

Kickaha did so, holding nothing back except what the Great Mother had said about the scaly man. Red Orc might know something of what his "guest" had said and done while with Manathu Vorcyon. It did not seem likely, but he did not know what kind of espionage system his "host" might have.

When Kickaha had finished, Red Orc said, "I did not want to drag her into my affairs. Not yet, anyway. But she did it when she snatched you away from me. By the way, she did not gate you through to the forest because she was considerate of you and wanted you to have time to get adjusted to her world before she met you. She did so to protect herself. If I had implanted a small atom bomb in you and set it to explode as soon as you arrived in her world, she would have been beyond its range."

He laughed, then said, "But I don't have that capability. To make atom bombs, I mean. If I wanted to take the time and do the research to find the data for making one and then go through the long tedious process of mining the metals needed and building a reactor . . . you get the idea."

He drummed his fingers for a moment before speaking again.

"Two days should be enough for you to recover. After that, ready or not, you will go out again. And this time I will launch you through a series of gates that I am sure Manathu Vorcyon has not trapped."

Kickaha had not yet eased his grief when he stepped through the gate the Lord had picked for him. At the second gate, he had time to slip a battery into his beamer before being shunted to the next station. Within three minutes, he had passed through five gates. One of these was in a cave high on a mountain. Before he was passed on, he glimpsed a valley at the bottom of which was a river. Near it was a tiny village and above that was a castle. He cried out with the joy of recognition. It was the keep of Baron von Kritz, an enemy of his when he had lived on the Dracheland level of the World of Tiers, the world he loved most. And then he was in the next station.

But this was not the place described by Red Orc. It was a windowless cell with a heavily barred jailhouse door, and it was bare of furniture except for a toilet, a washbowl with a soap dish, towels on a wall rack, and a pile of blankets in one corner.

It did have an occupant whom Kickaha recognized at once, though the man was unclothed.

Eric Clifton!

The Englishman was standing in a corner and looking confused.

Before either could say anything, Kickaha felt his senses leaving him. Clifton was now down on his knees, his face going slack. When Kickaha regained consciousness, he was lying on the floor. Like his cellmate, he was nude. And his beamer, holster, belt, and backpack were gone.

He struggled to his feet. Clifton was beginning to stir. Kickaha looked through the bars and gasped.

The scaly man was standing outside the cell.

12

I did not think that anyone save me could have been spared death from the flood," Eric Clifton said softly behind him. "But it might have been better if you and I had perished in it. Now we are in the merciless hands of a demon from Hell, perhaps the Prince of Darkness himself. Our very souls are in extreme peril."

Kickaha was aware of the words, but he was too intent on studying his captor to take in their full meaning. Close up, the creature looked even more monstrous and dangerous than when in the "coffin." The massive muscles and thick skeleton were a Hercules'. The gold and green scales of his skin gleamed in the naked light above him. Around his neck from just below the jaw and to the shoulders were interlocking bands of bone on the surface of which were the snakish scales. And lines on his face revealed what Kickaha had not seen before. Bony plates underlay the scales there, too. But they seemed to be of thinner bone than on his neck and body.

Now, the scaly man opened his mouth to reveal long sharp teeth like a lion's, though the canines were much shorter.

No fruit or vegetable eater, this thing, thought Kickaha. However, bears had a predator's teeth, and their diet was more vegetarian than carnivorous.

The long and very narrow tip of its tongue slid out like a

reptile's. It was a green tendril extending from a red tongue that looked like a man's.

Its large, green eyes were set an inch or so farther back than in a human skull. Though they reminded Kickaha of a crocodile's, they had eyelids that blinked regularly.

Behind him, on the other side of the hall, were two cells similar to his.

"How long have you been here?" he said softly to Clifton.

On hearing Kickaha's voice, the creature's flat ears moved outwards and formed cups.

Clifton whispered, "Since two days ago. I came close to drowning in the flood, and I was much battered. But I did manage to grab a treetrunk and float far down the flood. I was swept over the edge of a great cataract but still survived, thanks to God and my guardian angel. However, I was carried to the very deeps of the chasm, so deep that its top was a very thin ribbon of light and I was in the darkness of the bowels of Hell. I like to have died of the heat and the moisture, but I strove to reach the shore of the waters, which had become a mere river again by then. I groped around blindly, and, once more, God and my guardian angel bestowed salvation upon me."

The scaly man had moved forward, closed his huge hands on two bars, and was eyeing the captives intently. Kickaha was startled when he saw on the creature's right index finger the ring Clifton had worn in the pit. He turned swiftly and glanced at the Englishman's right hand. The ring was gone. He turned back to face the scaly man. If he had taken the ring from Clifton, he had made it larger so that it could fit his huge finger.

Kickaha said, "Cut the lengthy narrative. How did you get here?"

"God bless us all! I did not think we were short of time in this prison. To be brief, I climbed as high as I could, falling several times but only short distances, until, thoroughly exhausted, I found a ledge large enough for me to sleep on despite my fatigue."

"I told you to get to the point."

"When I awoke, I felt around the ledge and discovered that it projected from a cave. I heard running water inside. I was very thirsty and too high above the river to get a drink. So I went into the cave, very slowly, you may be sure, sliding my feet along the rock floor and making sure that I was not at the edge of an abyss. Presently, I came to a cataract within the cave itself. And then light blazed around me. I was on a high mountain in another world. In short, I had gone through a gate hidden in a cave in the chasm. Placed there by some Lord long ago after the battle on that planet between Los and his son, Red Orc."

"That could have been many thousands of years ago," Kickaha said. "Probably, a Lord named Ololothon did it."

"Yes. But I did not stay more than a few seconds on the projection of rock high on the mountain. I was gated to a another place, then another, then another. That was the last stage. I arrived in this cell inside the circle you see drawn on the floor in that corner. I advise you not to enter that circle because somebody else might be gated through at any moment. If you were standing within it when that happened, an explosion might occur."

For the first time, Kickaha noticed the orange circular line in the corner. He said, "I doubt that would happen. If this cell is equipped with sensors, and most gates are, the gate would not be activated as long as anyone was already in that circle."

"But you don't know that there are sensors in this cell."

"What happened to your ring?"

"Oh, shortly after my arrival here, I became unconscious. I suppose it was gas released by the demon. That would account for my becoming unconscious immediately after I'd entered the cell. It would also account for both of us becoming senseless when you entered. That thing came into the cell afterwards and removed our clothes and possessions. Anyway, when I woke up after arriving here, the ring was gone. He is now wearing it."

Clifton pointed at the creature's finger.

"I saw it," Kickaha said. "Now . . ."

The scaly man spoke then with a deep resonant voice while the tendril flopped around in his mouth. His words were an incomprehensible gabble. When he stopped speaking, he cocked one ear toward Kickaha as if he expected a reply.

Kickaha replied in Thoan, "I don't understand you."

The scaly man nodded. But to him a nod must mean a no. He turned away and shambled off down the corridor.

"Now," Kickaha said, "you never finished your account of how you got into the Lords' worlds."

"I . . ."

Clifton stopped, and his jaw dropped. Kickaha turned and saw that a cell across the hall from his had just been filled. The man in it was crumpling, his knees sagging. Then he lay on his side inside the circle where he had appeared. Kickaha recognized at once the long bronze-reddish hair and the angelically handsome face.

"Red Orc!"

Clifton gasped, and he cried, "The devil has caught the devil!"

An alarm must have been set off somewhere to notify the scaly man. Kickaha heard his heavy footsteps and then saw him coming down the corridor. Just before the creature got to Red Orc's cell, Kickaha became unconscious again.

He woke befuddled, deaf, and against the wall opposite the barred door. His head felt as if it had swelled to twice its normal size. Smoke stung his nostrils and made his eyes smart, but it did not have the odor of gunpowder. He reached out on both sides of him. His right hand touched, then moved up and down, flesh and ribs. By his side was Clifton, still knocked out. He was blackened with smoke and smeared with blood and fragments of bloody flesh. When Kickaha looked down at his own body, he saw that he was also blackened and bloody. Still stunned, he flicked gobbets of flesh from his chest, stomach, and right leg. What had happened?

By then, the smoke had drifted out of the cell and down the corridor. The bars of the door were coated with blood; pieces of skin and muscle clung to the bars and lay on the floor. An eye was on the floor near Kickaha's feet.

Slowly, he came out of his daze. He tried to get to his feet, but he was trembling so much that he could not do it. Also, his back hurt, and his legs were strengthless. He closed his eyes and sat against the wall for a while. When he opened his eyes, he had a clear idea of what had to have happened. Not Red Orc but a clone sent by Red Orc had been caught in the scaly man's trap. But that meant that the Thoan had sent his clone after Kickaha, for what purpose he did not know.

No. Kickaha, his brain now starting to operate on all cylinders, realized what the purpose was. Red Orc had detectors that told him that he, Kickaha, had been taken away from the course set for him by the Thoan. Red Orc must have been surprised—and very alarmed—when Kickaha had once again vanished. But Red Orc had sent a clone along the same path after Kickaha. How quickly he must have acted! He had placed a bomb in the clone's backpack, a bomb set to explode a few seconds after its carrier reached the point at which Kickaha had been snatched away. The clone, of course, had not known that Red Orc had put the bomb in the knapsack.

Though Red Orc could not have known what was occurring after Kickaha had vanished from the detectors, he had guessed that only an enemy would do it. He might have reasoned that Manathu Vorcyon had abducted Kickaha again. Whoever was responsible, he or she possessed a device Red Orc lacked. So that person must be destroyed even if Kickaha was also turned into a shower of fragments.

Despite his pain and violent shaking, Kickaha got up and limped to the door of his cell. The bars of the clone's cell had been bent outward. The vagaries of the explosion had left a leg, severed at the upper part of the thigh, standing against the bars, a hand lying on the floor outside the bars, and what looked like a rib.

He pressed his shaking face against the bars and looked down the corridor. The scaly man was standing about twelve feet from the door of Kickaha's cell, but he was moving his head vigorously up and down and to both sides. It was as if he was trying to move the scattered pieces of his brain back into their previous positions. Though he was clean of blood and gobbets, his bright gold and green scales were dulled by smoke.

Kickaha turned to look at Clifton. The man's eyes were open, and his mouth was working. Kickaha still could not hear anything. He started to walk toward the Englishman but never made it. His senses faded.

When he awoke, he was lying on his back on a bed in a big room. Its ceiling and walls were huge screens displaying unfamiliar animals and many scaly men and women moving through exotic and brilliantly colored landscapes. All of his pains and the shaking were gone. As he sat up, he could hear the rustling of the sheets. He pushed away the covers to expose his legs. The smoke, blood, and flesh pieces had been washed off.

Near him, Eric Clifton lay on a similar bed under a glowing crazy quilt just like his own. Kickaha was noting that the room had no windows or doors when a section of the wall sank into the floor. The scaly man entered. For a moment, he turned his head. The profile was an unbroken arc from the back of his neck to just below his lower lip except for the small protrusion of the tip of his nose. The line described by his profile was like the somewhat flattened arc of a mortar shell. The insectile appearance was increased when he came straight on to Kickaha's bed. But when he stopped in front of the bed and spoke, he seemed more human than insect. The tone of his voice and his eyes sounded as if they were expressing concern.

"I don't understand," Kickaha said.

The scaly man lifted his hands and turned their palms upward. But if that gesture meant that he also did not know Kickaha's speech, he certainly was not going to be frustrated.

During the next two months, Kickaha and Clifton spent at least four hours a day teaching Thoan to him. Meanwhile, they lived in luxurious rooms a story above the hospital room and were served food, some of which was tasty and some of which repulsed them. They also exercised vigorously. And the scaly man had returned Clifton's ring, now resized to fit the Englishman's finger.

Their host's name was Khruuz. His people had been called Khringdiz. He, the lone survivor, had never heard of Thokina, the name given his kind in Thoan legend. But Kickaha thought that the Lords had adapted Khringdiz to their own pronunciation.

They were deep underground below the "tomb"—itself very deep—to which Kickaha and Anana had gated. Khruuz did not know why they had been transported to his place of millennia-long rest. But when Kickaha told him that he had used the Horn of Shambarimem, a sonic skeleton key to all gates, Khruuz understood. He said that it was still an accident that they had gone through the gate there. What had happened was that the gate, like many closed-circuit gates, had a "revolving node." Anywhere from ten to a hundred gates were continuously "whirled" in the node. The gatee might be passed through any one of them, his entrance being determined by which one he encountered when a gate became activated by an energized portion of the node. The Horn had been blown just as a "crack" or flaw opening to the tomb had come by in its rotation. The flaw was not a true gate, that is, it had not been made by a Lord, but existed in the fabric. But the Horn had made the difference.

"That means that Red Orc might know how to get into here," Kickaha told Khruuz. "You used a series of gates to trap us and the Thoan's clone. If he has detectors, and I think he does, he may get into here. Or he may send another clone, somebody, anyway, with a bomb a thousand times more powerful than the one the clone carried. Of course, he can't know just where the clone went or what happened after he got here."

By then, Khruuz had heard everything that Kickaha knew about Red Orc. He had also been told as much of the history of the Thoan people as Kickaha knew.

Khruuz spoke in his heavily accented and just barely understandable Thoan. His tongue-tendril now and then struck parts of his palate and formed sounds that were not in Thoan and probably only in his language.

"I have closed all the gates for the time being. That keeps anyone from coming in, but it also does not permit me to gather information from the outside."

Khruuz had told Kickaha that parts of the outline of the legends about the Khringdiz were close to the truth. But the details were usually wrong. When the Thoan people had killed off all of the Khringdiz except for him, he had made this underground retreat. After being there for a while, he had stopped the molecular motion of his body and settled down for a very long "sleep." The fuel to drive the machine for maintaining the chamber, to record the events on various parts of various universes, and to "awaken" him was nuclear power. When the fuel was almost gone, the machinery would bring him out of molecular stasis.

"By then," Khruuz had said, "the probabilities that the situation would be considerably changed were high. The Lords might have died out. Their numbers were comparatively few at the time I went into stasis. And their descendants, if these existed after such a long time, might be different in culture and temperament. They could be much more tolerant and empathetic. Or some other sentient species, higher on an ethical level than the Lords, might have replaced the Thoan. In any event, whoever inhabited the universes might be willing to accept me, the last of the Khringdiz. If such was not the situation, I would have to deal with the evil as best I could.

"My fuel would have lasted for some time yet. But I had also set up the security system so that any intrusion into the chamber would awaken me. You entered, and I was brought out of stasis prematurely. But the process takes some time. It did not bring me out of stasis in time for me to speak to you. You got away because of the Horn. That, by the way, must contain machinery the design for which was stolen from my people. The Thoan did not have such technology."

"What?" Kickaha had said. "The Horn was invented by the ancient Lord, Shambarimem!"

"This Shambarimem must have gotten the data from one of us, undoubtedly after he killed the Khringdiz who owned it. But instead of sharing it with his fellow Lords, he kept it secret. He incorporated it in the artifact that you called the Horn. That has to be what happened."

"But there must have been other designs or even the machinery itself!" Kickaha had said. "If the devices for opening gates or flaws were used by the Khringdiz, surely some would have fallen into Thoan hands!"

"No. They were few and well guarded. They gave us an advantage over the Thoan because we could enter their gates and flaws. But those of us who survived the initial onslaught were too few to use the openers effectively. At last, only I survived. However, those who did have the openers must have destroyed or hidden all the designs and the machines before they were hunted down and killed. You know the rest of the story."

"So, Shambarimem lied about inventing the Horn," Kickaha had said. "There goes another legend into the dust!"

Khruuz had shrugged his massive shoulders in a quite human

gesture. He had said, "From what you tell me and from my experience since being awakened, it's evident that the Lords are still here and that very few have changed."

Kickaha had said, "You'd like to get revenge, wipe them out?"

The scaly man had hesitated, then had said, "I can't deny that I would be happy if all my original enemies, the Lords who existed when we were being exterminated, were to be killed and I was the one who did it. But that is impossible. I must somehow make peace with them. If I cannot do that, then I am doomed."

"Don't feel hopeless," Kickaha had said. "I am the enemy of almost all Lords because they tried to kill me first. They must be killed before there will be peace in all the universes. You and I would make wonderful allies. How about it?"

The scaly man had said, "I will do my best to help you. You have my word on that, and, in the days when there were other Khringdiz, the word of Khruuz was enough."

Kickaha had asked him if he knew how the Thoan came into being. Khruuz replied that his people would never have made beings so unlike themselves.

"Some questions have no answers," Khruuz had said. "But our universe was not the only one. Somehow, the Thoan broke through the wall between our universes. Instead of treating us as if we were peaceful and nonviolent sentients, which we were, they behaved as if we were dangerous animals. We were treacherously attacked and, in the first blow, the Thoan wiped out more than three-quarters of us. We survivors were forced to become killers. The rest of the story you know."

"And now?" Kickaha had said.

"When I opened a gate and connected it to a circuit, I had no way of knowing if the Thoan were still violent beings. So, I decided to collect various specimens. You two were the first to be caught. I did not know that you were not Thoan but from a planet that did not even exist when I took refuge. The third was a Thoan. You know what happened then."

"We can help you, and you can help us," Kickaha had said. "Red Orc must be killed. In fact, all those Lords who would slay us must be killed. But, first, I have to get into Zazel's World before Red Orc does."

"He really intends to destroy all of the universes and then make his own?"

"He says he does. He's capable of doing it."

Khruuz rolled his eyes and spat, his tongue-tendril straight out from his mouth. At that moment, he looked serpentine. Kickaha told himself to quit comparing Khruuz to insects and reptiles. The Khringdiz was as human as any member of Homo sapiens and much more human than many of them. At least, he seemed to be so. He could be lying and so hiding his true feelings.

Man, I've tangled with too many Lords! he thought. I'm completely paranoiac. On the other hand, being so has saved my life more than once.

Khruuz had promised to study the data re gates, which his bank contained. He had set his machines to scan that section, to abstract significant data, and to print it out. That took only two hours, but he had an enormous amount of data to read in the—to Kickaha— exotic alphabet of the Khringdiz.

"Most of this is what my people knew about gates," the scaly man said. "But I assume that the Thoan made some advances in their use since I went into the long sleep. I was trying to get information on these when I had to close my gates. Unfortunately, Zazel must have made his Caverned World after that. However, we may yet find out something about his gate setup. Not until Red Orc is dealt with, though."

"If we do that, we won't have to worry about getting into Zazel's World," Kickaha said.

"Yes, we will. Some other Lord might get the creation-destruction engine data. The data should be in safe hands or destroyed. Though it makes me shudder to think of doing that to scientific data, it is better than chancing that it might be stolen or taken by violence."

Kickaha thought for a moment, then said, "At one time, every Lord must have had the engine. Otherwise, how could they have made their own private universes? What made them all disappear? Why don't at least some of them now have the data for making the engines?"

"You're asking the wrong person," Khruuz said. "I was out of the stream of the living for thousands of years. There may be some Lords who have the engines or the designs for them, but they don't know it. As for your first question, I think that every Lord who successfully invaded another's universe destroyed his enemy's creation-destruction engine. The successful invader would not want others who might invade during the owner's absence to find one. And then another Lord would slay the previous invader. In time, very few engines would be left. But I really don't know."

Several weeks after this conversation, Khruuz summoned Kickaha and Clifton to a room they had never seen before. This was huge and had a domed ceiling. The ceiling and walls were black but strewn with tiny sparkling points and lines connecting them. They formed a very intricate web.

Khruuz waved a hand and said, "You see here the results of my data-collecting. The points are gate nodes, and the lines connecting them show the avenues traveled between and among gates. Those lines are drawn there just for the sake of the viewer. They separate the gates so that the viewer may more easily distinguish among them. Actually, the transit time between one gate and the next is zero."

Kickaha said, "I saw a gate map once when I was with Jadawin in his palace. But it was nowhere nearly as complicated as this. Isn't it something!"

Khruuz's dark eyes regarded Kickaha. "Yes, it is something, as you say. But what is displayed is a map of all nodes known to me. Mostly, they're Khringdiz gates, and the majority were opened into Thoan universes when my people were still battling the enemy. Thus, many of them connect with various Thoan gates, though the connection was done by accident."

Khruuz admitted that he did not know where many of the nodes and routes were. If someone took these from Khruuz's world, that person would have to go in ignorance to where the routes took him. And there were many nodes that intersected with closed-circuit routes.

"Is there a chance that a Khringdiz route might end at a gate leading into the Caverned World?" Kickaha said. "From what I've heard, there's only one gate, or there was one gate, giving entrance to Zazel's World. But what if there's an ancient gate to it made by the Khringdiz?"

"There is a chance. But I don't know what gate, if any, would take you there. It might take you a hundred years to travel every gate and route, and you still would not find the right one. Moreover, your chances of survival during this search would be very small."

"But Red Orc must think that there is one. Otherwise, why would he have sent me out to find it?"

Eric Clifton said, "You should know by now that he seldom tells you the true reason for what he does."

"I guess so. But he didn't have to lie about that."

During their time with Khruuz, Kickaha insisted that Clifton finish his often-interrupted narrative of how he had gotten into the Thoan universes.

"Where was I? Oh, yes! First, a recapitulation of the events leading up to the point at which the flash flood stopped my telling of the tale."

Kickaha sighed and sat back. There was no hurry just now, but he wished Clifton were not so long-winded.

"The madman Blake described to his friend the vision he had had of the flea's ghost, which you and I now know was of the Khringdiz. I was so fascinated by this that I drew a sketch of the scaly man as described by Mr. Blake. I showed it to my closest friend, a boy named Pew. He worked for a jeweler, a Mr. Scarborough. He showed my sketch to his employer, and Mr. Scarborough showed the drawing to a wealthy Scots nobleman, a Lord Riven, who then ordered that a ring be made based on the sketch. But poor stupid Pew stole the ring. Knowing that there would be a hue and cry and that he would be the most suspected, he gave the ring to me to hold for him. That shows you how brainless he was. At that time, I had not repented of my sins and sworn to God that I would no more lead a dishonest life."

Kickaha, his patience gone despite the abundance of time he had, said, "Get on with it."

"Very well. The constables searched for Pew, who had taken refuge with the gang of homeless street boys he had joined before working for Mr. Scarborough. But the constables found him, and he was killed while fleeing from them. A shot in the back of the head, I believe, sent the poor devil's soul downward to Hell.

"That meant, as far as I was concerned, that I owned the ring. But I knew that much time would have to pass before I could chance selling it. And it would be better if I went to a far-off city before I attempted that transaction. But I could not quit my employer, Mr. Dally, the bookseller and printer, immediately. I would be suspected, and the constables might discover my association with George Pew. If I was convicted, I would hang."

Baron Riven was determined to find the ring and the person who had stolen it. One of his agents questioned Clifton about the theft. The agent had unearthed the fact that Clifton was one of

Pew's closest friends, perhaps his only friend. Clifton was terrified, but he denied everything except knowing Pew. That was a lie Clifton knew would be eventually exposed. One night, shortly after the interview, he fled, his destination the city of Bristol. He planned to board any ship that would carry him out of England. He had no money, so he would have to find work aboard as a cabin boy. Or any job he could get.

"I snatched a purse and with the money got lodgings in a cheap dockside tavern," he said. "I also applied at a dozen ships for work to pay for my passage. Finally, I got one as a cook's helper aboard a merchantman."

The night before he was to ship out, while he was walking the streets near the waterfront, he felt a hand on his shoulder and then a pinprick in his neck. He tried to run away, but his legs failed him, and he fell unconscious onto the cobblestones. When he awoke, he was in a room with Lord Riven and two men. He was naked and was strapped to a bed. The baron himself injected a fluid into one of Clifton's arteries. Contrary to Clifton's expectation, he stayed conscious. When Lord Riven questioned him about the ring, Clifton, despite his mental struggles, told him the truth.

"A truth drug," Kickaha said.

"Yes, I know. My sack, containing my few worldly possessions, had been examined. The baron now wore the ring. I expected to be turned over to the constables and, eventually, hanged. But it turned out that the baron did not want the authorities to know about me or the ring. He ordered his men, very rough and brutal-looking scoundrels, to cut my throat. He tossed them some guineas and started to walk to the door with a splendidly decorated and large leather bag in his hand. But he stopped after a few steps, turned, and said, "I have a more severe punishment in mind for him. You two leave now!"

They did so quickly. Then he took out from his bag two large semicircular flat pieces of some silvery metal.

"Portable gates!" Kickaha said.

"Ah, then you know what I am talking about?"

"They're the means I used to get into the universe of the World of Tiers," Kickaha said.

"Ah! But I did not have the slightest idea then what their purpose or origin was. I thought that they were tools of torture. In a way, they were just that. He placed their ends close together on the floor so that they formed a slightly broken circle. Then he untied me. I was too terrified to resist, and I wet my pants again though I believe that I had emptied my bladder when I awoke tied to the bed."

Lord Riven untied the Englishman, leaving his hands bound behind his back but his feet free. Then he picked up Clifton by the back of his neck with one hand. He carried him as if he were a small rabbit and stood him inside the two crescents. He told Clifton not to move unless he wanted to be cut in half.

"My teeth were chattering, and I was shaking violently. Though he had warned me not to speak, I asked him what he intended doing to me. He replied only that he was sending me directly to Hell instead of killing me first."

Clifton believed that he was in the power of a devil, perhaps Satan himself. He begged for mercy, though he expected none. But Lord Riven bent down swiftly, shoved the ends of the semicircles together with his fingertips, stood up, and moved back several feet. For several seconds, nothing happened.

"Then the room and the baron disappeared. Actually, I was the one to disappear, as you well know. The next second, I was aware that I was in another world. It did not look like Hell. There were no capering devils or flames issuing from the rocks. But I was indeed in Inferno. It was a dying planet in one of the worlds of the Lords."

He paused, then said, "Remembering that calls up the absolute panic and horror possessing me then. But I managed to get my hands unbound, and I managed to live, though I experienced the torments of the damned."

"What year was it that you gated through?" Kickaha said.

"The year of Our Lord 1817."

"Then you've been about one hundred and seventy-five years in the Thoan worlds."

"Good God! That long! I've been so busy most of the time."

The Englishman sketched his life since then. He had been many places, had passed safely through many gates, had been a slave many times to both Thoan and humans, had been a chief of a small tribe, and had finally settled down into a comparatively happy life.

"But then I got an itch for adventure. I took a gate that led me eventually through many worlds until I fell into the trap, the pit, set up by Red Orc. I did not know whose it was until I saw the man who appeared in Khruuz's cell and was blown to bits."

He paused briefly, "That man looked exactly like Lord Riven."

"I had guessed that," Kickaha said. "The baron was Red Orc, living at that time on Earth I and disguised as a Scotch nobleman."

13

*T*hough Kickaha kept busy so that he would not think about Anana, he could not keep her out of his mind. With the images of her came anguish and fury. By now, the Thoan should have finished his memory-erasing on Anana, and she would think that she was only eighteen years old.

Red Orc would explain to her that she had had amnesia and was now in his care. Or that she had been given as his ward to him by her father and then had suffered a memory loss. He would make sure that she did not learn how many millennia had passed since that supposed event.

Even now, he might be attempting to seduce her. Or he might be forcing her to his bed. Kickaha tried shutting out the visions of her making love to Red Orc. But it was not as easy as pulling down a window blind.

Two months passed. On the third day of the third week of the third month (a good omen, if you believed in omens) Khruuz told Kickaha and Clifton to come to the gates-display room. The vast chamber was unlit except for the light-points on the ceiling dome and the walls. They were much brighter than during the first visit. A single light illuminated Khruuz and the control panel before which he sat. When they entered, he rose with an expression that the two knew by now was intended for a smile.

He rubbed his hands together just as humans did to express their joy or high satisfaction. "Good news!" he said. "Very promising!"

He stabbed a finger at the ceiling. Bending his neck, Kickaha saw a huge point that had not been there when he was in the chamber. Many lines ran from it to many smaller points. He also saw that one bright point had changed from white to orange. Several lines leading to it were also orange. One of them ended at the big point.

"The orange point leads to Zazel's World—if my calculations are correct."

"Are you sure?" Kickaha said.

Khruuz sat down before the huge indicator-control panel. "I just said that I was not sure. If the computer is correct, I'm sure. But I don't know if it is correct. The only way to know will be to gate someone to it."

"How did you do it?" Kickaha said.

"I set the computer to tracing all the lines you see in this room. Since you were here last, many new points and lines have been added."

"But you said that you had shut down all the gates leading to here because of Red Orc," Clifton said.

"True. I had. But I took the chance that Red Orc would not detect the new gates I opened. These were opened for some microseconds before closing down. In that time, the computer did its tracing. The results of millions of tracings in the microsecond intervals are now displayed."

Kickaha wondered what it was that made the Khringdiz believe that he had found the gate to the Caverned World. Before he could ask, Khruuz said, "Look at the point that is far larger than the others. Now, do you see the orange line leading from it to the smaller orange point? The large point is a cluster of points so close together they look to your eye as if they were one point."

He looked up and smiled again. "The big point represents something I do not believe that the Thoan know about."

"Is that the all-nodes gate you asked me about two months ago?" Kickaha said. "I wondered about that, but you didn't say anything more when I said I'd never heard of it."

"Your answer was enough, even though you are only an expert on gates by experience. But you are not a scientist. Also, if Red Orc knew of the revolving or all-nodes gate, he would have used it."

He said something into the panel, and the screen before him showed a different display. In its center was a big light, the cluster of points that made up the all-nodes gate. Now Kickaha could see a small separation among the points.

Khruuz said one word in his harsh language. The screen zoomed in toward the point until the image almost filled it. By it appeared a word in small Khringdiz letters.

"That indicates the gate in the all-nodes cluster that leads to two places, what you call cracks, in the 'wall' of Zazel's World. Note that the faults are much dimmer than the active gates. One fault is a once-active gate; the other, a weakness that was in the wall when that universe was made. The once-active gate was the gate that was closed, I believe, by the creature that rules the Caverned World. That being—you said his name is Dingsteth—not only closed the gate, he moved the fault. That implies great knowledge and a vast power source. Even my machines are not capable of doing that. But my machines can detect that the fault has been moved. Look closely. I'll turn the power up so that it may be better seen."

He spoke another word. A very faint line appeared. One end was at the dim point, and the other end was at an even dimmer point.

"Traces of the operation," the scaly man said. "There are thousands of light-points on the chart. But this is the only one showing the path of a gate or fault that has been moved. Of course, what Dingsteth did was to shut down the shearing trap in the one-way gate that Red Orc had used to get into his world. Then he made it into a two-way gate just long enough to disintegrate the hexagonal structure. He would not have to leave his own world to do that since the beamer rays he used on the inner side of the metal hexagon would disintegrate it in his world and in the other.

"After doing this, he remade the gate into a one-way entrance. Having done that, he moved the fault to another location, a feat beyond the power of present-day Thoan technology. That's why Red Orc could not find it on the Unwanted World. What you saw through Manathu Vorcyon's device was, as you realized later, a false light."

"That's wonderful!" Kickaha said. "But what about the one-way gate through which Dingsteth let Red Orc out of the Caverned World?"

Khruuz held his opened hands palms up in another human gesture. "It's been closed down, made into a no-way fault. I doubt that Red Orc has detectors sensitive enough to locate the fault. The lack of these also accounts for his failure to detect the entrance gate and the path it made when it was relocated. Even though the gate had been a two-way momentarily, the creature had means to cancel the trace of the two-way gate's existence. But you'll have to reopen the exit gate after you get in there."

"I'll handle it!" Kickaha said. "Let's get going!"

"Not so fast. Here's the machine that will open, or should open, the entrance point Dingsteth closed."

Khruuz said something, and a drawer slid out from the wall below the control panel. From it, he took a black metallic cube, four inches across. An orange button was on its top; the bottom part was curved; a strap dangled from one side of it.

"The key to the gate to the Caverned World," Khruuz said. "Your Horn of Shambarimen is the only other key."

He held up the black box. "I inherited this from a friend, a great scientist, who was killed a few days after he gave it to me. As far as I know, it's the only one in all the universes."

"Strap this gate-opener onto your wrist. Without it, you might as well stay here."

The preparations for the trip took two days. Eric Clifton argued that he should go with Kickaha. Khruuz said that the chances were high that Kickaha would fail in his mission. If Clifton went with Kickaha, he might die, too. Khruuz needed Clifton's knowledge of the universes of the Lords if he was to be effective in the battle against them.

"Besides," Khruuz confessed to Kickaha when Clifton was not present, "I would get very lonely, even if he is not a Khringdiz."

Thus, though impatient, Kickaha had to wait until Khruuz told him when the correct time for entering the all-nodes gate arrived.

"The node does not really revolve," the Khringdiz said. "But I use 'revolve' as a convenient term. Launching you requires exact timing. You have an interval of twenty seconds to get into the node and to take the gate that should lead you to the fault in Zazel's World. If you are delayed by ten microseconds, you'll enter another gate taking you to somewhere else."

The Khringdiz had built a nine-angled metal structure to mark the place for Kickaha to enter. An hour before the time to go, Kickaha put on an oxygen mask, an oxygen bottle, a pair of dark goggles, weapons, a backpack filled with supplies, and, strapped to his left wrist, a watch containing the device for opening the fault. Kickaha called it "the can opener." On top of it was an orange button.

Eric Clifton was there to see his fellow Earthman off. "God be with you," he said, and he shook Kickaha's hand. "This is a war against the Devil, so we are destined to win."

"God may win against Satan," Kickaha said. "But how about the casualties along the way?"

"We will not be among them."

A display in Khringdiz numbers on the wall indicated the time. Kickaha had learned what these meant. When he had two minutes to go, he checked a Khringdiz watch on his right wrist. It was synchronized with the wall instrument. He stood before the nonagonal structure, and, when he had thirty seconds to go, made ready to enter the gate. Though Khruuz had told him that he would meet no else, Kickaha had unstrapped the beamer in his holster.

Khruuz said, "Get ready to go. I'll give the word twenty seconds from now."

It seemed that he had just quit talking when he shouted in Thoan, "Jump!"

Kickaha leaped. He passed through the nonagon and was momentarily bewildered. He seemed to be stretched far out. His legs and feet looked as if they were very elongated. His feet were at least twenty feet from his torso. His hands, at the ends of beanpole arms, were ten feet from his shoulders.

He felt, at the same time, a shock, as if he had fallen into a polar sea. His numbed senses began to fade. Khruuz had not told him that this would happen—but then, Khruuz did not know what would happen. It was up to him, Kickaha thought, to do what was required.

He was enveloped in a dim greenish light. His rapidly chilling feet felt as if they were on a floor, but he could not see it. Nor were there any walls around him. It was like being in an invisible fog.

Then a slightly brighter light glowed behind the dusk. He walked toward it, if "walking" was the right word. More like wading through molasses, he thought. He did not know how many seconds had passed since he had entered this place—if it was a place. But it was no use wasting time in looking at the wristwatch. Either he got there in time or he did not.

The greenish dusk brightened; the light on its other side—if there was any such thing as another side here—increased. That should be the node "revolving" there. The light should be the gate he wanted.

Then the light began to fade. He strove to step up his pace. By all the holies! He had thought that twenty seconds were more than enough time to get to the gate. But now it seemed an impossibly short time. And he was beginning to feel as if his stomach, lungs, and heart were as distorted as his limbs. He felt very sick.

If he vomited in the mask, he would be in a bad way indeed.

Then the light was around him. Very slowly, or so it seemed to him, he reached for the opening device given him by Khruuz. It, too, was distorted. His right hand missed it altogether. He felt close to panic, a cold panic sluggishly moving up from wherever panics came from. He did not have much time to press the button. At least, he thought he did not. But he was sure that if he did not activate the little machine very quickly, he would not be within his allotted time.

He reached across his chest and felt his left shoulder, though that, too, took time to find. How many seconds did he have left? Finally, his fingers touched his shirt. He slid them downward, at the same time seeing an arm bent in a zigzag course, as crooked as the cue stick W. C. Fields had used in a movie, the title of which Kickaha could not remember. Then his middle finger was on the button, which had a concavity on top of it that had not been there when he had leaped through the gate. But he pressed on it.

Now, he was in a tunnel illuminated with a first-flush-of-dawn light. He no longer felt sick; his legs and feet had snapped back to their normal size. The cold had given way to warmth. He breathed easily then. Maybe he had been holding his breath while he was in that awful space. His wristwatch told him that he had been in the half-space or no-space for eighteen seconds.

He turned off the oxygen and removed the mask and bottle. Immediately, he noticed that the air was not moving. It was hot and heavy and gave the impression of having died a long time ago. After putting the oxygen equipment down at his feet to mark the point of entrance, he looked around. The tunnel went through smooth crystalline stone and was wide enough for twenty men to march abreast. In the middle of the floor was a shallow and curved ditch filled with running water. Some sort of thick lichen grew on the walls and ceiling in large patches. The dim light was shed by greenish knobs on the ceiling, walls, and floor. Hanging from the ceiling or lying on the floor were the dried-out bodies of six-angled insectile creatures. He had no idea of their function or of what had killed them.

The strangest feature of this tunnel, though, the one giving him the most pause, was the characters moving slowly in a single-file parade along each wall. They were black and four inches high and slightly above his eye level. When they came to a lichen patch, they disappeared but emerged from beneath the patches on the bare spaces. They could be symbols or alphabet or ideogram characters. That some looked vaguely familiar, resembling some Greek, Cyrillic, Arabic, and Chinese writing, did not mean anything. They were coincidences.

The still air continued to oppress him. He decided to scratch a big X on the wall as a starting point. Then he placed the oxygen mask and bottle in his backpack.

Now, which way should he go?

Upstream was as good a direction as any. That was also the way in which the characters were going.

For five hours, he walked steadily through the tunnel in a silence that filled his ears with a humming. The only living thing was the luciferous lichen. But it could be that the knobs were also live plants. Every half-hour, he stopped to scratch an X upon the wall. The air continued to be hot and thick, and he often was tempted to use the bottle. But he might need it for an emergency.

By now, he was convinced that he was in Zazel's World.

Though the Thoan legends were sketchy in their descriptions of it, they certainly sounded like the tunnel he was in. Jubilation at having done what Red Orc had found impossible to accomplish spurred him on. He'd show the bastard.

Near the beginning of the sixth hour of his walk, he came to a fork. A tunnel opening was on his left, and one was on his right. Without hesitation, he took the left one. He regarded the left as lucky—to hell with the superstitions concerning sinistrality—and he was betting that the chosen avenue would lead him to the heart of this planetary cavern. He found evidence for this when he came across the first of many animal skeletons. They strewed his path as he stepped past or over them. Some seemed to have died while locked in combat, so intertangled were their bones. Alarmed, he started to jog. Something bad had happened.

A few minutes later, he stepped over bones and through the tunnel exit into a gigantic cave. It was lit by the knobs, which were much more closely placed than those in the tunnels. But their illumination did not enable him to see very far into the cave.

He walked down a slope and onto the flat stone floor. Here, as in the tunnel, lay the bones of many different kinds of animals and birds. The plants once growing here had been eaten down to the soil on the stone floor. However, enough fronds and fragments were left for him to identify them as of vegetable origin. He supposed that the animals had devoured the dead or dying plants. But they had killed each other off before all the plant remnants could be eaten.

On the wall nearest him, the symbols moved in their arcane parade as far as he could see.

According to what he had heard, the entire world was a colossal computer. But Zazel had made fauna and flora to decorate his large caves and to amuse him. They and the computer had failed to preserve his desire to live, and he had committed suicide.

Where was the operator of this place, the sole sentient, the lonely king, the artificial being whom Zazel had left to watch over this dismal universe?

Kickaha called out several times to alert Dingsteth if he should be within hearing range. His voice echoed, and no one answered him. He shrugged and set out for the other end of the cavern. When he looked back, he could not see the entrance. The shadows had taken it. After another hour, he came to the end of the vast hollow and was confronted by six tunnel openings. He took the one on the extreme left. After thirty-five minutes, he came to another. The same spectacle as in the previous place was before him. The bones and shreds of plants lay together in the silence.

But the train of symbols still moved along the walls and disappeared into the darkness ahead. The computer was still alive. Rather, it was still working.

Nowhere had he seen any controls or displays. To operate the computer, he figured, you had to speak to it. He did not have the slightest knowledge of how to ask it questions, and the strange symbols were unreadable. Probably, Zazel had made his own language to operate the machine. That meant that Kickaha's mission was a failure. Worse, he was stuck in this godawful place with only enough food to last him twelve days. If, that is, he ate very lightly.

He thought, if I can find Dingsteth or he finds me, it'll be fine. That is, it'll be okay if he cooperates.

Dingsteth, however, was beyond helping anybody, including himself. Kickaha found what was left of him in a chair carved out of stone and on the floor in front of the chair. The bones had to be his. They were of a bipedal manlike being, but too different in many respects to be a genuine specimen of Homo sapiens. Among the bones were tiny plastic organs and wires attached to them. The skull, which had fallen into the lap, was definitely not a man's.

I'm very lucky to have found this place so soon after I got here, Kickaha thought. After all, when I came to this world I was gambling that I'd find Dingsteth. I could have wandered through this maze, which probably goes for thousands of miles throughout this world of stone. But here I am in the place I was looking for. And in a relatively short time, too.

On the other hand, his luck hadn't been so good. The only one who could tell him where the engine data was was no longer talking and never would.

Kickaha could find nothing to reveal how Dingsteth had died. The skull and skeleton bore no obvious marks of violence. Maybe he had become bored with his futile and purposeless life and had taken poison. Or it could be that Zazel had constructed Dingsteth so that he died after a certain span of time. Whatever had killed him, he had left behind a world that was running down.

Kickaha said loudly, "I just don't know!" And then he howled with frustration and rage and seized the skull and hurled it far across the floor. That did not help his predicament any, but it did make him feel a little less angry. His voice and his cry were hurled back at him from the faraway walls. It was as if this world were determined to have the last word.

He was galled by the thought that Dingsteth's death did not mean that the creation-destruction data would never be available to anyone. If Red Orc got here, he might be able to operate the computer. He was a scientist, and he was intelligent enough to figure a way to communicate with the computer. Kickaha certainly could not hang around here until the Thoan arrived, if he ever did.

He smacked his fist, not too hard, against the back of the stone chair. He shouted, "I'm not beaten yet!"

14

*T*he symbols on the wall could be going in a circuit and ending up where they had started. But they might be heading toward a control room. He decided to go deeper into the cavern-tunnel complex. A little more than a mile was behind him when he stopped. The light-shedding knobs and lichen here were turning brown. At least half of the knobs had fallen from the ceiling to the floor, and the rest looked as if they would not be able to cling to the ceiling much longer. If this rot spread, all the tunnels and caves would be totally dark, and the plants' oxygen production would cease.

Unable to give up any project easily, he walked onward, marking the wall with an X every hundred feet. The rot had now become almost complete. There was plenty of fresh water, though. No, there was not. Ten minutes later, the stream had quit running. Within five minutes, the groove in the middle of the floor was filmed with water. Even that would soon be gone in the increasing heat.

By now, so many knobs were dead that he could see only five feet in front of him. He stopped again. What was the use of pushing on? This world would soon be dead. Though the characters were still moving along on the wall, that meant only that the great computer had not completely died. It would probably keep working as long as its energy supply did not run out. That might be for an unguessable number of millennia.

He turned around and began walking toward the huge cave. To make sure that he was following the right path, he had to stay close to the wall marked with X's. After a few minutes, he was forced to take his flashlight from his backpack. He attached this to his head with a band and walked faster. Then the air became so heavy and oxygenless and his breath so short that he brought the bottle out of the backpack and carried it by a strap over his right shoulder. After putting the mask over his face, he turned on the air. Now and then, though, he would turn it off and slide the mask to one side. He was able to get along without the oxygen for a few minutes before he had to replace the mask and breathe "fresh" air.

At least, no one would have to worry that Red Orc would possess the engine. That made him feel better. He could now dedicate himself completely to killing the Thoan and rescuing Anana.

Following the X's, he finally came to the huge cave. They ceased then because he had seen no reason to mark the wall here. He would continue to its other side and find the X marked by the mouth of the tunnel from which he had entered the cave. Instead of going along the wall, he walked through the center toward the middle tunnel. The headbeam fell on the dead pieces of plants and the bones of the animals, some of which were very curious. Then, he stopped.

There was the stone chair. But where was the skeleton of Dingsteth?

He went close to the empty chair and turned around and around to flash his light throughout the cavern. It did not reach to the ceiling or the walls. He walked in the direction in which he had hurled the skull. Though he inspected a wide area where it could have fallen, he could not find it.

He removed the oxygen mask.

"Dingsteth! Dingsteth!" he called again and again. The name roared back at him from the distant walls. When the echoes had ceased, he put the mask back on and listened. All he heard was his blood thrumming in his ears. By now, though, the hidden watcher must know that the intruder was aware that he was not the only living creature in the Caverned World.

Kickaha waited for five minutes before shouting out the name twelve times. Echoes and then silence came once more.

He called out, "I know you're here, Dingsteth! Come out, wherever you are!"

Presently, he went to the chair and sat down. He might as well be comfortable, if a stone chair could be that. He waited the ten minutes he had allotted himself. After that, he had to get going. Someday, though, he would come back with much larger supplies and resume the search. Khruuz would probably be with him and would determine if he could do anything to get this world's electrical juices to flowing again.

Two minutes had passed. He was thinking that that was enough time to wait, since he was not absolutely sure that he had enough air. Then he straightened up. His eyes tried to pierce the darkness beyond the beam. He thought that he had heard a very faint chuckle. He stood up and turned around slowly. Before he had completed a three-quarters circle, he was struck hard on the right side of his head. The object hurt him but did not daze him. He jumped forward and reached up and turned off the headlight. Then he ran forward about ten steps more and flopped onto the hard floor.

His beamer in his hand, he listened. He knew what had hit him. As he had dashed away from the chair, he had seen, out of the corner of his eye, the skull of Dingsteth rolling out into the blackness.

He listened as if his life depended upon his ears—which, indeed, it did. After a few seconds, another chuckle, louder this time, came from behind him. He rolled away for a few turns, then crouched. Whoever had thrown the skull probably had means for seeing without photonic light. So did he. After removing the backpack and groping around in it, he brought out a pair of goggles and put them on. He moved a small dial on the flashlight and looked through the goggles in the ghostly light.

No one was visible. The only hiding place would be behind the stone chair. But the attacker would know that Kickaha knew that. Where else could he—or she—hide? The water channels in the cave were deep enough for a stretched-out man to conceal himself. The nearest was thirty feet away.

Hold it a minute! Kickaha thought. He who jumps to conclusions is often concluded. The attacker may be figuring out what I'm thinking. So he really is behind the chair. He pots me while I'm on my way to check out the water channels. But then, he could have done it easily any time. Why did he throw the skull at me and thus give me warning?

Whoever's doing this is a Thoan. Only one of them would play with me as a cat would play with a mouse. However, I'm no mouse, and the Thoan must know that. The higher the danger, the more the fun in the game. That's what he's thinking. So, let's give him a lot of fun and then have the last laugh. ·

It's highly probable, of course, that more than one is lurking out there. If the game starts to go against the skull-thrower, his buddy shoots me.

He could do nothing about that for the present. He would keep watching for other players, however.

He rose, whirled three times, holding the backpack out like a throwing hammer, and hurled it at the chair. The pack fell by the side of the stone carving. No one poked his head from behind it or looked around its side. Then he switched the night-vision light to photonic, hoping to startle his enemy into betraying himself. A glance showed that no one had fallen for the trick. He switched back to night vision.

He approached two channels cautiously, looking back quite often. These were empty for as far as he could see in the light beam. But his attacker or attackers could be in the darkness. He felt the dial on the side of the beamer barrel near the butt. Without looking down at it, he advanced it to what he guessed would be a two-hundred-yard range. Suddenly, he started spinning, the trigger pulled all the way back. The beam from its end, a black pencil as seen through his goggles, described a circle as it pierced into the darkness. If anyone was hit, he did not yell.

Just as he completed his spin, he ran toward the chair. At the same time, he released his pressure on the trigger. Too much battery energy had already been expended. Anyone behind the chair would hear his pounding footsteps and would know he would have to do something quickly.

A goggled head followed by very broad shoulders rose from behind the carving. Even before his chest reached the top of the chair, his beamer was spitting its ray. Firing, Kickaha threw himself down. The stone floor smoked an inch from his left shoulder. But his ray had gone through the Thoan's neck and beyond. No doubt of that.

He rose and made a wide curve while walking toward the chair. Though he could hear his own soft steps, he doubted that the fallen man could. He also doubted that the man could hear cymbals clashing next to his ear.

While approaching the chair, he glanced behind and to both sides of him. If there was another enemy out there, he should have fired by now. However, he could be lying wounded in the dark, though not so hurt that he was out of the action permanently.

After making sure that his beam had gone through the man's neck, Kickaha took off the corpse's goggles. As he had thought it would be, the face was Red Orc's. But the real Red Orc could have sent a clone in his place. Kickaha would never know unless he ran across another one and that one confessed that he was the original Red Orc.

Unlikely event, Kickaha thought. This one, though, did not have the Horn. Would Red Orc let it out of his sight? No, he would not. So, it seemed probable that the dead man was a clone. But he could not have gotten into this world without the Horn. Thus, Red Orc had blown the Horn and then sent this clone through. Or was he along with him and now somewhere in the darkness?

Few things were ever certain.

He picked up the man's beamer and held it so that the headlight showed him its every detail. Its dial was set on stun range within a hundred feet. That meant that he had intended to knock his enemy out, not kill him. Whoever he was, he had been having fun by playing around with his enemy. When the Thoan tired of that, he would have stunned the Earthman and taken him back to Red Orc's headquarters as a prisoner.

Quickly, though frequently looking around, Kickaha took the man's oxygen bottle, beamer, battery pack, headlight, food rations, and canteen. Waste not, and you might not get wasted. As he left the cave burdened with two backpacks and went into the tunnel, he wondered if Red Orc could be in this tunnel and waiting for him, hoping to ambush him.

Kickaha switched to the night-vision light and, goggled, walked more swiftly. The long journey was uninterrupted. No other person suddenly appeared ahead of him. Nor did his frequent glances backward show him any follower.

Sweating, his nerves still winched up tight, he got to the last X, the mark showing where he had come through the gate. He stood before the wall and uttered the code word Khruuz had given him. He was not looking forward to going through the cold and twisted and terrifying ordeal of the core-gate again. To his surprise, he was spared that. He stepped through the wall and was immediately in a forest.

He looked around and groaned. The trees were like those he had seen when he had gated to the world of Manathu Vorcyon. Before he could adjust to the unexpected, he was surrounded by big brown men with long straight glossy-black hair, snub noses, and black eyes with epicanthic folds. Their long spears were pointed at him.

"Hey, I'm the Great Mother's friend!" he said. "Don't you know me?"

Though they obviously did know him, they said nothing. They marched him through the forest. An hour later, they entered a clearing in the center of which was the gigantic tree in which Our Lady lived. Forthwith, he was conducted into the arboreal palace and up the winding stairway to the dimly lit sixth floor. They left him standing before a big door.

"You may come in now," Manathu Vorcyon said from behind the door. He pushed the polished ebony door open. Light rushed out upon him. He squinted, then saw a large round table in the center of a luxuriously furnished room. The giantess was on a large well-padded chair facing him. On one side of her was seated Eric Clifton; on the other, Khruuz, the scaly man.

He said, "I've had a lot of surprises, but this one jolts me the most. How in hell did you two get here?"

She waved a hand. "Sit down. Eat. Drink. And tell us of your adventures in the Caverned World. Under other circumstances, I would allow you time to bathe and to rest before dining. But we are very eager to know what you discovered."

Kickaha sat down. The chair felt good, and he was suddenly tired. A sip of yellow wine from a wooden goblet gave him a glow and pushed away his fatigue. While he ate, he talked.

When he was done, he said, "That's it. Red Orc can now get into that world. A lot of good it'll do him. As for his finding the way in, I don't know how he did it."

"Obviously," Khruuz said, "he put some kind of tracer on your passage from my place to Zazel's World. That is not good news. He has means of tracking he did not have before. That is, to my knowledge."

"He can track intergate passage to my world, too," Manathu Vorcyon said. "Especially since he has the Horn."

"But I doubt that he has the device I used on the Unwanted World," Kickaha said. "Okay, I've told you my story. How did you three get together?"

"It was Khruuz's idea," the Great Mother said. "He sent Eric Clifton as his envoy to me to propose that we band together against Red Orc."

"And I set up the gating from Zazel's World so that you would come directly here," Khruuz said.

"Your world is unguarded now?" Kickaha said. "Red Orc'll . . ."

"Try to get into it," Manathu Vorcyon said. "But he does not know that it's unguarded. Anyway, Khruuz has set up traps."

Though Khruuz's face was so nonhuman, it showed a quite human annoyance. He said, "I believe that Kickaha was addressing me and expected me to reply."

The giantess's eyes opened. She said, "If I offended you, I regret doing so, though I did not intend offense."

Kickaha smiled. Already there was friction, however slight, between the two allies. Manathu Vorcyon was used to doing exactly what she wanted to do. That included interrupting people when they were talking. Apparently, Khruuz was not used to being regarded as an inferior. To Manathu Vorcyon, everybody else was inferior. Was she not Our Lady, the Great Mother, the Grandmother of All? Did not everybody in her world and the others regard her with awe? Even Red Orc had not contemplated attacking her until recently. And that was only because she had entered the battle early.

"If I am not speaking out of turn," Kickaha said, carefully keeping sarcasm out of his voice, "I suggest that our best defense is attack against Red Orc. We shouldn't wait until he storms into this world or any other. We should go after him with everything we have."

"Good thinking, although it's superfluous," she said. "We have already decided that is the best policy. We also agree that you should be our spearhead."

"I'm used to being cannon fodder," he said. "It started during World War II—that was on Earth when I was a youth—and it's never let up since. But I won't be used as a mere pawn. I insist on full membership in this council of war. I've earned it."

"There was never a thought that you would not be an equal in the council," she said smoothly. "However, it has been well known for millennia that a military committee is useful only for advice. An army must have a single leader, a general who makes quick decisions, whose orders are to be obeyed even though the soldier questions that they are the right thing to do.

"You, Clifton, have no military experience. You, Kickaha, are essentially a loner, a man of action, one excellent, perhaps unexcelled, in situations involving very few persons. You are no master strategist or, at least, have had no experience in planning strategy. You, Khruuz, are an unknown element, though your ability to survive when all your people died is testimony to your wiliness. You also must be an invaluable repository of scientific and technological knowledge. But you really do not know humans or their past and present situations. Nor have you had any experience as a military leader."

She paused, breathed deeply, then said, "The choice of your leader is obvious. I have all that you lack and also those abilities you do have."

The others were silent for a minute. Then Kickaha said, "I don't give a damn about being the general. That's not my style. But I insist I not be treated like a sacrificial piece on a chessboard. When I'm in the field, I make my own decisions, right or wrong, even if it goes against orders. The foot soldier is the only guy who knows what's needed in his immediate area."

He took in a deep breath, then looked straight at Manathu Vorcyon.

"Something is sticking in my craw, choking me. It's a bone I have to pick with you."

"I expected this," she said. "If you had kept silent about it, I would not have respected you."

"Then I'll say out loud for Clifton's and Khruuz's benefit what's bugging me. You sent me to the Unwanted World to locate the gate to Zazel's World. You gave me a gate detector. But you didn't tell me the detector was a fake or that it was a booby trap. You knew that it would explode after a certain time. And . . ."

"No. It would explode only when Red Orc or his clones came within a certain distance of it. And after a certain time interval. I did not know the pattern of his electrical skin fields or what his body mass was. But, using your descriptions of his physical features, I estimated his probable mass. I doubt that that was off more than a pound or two."

"You didn't care if I was killed, too!" Kickaha blurted.

"No. I cared very much. That is why the bomb was set so that it would not go off until the one who took it from you was out of range of you. Out of killing range, anyway."

"But you didn't know if the person who took it away from me was Red Orc or not!"

"Whoever did take it was likely to be your enemy."

"Well," Kickaha said slowly and less vehemently, "I suppose you want an apology from me for suspecting you didn't care if I was killed as long as Red Orc bought the farm."

"What does . . . ?"

"In English, it means dying in combat."

"Ah! But, no, I don't wish for an apology. No reason to give me one. You didn't know all the facts . . ."

"Damned few facts," Kickaha muttered. "In fact, none."

"I had to expose you to a certain amount of danger. You are used to that. As it turned out, you were only stunned."

She looked at the others. "You agree that I am the general in this war?"

Khruuz shrugged. "You have presented your case logically. I cannot argue with you."

"Thanks for even allowing me my say," Clifton said. "Who am I to question you three mighty ones?"

"Kickaha?"

"Agreed."

"Very well. Here is what I have in mind as our next move."

15

Kickaha was on one of Red Orc's properties, Earth II.

Just exactly where he was there, he did not know. He had gated through, courtesy of the Great Mother, to an area on Earth II corresponding to the California region on Earth I.

"Red Orc has forbidden any Lord to enter either Earth," Manathu Vorcyon had told him. "But, as you know, other Lords, including Jadawin and Anana, made gates to both these worlds and entered them.

"Long ago, I made several gates there for possible future entrances, though I have not used any so far. You will take the gate on Earth II closest to where you think Red Orc has a palace. It's possible that he has discovered this gate and trapped it."

"How well I know that."

Before stepping through the glindglassa, he had been embraced by her. For a few seconds, his head was buried in the valley between her breasts. Ah, delicious sensation!

After releasing him, she held him at arm's length, which was a considerable distance. "You are the only man who has ever rejected me."

"Anana."

She nodded and said, "I know. But you'll get me in the end."

"It's not your end I'm thinking about."

She laughed. "You're also the only man whom I could forgive. But you have forgiven me for placing you in such danger without telling you. On your way, and may the luck of Shambarimen be with you."

The legendary Hornmaker's luck had run out eventually, but Kickaha said nothing about that. He stepped through the seeming mirror into a warm desert of rocks and few plants. Behind him was the boulder holding the gate. He looked around and saw only some buzzards, weeds, more boulders, and some angular rock formations, strata that had been tilted upwards. When and where had he seen them?

The sky was cloudless. The sun was at a height that made him believe that the time was around ten in the morning. The air seemed to be a few degrees above 75° Fahrenheit.

The Great Mother had not been able to tell him how close the gate was to the area corresponding to the Los Angeles region of Earth I. Nor did she know in what direction it was from that place.

As usual, on my own, he thought. But that was a milieu he loved.

He had been facing west when he came out of the boulder. South was on his left hand. He always favored the left, his lucky side. If he found out that he was going in the wrong direction, he would just turn around and head the right way. He walked down the rough and exotic rocks, slipping a few times though not falling, until he got to more or less level ground. During this, he passed close to a diamondback snake, whose warning rattle made him feel comfortable. He was, in a sense, home. However, the last time he had really been on his native planet and in Los Angeles, he had not liked it. Too many people, too much traffic, noise, sleaze, and foul air.

A little later, he came across a huge tarantula. Its tiny vicious eyes reminded him of some of the black-hearted villains he had encountered in many worlds. That, too, warmed him. Meeting them had sharpened his survival skills; he owed them a debt of gratitude. Too bad they were all dead. He could not now thank them.

He wore a wide-brimmed straw hat for shade, a dark maroon shirt open at the neck, a leather belt, baggy black pants, black socks, and sturdy hiker's shoes. A holster holding a beamer was at his side, and a canteen full of water hung from his belt on his right. His backpack was stuffed full with items he considered necessary for this expedition.

Shortly after he began walking on the road, he stopped. Of course! Now he knew where he was. Those stone formations and boulders! How many times he had seen them in Western movies! They were the Vasquez rocks, an area used many times in shooting those films. Thus, his destination was south, though he did not know how far away. He set out confidently in the direction of the 30th parallel.

Ahead of him was what Earth I called the Los Angeles area. The geography was the same as on Earth I, but its architecture and inhabitants were different.

After a while he came to a well-traveled and wheel-rutted path. Five miles or so had spun out from his feet when he heard something behind him. He turned around and saw a cloud of dust a half-mile north. It was boiling up from a body of men on horseback. Their helmets flashed in the sun. Two men at the front of the cavalcade held aloft flapping banners on long poles. And now the reflection from lanceheads struck his eyes as if it were from sunbeam javelins. It twanged nerves that evoked images of the many raids he had made when with the Bear People tribe on the Amerind level of the World of Tiers. And when he had been in jousts on the Dracheland level of that same world. The flashing lights were transformed into the blood-thumping calls of war horns.

However, the last thing he wanted was to be arrested by soldiers. His clothing would make them curious. If they paused to question him, he would not be able to answer them in any tongue they knew. In this world, a suspicious alien equaled the calaboose.

The country on his left was flat, but a wash was forty feet away. The hills on his right were a hundred and fifty feet from him. He ran toward the dry streambed, hoping that the cavalry would not see him. But if he could see them, they could see him. Too bad. Nothing to do about it except run.

He jumped into the wash, turned around at once, and looked over the edge of the bank. His head was partly hidden by a clump of sagebrush. Presently, the standard-bearers rode by. Each of their crimson flags bore the figure of a huge brown bear with relatively longer legs than a grizzly's. The face was also relatively shorter than a grizzly's.

Maybe the giant short-faced bear that died out on Earth I has survived here, he thought.

The officers behind the standard-bearers were clean-shaven and wore round helmets with noseguards and curved neck-protectors, topped by black plumes—something like the armor of ancient Greek warriors. They also wore plum-colored capes and crimson tunics with gold braiding on the fronts. Their legs were bare, and their feet were shod in leather sandals. Scabbards with short swords were on their broad crimson-chased belts. Their body armor, casques something like those of the Spanish conquistadores, was in a basket behind each rider. It was too hot to don these unless a battle was coming up.

Actually, the sun was too strong for wearing helmets. But he supposed that their military regulations required them on even when the heat forbade them.

The dogfaces carried spears in their hands and long swords in their scabbards. They were as clean-shaven and as dark-skinned as the officers. But whereas the officers had short hair, the rank-and-file had long, dark, wavy, and unbound hair. They did not look Mediterranean. Their faces were broad and high-cheekboned, the eyelids had slight epicanthic folds, and their noses were, generally, long. A dash, perhaps only a savor, of Amerind ancestors, he thought.

About two score of archers followed these out of the dust cloud.

Behind these came a number of men and women on horseback or driving wagons loaded with bundles of supplies. They wore soiled, yellow, high-crowned, floppy, wide hats. Their varicolored tunics were dust-smudged, and they carried no weapons. They were undoubtedly American Indians and were civilian servants or slaves. Behind this section rode a few companies of lancers and archers.

"They've got horses," Kickaha mumbled. "I need a horse. Ergo, I'll get a horse. But I suppose they hang horse thieves just as they did in the Old West. Well, it won't be the first time I stole a horse. Nor the last, I hope."

After the group had passed, the dust had settled down, and he was sure no soldiers were coming back to get him, he went back to the road. He walked for an hour in the increasing heat. When he saw two men ride down from a pass in the hills on his right, he increased his pace. By the time the two had gotten to the road, he was only forty feet from them. He called out to them, and they reined in their horses.

Two tougher customers he had never seen. Their hats were like the wagon drivers'. Their black and food-dotted beards flowed down to their chests. Their black eyes were hard, and their hawk-like faces were sun-seamed and looked as if they had never smiled. They wore dirty blue tunics and full, leg-length boots. Quivers full of arrows hung from their backs; their bows were strung; their scabbards held long swords and long knives.

Kickaha put his pack down, reached in, and brought out a small ingot of gold. Holding it up and pointing with the other hand at the nearest animal, he said, "I'll give you this for a horse."

Of course, they did not understand his words, but they understood his gestures. They spoke softly to each other, then turned their horses and charged him, swords in hand. He had expected this, since they looked to him like outlaws. His beamer ray, set at stun power, knocked them off their steeds. He caught one horse by the reins and was dragged for a few feet before it stopped. The other animal kept on running. After doffing all his clothes except for his pants and donning the stinking boots and tunic of the larger man, he rode away. He also had the man's bow and quiver. He had kept his own pants because they would ease the chafing from riding. He had left the gold ingot on the ground by the unconscious bandits. They didn't deserve it, but what the hell?

The ride was far longer than he wanted, because he did not press his horse, and he had to find water and feed for it. As he neared the city, he encountered an increasingly heavier traffic. Farmers with wagons piled high with produce were going into the city, and wagons holding bales of goods rattled out of it. Once, he passed a slave caravan, mostly Indian men and women linked together by iron collars and chains. The unchained children followed their parents. Though he felt sorry for the wretches, he could do nothing for them.

Finally, he came to a pass that led down to the city, which was still some miles away. By then, he had exchanged some gold for local money, round copper or silver coins of various sizes and values. On each was stamped the profile of some big shot and circling close to the rim were three words in an alphabet unfamiliar to him.

This was a large city by the citizens' standards, he supposed. His estimate was approximately one hundred thousand to one hundred fifty thousand population. It had a few squalid dwellings on the edge of the municipality. Their number increased as he rode closer to the ocean, though it was still miles from where he was. Here and there among these shacks and rundown stores were walled estates with huge houses. The streets seemed to have followed the paths of drunken cows until he was halfway along what would be the Hollywood Hills on his native planet. Then the dirt streets straightened out and became paved with large hewn-stone blocks.

Here and there were some tall, square, white stone buildings with twin domes, large front porches, and columns bulging in the middle and covered with the carved figures of troll-like heads and of dragons, lions, bears, and, surprisingly, elephants. Or were they mammoths? The streets were unpaved in this area. Narrow ditches along their sides were filled with water that stank of sewage. He supposed that there were stone-block or cobblestoned streets nearer to the coast, but he did not have time to see them.

This city had its equivalent of the L. A. smog. The smoke from thousands of kitchen fires hung heavy over the valley.

While he rode, he had been using his gate-detector. The light in it did not come on until he swept the "Hollywood Hills" area. Unlike the hills he had seen while on Earth I in 1970, these slopes were bare except for a score or so of mansions. Emanating from one on the very top of a hill were several bright spots. Gates.

He could not be sure, but he thought that the large white building topped by two domes was where the Griffith Observatory would be on his native planet. If he remembered correctly what he had been told while in Los Angeles, a road led up through a park and ended at the observatory. It seemed probable that, on this world, a private road to the same spot would have been laid out to the mansion. There was only one way to find out.

It took several hours of searching to find it, because he could not ask directions of passersby. Finally, he came to a dirt road that led him to a road paved with large flat stones. That led toward the ocean and followed a course at the foot of the hills. But a road that wound to the top of the hill was dirt. He rode unhurriedly up it. The steep slope would be hard on a horse if it galloped or even cantered.

While he was on a narrow lane flanked by tall trees, he figured out what he would do when he got close to the mansion. Though Red Orc lived in it now and then, he was probably unknown to most of the citizens. He had bribed some prominent citizen to front for him and to put the property in his name. Red Orc might not even leave his grounds. The mansion would be well guarded, and any entrance gates in the house would be trapped.

At this moment, the Thoan might not be in the house. He was said to have other houses on several continents of Earth II. He gated from one to the other, depending upon what area he was interested in at the time. His spies reported indirectly to him on the current state of affairs in that part of this world, and he no doubt also read the news periodicals.

Though the creator and hidden observer of both Earths, Red Orc made it a policy to interfere as little as possible with human affairs. The planets were his studies. He had made both in the image of his own planet, that is, the geological and geographical image of his now-ruined native world. But they had been been copies of his world when the human inhabitants were in the Early Stone Age.

He had made artificial humans, then cloned one set, and put one on Earth I and one on Earth II. Each was exactly like the other in genetic makeup, and each had been placed in the same geographical location as the other. They were both in the same primitive state, and each of the corresponding tribes had spoken the same language. Thus, those placed in, say, what would be Algeria on Earth I and the exact same area on Earth II, would speak the same language.

Red Orc had observed the tribes on both Earths during the last twenty thousand years. Some Thoan said it was thirty thousand years, but no one except Red Orc knew the correct period of time. Whatever the date, he had watched the prehistory and history of humans on both planets. He had not devoted all of his time to observation there. He apparently just dropped in now and then to bring his information up to date. Or to conduct some of his nefarious business.

Both planets were vast experiments in divergence. Though the various tribes had been, in the beginning, the exact counterparts of their duplicates on the other planet, including not only their physical forms but their languages, customs, and even names, there was a great difference after twenty thousand years.

Kickaha did not have time to compare in detail how these people had diverged from those of Earth. Red Orc might have spies watching for him. The Thoan left as little to chance as possible; he guarded his own rear end. For all Kickaha knew, word of his coming might have reached Red Orc days ago.

So be it.

Halfway up the road, he came to a high stone wall across it and extending up into the hills. A dozen armed men were lounging in front of the gate. He turned around and rode back into town. There he managed to trade some of his small coins for lodging for his horse. The owner of the stables did not seem very curious. There were too many foreigners in this harbor city for him to be surprised to meet one, even out here, miles from the metropolitan area.

Or it could be that he had been told by a Red Orc agent to pretend indifference.

Kickaha walked back to the bottom of the hill and went into the woods a few yards from the road. Here he waited for nightfall, meanwhile napping and then eating his own rations and drinking from his own canteen. Though he was theoretically immune to any disease, he did not want to chance the local food or the water. After a long time, midnight came. By then, the sky was overcast. But he wore the headband and its attached night-vision device. He worked uphill through the trees some distance from the road until he came to the wall. Though it was ten feet high, he got over it easily by throwing a grappling hook and climbing up the rope.

When he was on top and had drawn the rope up, he took from the backpack a sensor-detecting instrument given him by Khruuz. He swept the immediate area with it. It registered nothing. That only meant, however, that any sensors planted out there were not active. There could be plenty of passive detectors camouflaged as rocks or tree bark. It did not matter. He was pressing onward and upward.

He let himself down to the ground and whipped the hook free. After coiling it and hanging it from a strap on his belt, he climbed up almost vertical slopes. Then he came to less steep ground. Again, he swung the sensor-detector in a semicircle. Its light, set within a recess, did not come on.

After he had climbed to the top of another stone wall, he used the detector again. Now, its indicator glowed. He set it to determine what frequency the detectors were on. Having done that, he rotated a dial on the machine's side until it matched the frequency. Then he pressed a recessed button in its side. Immediately, the inset light turned off. The machine had now passively canceled the transmitted waves so that they would not register his body. But the alarms in Red Orc's house might go off if this action was detected.

He was, he thought, in a tiny canoe moving on a river of uncertainty and ambiguity, a craft leaking from holes, with the paddle on the point of breaking. But if it sank, he would swim on upstream.

He wiped the sweat from his forehead and drank deeply from the canteen. This he had emptied and refilled a dozen times during his trip with water from clean streams flowing from the hills. He pushed through the thick bushes among the trees for a few yards, stopping when he saw the lights in the upper-story windows of the great mansion. The ground floor had no windows. Like those large houses in the valley, this building was constructed of white stone blocks.

Kickaha removed his night-vision goggles and looked behind him and down. The valley was in darkness except for a few widely scattered lights, probably clusters of torches. He resumed his walk toward the east side of the house. The ground was level, and the gravel path he was following wound through beds of flowers. Forty feet from the house, the lawn began. Glancing at his detector now and then, Kickaha proceeded to the corner of the house and stuck his head around it. Lit by torches set in brackets on the front wall was a wide porch. Along the front edge of the porch were seven columns covered by carved figures.

Two spearmen stood before the eight-foot-high arched door-way.

He took two minutes to stun them with the beamer, tie their hands behind them and their feet together, and slap tape on their mouths. He did not know when the change of guard would be and did not care. There was no lock on the big iron door. Since it resisted his push, he supposed that it had been barred from the inside. His beamer cut through the door and the big rectangular wooden bolt behind it.

The only noise was the sputter of melting metal and the clang as the bolt and metal bracket on the other side fell onto the floor. He had to push them aside when he entered. He stepped inside a well-lit room big enough to hold a medium-sized sailing ship. The illumination was the sourceless lighting of Thoan technology. Cool air was blowing from a wall vent near him.

No one appeared to defend the house. After searching through the ground floor and finding no one there, he went up a wide staircase to the second story. There he found the room in which Anana had been subjected to the memory-uncoiling. It was as empty of people as the first floor. The third revealed nothing useful except the lights he saw through his gate-detector. So far, he had found gates on every floor, ten in all. Red Orc believed in having many escape routes close at hand.

The "attics," the twin domes, were entered by trapdoors in the ceiling of the third story. Though he did not expect to find anything significant there, he was wrong. Each dome housed an airboat. If Red Orc failed to get to a gate fast enough, he could use one of these to escape. Kickaha got into the cockpit of one and reacquainted himself with the controls and instruments. Having done that and started the motor, he pushed the button that energized the control mechanism of the dome door. It slid to one side, showing a still-cloudy sky.

The airboat lifted and pointed toward the doorway. He was going to fly back to the Vasquez rocks and regate there to Manathu Vorcyon's World. Since he was one hundred percent sure that all the gates in the house were trapped, he would take none. He was beginning to feel that Red Orc had guessed that he would break into the house. It was a wonder that the Thoan had not fixed it so that the house would blow up when any unauthorized person entered it.

He pressed down on the acceleration pedal. The craft surged forward, pressing him against the back of the pilot's chair. He should go slowly until he was out of the dome, but he was in a hurry.

That haste was his undoing. Or maybe it wouldn't have made any difference.

In any event, when he saw the shimmering, which was a few inches outside the dome-hangar door, it was too late to stop.

He howled, "Trapped!"

The airboat passed through the shimmering curtain, the gate that Red Orc had set to be triggered when the craft approached it.

16

Just as he bulleted through the veil, he pressed two buttons to fire big and powerful "cannon" beamers, one on each side of the nose of the boat. Whatever was waiting for him on the other side was going to be blasted. Metal would melt, and flesh would be a cloud of atoms.

No, they would not. The cannons failed to spit out the ravening beams that destroyed everything in their range.

He should have checked them out before taking off. Red Orc had deactivated them.

Though furious at himself for not testing the beamers, he did what was needed to keep the airboat from slamming into the opposite wall of the gigantic hangar he had shot into. His foot lifted from the acceleration pedal. At the same time, he turned the magnetic retro-fire dial to the full-power position. His body surged forward slightly, but the pressure was so intense he felt crushed. The magnetic restraining field kept him from breaking his chest bones against the steering wheel. Its nosetip almost touching the wall, the boat had stopped.

He slid back the canopy and looked over the side of the cockpit. About fifty feet below was the hangar floor. Parked at the rear of the vast room were two score airboats of different sizes and a zeppelin-shaped and -sized vessel. On the floor near the front of the building, a dozen men were aiming their beamers at him. What he had thought was a wall was the upper part of the closed hangar door.

Red Orc walked out of the small doorway near the big one. He stood well back of the armed men and looked up. Though he seemed small at this distance, his voice was loud.

"Bring the boat down slowly, and give yourself up! If you don't, I'll detonate the bomb in your boat!"

Kickaha shrugged and then did as ordered. This was most probably the stonewall end of his life. He was sure that the Thoan did not need the Trickster anymore. Besides, his enemy had slipped away from him so slickly so many times that he would no longer chance his doing it again.

But then you never knew about Red Orc, a slippery and unpredictable customer himself.

Kickaha turned off the motor. At the command of the soldiers' officer, he threw his backpack and weapons out. Red Orc would now have a gate-detector for his own use. He'd be one up in the ever-shifting conflict between himself and his foes, Khruuz and Manathu Vorcyon. Kickaha got out of the cockpit and stood, hands held high, while the officer ran a metal detector over him and patted him down. The officer spoke in Thoan, and Kickaha put his hands behind his back. The officer used a hold-band to secure his wrists together.

A woman walked through the doorway and then stopped by Red Orc's side. She was beautiful. Her long straight black hair fell past her shoulders. Her dress was a simple red shift; her feet were sandaled.

Kickaha cried, "Anana!"

She looked blankly at him and questioningly at the Thoan.

"She doesn't know you, Kickaha!" Red Orc said. He put one arm around her. "I haven't told her about you, but I will. She'll find out what a vicious and murderous man you are. Not that she'll be very interested in you."

Many bad things had been happening to Kickaha. This seemed the worst to him.

Red Orc told the officer to take the prisoner away.

"We'll see each other soon," he said. "Our final talk will be, in a sense, our last one."

In a sense? What did that mean?

Anana was looking straight at him. Her face showed pity for him. But that would soon change to repulsion when the lying Thoan told her what a cowardly backstabbing lowlife he was.

"Don't believe a word he says about me!" Kickaha shouted at her. "I love you! You loved me once, and you'll love me again!"

She pressed closer to Red Orc. He put his hand on her breast. Kickaha surged forward but was brought to his knees by a beamer butt slamming the back of his head. Dazed, his head hurting, and with vomit rising, he was marched away. Halfway to the building that would be his prison, he got the dry heaves. But his guards urged him on with kicks.

Even though sick, he observed the land around him and the big building he was headed for. It was in a large clearing surrounded by trees. These were growing so closely together that their branches interlocked, moving up and down and sometimes bending around other branches. They looked as if they were feeling each other up. He did not need to be told that they were watchdog trees. Whether or not they just held an escapee or ate him, they were tough obstacles.

The sky was blue and clear except for some very high and thin clouds. The sun was like Earth's. That meant nothing, because many suns in many worlds looked like the Terrestrial sun. Some were as large as the sun; some, very tiny though they looked large.

The guards were tall blue-eyed men with Dutch-bobbed brown, red, or blond hair. They wore yellow calf-length boots and baggy green knee-length shorts attached to a harnesslike arrangement over their shoulders. Broad leather straps running diagonally across their chests bore metal sunburst badges.

Kickaha had never seen such uniforms before. For all he knew, he could still be on Earth II but in a place distant from the "Los Angeles" area.

The building into which he was conducted was onion-shaped, and its front bore clusters of demonic and snakelike figures locked in combat or copulating.

He was marched between two squads through a vast foyer and then halted before an elevator door. Its door did not open. Instead, the shimmering of a gate appeared, and he and one squad walked through it and into a large elevator cage. It was the only one he had ever seen furnished with a washbowl, its stand, a rack with towels, a toilet, a fully rotatable blower, a shower head, a floor drain, and a chair on which was a roll of blankets. The cage accelerated upward for several stories. When it stopped, he expected the door to slide open. But it lurched sideways and began to move swiftly on the horizontal plane.

Presently, the cage stopped. The squad marched out through a shimmering that had appeared over the doorway. As soon as the last man had left the cage, the gate vanished.

So, the cage was also his prison cell. An hour after entering it, he saw a small section of the wall slide up. A revolving shelf came out of the recess. His meal was on it. Okay. He had been served before in just such a manner. And he had gotten more than once out of what seemed to be an escapeproof chamber.

He did not eat for several hours. Though he had recovered somewhat from the blow on the head, he still felt sick. Most of that, though, was because Anana no longer knew him and might never know him again.

When he had seen her in the huge hangar, her face had looked, in a subtle way, much younger. It was as if, without his realizing it before, every hundred years of her millennia-long life had placed another microscopically thin mask of age on her face. Yet, she had always looked young to him. Not until the memory-uncoiling had taken her back to when she was eighteen years old had the real difference become apparent. Though still aged, she was now unaged. What previously could not be seen had been made visible. And a long-dead innocence had been reborn. Only he, who knew her so well, could have perceived the lifting of the years.

A square section of the wall glowed, shimmered, then became a solid picture. He saw Red Orc, nude, sitting on a chair behind a table. Behind the Thoan, by the opposite wall, was a huge bed.

He lifted a cut-quartz goblet filled with red wine. He said, "A final toast to you, Kickaha. You led me a hot chase and a quite amusing one. To be frank, you also worried me now and then. But you made the hunt more interesting than usual. So, here's to you, my elusive but now doomed quarry!"

After sipping the wine and setting the goblet down, he leaned back. He looked quite satisfied.

"You did what I could not do during my intermittent searches: you found a way into Zazel's World. But that was because I was too close to the problem. You were fresh. However, I owe you thanks for what you did for me, and you're one of the very few I've ever felt gratitude toward. In fact, I owe you double thanks."

He reached out a hand to something Kickaha could not see. When he brought it within vision, it held the gate-detector device.

"I also owe you great gratitude for your gift even though you were not so willing to tender me this. Thank you, again."

"You call this gratitude?"

"I haven't killed you, have I?"

He sipped again, then said, "I don't know what happened to my son, that is, the clone I sent after you into the Caverned World. I suspect that you killed him. You will tell me in every detail what did happen."

To refuse to tell the Thoan of his experiences there would be useless, even stupid. Red Orc would get it out of him and cause him unendurable pain while doing it. Reluctantly, Kickaha described how he had traveled to the place and what had occurred there. But he did not mention Clifton or Khruuz.

Red Orc looked neither frustrated nor angry. He said, "I believe some of your story, but I'll wait a while for verification for my son Abalos to return. Whether he does or not, I will get into Zazel's World in time. I have no doubt that I'll be able to reactivate it, though it may take a while."

"Time is what you don't have. After all, Manathu Vorcyon has come out from her isolation. She is now your great enemy."

"I was going to tackle her someday anyway."

Kickaha quoted an ancient Thoan saying. "He who is forced to begin attack before he planned to do so has no plan."

"It was Elyttria of the Silver Arrows who said, 'Old sayings are always old but are not always true.' "

Kickaha sat down in the only chair in his room. He grinned, and he said, "Let's quit trading epigrams. Would you be kind enough to tell me exactly how you intend to proceed against Manathu Vorcyon? After all, I'll never be able to warn her. And then would you tell me what you've got in store for me? I like to be prepared."

"I will do the latter, though not completely," Red Orc said. "I'll not tell you one of the things I plan for you. You can watch me do it."

The Thoan stood up and called out, "Anana!" Then he said, "From now on, you'll be able to see what takes place in this room and hear everything. The transmission from your room will be stopped."

A minute later, Anana, as nude as the Thoan, walked into the room. She went into his arms and kissed him passionately. After which, he led her to the bed.

Kickaha yelled, "No! No!" and struck the screen area with his fist. All he did was to hurt his hand, but he did not mind that. Nevertheless, he used the chair to strike the screen many times. Neither the wall nor the chair was damaged. Then he unrolled the blankets and wrapped them around his head and stuck the ends of his little fingers into his ears. When he did that, the sound volume was raised so high that he could hear everything.

He screamed to drown out the noises until his throat was too hoarse to continue. After a long time, the sounds ceased. He came out from under his covers to look at the screen. It was now silent and blank. He croaked a sound of relief. But his mind was still displaying the images and voicing the noises.

Suddenly, the area glowed, shimmered, and became a picture. This one was a replay. Evidently, Red Orc was going to run it and, probably, future scenes over and over again until Kickaha went berserk or withdrew into himself.

He gritted his teeth, pulled up his chair to face the wall, and, mask-faced, stared at the images. He did not know if he could concentrate enough to summon up certain mental techniques he had learned a long time ago. While living with the Hrowakas, the Bear People, on the Amerind level of the tiered planet, he had mastered a psychological procedure taught by a shaman. Many years had passed since then. Despite this, he had not forgotten the methods any more than he had forgotten how to swim. They were embedded in his mind and nerves.

Doing them with the needed concentration was the main problem now. It was not easy. He failed after starting them seven times. Then he grimly focused on the movie and did not quit that until hours later. If Red Orc was watching him—he undoubtedly was—he would be puzzled by his prisoner's attitude.

Seeing the film over and over hurt Kickaha as he had never been hurt before. Tears flowed; his chest seemed to be a cavern filled with boiling lead. But he would not quit. After a while, his pain began to ooze away. Later, he became bored. He had attained enough objectivity to see the film as a pornographic show in which the characters were strangers. He felt as if his only punishment was to be doomed to watch the same movie over and over forever.

Now, he was able to start the internal ritual. This time, he succeeded. The screen area suddenly disappeared. Though it was still there to see and to hear, he no longer saw nor heard it. He had shut it out.

He thought, Absakosaw, wise old medicine man! I owe you much. But he could never repay Absakosaw. He and his tribe had been slain by one of Kickaha's enemies. Kickaha had killed their killer, but revenge did not make the Bear People rise from the dead.

Three days passed. The screen area remained blank. On the morning of the fourth day, it came alive. This time, the scene was a different bedroom but with the same actors. It was obvious that Anana was deeply in love with Red Orc. But then she had always been lusty, and she had no reason she knew of to hate the Lord. Nor did she know, of course, that she was being observed.

Either this transmission was a new one or Red Orc had figured out why Kickaha never paid attention to the film. In any event, it was getting through to Kickaha in more than one way. Again, he sat for hours staring at the wall until he was bored. After this, he used Abakosaw's system. When he rose from the chair, he saw only the wall. However, occasional images from the film would pierce his mind. He might be worn down eventually and be unable to make the blanking-out work.

The fifth day, while he was exercising vigorously, he heard the Thoan's voice. He turned. The screen was active. But it did not display the scenes that had driven him close to insanity. Red Orc's head and shoulders filled the screen. That confused Kickaha for a few seconds until he realized what had happened. Only the films were blocked from his mind, and he would receive anything else coming from the wall.

Red Orc said, "You are elusive in more ways than the physical.

I'd ask you to teach me your technique, but I have my own. And I could get you to tell me that without rewarding you with a month or so free of mental torture. I'm sure that you have held certain items of information back from me. You've been pleased, perhaps smug, because you've done this. You're going to go to sleep now. When you wake up, I'll know everything you know. Know, at least, those items you've been keeping from me."

The screen faded into blackness. Everything faded. When Kickaha awoke on the bed, he knew that he had been made unconscious, probably by gas. Then he had been questioned. Red Orc had used some sort of truth drug and gotten out of him everything, including the facts about Khruuz. That must have startled and alarmed him considerably. The appearance of the scaly man was something he could not have anticipated.

After Kickaha had eaten his dinner and placed the tray of dirty dishes on the swing-out shelf, he found out what else Red Orc had done. The screen came on. Again, Red Orc and Anana made passionate and polymorphous-perverse love. Grimly, Kickaha went through the old Hrowaka's methods. But this time, five hours went by without his being able to blank the screen out.

Suddenly, it stopped in the middle of the tenth replay. The Thoan's head appeared.

"By now, you have concluded that I canceled the effects of your technique. I did so, of course, with hypnotic commands. You remember the methods, but you can't make them effective."

Kickaha managed to control himself and not throw the chair at the screen. He tried to smile as if he did not care. Instead, he snarled.

"I have decided not to wait for Absalos to return from Zazel's World," Red Orc said. "Your story that you killed him is probably true. I'll find out when I get there. I will be gating out to there in a few minutes. When I come back, I'll have data to make the creation-destruction engine. After that, you and all my enemies and billions who have never heard of me will die. So will their universes. Even my Earths will perish in a beautiful display of energy. I've run them as experiments, but I can now predict what's going to happen to their people. Earth I humans will kill almost all of themselves with their brainless breeding, poisoning of land, air, and sea, and, in the end, the collapse of civilization, followed by starvation. Then the survivors, though plunged into savagery, will start the climb back to civilization, science, and technology, only to repeat the same story.

"This will also eventually happen on Earth II. Why should I continue the experiments when I know by now what the results will be? I'll use the energies of the disintegrated universes to make a new one. One only. This will be the ideal world, ideal for me, anyway.

"I may take Anana with me to my new world. But I may not. While I am gone on my trip, she'll be kept occupied. My son, Kumas, will have her. She will love him as much as she loves me because she won't know the difference."

He paused, smiled, and said, "That she won't know the difference shows something about true love, doesn't it? It's a philosophical problem in identity. I would like to discuss it with you, though I believe that the discussion would not last long. You're a trickster, Kickaha, but you do not know Thoan philosophy. Or, I suspect, Earthian philosophy. You are, basically, a simple-minded barbarian."

He turned his head to look at something. Perhaps, Kickaha thought, he was checking the time on a chronometer. What did it matter what Red Orc was doing? It didn't, but he was always curious about anything he could not explain.

The Thoan turned his head back to look at Kickaha.

"Oh, yes! Enjoy the movies!"

He walked out of Kickaha's view. Immediately after, the screen shifted to a room in which Red Orc—or was it his clone?—and Anana were at the peak of ecstasy.

Kickaha tried to become deaf, blind, and unfeeling steel. He failed.

There was more than one way to skin a cat. Or, as the Thoan saying went, more than one direction in which to fart. He had used only one of the three techniques taught him by the shaman, Absakosaw.

He sat down and, once more, watched the films. He was going to sit here until he got bored. Then, he would think of Anana and Red Orc as puppets operated by strings. After a while, they should cease being human—in his mind, anyway—and become mere wooden dolls with articulated limbs.

However, as long as the amplified noises came from the screen, he would have much difficulty ignoring that. The sounds that Anana made kept moving the course of his thoughts back to when he and she had been making love. Just as he was on the edge of giving up and trying some other technique, the screen went blank.

A second later, the Lord's face appeared.

"Kickaha! I am Kumas, Red Orc's son!"

Kickaha shot up from his chair. He said, "Are you? Or are you Red Orc playing another trick on me?"

The man smiled despite the strain on his face.

"I don't blame you. My father breeds suspicion as some breed worms for fishing."

"If you are indeed his son . . . his clone . . . how can you prove that? And what if you are? What do you want of me?"

"Partnership. My father has gone to Zazel's World. He has left me in charge because he trusts me most, though that is not saying much. I have always been obedient to him and never shown any sign of ambition. He thinks I am shy and reclusive, far more interested in reading and in writing poetry and in gaining knowledge. In that, he is partly correct. But I have hated him as much as my brothers do. Unlike them, I have succeeded in hiding my true feelings."

He stopped for a moment while he obviously made an effort to slow down his rapid breathing.

Kickaha said, "You want me to help you kill him?"

Kumas gulped audibly and nodded. "Yes! I know much about you, mostly from my father, though I do have other sources of information. I admit that I do not have enough confidence in myself to carry out my plans."

"Which are what?"

Kickaha's heart was beating hard, and he had to control his own heavy breathing. The situation had suddenly changed from hopelessness to hope. Unless, that is, the Thoan was playing another game with him.

"We'll talk about that now. I'll show you that I am not my father by doing something he would not do. Watch!"

Suddenly, a door-sized area of the wall near the screen shimmered.

"Step through the gate into my room."

Though Kickaha was still suspicious, he could not refuse this invitation. He went through the shimmering to find himself in a large room. It was Spartan in its decorations and furniture. Along all the walls were shelves filled with books, rolls of scripts, and computer readout cubes. The bed was old-fashioned, one of those that hung from the ceiling by chains. By the opposite wall was a desk that ran the length of the room.

Kumas, if he was truly Kumas, was standing in the middle of the room. A beamer was on the edge of the desk near Kickaha. He could get to it before the Thoan could. Kumas spread his hands out and said, "See! I have no weapons except that beamer. To prove that I trust you, I'll not stop you from having it. The battery is in it; it's ready to fire."

Though he moved nearer the weapon, Kickaha said, "That won't be necessary—as of now, anyway. Where's Anana?"

Kumas turned toward the empty space of the wall just above the desk. His back was to Kickaha. He said, "Sheshmu," Thoan for "open." The area became a screen showing Anana and several women swimming in an enormous outdoor pool. Anana seemed to be having fun with them. Their cries and shrieks and chatter came clearly.

Kumas spoke another word, and the volume shrank to a barely heard sound.

"As you see, she is quite happy. She has accepted my father's lies that she was rescued by him from Jadawin when Jadawin—so my father said—invaded her parents' universe. She believes that she is only eighteen years old, and she is deeply in love with my father."

Kickaha's chest was, for a moment, again filled with a searing-hot liquid. He murmured, "Anana!" Then he said, "What'll happen when she finds out he's lied? She'll eventually find discrepancies in his story. How's he going to keep her from reading histories or overhearing somebody saying something that'll not contradict what he says?"

Kumas had been looking curiously at him. He said, "I expected you to be concerned only with how we were going to dispose of my father. But your first concern seems to be about Anana. You must really love her."

"No doubt of that! But will she ever love me again?"

Kumas said sharply, "That remains to be seen. Just now, if you'll pardon me, we have something much more important. If we don't do that, you and Anana won't have any future. Neither will I."

"Agreed. It'll be hard not to go to her, though. Very hard. But you're right. Let her stay happy until the time when she must be told the truth."

They sat down at a table. Kickaha outlined his story to the

Thoan. When he told him that Red Orc planned to disintegrate all the universes and to start over with a new one, he saw Kumas turn pale and start to shake.

The Thoan said, "I did not know that, of course. He told that only to you because he thought that you would never be able to pass it on."

"That can wait," Kickaha said. "How many of your brothers are left, by the way?"

"Four of us unless you really did kill Absalos."

"I did."

"Three out of the original nine still live. Ashatelon, Wemathol, and myself. Ashatelon and Wemathol insist on accompanying us to the Caverned World. They want to be in on the kill."

"The more the merrier," Kickaha said.

But he was thinking that he could not trust any of the clones, though Kumas seemed to be different from the others. Red Orc might have done some genetic tampering with the clones. Or perhaps environment counted for more than the Lords thought it did. In any event, he would have to watch them closely, though he doubted they would be a danger to him until Red Orc was out of the way. They were afraid of their father, and they would need a leader who was not the least bit scared of him. Then, like jackals who'd helped the lion during the hunt, they might fall upon Kickaha.

Kumas resumed talking, "At least four of my brothers so far have died when our father sent them on suicidal missions. Kentrith was sent into Khruuz's world not knowing that a bomb was in his backpack. We were not aware of it until our father told me about it. He laughed all the while. You would think that he would be kind to us since his father was so cruel to him. But that did not happen. Los seems to have twisted him so much that he takes an especial pleasure in tormenting his own sons. Sometimes I think he brought us into being just so that he could, in a certain way, torture himself."

"What do you mean?" Kickaha said.

"He hates himself, I am sure of that. By punishing us, he is punishing himself. Does that idea seem too farfetched to you?"

"It could be valid. But I don't know if it is. Right or wrong, it doesn't change a thing. You've swept this room for recording devices he might've planted?"

"Of course. So, that leaves me and Ashatelon and Wemathol. Those two are what my father wanted, men of action. I disappointed him because I was too passive. He didn't understand it. After all, I was his genetic duplicate. So, why didn't I have his nature? He tried to explain it, but . . ."

Kickaha cut in. "We can always talk about that later. But if we don't stop your father dead in his tracks, and I do mean dead, we won't have a later time."

"Very well. He is now in the Caverned World, if what he told me is true, and I can never be sure about anything he tells me. He should be there a long time. Reactivating that world won't be easy. Our logical next step should be to attack him while he's there. First, if it's possible, we should seal up all gates there except the one we use for entrance. Don't you agree?"

Kickaha nodded. But while listening to Kumas, he could not keep from thinking about Anana. What if she could not love him again? It was then that an idea pierced him like an arrow made of light. If it worked, it would turn her against Red Orc.

He said, excitedly, "Kumas! Listen! We're going to fix your father. In one way, anyway. He seems to anticipate just about everything, but he won't have foreseen this. At least, I hope not. Here's what we're going to do before we leave."

An hour later, Kumas left the room to be with Anana. Kickaha watched them via a screen. By then, she was out of the pool and in a green semi-transparent dress, her long black hair done up in a Psyche knot. She was reading from a small video set while sitting on a bench in the flower garden. She looked up when Kumas stopped before her. He handed her the cube he and Kickaha had prepared. He talked to her for a while, then walked away. Frowning, she held the cube in her hand for a long time.

Kickaha turned the screen off when Kumas walked into the room.

"Do you think she'll look at it?" he said.

Kumas shrugged his shoulders. But he said, "Would you be able to resist doing it?"

"That depends upon whether or not he made her promise not to listen to any derogatory comments about him. If he did, she probably won't watch it. But I'm betting the Bluebeard syndrome will overwhelm her. She'll drop the cube into the slot and turn on the screen. I hope so, anyway."

"Bluebeard syndrome?"

Kickaha laughed. He said, "Bluebeard was the villain in an old folktale. He married often and killed his wives and hung them up to dry in a locked room. But he had to go off on a trip, so he told his latest wife she could use the key he'd given her. It would open every room in the castle. But she was definitely not to unlock one room. Under no circumstances was she to do that. Then he took off.

"Naturally, her curiosity overcame her wifely duty to obey him. So, after fighting temptation for some time, she surrendered to it. She unlocked the room where the former wives hung from hooks. She was horrified, of course. She told the authorities, and that was the end of Bluebeard."

"We Thoan have a tale similar to that," Kumas said.

"If Red Orc just commanded her not to pay any attention to anything bad she hears about him from his sons, she'll do it anyway. But if she gave her word . . . I don't know. In her mind, she's eighteen years old. The Anana I knew would hardly have waited until he had left her to find out just what it was he didn't want her to know. But eighteen-year-old Anana must have been a different woman from the older woman."

"We'll find out when we come back," Kumas said. "If we do come back."

17

*H*ere we are," Kickaha said cheerily. "Back in the land of the dead."

He and the three clones, the "sons," were in the tunnel of Zazel's World where he had entered it on his first mission. They had not passed directly from Red Orc's mansion to this place. The first step, a comparatively easy one, had been to find a gate to Manathu Vorcyon's World. The Great Mother had told Kickaha before he had been sent on his first passage to Khruuz's World that she was again setting the trap that had whisked him away to her world. He could return to her through that.

On entering the Great Mother's world, the party was in the forest surrounding the great tree in which she lived. Again, warriors appeared from the trees and led them to the palace-tree. After a series of conferences with her, they were sent on to Khruuz's universe. They landed in a room cut out of rock and with no windows or doors. A few minutes later, the gate passed them on to a prison cell. This was in Khruuz's underground fortress. The scaly man had set up a shunt in the gate-passages. This had allowed him to seal all the immediate entrances to his world. But they would be opened when Eric Clifton's instruments told him that the preliminary gate was occupied. Khruuz had gone to Zazel's World, and Clifton had been left behind to monitor the gates.

The Englishman had released them from their cell after he was sure that Kickaha was not the captive of Red Orc's sons. Kickaha had told him immediately of events to the minute he had left for here. Then, Clifton had told his news about Khruuz.

"Or, at least, he started to go there," Clifton had said. "He intended to use the same route you used when you gated there."

"How long has he been gone?"

"Ten days."

Clifton had rolled his eyes and looked mournful.

"It seems to me that he should have been back five days ago. However, he might have tried to reactivate the world. I didn't know it was dead until you told me, and he wouldn't find out it was until he got there."

"I don't know what he's up to," Kickaha had said. "He should've waited for us. Maybe he thinks he can do just as well without us. I don't know."

"You're suspicious?" Clifton had said.

"Khruuz has never proved that he's trustworthy. On the other hand, he's given me no reason to suspect him. He seems to be very friendly, and he sure needs us. Did need us, anyway. Maybe something's happened so he doesn't need us anymore. But what could he have up his sleeve?"

"His hatred for the human species?"

"He hates the Lords. He wouldn't be human if he didn't. But then, he's not human. Why should he have anything against us *leblabbiys*? We never did anything to him."

"We do look just like the Lords," Clifton had said. "Hatred is not by any means always rational."

"But he's never shown anything but friendliness toward you and me. He'd have to be a hell of an actor to repress his hatred all this time."

"That may be significant. I wouldn't blame him a bit if he

frothed at the mouth when he spoke about them. But he seems to have a self-control cast in bronze. Is that in itself suspicious?"

"It could be," Kickaha had said. "But, for the time being, there's nothing we can do about it. We go ahead without him."

An hour later, the war party had gated out to Zazel's World, not knowing what reception it might get at its destination. The tunnel, however, was empty. There was one difference, no small one, from Kickaha's first trip. The symbols were again marching along on the tunnel wall.

He said, "Somebody's had some success resurrecting this stone carcass."

"Let's hope the somebody is not Red Orc," Kumas said.

To avoid their confusing Red Orc with the clones in a situation where individual identity was crucial, the clones had changed the color of their hair to purple. They also wore orange headbands and carried light-blue backpacks.

"That those characters on the wall are moving again means that either Khruuz or Red Orc has started the computer up again," Kickaha said. "Let's find out who did it."

This time, he was not going to walk the wearying and time-consuming tunnels. The four men had gated from Red Orc's palace riding small foldable one-seater airboats weighing thirty pounds. They were more like motorcycles than the conventional airboats. But the oxygen and water tanks and the case of supplies and the "small cannon" beamers fixed to the fuselage nose put a strain on the tiny motor.

Their craft were cruising at thirty miles an hour. Nevertheless, in these close quarters, the boats seemed to be going very swiftly.

Through his goggles, the infrared light made the tunnels even more ghostly than in photonic light.

In less than an hour, he saw the two-tunneled fork ahead. He held up his hand and stopped the boat.

"What in hell!"

The entrance to the left-hand tunnel was blocked with a single stone. The symbols disappeared there. But those on the other wall kept marching into the right-hand tunnel.

He got off the craft to inspect the stone. It was smooth and contained many fluorescent chips. It also merged with the sides of the entrance as if it were stone grown from stone. Or as if a stone-welding instrument had been used.

He took from his backpack a square device with a depth indicator on its back. After pressing the front part against the stone, he said, "There's thirty feet of solid stone there. Beyond that is empty space, the continuation of the tunnel, I suppose. Someone has set it up to make us go where he wants us to go."

Kumas's voice came over the tiny receiver stuck to Kickaha's jaw. "I hope Khruuz did it."

"Me, too. But we can't do anything except follow the route so thoughtfully laid out for us. From now on, you and I, Kumas, will be as close to the ceiling as we can get. Ashatelon and Wemathol, you keep your boats several inches above the floor and about ten feet behind us. That way, we can have maximum firepower and yet not shoot each other. I'll be slightly ahead of Kumas."

Although he did not like having the Thoan at his back, he had to be the leader. Otherwise, they would believe he was a coward. He had told Kumas to stay at his side because he was not at all certain that Kumas would know what to do in a fight unless he had orders.

Five minutes later, they decelerated quickly and then stopped. The entrance to the cave was also blocked. But a new hole had been made in the wall by the mouth of the cave. It led at right angles to the tunnel they were in. The symbols had reappeared on the previously blank part of the wall.

"Onward and inward," Kickaha said. "Keep your eyes peeled and your fingers on the firing button. But make sure you don't shoot unless you have to."

"If our father did this," Kumas said, "we're done for."

"Many a Lord has thought that after setting a trap for me," Kickaha replied. "Yet, here I am, as healthy and unscarred as a young colt. There my enemies are, dead as the lion who tackled the elephant."

"A braggart is a gas balloon," Wemathol said. "Prick him, and he collapses."

Ashatelon spoke harshly. "This man is not called the Slayer of Lords, the man who won the war against the Bellers, for nothing. So why don't you keep your sneering to yourself?"

"We'll discuss this later with knives," Wemathol said.

"Nothing so heartening as brotherly love," Kickaha said. "You Thoan make me sick. You think you're gods, but you haven't graduated from the nursery. And you wipe your asses just like the lowest of *leblabbiy*, though you don't do as good a job of it. From now on, no more squabbling! That's an order! Keep your minds on our mission! Or I'll send you back to your nurses to wipe your noses!"

They did not speak again for some time. The boats took them along a tunnel for a mile before another stone blocked their passage. But this was not stone-welded. The separation between it and the tunnel wall was obvious. Nevertheless, the men were stopped.

Either the symbols had ceased moving or they were somehow slipping through the blocking stone.

Again, Kickaha used the depth sounder. Looking at the indicator, he said, "It's ten feet deep. Then, emptiness."

"Do we turn back?" Kumas said.

"And wander around here until we run out of food?" Wemathol said.

"Maybe we should use the cannon to melt our ray through," Ashatelon said. "That might use up much of the battery energy. But what else can we do?"

"We'll blast our way in," Kickaha said.

They did as he ordered and took turns in beaming the stone. Under the force of the rays, the stone melted swiftly and lava ran out on the floor below. Scraping the semiliquid away from the stone was hot and hard work. Their small shovels made the labor longer, but it had to be done. Sweating, making sure they did not come within range of the narrow beams, they succeeded in throwing the glowing stuff away from the tunnel entrance. When one craft had used up half of the battery, the second boat moved in. But a minute after the second boat had started its melting, the stone began to roll into a recess in the wall.

Kickaha told Ashatelon to turn off his beamer.

"It's a wheel!" Kumas cried.

"Tell us what we don't know, stupid," Wemathol said.

They backed the boats away and then waited. The craft noses were pointed at the opening, and the pilots had their fingers on the FIRE button.

"Be ready to shoot," Kickaha said. "But don't be trigger-happy."

"Why would anybody except Red Orc have closed the entrances?" Wemathol said.

"I don't know. Maybe Khruuz did it, though I don't know why. Just don't assume anything."

The huge wheel had completely moved within the wall recess. Beyond that was a cave.

Kumas had removed his goggles at Kickaha's order. He was to determine if photonic light was present. He said loudly, "The cave is lit up!"

The others now took their goggles off. The brightness from the cavern was much stronger than could be given by luminiferous plants. There were no shadows, so the illumination seemed to have no source. That meant that a Thoan was providing it. Maybe.

Now, they could see that the cave was gigantic. Cool air brushed their bodies. To test it, Kickaha took off his oxygen mask and breathed deeply. Though the air was delightfully fresh, he said, "We'll keep our masks on for a while."

He could not see the distant walls and ceiling of the cave, so vast was it. But he could see strange-looking plants, some of them tree-tall, growing from the soil on the floor.

Kumas said, "Red Orc is waiting for us in there."

"Somebody is," Kickaha said.

"You go first," Kumas said.

"Of course!" Kickaha said loudly. "If I waited for one of you to lead, we'd sit here until we starved!"

"No man calls me a coward!" Ashatelon said.

Before Kickaha could stop him, Ashatelon had shot his boat forward and through the opening. But he did not stop at once. Instead, he accelerated until he seemed to be going at the maximum speed of the craft, fifty miles an hour. The boat rose. For a moment, it was out of sight. Then it appeared and, a moment later, hovered a few inches above the floor and ten feet in from the entrance. Its nose was pointed toward them.

"Now you may know who's a coward!" Ashatelon bellowed.

His words echoed from the distant walls.

Kickaha's boat moved into the cave. He looked around. A green lichenous stuff covered most of the wall behind him. Somehow, the plants had been given a new life. Or else they had never been dead in this cave. The walls near them were about two miles apart, and the ceiling was about a hundred feet high. The other end was so far away that it shrank to a point. The symbols paraded on both walls and toward the end of the cave until they were too small to see.

The other two Thoan entered. "No one here," Kumas said. He sounded very relieved.

"Someone rolled that wheel aside," Kickaha said. "We'll go on."

He started to press his foot down on the acceleration pedal.

Then, he felt wet drops on his bare skin and a fine mist was around him.

When he woke up, he was inside a square cage made of bars. Above him were bars through which he could see the cave ceiling. High above these was the cave ceiling. Or of some cave somewhere. He got slowly to his feet, becoming aware that they were unshod while he did so. His clothes had been removed and were nowhere in sight. The cage floor was solid metal. In a corner was a pile of blankets. In another was a metal box, and the third corner held another box, the top of which had a toilet seat hole. In the center of the metal floor was a painted orange-lined circle with a diameter of three feet.

And there were other cages, widely separated, arranged in a circle. Six, including his. Inside each one was a man. One of them, however, was not a member of Homo sapiens.

"Khruuz!" he said hoarsely. He gripped the bars facing the inner part of the circle. For a moment, he was weak and dizzy. Despite wearing oxygen masks, he and the Thoan had been gassed. The gas must have been of the kind that did its dirty work through the skin.

"Must've been sprayed through holes in the wall behind us," he murmured to himself. "It doesn't matter how it was done. We're here."

Red Orc wasn't the one responsible for their captivity. He was in the cage directly across from Kickaha's. Like the others, he was unclothed. His face pressed against the bars, he was smiling at his archenemy. Did that mean that he was pleased that, at least, the others were also caged? Or did it mean that he was enjoying a secret? Such as that he had brought them here and was now posing as a prisoner? But why would he do that? Time would reveal the truth.

The three clones of Red Orc were in the other cages. Wemathol called out, "So much for your brags, Kickaha!"

He spat through the bars.

Kickaha ignored him. He was about to speak to Khruuz when a . . . creature? thing? semihuman? walked slowly and dignifiedly into the center of the circle. A second before, it had not been present. Where had it come from? A gate, probably.

Though he had never seen it before this, Kickaha knew that it had to be the thing he had thought was dead.

He cried out, "Dingsteth!"

It faced Kickaha, and it said, "Neth thruth," Thoan for "I am it." Carved jewels, not teeth, flashed in its mouth.

Kickaha had heard about Dingsteth from Anana and Manathu Vorcyon. According to them, Dingsteth was an artificial creature made by Zazel as a sort of companion and manager. Before Zazel had killed himself, he had charged his creation to stand guard on and to preserve his world. Just why he would want to keep the dreary universe going, no one knew.

Now, the fabled being was standing before Kickaha. It was bipedal and six feet tall. Its skin was lightly pigmented, a Scandinavian pink. It walked slowly because it had to. The shiny flesh rings around its shoulders, hips, elbows, knees, and wrists did not allow the free movement humans had. Its head, neck, and trunk were proportionally larger than those of a man. The skull was almost square, and the lips were very thin.

Where a man's genitals would have been was smooth skin.

The thing said, "You know my name. What is yours?"

"Kickaha. But I thought this world had died and you with it."

"You were meant to think that," it said, pronouncing its words in a somewhat archaic manner. "But you and the others were too persistent. So, I was forced to take appropriate action."

It paused, then said, "I thought the gate was closed."

"This thing intends to keep all of us here forever!" Red Orc shouted. "Dingsteth! I came here in peace!"

Without turning around, the thing spoke to the Thoan. "You

may have, and you may not have. The being who calls himself Khruuz says that you are very cruel and violent and obsessed with the desire to have the data for my master's creation-destruction engine. He says that you will destroy all the universes, including Zazel's, to have the energy to make a new world for yourself only."

"He lies!" Red Orc said.

Dingsteth continued to look at Kickaha.

"The semihuman calling himself Khruuz may be lying, and he may be telling the truth. He says that he can bring me proof of his words if I let him return to his own world. But you, Orc, promised to come back soon after I gated you out of here so long ago. You did not. Therefore, you lied to me.

"How do I know that this Khruuz is also not a liar? How can I be sure that you are not all liars? You, for instance, Kickaha. You and Khruuz and the others may never return if I let you leave this world. Or you may come back intending to force me to reveal data that you should not have. I do not know if you are a liar, but you are certainly capable of senseless violence. I saw you throw away the facsimile of my skull. And I saw you kill a man, though that act was in self-defense. Or appeared to be."

Dingsteth walked away from the circle of cages. Kickaha watched him go to a place twenty yards away. It stopped near a "tree," a scarlet plant the branches of which grew closely together and extended to an equal distance from the trunk. Near this cylindrical tree was a large round stone. The keeper of this world was equidistant from the tree and stone. It turned its back to the prisoners. It must have spoken a code word because it vanished suddenly.

He called to Khruuz, who was two cages away from his, "How did it catch you?"

"Gas. Your question should have been, 'How do we get out of these cages?' "

"Working on it now," Kickaha said. "But I admit that this is one of the toughest problems I've ever had to solve."

"You mean that we have ever had," Khruuz said.

Red Orc said, "Yes, we! I propose that, until we do escape, we put aside our hatreds and cooperate fully."

"I won't put them aside," Kickaha said. "I won't allow them, however, to keep me from working with you."

Kumas said, "We're doomed."

"Weakling!" Ashatelon said. "I am ashamed to be your brother. I have been since we played together as children."

Wemathol called, "You're really cooperating, Ashatelon!"

Khruuz's deep and rough voice stopped the snarling and snapping. "Hearing you Thoan makes me wonder how you ever succeeded in conquering my people. I do not believe that the Thoan who killed all of us except myself could be your ancestors.

"I suggest that we act as a harmonious whole until we have dealt with Dingsteth—nonviolently, I hope."

"Don't ask them to give their word they won't stab you in the back before that's done," Kickaha said. "Their word is as worthless as a burning piece of paper."

"I know that," Khruuz said. "But our common danger should be the cement binding us together."

"Ha!"

Red Orc said, "Does anyone have any ideas?"

"Dingsteth may be listening, probably is right now," Kickaha said. "So, how do we share ideas if it's going to know what we plan to do? We have no paper to write on, and we couldn't throw notes from cage to cage even if we did have paper. They're too far apart. Besides, Dingsteth'll be watching us."

"Sign language?" Kumas said. The others laughed.

"Think about it, dummy," Wemathol said. "How many of us know sign language? It'd have to taught by one who knows, if any of us do. And we can't do that unless we shout at each other.

Dingsteth would hear us and learn along with the rest of us. Thus . . ."

"I get the idea," Kumas said. "I was just thinking out loud, you worthless, do-nothing, gasbag lout. What's your ingenious idea?"

Wemathol did not reply.

Very little was said for the rest of the day. Night came when the sourceless light was turned off, and the only illumination was from the plants. Kickaha slept uneasily on his pile of blankets, not because he lacked a bed but because he could not stop thinking about how to get out of the cage and what he would do after that. Finally, sleep did come, laden with dreams of his life with Anana. Some of them were nightmares, fragments of desperate situations they had been in. On the whole, though, they were pleasant.

During one dream, he saw the faces of his parents. They were smiling at him and looked much younger than when they had died. Then they receded and were lost in mists. But his feeling about them was happy. He awoke for a while after that. There had been a time when he wondered if they were his biological mother and father. It had been hinted by some Thoan that he was adopted; his true parents were Thoan, possibly Red Orc himself. He had seriously considered questing for the truth when he had time for it. Now, he did not care. The biological parent was not necessarily the real parent. Loving and caring made the real father and mother. The poor but decent couple who had raised him from a baby on an Indiana farm were the ones he had known and loved. Thus, they were the only parents about whom he cared. Forget the quest.

Dawn, a less bright light than yesterday's, sprang into being. No false dawn here for Dingsteth. An hour later, it appeared between the tree and the stone and walked into the circle. It was careful not to come close enough to be reached through the bars.

Without the preliminary of a greeting, it spoke. "I heard your talk about escape plans. I have run the possibilities of your succeeding in that through the world. It gives you more than a

99.999999999 percent chance of never doing that. It is trying now to locate what it is that you could do that so that the percentage will be 100 percent."

"It has to have complete data from you to calculate that," Kumas said. "You cannot ever know that."

"Make it easier for us!" Wemathol howled. "Blab everything, you anus's anus, king of the cretins!"

Kumas, looking chagrined, lay down on his blanket pile. He refused to say a word after that.

"Nevertheless, I am attempting to consider all factors," Dingsteth said. "Unfortunately, my creator did not install a creator's imagination in me."

"We'll be glad to help you find what you're looking for!" Wemathol yelled.

Dingsteth turned toward Wemathol. "You would? That is most kind of you."

It had to wait until the laughter of the caged men had ceased before it could make itself heard. Even Khruuz vented his short barking laugh.

"That's some kind of human joke, I suppose. I don't understand such. An hour from now, you will hear a signal. You, Kickaha, will immediately stand in that circle on the floor of your cage. You will be gated to an exercise and shower area. After you have returned to the cage, the signal will again sound. You, Wemathol, will go first."

It named off each man in turn, made sure that they understood the arrangement, and returned to the gate by the tree. After it had disappeared, Ashatelon said, "It's taking good care of us, though I can't say much for the food. I wonder why it cares at all about our condition?"

"Its seeming concern for us is built in," Red Orc said. "It's part of its command complex. But Zazel put that in for his own good reasons. We may regret that Dingsteth did not kill us at once."

"We shouldn't give a damn about Zazel's reasons just now," Kickaha said. "Let's take advantage of them as soon as possible."

Easier said than done, as the old Terrestrial saying went. By the time that Kickaha had been transported to the exercise area, he had not heard or said anything that might help them. He found himself in a space cut into the stone. It had no exit or entrance—except for the gate that had brought him there—and was ventilated from narrow slits along the walls. Its ceiling was fifty feet high, it was fifty feet wide, and it was a half-mile long. At either end was an unwalled shower, a fountain, a commode, and a heat-dryer.

He warmed up before running swiftly up and down the room for five miles. After a warming-down exercise, he drank, showered, and dried off standing before the blower, after which he stood in the circle and was gated through to the cage. Another loud hooting came, and Wemathol got into his circle.

On the third morning of this routine, Kickaha asked Dingsteth what it planned to do with them eventually.

"You will stay caged until you kill yourself or die through accident, though I do not see how accidents can occur."

It was some time before the hurricane of protests trailed away. There was a silence for several minutes. Then Wemathol said, "We'll be here forever."

Dingsteth said, "Forever is only a concept. There is no such thing. However, if you had stated that you would be here for a very long time, you would be correct."

"We'll go crazy!" Kumas screamed.

"That is possible. It won't make any difference about your longevity."

Kickaha spoke calmly, though he did not feel like doing so. "Why are you doing this?"

"Zazel's commands are to be obeyed. I myself do not know why he left such orders. I surmise, however, that at the time he gave them to me, he did not foresee that he would one day kill himself. He is dead; his commands are not."

Kumas fainted. Wemathol hurled at Dingsteth every item in his large treasury of insults and obscenities. When he had run through them, he started over. Ashatelon bit on his arms until blood came. The other three said nothing, but Red Orc stared through the bars for a long time. Khruuz wept, a strange sight for the humans, since his insectile face looked as if it hid no more than an insect's emotions. Kickaha leaped up and hung from the bars and grimaced and hooted as if he were an ape. He had to express himself in some way. Just at the moment, he felt as if he had shot backward along the path of evolution. Apes did not think of the future. He would be an ape and not think about it.

He would later realize just how twisted his logic was. Just then, it seemed to be quite reasonable. It was only human to go ape.

18

*H*e had completely recovered by the next morning. Now, looking back at yesterday, he thought that being an ape had been fun. All he had lacked to be a true anthropoid was a fur coat and fleas.

Nevertheless, that brief fall from evolution's ladder was a warning. For too many years, he had been under extreme stress and in near-fatal situations. The breaks between them had been too short. It was true that he seemed almost always to be in top physical and mental condition, ready to take on the universe itself, no holds barred, anything goes. But, deep within him, the multitudinous perils, one after the other, had demanded high payment. The latest and worst of the shocks, Anana's permanent memory loss and then an inescapable sentence to life imprisonment, had been the one-two punch knocking him out of the ring.

"Only for a little while," he muttered. "Once I get in shape again, get a long rest, I'll be ready to fight anything, anybody."

Some of his cage-mates were still suffering. When Kumas was addressed by the others, he only grunted. All day long, he stood, his face pressed against the bars, his hands gripping them. He ate very little. Ashatelon cursed and raved and paced back and forth. Wemathol muttered to himself. Only Khruuz and Red Orc seemed to be undisturbed. Like him, their minds were centered on escaping.

Fat chance! He had tried again and again to summon up from his reservoir of ingenuity a possible means to break out. Every idea was whisked off by the hurricane of reality. This prison, compared to Alcatraz, was off the starting blocks and over the finish line before Alcatraz could take a step.

Thirty days passed. Every afternoon, Dingsteth visited them. It spoke for a few minutes to each prisoner except Kumas. He turned his back to it and refused to say a word.

Red Orc tried to talk it into releasing him. Dingsteth always rejected him. "Zazel's orders are clear. If he is not here to tell me otherwise, I am to hold any prisoners until he returns."

"But Zazel is dead. He will never come back."

"True. That makes no difference, however. He did not inform me as to what I should do with prisoners if he died."

"You will not reconsider in light of the changed situation?"

"I am unable to do so."

Kickaha listened closely to the dialogue. The next day, while running in the exercise room, not even thinking of his problems, an idea exploded in his mind. It was as if his unconscious had lit a firecracker. "Might work," he told himself. "Couldn't hurt to try. Depends upon Dingsteth's mental setup."

The following day, when he saw his captor walking stiffly into the circle of cages, he called to him.

"Dingsteth! I have great news! Something marvelous has happened!"

The creature went to Kickaha's cage and stood close, though not close enough to be grabbed. "What is it?"

"Last night, while I was dreaming, Zazel's ghost came to me. He said that he had been trying to get through to you from the land of the dead. But he can only do that in dreams. You don't dream."

Kickaha was guessing about that. But it seemed probable that its brain would lack an unconscious mind.

"Since you don't dream, but I am a blue-ribbon dreamer, Zazel, his ghost, that is, used me as his medium to communicate to you!"

Dingsteth's features were incapable of expressing puzzlement. Nevertheless, they managed to hint at it.

"What does 'blue ribbon' mean in the context of your statement?"

"It's a phrase for 'excellent.' "

"Indeed. But what is a ghost?"

"You don't know about ghosts?"

"I have great knowledge, but it is impossible for my brain to hold all knowledge. When I need to know something, I ask the world-brain about it."

"Ask them about ghosts and spirits and psychic phenomena. Now, here's what happened last night. Zazel . . ."

After Kickaha had finished his story, Dingsteth said, "I will go to the world and ask it."

It hurried away. As soon as it had vanished through the gate between the tree and the stone, Red Orc said, "Kickaha! What are you . . . ?"

Kickaha held a finger to his lips while shaking his head slightly. "Shh! Bear with me!"

He paced around the cage. His thoughts were like a swarm of asteroids orbiting a planet. The center of the planet was the idea that had suddenly come to him yesterday. It was a bright comet born in the darkness of his unconscious mind and zooming into his conscious mind, the bright planet—colliding with it, turning it into fire for a moment.

I should have been a poet, he thought. Thank God I have sense enough, though, not to tell others the images, the similes and metaphors springing up in my brain. They would laugh at me.

Having veered away from the subject of importance to his own self, a failing common to everyone, his mind returned to it. What would he say when Dingsteth came back to tell him he was full of crap?

The ruler of the Caverned World did return within five minutes. When he stood before the cage, he said, "The world informs me that there are in reality no such entities as ghosts or spirits. Thus, you are lying."

"No, I'm not!" Kickaha shouted. "Tell me, when was the data about spiritual things put into the world-brain?"

Dingsteth was silent for a few seconds. Then it said, "It was approximately twelve thousand years ago as time was measured in Zazel's native world. I can get the exact date for you."

"See!" Kickaha said. "The data has long been obsolete! Since then, it's been discovered that what was thought to be a superstition is fact! There are indeed such entities as ghosts and other kinds of spirits! About two thousand years ago, a Thoan named Houdini proved that there are ghosts. He also proved that they can communicate with us, but it's seldom that we can communicate with them. The ghosts appear to highly sensitive and gifted individuals, such as myself, and make their wishes known. Their method of communication is like a one-way gate. They can speak to us. We can't speak to them!"

He glanced around. By now, all except Kumas were gripping the bars and looking intently at him.

"If you don't believe me, ask them! They'll tell you that what I said is true? Isn't that right, men?"

None of them may have guessed rightly what he was heading for. But they were intelligent enough to play along with him. Kumas might not, but when Dingsteth asked him if Kickaha was telling the truth, the Thoan lay silent on his blankets and stared up through the bars. The others swore that what Kickaha claimed had indeed been public knowledge for a very long time.

"In fact," Red Orc said, "this same Houdini confirmed the existence of ghosts through scientific-psychic experiments. He was able several times to see them, though faintly. But the dead sometimes come through more or less clearly in dreams."

He looked at Kickaha as if to say, "Who the hell is Houdini?"

Kickaha held up a hand and formed an O with the fingers while Dingsteth's back was turned to him. He was delighted that the Thoan had caught on so quickly.

Khruuz spoke loudly. "My people lived before the Thoan! We knew that there were spirits long before the Thoan became aware that we existed!"

Kickaha hoped that the clones did not get so enthusiastic that they made up "facts" that could be exposed as untruths. This game had to be played coolly and close to the chest. When Dingsteth wheeled around to see Khruuz, Kickaha gestured at Ashatelon and Wemathol to say little. Then he stopped. It had occurred to him that Dingsteth's monitor cameras would photograph him.

If the creature did view the films and it had questions about the gestures, it would get some kind of hokey explanation from him.

Wemathol and Ashatelon told the creature that everybody had known for millennia that there was a spiritual world and that ghosts now and then did communicate through dreams. They were, however, more scornful of Dingsteth for its ignorance than Kickaha wished them to be. They could not resist their impulses to insult and demean.

If Dingsteth was affected by them, it did not show it. After turning its back to face Kickaha, it said, "Describe Zazel."

Canny creature! Not so guileless as it seemed.

To put off the answer until he could think of an acceptable one, Kickaha said, "What do you mean? Describe his physical features? His face? His height? The relative proportions of his limbs to his trunk? The color of his hair and eyes? Whether his ears were small or large? How big a nose he had and what its shape was?"

"Yes."

Kickaha breathed in deeply before speaking, hoping to suck in inspiration of mind as well as breath. He spoke loudly so the others could hear him clearly.

"Ah, well, he was shrouded in a mist so I couldn't make out his face clearly. The dead appearing in mists or not clearly to the dreamer is, as I've said before, a common phenomenon. Isn't that right, men?"

"Yes, indeed!"

"No doubt of it! It's been proven!"

"If Houdini were here, he'd tell you himself that it's true!"

"We Khringdiz had the same experiences!"

Kumas rose from his blankets, went across his cage, and screamed, "You're all crazy!" after which he lay down again.

Dingsteth said, "He invalidates your statements."

"Not at all," Red Orc called. "His mind is sliding down into insanity. You will have noticed that he said 'all,' meaning everybody here, you included. You know you're not insane. The rest of us know we're sane. Therefore, his statement is that of a mentally unhinged man and so does not coincide with reality."

"That seems reasonable," Dingsteth said. "I know that I am quite rational."

He spoke to Kickaha, "What did Zazel say?"

"First, he greeted me. He said, 'Niss Zatzel.' "

Wemathol groaned. He thought that the *leblabbiy* Earthman had really goofed up.

" 'Niss Zatzel.' I didn't know what he meant. Then I realized that he was speaking the Thoan of his time. He was saying, 'I am Zazel' in the form of his tongue when he lived. Fortunately, the language has not changed that much. I could understand almost everything he said. When I couldn't, I could figure it out from the context. Also, his words did not come through the mists without some distortion, some muffling, too. Both the appearance of ghosts and their voices come through as if a slightly malfunctioning gate were transmitting them."

"I am pleased to find that out. 'Niss Zatzel.' You are not a

Thoan, hence you would not be likely to know the ancient language."

Kickaha decided to quote Zazel's supposed words indirectly from here on. About all he knew of the archaic Thoan was a few words Anana had told him. He was glad that he remembered some of their conversation, which had taken place long ago.

"What did he say after that?" Dingsteth said.

Kickaha spoke slowly, his thoughts only a few words ahead of his tongue.

"He said he had learned much from the other spirits and from the Supreme Spirit who rules their land. He sees now what errors and mistakes he made while in the land of the living."

Don't get carried away, Kickaha told himself. Make it effective but short. The less I say, the more chance I won't say something that'll betray me.

"To be brief, he told me that he could not get in contact with you except through a human who was open to psychic channels. That one was me. It took him some time and energy to do it since I was emotionally upset about being imprisoned. Finally, last night, he did it in a dream of mine. He told me to tell you that we should be released and treated as guests, though Red Orc is to be watched carefully because he's dangerous. But you are not to give anybody the data on the creation engine. You should destroy it and then let each of us go our own ways."

After a slight pause, Kickaha said, "He also told me, insisted, in fact, that the Horn of Shambarimen, which you took from Red Orc, should be given to me. It is my property, and, as Zazel said, I won't misuse it."

Red Orc's face paled, and it twisted into a silent snarl. But he dared not say anything that would make Dingsteth refuse to release him. On the other hand, Kickaha had to include the Thoan in the people to be freed. If he did not, Red Orc would expose him for the liar he was.

"Zazel ordered that you erase all the data about the engine because it's a great danger to every living thing in every universe. You must do this immediately. And you must make sure the data is not retrievable. By that, he means that none of it is to be left stored in the world-brain. No one'll be able to call it up from the world.

"Then, you will let us out of our cages and permit us to gate out of this world. But Zazel ordered that Red Orc's weapons not be given back to him and that his airboat be stripped of its beamers. We will fly our machines to the departure gate. All of us will leave together and gate through to Red Orc's palace on Earth II."

Red Orc glared. He knew why Kickaha was making these terms.

Kickaha continued, "Zazel did not tell me why he wants us to do that. He must have some reason he didn't care to tell me. But it'll be for the best, I'm sure. The dead know everything."

Dingsteth did not speak for several minutes. Its eyes were as unmoving as those in a statue, though it did blink. It did not shift slightly or twitch minutely as a human would have done in that rigid posture. The caged men, Kumas excepted, did not take their gazes from him.

Kickaha murmured to himself, "Is Dingsteth going to buy it?"

His fabrication would not work on any Thoan or most Earth-people. But the creature was not human, and it had had almost no experience with the supreme prevaricator species, Homo sapiens.

At long last, Dingsteth spoke. "If Zazel ordered it, it will be done. If only I could dream, he might speak to me!"

For a moment, Kickaha felt sorry for it. Maybe it was more human than he had thought. Or maybe it just wanted to be.

They would be released within an hour, and they would be gated to the cave wherein their craft were stored. But it took longer to carry out "Zazel's instructions" than Kickaha had antici-pated. The unforeseen, as so often happened, took place. Khruuz was the first to be gated through to the place where Dingsteth had put the aircraft. Kumas was to follow Khruuz, after which Red Orc would be transmitted to the storage place. Kickaha had requested this gating order because he wanted Red Orc not to be the first in the storage place. No telling what that wily bastard could do if he were alone or had only his clones to deal with. But Khruuz was powerful enough to overcome him if the need arose.

The Khringdiz disappeared from the circle in his cage. Dingsteth had trouble getting Kumas to obey its orders. Kumas, lying on his blankets, turned his back to Dingsteth. Finally, Dingsteth said, "I have means to make you do as I wish. They involve much pain for you."

For a half-minute, Kumas was silent. Then, his face expressionless, his eyes dull, he rose. He shambled to the center of the circle and stood in it. Dingsteth pointed one end of the small instrument in its hand at the circle and pressed a button. Though the radio signal from it started the process, five seconds would pass before the gate was fully activated.

Kumas must have been counting the seconds. Just before he would have vanished, he moved to one side and stuck his right leg beyond the circle.

Then, he was gone. But the leg, spurting blood, remained in the cage. It toppled over immediately.

"Killed himself!" Red Orc shouted. The other humans were silent with shock. Dingsteth may have been, but it did not show it. It said, "Why did he do that?"

"It's as I told you," Kickaha said. "He was crazy, poor bastard."

Dingsteth said, "I do not understand the instability and twisted complexities and frequent malfunctionings of human beings."

"We don't either," Kickaha said.

Dingsteth put off cleaning up the mess until after his "guests" had left his world. Or, perhaps, it was not going to bother with it. It gated the others to the cave in which their aircraft were stored but sent them to a different circle in the cave from the one originally intended. When Kickaha stepped out of his circle, he saw the Thoan's body in a circle nearby. After a glance at it, he was busy getting ready. That did not take much time. When they were all mounted on the seats of their boats, Dingsteth opened a door to the cave by speaking a code word. A section of the wall slid into the recess, and they flew out into a tunnel. Dingsteth had given them directions for getting to the gate that Red Orc had used for entrance to this world. Red Orc rode behind his clones; Khruuz and Kickaha, behind him.

Twenty minutes later, they were at the gate. Kickaha dismounted from his boat and brought out of his backpack a wrist-binding band. Before Red Orc could react, the clones and Khruuz had seized him. He might have gotten away from Ashatelon and Wemathol, but Khruuz was as strong as a bear. Obeying the orders Kickaha had whispered in the hangar-cave, the Khringdiz held the Thoan's arms behind him, and the clones gripped Red Orc's legs. Dingsteth, watching them via the world-brain, must have wondered what was going on. Kickaha quickly secured Red Orc's wrists together at his back.

Exultantly, Kickaha took the Horn from his pack and blew the seven notes. Immediately, a section of the wall shimmered. Red Orc, who had been silent throughout, was hurried by Khruuz into the gate. A minute later, all were in the palace that held Anana. They were busy for a little while defending themselves against the guards, who had attacked them when they saw that their master was a prisoner. That did not take long. A few beamer shots killed some, and the others scattered.

Soon, however, the guards rallied and took up defensive positions. It looked as if the invaders would have to take the place by room-to-room fighting. But Kickaha called for the captain, who replied from behind a barricade of furniture in a hall. After Kickaha, Wemathol, and Ashatelon talked to the captain, they made an agreement. The captain then conferred with his lieutenants and some of the rank and file. The parley took over an hour, but the result was that the guards swore loyalty to Kickaha and the clones. They did not love Red Orc and did not care who paid them, especially since Kickaha had doubled their wages and reduced their working hours.

Kickaha was delighted. "I'm sick of bloodshed. Necessary or unnecessary, it goes hard against my grain. Besides, some of us would've been killed if they'd put up a fierce resistance. One of us might've been me."

Wemathol and Ashatelon did not trust the soldiers. To prevent assassination or mutiny, they took some guards aside. These were promised large sums if they would spy on their fellows and report any likely troublemakers or actual plots. Then the clones, not telling Kickaha what they were doing, approached other guards to keep their eyes on Kickaha's spies. He found out about this when some of the clones' spies informed him of this. They expected a reward for the betrayal, and they got it.

Kickaha then hired other soldiers and some servants to watch the clones. For all he knew, though, the clones had taken into their secret service the same people he employed. These would spy on him. Undoubtedly, Wemathol and Ashatelon also had their own agents to spy on each other.

This made him laugh uproariously. If the process kept up, all of the guards and the servants would be double or triple or even quadruple agents.

After making reasonably sure that the guards would give no immediate trouble, Kickaha visited Anana. She was in the garden and in a lounging chair by the swimming pool, which was large enough to be a small lake. The sun of Earth II, near its zenith, blazed down on her. On a small table by her was a tall glass containing ice cubes and a dark liquid. Though the noise from the dozen or so women attendants in the water was a happy one, she did not look contented. Nor did she smile or ask him to sit down when he reintroduced himself.

"By now," he said, "Wemathol has told you the truth. I sent him ahead of me to explain what's really happened to you because I didn't think you would listen to me at all. But I'm ready to tell you all over again what Red Orc did to you and to add any details Wemathol left out."

Her voice was dull, and she did not look directly at him. "I heard him through to the end, though it cost me much not to scream at him that he was a liar. I don't wish to hear your lies. Now, will you go away and never come back?"

He pulled up a chair and sat down.

"No, I won't. Wemathol told the truth, though, being Thoan, it may have hurt him to do so."

He longed to take her in his arms and kiss her.

She looked at him. "I want to speak to Orc in person. Let him tell me the truth."

"For Elyttria's sake!" he said, speaking more loudly and impatiently than he had intended. "Why bother with that when he'll only lie!"

"I'll know if he's telling the truth or not."

"That's illogical! Irrational!"

He tried to master his anger, born from frustration and despair.

She said coldly, "I do not tolerate a *leblabbiy* speaking to me like that. Even when he has me in his power."

"I . . ."

He closed his mouth. This was going to be very difficult and would require great self-control and delicacy.

"I apologize," he said. "I know the truth, so it's hard for me to see you so deceived. Very well. You may speak to Red Orc face to face."

"You'll be watching us, hearing us?"

"I promise you that no one will be observing you two."

"But you'll be recording us. Then you'll run off the tape and still not be lying to me."

"No. I promise. However . . ."

"What?"

"You won't believe me. But Red Orc might kill you unless you're guarded."

She laughed scornfully. "He? Kill me?"

"Believe me, I know him far better than you do. He could revenge himself on both of us by breaking your neck and depriving me altogether of you."

"I would never have loved you, *leblabbiy*. So how could he deprive you of me?"

"This is taking us in a circle. I'll give you what you want. You'll be in a room with Red Orc, and neither human nor machine will be watching or listening to you two. But there'll be a transparent partition between you and him. I won't take any chances with him. That's my decision, and it's unchangeable."

Khruuz was not human. He could monitor Anana and Red Orc. In a literal sense, no human or machine would observe them. But I can't do that, he thought. I've never lied to her.

For the same reason, I'll also not carry out a plan I had. Putting Wemathol or Ashatelon in their father's place and having one of them pretend to be a repentant and now truthful Red Orc . . . that's out, too. But the temptation is so powerful it hurts me deeply to reject it.

Anana did not seem to be grateful even when he told her that she could take all the time she wanted for the meeting. That turned out to be two hours. When she came out of the room, she was weeping. But, as soon as she saw Kickaha, she managed to make her face expressionless. A Thoan did not show "weak" emotions before a *leblabbiy*. Instead of responding to his questions, she walked swiftly to her room.

Red Orc had been held in the room in which he had talked to

Anana. Kickaha went to it and sat down on the chair she had occupied. That it was still warm made him feel as if he had touched her.

He looked through the transparent metal screen at the Thoan, who met his gaze unflinchingly.

"You have won this round," Kickaha said. "Big deal. You're not going to get out of this alive. Not unless I decide you will. You do have a chance, but I won't lie to you. I find it almost impossible to kill a man in cold blood or to order others to do what I'm not willing to do. Believe me, your clones want to torture you for a long time before killing you. They can't understand why I won't let them do it."

The Thoan was silent for a moment before replying. He said, "I don't understand either. As for escaping from here, you ought not to be so sure. We are alike in many respects, Kickaha, more than you admit, I believe. But that's nothing to waste time with. You've opened a door for me, if I understand your implications. That opening, however, won't be freedom for me. You just will not kill me, but you will keep me prisoner or attempt to do so until I kill myself from frustration and boredom. Correct?"

Kickaha nodded.

"You stupid *leblabbiy!*" the Thoan screamed. His entire skin was suddenly a poisonous red, and his face was knotted with fury. He shook his fist at Kickaha, then he spat. Tiny bubbles quickly gathered at the corners of his mouth, broke, and were replaced by other bubbles. His eyeballs were shot with blood; the arteries on his forehead swelled as if they were cobras puffing up their hoods. And then he began banging his forehead against the screen.

Kickaha had jumped with surprise when Red Orc screamed and had stepped back. But he now went up to the screen to observe the Thoan closely. Blood was running from his forehead and spreading over his face. Blood had smeared the screen. He truly looked red with a capital R. Though the Thoan had earned his title primarily because he had shed so many people's blood, he was also known throughout the many universes for his rages. They did not happen often, because of his glacial self-control. But when they did erupt, they were fearsome to behold.

This, Kickaha thought, was the granddaddy of all furies.

If it was true that the child was the father of the man, ancient hurts were thrusting themselves up from his soul. Though the very long-lived Lords remembered only the most significant events of their remote past, Red Orc had never forgotten his earliest years, his hatred of his father, his deep love for his mother, and his grief when she had been killed. Nor the numerous frustrations and disappointments since then. His many victories had never canceled these.

Watching the Thoan, who was now tearing at his face with his fingernails and still screaming, Kickaha wondered why the Thoan had not tried some system of mental healing. Or perhaps he had, but it had not been successful.

Now Red Orc was rolling over the floor until he banged against a wall, then rolled back until stopped by the opposite wall. He was, however, no longer screaming. Blood from the scratches and gashes on his face, chest, stomach, and legs marked his passage on the floor.

Suddenly, he stopped rotating. He lay on his back, his mouth gaping like a fish out of water. His legs and arms were extended to form a crude X, and he was staring at the ceiling.

Kickaha waited until the Thoan's massive chest was no longer rising and falling so quickly. Then he said, "Are you over your tantrum?"

Though Red Orc did not reply, he did rise to his feet. His face was composed under the blood covering it. After a minute, during which he stared at Kickaha, he spoke calmly.

"I know what you are going to propose. If I am to stay alive, I will have to tell Anana the truth about what I did to her."

Kickaha nodded.

"I need some time to think about it," the Thoan said.

"Okay," Kickaha said. "You have ten seconds."

For a moment, Kickaha thought that Red Orc was going to rocket off in another rage. He had pressed his lips together, and his eyes began looking crazy again. But then he breathed out deeply and smiled.

"I was thinking about a week to make up my mind. Very well. No, I will not tell Anana the truth."

"I didn't think you would," Kickaha said. "However, I have another offer. If you accept it, you'll escape lifelong imprisonment. But the offer depends upon an answer to my question. Did you store Anana's memory? If you did, can you give it back to her?"

19

Red Orc sat still, his eyes focused on a point a few inches from Kickaha's head. That he did not answer at once showed that he was going to be very careful about what he would say.

Kickaha tried to think as the Thoan was thinking. Red Orc knew whether or not he could give Anana's memory back to her. He was wondering if he should lie. If he was able to restore her memory, he would say that he could not do so. Though a no from him would confine him for life in a seemingly escapeproof cell, Kickaha had found a way to get out of Dingsteth's cages. What the *leblabbiy* could do, he, Red Orc, could do.

If he said yes, only he would operate the machine. Anana would be in his power, and he could kill her with a jolt of electricity or whatever else was available. He would not enjoy his revenge long. A few seconds later, he would die.

Finally, he said, "No. I cannot restore her memory. Even if it could be filed, it would take a vast storage space, a capacity that only Zazel's World would have. And I am not certain of that. Destroying is far easier than creating."

"You should know," Kickaha said. "You have taken Anana's memory from her. What's been done to her can be done to you. How would you like to be stripped of your memory?"

The Thoan shuddered slightly.

"I'll see to it that the memory-uncoiler takes you back to when you were only five," Kickaha said. "You were, if my informants are to be believed, a loving person at that age. That way, I don't have to kill you—I hope I don't—and you'll be given a second chance. You'll not be confined to a cell, but you won't be allowed to go out of this palace. Or wherever you're kept. Not until I'm one hundred percent satisfied that you'll stay on the right path, that you're a real pussycat.

"Maybe it'd be better to take you back to the age of three. Or even two. That'd make it easier for us to help you form a different persona or at least reshape you. Your destructive tendencies could be channeled into creative drives. Despite what you said, it's sometimes easier to create than destroy."

"Thousands of years of knowledge and experience lost," Red Orc murmured.

Kickaha had expected that the Thoan would go into another rage. But the first one seemed to have exhausted him.

"It happened to Anana."

The Thoan breathed deeply, looked at the ceiling, then into Kickaha's eyes.

"But you forget something. Only I know how to operate the memory-uncoiler."

"I haven't forgotten," Kickaha said. "You'll be injected with a hypnotic that'll make you answer all questions."

"That won't do anything to me," the Thoan said. He smiled. "I have taught myself certain mental techniques that will automatically block out the effects of any hypnotics available to you."

"I won't hesitate to cause you such pain you'll be happy to tell me much more than I want to know about operating the uncoiler. I've seldom tortured a man before this, only when it was absolutely necessary to save lives. Do you doubt that?"

"You're a man of your word," Red Orc said sarcastically. "But whose life are you saving if you torture me?"

Kickaha grinned. "Yours. However, I don't have to torture you. I have another card up my sleeve. I won't have to hurt you, physically, that is. Khruuz will be able to figure out how to operate the machine."

It was the Thoan's turn to grin. "I anticipated long ago that someone with the Khringdiz's knowledge might be available. The machine will not turn on until it has identified me as the operator. It must read my voice frequencies and pattern of intonation. It also requires my handprint, my eyeprints, my odorprint, and a small patch of my skin so that it may read my DNA. It also must receive a code phrase from me, though you will be able to get that out of me by torture. That will not be necessary. I'll give you the code phrase, much good it will do you."

"And?" Kickaha said.

"Ah! You have anticipated another barrier to operating the machine. You are right in doing that. Certain numerous components of the machine, after a certain delay, will explode unless I am the operator. That will disintegrate the machine and annihilate everything within three hundred feet of the blast and do extensive damage for another three hundred."

"That's a lot of trouble," Kickaha said. "What you did, you set up the self-destruction system to keep your clones from being able to use it, right?"

"Of course, you idiot!"

"This idiot will find a way to fool the machine," Kickaha said. "You're holding back one item of information about how the machine identifies you. It's something that marks you as different from your duplicates. I can get that out of you if you hurt enough. I don't like the idea, but, as I said, I'll use torture. It's a tool that almost always works."

"It would get you what you want. But that information would not aid you one bit. The machine would explode even if you used Ashatelon or Wemathol."

Red Orc paused, then said, "My sons could be the operators if it were not for one insurmountable factor. I may as well tell you what it is since I don't care to be disintegrated, and it is the factor that makes it impossible to use the memory-stripping on me. Not even I can cancel it. If I am the person whose memory is to be stripped, the machine will blow up. It will know that I am the subject because it can detect my age. The clones are much younger than I. Therefore, the machine will be triggered when it reads the age difference."

"How can that be?" Kickaha said. "Your body cells are replaced every seven years. It won't be any older, within a seven-year limit, than your clones' bodies."

"True. But the machine will scan my memory before it starts the stripping process. That will determine that I am indeed the original person, because my clones have shorter memories. There is nothing that I can do about that. I cannot remove that circuit without causing the machine to explode. That is a command that, now that I've installed it, cannot be canceled."

Red Orc stood up. "I'm tired of this. Gate me back to my cell."

Kickaha also rose from his chair. "You're leaving when I'm having so much fun?"

Red Orc was now standing inside the circle on the floor, waiting to be transmitted to his cell. He called out, "Take my advice, Kickaha! Watch Khruuz! Do not trust him!"

As Kickaha left the room, he admitted to himself that he was stymied. The situation was a Mexican standoff. Red Orc was suicidally stubborn. Though he'd been offered a deal far better than he deserved, he'd rather die than lose his memory and, thus, his precious identity.

Kickaha went to the control room, a huge chamber with a very deep carpet on which were various mathematical formulae. The Khringdiz was sitting on a chair before a panel with many displays and controls. He wheeled his seat around and looked up at

Kickaha. "It seems that you must either kill him or imprison him until he dies."

"Keeping him locked up is a bad idea. Sometime during the thousands of years he may yet live, he'd find a way to escape. I hate to think of him on the loose again."

"My advice is to end his misery."

"Misery?"

"Yes. Sometimes, so I've been told, he is quite calm, at one with himself because he feels superior to all other humans. Then, he is even kind to people. He believes that he is truly a god. But this feeling only lasts a certain time. He tortures himself because he cannot make himself peaceful and serene. He cannot get people to love him, though this feeling largely comes from the unconscious, and he is not aware of it. By love, I don't mean sexual love—that is, lust. During the thousands of years he has lived, he has not found a way to be at peace with himself or with others. He was driven to madness by others because he drove them to hate him.

"Now, he is given the opportunity to erase that madness, to start over again. But, despite his misery and suffering, he loves his madness. He cannot give it up. He thinks of himself as a very strong person, which he is in many respects. Yet, he is also what he despises most, a weakling."

Kickaha laughed loudly, then said, "Thank you, Dr. Freud!"

"Who?"

"Never mind. But, though nonhuman, you certainly seem to know much about the human psyche."

"I'm convinced that there is not a significant basic degree of difference between any two sapient species or among the members of the same species."

"You may be right. Anyway, I gave Red Orc a most generous offer, considering what he's done. He isn't going to accept it. That's that."

Khruuz rolled his huge eyes upward. Kickaha did not know

what that meant. Disgust? Wonder at the craziness of human beings?

The Khringdiz said, "Red Orc was trying to make you suspicious of me when he told you to watch me. I hope that you dismissed his warning for what it is, a lie."

"Oh, sure. I know what he's doing," Kickaha said. "He's always in there pitching."

Damn Red Orc! he thought. He's brought up from the deep of my mind what's been lurking down there. I knew it was there—I'm never entirely without suspicion—but I just had no valid reason at all to suspect Khruuz of evil intentions. I don't have any now. I should rid my mind of Red Orc's warning—though, come to think of it, Manathu Vorcyon did say that I might trust the Khringdiz too much. But she admitted that she didn't have any basis for her remark. Except that you shouldn't trust anybody unless they'd been through the fires with you and maybe not even then.

Usually, I breathe in suspicion with the air. But Khruuz had such impressive credentials for hating the Lords. I don't doubt that he has. But who else does he hate? All humans? Could he be as crazed as Red Orc but have much better control at concealing his feelings? I certainly can't accuse Khruuz. No basis for doing that.

But it's possible he's up to something I won't like at all. How do I determine what he really thinks and feels? I could lock him up, keep him out of the way. But I need him badly, and I'd be unfair and unjust if I imprisoned him without good reason.

Ah! Idea! Ask him to submit to a lie detector! No. He might be able to fool the machine or any truth drugs through mental techniques. If Red Orc can do that, Khruuz probably can do it. Anyway, his metabolism and neural reactions probably differ from those of humans. The machine or the drugs wouldn't work as they do with us. If I ask him to volunteer, I'll mightily offend him. I just can't do that. Or should I do it anyway?

He looked at the Khringdiz and wondered what was going on in that grasshopper head.

Khruuz said, "Do you plan to execute Red Orc soon?"

"I haven't made up my mind. He should be killed. But I hate doing it—that's my weakness—and I'd have to do it personally, press the button to flood his cell with gas or whatever. I won't delegate it to someone else. That's a coward's way."

"I do not see that it is," Khruuz said. "Do you yourself kill the animal that others serve you on the table?"

"I usually kill my own meat. But you have a point. Not much of one, though. Red Orc is not an animal despite what many say about him. And despite the fact that he intended to kill me and then eat me as if I were an animal."

"I hope you soon resolve your dilemma," the Khringdiz said. "Meanwhile, I have been thinking that I should return to my world and stay there for a while."

Red Orc's warning was a hand plucking at his mind as if it were made of harp strings. The music—discord, rather—was high notes of suspicion. Damn Red Orc again! But he said calmly, "Why?"

"As you know, I've been trying to get through Red Orc's access codes here to enter various sections of the computer. His data banks may have the information we need to make another memory-uncoiling machine and to operate it. If so, we can strip him of his memory to any age we select, and thus avoid the unpleasantness of executing him. But there's another far more compelling reason. He may be lying when he says that he has not stored that part of Anana's memory that he took from her. It may be in the bank. If it is, we can give her memory back to her."

Kickaha was so excited that all thoughts of doubt about the Khringdiz scattered like a flock of birds under gunfire. After all, what evidence did he have that Khruuz was plotting something sinister? Not a bit. The Khringdiz had been invaluable in the conflict with Red Orc. Moreover, he was a likable person despite his monstrous features.

"Do you really think so?" he said.

"It is possible. We cannot afford to ignore anything no matter how difficult it may be to obtain it. It is well worth the time and the effort."

"I could kiss you!" Kickaha cried.

"You may do so if it pleases you."

"I should have said I feel like kissing you," Kickaha said. "I was speaking emotionally, not literally."

"But I need to go to my planet," the Khringdiz said. "I have an enormous amount of data stored there, data inherited from my ancestors and data stolen or taken from the Thoan. There is much there of which I am not aware. It's possible that I might not only find the means there to crack Red Orc's codes, but find data on building memory-uncoiling machines. Who knows?

"Also, our friend, Eric Clifton, must be very lonely. I will transmit him to here so that he will have human companionship."

"Oh, man!" Kickaha said.

"What?" Khruuz said.

"Nothing."

"I've noticed that, when you humans say 'nothing' in the context of your conversation, you mean 'something.'"

"Very observant of you," Kickaha said. "But, in this case, I was struck by a completely irrelevant thought. Something I'd forgotten to do, that's all."

His suspicions of the Khringdiz had been like a bag of garbage he'd thrown from the beach into the ocean. It had drifted off, almost out of sight, and then a tidal wave had picked the bag up and hurled it back against him, knocking him off his feet.

He said, "That's damned decent of you, considering Clifton's feelings. But I'd rather he stayed with you for a while."

"Why?"

Kickaha was taken aback. Mentally, he stuttered. But a second later, he said, "Clifton can't help you with anything technological, I think. But he can be helpful in other matters. As for companionship, you need that, too. And Clifton likes you. Also, I'm sure there are things you could tell him, enlighten him. He's intelligent and eager to learn."

Weak, weak! he thought. But it's the best I could come up with. I hope what I said doesn't make Khruuz suspect that I suspect him.

"Very well," Khruuz said. "He stays. I like Clifton, and he does provide companionship. But he must want to be with his own kind, and I offered to send him here because of that."

He paused, then said, "I thank you for considering my feelings of loneliness."

"You're welcome," Kickaha said. The Khringdiz certainly did not behave as if he wished to get Clifton out of the way. If Khruuz was up to no good—but why should he be?—he could easily kill Clifton, who would not be on his guard.

"I would like to return immediately so that I may get started quickly on the research," the Khringdiz said. "I'm eager to grapple with the problem."

He punched a button on the control panel and rose from the chair. Suddenly, the room seemed to crackle with emotional static. Khruuz was smiling, but that did not make his face seem less sinister. It looked that way no matter what his expression. The tendril on the end of his tongue was writhing; his stance was subtly changed. Like a lion who's been drowsing but has just smelled a strange lion, Kickaha thought. He's ready to defend his territory. Ready to charge the intruder.

But the Khringdiz spoke calmly. "You are making much from nothing. I sense that you have unaccountably become hostile. I cannot as yet easily read subtle human expressions or understand certain inflections of voice. But it seems to me that you—what should I say?—have become suspicious of me. Am I wrong?"

"You're right," Kickaha said as he withdrew his beamer from its holster and pointed it at Khruuz. "I may be completely wrong to doubt your intentions. If I am, I'll apologize. Later, that is. But the stakes are too high for me to take a chance with you. For now, you'll be locked up until I determine if I'm right or wrong. I'll explain later."

He waved the beamer. "You know where the gates to the special cells are. I'll be right behind you. Don't try anything. If you do, I'll know you're guilty."

"Of what?" Khruuz said.

"Get going."

They walked toward the door. Khruuz, instead of making a beeline toward it, veered a few feet to the left. Kickaha said, loudly, "Stop!"

The Khringdiz took two more steps, halted, and began to turn. Kickaha had his finger on the trigger. He had advanced the power dial on the side of the beamer to a setting for a more powerful stun charge. Khruuz, he calculated, would have more resistance to the normal charge than most human beings.

Khruuz was saying something in his native language while he turned around to face Kickaha. Then, he was gone.

For several seconds, Kickaha was too surprised to react. When he recovered, he smacked his forehead. "Code word! That's what he was saying! For God's sake! He'd set it up! Slick! They don't fool me often, but . . . !"

The Khringdiz had formed a gate inside a loop of the symbol for eternity, the figure eight, one of the designs on the carpet. Standing in the area of the gate, he had uttered the code word, and was now, most probably, in the underground fortress in his planet.

Clifton was doomed. Khruuz would kill him at once.

Kickaha strode to the control panel and called for an all-stations attention. Then he ordered Wemathol and Ashatelon to report to the nearest screen. A minute later, both their faces were in the panel screens. He told them what had happened. Both looked alarmed. Wemathol, distinguishable from his brother by his green headband, said, "What do you think he's planning to do?"

"I don't know," Kickaha said. "Listen! He may pop back through the gate or another gate at any moment. Can either of you set up a one-way exit gate covering the floor of this room? That'll stop him if he tries to re-enter."

Wemathol said, "We both know how to do that."

"Then get up here on the run, and do it!"

Ashatelon, wearing a crimson headband and crimson boots, was the first to appear. Several seconds later, his brother entered the room. Ashatelon, breathing hard, said, "The Khringdiz could have set up gates anywhere in the palace."

"I know that, but we can't cover the floors in every room! Can we?"

"Yes, but it would take time. If we did that, then the gates we use now would be closed. You could not transport food to my father, for instance. Not that I would mind if he starved to death."

"Besides," Wemathol said, "Khruuz could have set up gates in the walls. Or even in the ceilings."

"Just cover the floor of this room," Kickaha said. "Get to work, you two."

They seated themselves before control panels. Kickaha called the captain of the guards and told him some of the situation. "Put your men on a twenty-four-hour roving patrol. Work in three shifts. If the Khringdiz shows, shoot him."

He doubted that Khruuz would come back soon. He suspected that the scaly man would be returning to Zazel's World or trying to do so. Khruuz wanted the data for the creation-destruction engine as fiercely as Red Orc desired it. Or so it seemed reasonable to assume. Just why, Kickaha did not know. But he would not put it past the Khringdiz to use it to destroy all but one universe.

Doing that would make him the most solitary of all sentient

beings. Unless he had means for cloning himself and changing some of the duplicates into females. He might even have the data in his files for altering the genes of the clones. That would make a genetically varied people.

No use speculating. Get done at once what needs to be done.

He used a recorder to send a message to Manathu Vorcyon and had it taken by a runner to the gate that channeled to her world. She might come up with an idea for invading Khruuz's World. Kickaha did not like sitting around waiting for the Khringdiz to attack. Attack as soon as possible was his motto. By the time that the messager reported that the recorder had been placed in the gate, the clones had finished setting up the one-way exit gate over the control-room floor.

Wemathol said, "It does not interfere with the operation of the controls, however."

When Kickaha was convinced that there was nothing more to do, for the moment, anyway, he went to Anana's suite of rooms. The entrance to this was a door with a huge monitor screen on it. He called to her. The screen became alive. He saw her walking back and forth just beyond the door. A caged tigress, he thought, and even more beautiful. She hates me and would kill me if she could. That was a thought to choke his mind. Whoever would have thought that his beloved would one day tear him to bloody rags of flesh if she had the opportunity?

He asked for permission to enter. She stopped pacing and whirled around, her face twisted with anger.

"Why do you keep up this charade of politeness and of caring for me? You're the master here! You can do anything you wish to do!"

"True," he said. "But I would never harm you. However, I can't trust you—as yet. I'll be gone for a while. I don't have time to explain the situation to you, and it wouldn't change your mind about me, anyway. I'm putting you in a special suite for your own safety and for mine. Someday, maybe, you'll understand why I'm doing this. That's all."

He had intended to enter her suite and talk face to face with her. But he had changed his mind. He went to another screen section on the wall and called Wemathol and Ashatelon.

"New plan," he said. "Here's what you must do at once. Gate Anana into Cell Suite Three. Pick four trusted women servants to gate food and water and other necessary supplies to her and Red Orc while we're gone. Send all but fifty guards off on a paid vacation. Those left—and they must be the most trusted men you know—will continue the twenty-four-hour patrol. After that's done, close up the palace, bar all gates, lock all lower-story windows. I give you two hours and thirty minutes to do the job. Then report to me. Be ready to go to Zazel's World."

The clones started to protest that there was not enough time to carry out his orders. He said, "Do it!" and turned the screen off. Ten minutes later, he had sent another message to Manathu Vorcyon. This brought her up to date on the situation. Then he verified that Anana had been transmitted to the escapeproof suite. At the time he had set for them, Wemathol and Ashatelon appeared on their one-man airboats.

Kickaha said, "Let's go." He lifted the Horn to his lips.

20

*T*hey had expected a world made alive again by Dingsteth. But it was as dead as when they had left it. However, it was not quite as it had been during their previous visit. And it looked as if someone had blasted through a section of a wall. The new hole led to a very large cave containing live plants and animals and an area with chairs, tables, dishes, cutlery, a kitchen, and a bathroom. Dingsteth must have lived here, though there were no signs of struggle.

"Khruuz has been here," Kickaha said, "and he captured Dingsteth despite its traps. Nothing subtle or easy, just powered his way through them, destroying them. So, we go to Khruuz's World."

"Elyttria!" Wemathol said. "How do we get into his world? And would it be wise to go there?"

"No," Kickaha said. "Not if you want to live forever. We'll have no trouble, though, transmitting ourselves there. The Great Mother is helping us. She told me some time ago how we could do it. The way is now set up."

They flew back to the final X marking the gate through which they had entered. Here, Kickaha blew three times on the Horn. Manathu Vorcyon had also arranged that blowing it thrice at this point would alert her to open the passage to Khruuz's World.

Kickaha did not know how she did this, but the important thing was that she could. She was now willing to use the knowledge she had kept to herself for so many millennia.

After warning them, though unnecessarily, to be alert, Kickaha led them into the gate. They came into the many-tunneled place a long way from Khruuz's headquarters. Using the detector Manathu Vorcyon had gated to him days ago, Kickaha saw where the cluster of gates was located and rode off in that direction. Though the Khringdiz must have assumed that he had closed all the gates, they still glowed faintly in the detector and so could be found. The Great Mother had indeed provided well for them.

They had expected traps in the form of explosions, deadly gases, or gates switching them into a circuit or to a desolate universe. But they encountered none. Khruuz seemed to have assumed that no one could gate to his complex unless he permitted them entrance. Finally, after searching the scaly man's living quarters, which were empty, they got to the entrance to Khringdiz's control chamber.

Kickaha was the first to go into it. He halted; the others crowded around him. They stared at the smears of dried blood on the floor directly before the main control panel. Then Kickaha saw the body on the floor fifty feet from the stains. Clifton was lying there on his face. His outstretched hand still gripped a beamer. He had not been taken completely by surprise by Khruuz.

Kickaha strode to the body, noting on the way that there were no bloodstains between the smears and Clifton. Kneeling down, he put his finger on Clifton's neck. No pulse. He had not expected one. Clifton was wearing only a kilt, sandals, and a belt with a holster. On the back of the left arm was a cauterized hole, and close to the lower spine was a similar hole. He had been shot twice with a narrow beamer ray.

He turned the Englishman over. The two wounds in the front matched those in the back. Rising, he said, "Khruuz must've been in a hell of a hurry. He didn't even take the time to get rid of the body."

He ordered Wemathol to take the corpse into the hall some distance away and disintegrate it with the big beamers on his airboat. The Thoan put on his gas mask and began dragging the body from the room. Kickaha went back to the smears before the main control panel. He looked at them more closely.

"Clifton did get off some shots before he died. It looks as if Khruuz was wounded. But not bad enough to lay him low."

Again, he got down on one knee, and he examined one edge of the stains. He said, "Ah! Here's the imprint of the front part of a foot! It's not human! And it's not Khruuz's! Has to be Dingsteth's! He was standing close to Khruuz when the beamer fight was going on!"

Ashatelon got close to the half-print. When he arose, he said, "You're right. But was Dingsteth a prisoner, or did he come with Khruuz voluntarily?"

"I doubt very much he came willingly."

Ashatelon said, "Why would Khruuz take Dingsteth with him? If Dingsteth obeyed your orders, it would have erased all data about the creation engine."

He stopped, then said, "Oh, I see! I think I do, anyway. The data in the computer could be erased, Dingsteth having followed your orders. But it could be in Dingsteth's brain!"

Kickaha nodded. "I goofed up. I should have thought of that Dingsteth wouldn't have told me the data was in his mind unless I'd asked him if it was. Khruuz was smarter. He may even have thought of it when we were there. But he kept quiet about it for his own reasons."

The clone said, "He's hellbent for revenge. He's going to do what Red Orc meant to do! Destroy all universes except one!"

Kickaha said, "We don't know that for sure. But you're probably right. We're going back to the palace but not until we see Manathu

Vorcyon. Bad as the situation is, she may want to join us. I think Khruuz is already in the palace. He'll expect us to be treading on his heels. We may have hurried him so much he didn't take time to prepare for us. Let's hope so. In any case, we're going to take a detour, see Manathu Vorcyon first."

If the giantess was surprised by their sudden appearance, she did not show it. As soon as she had been informed of the latest events, she said, "I'm going with you. I have not left my world for many thousands of years, but I have not forgotten how to fight. It will take a few hours to get ready. Meanwhile, eat. You need the rest and the food."

What she did during this time, the others did not know. But when she appeared before them, she wore a suit like a firefighter's, a transparent globe over her head, gloves, and an oxygen tank on her back. A harness over her torso held at least a dozen weapons, some of them unfamiliar to Kickaha. Behind her were four servants carrying similar outfits. These were given to the men.

She is indeed the goddess of war, he thought. But Athena never looked so formidable. And it was at once evident that she had assumed command. Though Kickaha did not like that, he knew that it was best for all of them. Her millennia of experience made him look like, pun intended, a babe in arms.

"Follow me," she said, her voice coming through a speaker in her helmet. "We're going to a place where only I have been. You may put on the suits when we get to it."

They went up the winding staircase in the tree to her room. She spoke a code word. The glindglassa, the huge mirror, shimmered. Kickaha, the first in line behind her, stepped through it into a gigantic room with many doors. He did not have time to marvel at its many objets d'art, some of which must have been twenty thousand years old, nor at the stuffed bodies of men and women standing here and there, all arranged in various postures, their faces expressing a range of emotions. These, he supposed, were enemies she had killed during the ancient Time of Troubles. Unique mementos—and dust-free, too.

She led them from the room into a hallway at least four hundred feet long. Near its end, she turned into a fifty-foot-high entrance. Beyond it was a huge hangar housing scores of aircraft. At her orders, the four donned the clothes. The holsters on their harness, however, contained only the familiar: beamers, hand grenades, knives, and tasers. She told them how to snap the globes into the metal rings at the top of the suits and secure them with a tiny snap lock on the rim. Inside the globes were transmitters to bring in outside noises. She also gave them instructions on the operation of the oxygen apparatus. After their helmets were on, they heard her voice only through a transmitter-receiver attached to the globes.

A minute later, they got into a transparent-hulled vessel shaped like a blimp envelope minus the rudder and fins, but with top and bottom turrets. She showed them their posts and how to operate the big rotatable beamers spaced around the ship to be able to fire from every side of the craft. Two of them were instructed briefly on the operation of the retractable turrets. She pointed out the six foldable single-pilot craft secured along the hull.

"They operate just like those you rode into Zazel's World. Be ready to use them."

She got into the pilot's seat and instructed them in the use of the simple controls. After that, the others strapped themselves into the swivel chairs at the beamer stations. Wemathol occupied the bottom turret; Ashatelon, the top turret. Kickaha was the rear gunner. He preferred to be the pilot or, if he could not be that, the top turret operator. But the Great Mother had ordered otherwise. Like the rest of the crew, he took ten minutes familiarizing himself with the turret and beamer controls. Then Manathu Vorcyon lifted the ship from its landing supports and drove it slowly into the wall at the back of the hangar. The gate, unlike so many, did not display a shimmering as the vessel went through it.

For a moment, they were at an altitude estimated by Kickaha to be five thousand feet. The sun was bright, the blue sky was clear, and the land beneath was forest-covered. Whether or not they were still in Manathu Vorcyon's world he did not know. Then, they were suddenly surrounded by water and a feeble light from above. A minute later, they were again flying, this time in a moonless night.

The Grandmother of All certainly made it difficult for an enemy to track her through the gates.

Kickaha recognized the constellations. He had seen them every night while in Red Orc's stronghold. They were flying above Earth II. Their attack would be from outside the palace instead of inside it.

Manathu Vorcyon's voice came through his helmet receiver.

"In two minutes, we'll be within the palace! If you can take Khruuz alive, do it! He is the repository of knowledge that we do not possess. And he is the last living person of his species. He may plan to destroy all living creatures in all the universes. He cannot be condemned for his madness, though he cannot be excused.

"We Thoan cannot repay him for what we did to his people. Nevertheless, we cannot allow empathy or guilt to interfere in this. If you have to do it, kill him!"

A minute passed. She cried out, "We're going in!"

The night sky vanished. They were inside the well-lit and enormous dining hall for the guards and servants. Approximately forty corpses of guards, severed by beamer rays, were scattered through the hall. Three of the four maids left in charge of gating food to Red Orc and Anana were dead on the floor near a table. The overturned chairs and the half-eaten food on the dishes showed that they had been interrupted in their meal. The ten

remaining guards had either fled the palace or were dead somewhere in it or, perhaps, hiding.

By now, Kickaha thought, the alarms Khruuz must have set up
will have told him an intruder is in the palace.

The doorway into the dining hall was just large enough for the
vessel, despite its top and bottom turrets, to scrape through. Like
the dining room walls, ceiling, and floor, the hallway was blackened from beamer rays. The ship emerged into another huge room.
It was also blackened. The fried or severed bodies of five guards
sprawled there.

Manathu Vorcyon's voice came to Kickaha. "The fourth maid
was probably kept alive so that Khruuz could question her. He
would want from her the code words allowing him to gate through
whatever he wishes to send to Red Orc's and Anana's quarters."

Kickaha gritted his teeth. The scaly man could send explosives
or poisonous gas through the small food gates. Given enough
time, Khruuz might be able to figure out how to expand the food
gates to a size large enough to gate a person in or out. That is, he
might if he wanted them in his presence for some reason.

Sweat poured over him when he envisioned the scenario. He
groaned softly. A high imagination was both a blessing and a
curse.

". . . might have done that before he resumed his interrogation
of Dingsteth," Manathu Vorcyon said. "He may have the engine
data by now, or he may still be trying to get it out of Dingsteth.
That depends on how long he has been here, and what the situation is."

The ship squeezed through another hall. The scars and the
broken-off parts of the walls and ceiling showed that Khruuz had
entered the palace in a craft similar in size to theirs. But they were
quickly in another wide, long, and high room. This was for receiv-
ing many guests, even though Red Orc never gave parties. In its
center, sitting unoccupied and unlit, was a ship much like Manathu

Vorcyon's. But its hull was rounded fore and aft, and its bottom was flat.

"Khruuz has gone ahead on foot, because the hallways are too narrow for his ship unless he blasted his way through them," the giantess said.

Her vessel settled down. The bottom turret withdrew into the hull while Wemathol scrambled out of it. When the ship was resting on the floor just behind the scaly man's, she said, "Get out the fliers."

While the men were unfolding the aircraft outside the hull, she investigated Khruuz's vessel. It did not take her long. When she returned, she said, "Its door seems to be locked. Here is my plan. We go in two parties to make scouting forays. Kickaha, you and Ashatelon will go together down the nearest hall. Wemathol, you and I will go into the far hallway. That leads to the control room if what you told me about the layout, Kickaha, is correct. Report at once if you need help."

She told them the code words for unlocking the two doors of her craft and for turning the power on in the big vessel. Anybody who had to run for it would return to it and use it as the situation required. They would have no trouble operating it. The controls were clearly marked.

As Kickaha rode off with Ashatelon's machine by his side, he said, "You know, Khruuz may have already flown the coop. If he did, he probably left a bomb strong enough to blow this building to bits."

"You're the most encouraging man I've ever met," the Thoan replied. "Why don't you keep all that cheer to yourself?"

Kickaha laughed, though not as enthusiastically as he usually did.

In twenty minutes of cursory search, they had been in every room and corridor on the first floor in the eastern half of the palace. Kickaha reported their findings. Manathu Vorcyon's voice quickly followed his. She and Wemathol were in the second story and outside the door to the control room.

"We've found the fourth maid. She is lying in the hallway. Her body is covered with small burns, her eyes are burned out, and her head is sliced off. Evidently, she had to be tortured before she would tell him what he wanted to know. A very brave woman, though it was foolish of her not to reveal her secrets. She could have spared herself all the pain."

She paused, then said, "All of you come up here. I'll wait for you before I enter the control room."

When Kickaha and his partner got there, they found that Manathu Vorcyon's beamers had cut the door away from the wall. It was lying in the hall. She was now carving out a large circular area in the wall thirty feet from the doorway. It was large enough to admit her and the airboat.

"Kickaha and Ashatelon, make another entrance on the other side of the door at the same distance from it as this one."

While they were doing that with the large beamers of their vehicles, they heard the other section fall crashing into the room. Shortly thereafter, Kickaha rammed his flier into the section he and the clone had cut out. The impact would have knocked him off his seat if he had not been belted to it. The section fell inward and crashed onto the floor.

He looked through it, wary of a beamer ray or a grenade. The huge room contained many control screens and panels, but it also had many machines, their purpose unknown to him. He reported that he could see part of the room. No one was in his view, but he'd be happy to stick his head through the hole to see all of the room. He was relieved, however, when Manathu Vorcyon forbade that. Did he want his head sliced off just to show how brave he was?

She continued, "The part of the room I can see seems to be unoccupied. Nor do my sensors indicate any body heat in there.

Nevertheless, he may be shielded by something—if, that is, he is indeed in there. When I give the signal, we'll all go in at the same time. As I said, I prefer that we just wound him, but that will probably be impossible."

She held her hand up. Then she shouted, "Go!"

Kickaha pressed down on the acceleration pedal of his craft. It shot through the hole so swiftly that he was pressed back against the upright support behind him. Just as he entered the room, he raised the airboat so that it lifted in a tight curve to his right. His head almost touched the ceiling, which was forty feet above the floor. He straightened out the machine as his retrofield fired. It slowed down so abruptly that he was pushed forward against the restraining belt.

Ashatelon's vehicle, which had curved to the left, stopped in front of Kickaha's. It was so close to his that the cone noses almost touched. Ashatelon's flight path was supposed to end at a level lower than his partner's, but he had miscalculated. No time for reproaches. Kickaha was too busy looking around below him for Khruuz. He did not see him.

He grunted when he saw Dingsteth stretched out face down behind a massive machine set out a few feet from the back wall. Its hands were tied together behind its back. A trail of blood in front of the machine led around it to Dingsteth.

Khruuz must have walked out of the room before his pursuers got there or he had gated out of it. The latter, probably. His enemies had interrupted him just as he had shot Dingsteth. Since the Khringdiz did not have time to finish it off, he had fled through a gate or down the hallway.

Kickaha, along with the others, rode down to the console behind which Dingsteth lay, landed, and got off his craft. Manathu Vorcyon ordered Wemathol to stand guard by the doorway. She did not want Khruuz to surprise them by doubling back from a gate. Then she strode around the console. The others crowded behind her. Kickaha was turning Dingsteth over on its back.

He looked up as she stopped by him. "Beamed through a shoulder and a leg," he said. "His pulse is weak."

The giantess said, "Khruuz has not been gone long. Dingsteth's blood is fresh."

Kickaha started to stand up. A strange disorienting feeling passed through him. He seemed to be floating. It was as if he were in a very swiftly descending elevator. When he straightened up, he looked up through the giantess's helmet at her face, twisted with alarm. She opened her mouth. Before she could say anything, a great noise stopped her.

Then the floor came up at him. He struck it very hard, and it buckled and broke open against his fallen body. He was vaguely aware that the console was skittering over the floor, hurling aside Ashatelon, who had been standing at its corner. Something hit him hard in the back, and he lost consciousness. The last things he heard were a deep rumbling, a crashing like an avalanche, and his own feeble voice crying out.

21

*P*ain awoke him. His head, nose, neck, lower back, and right elbow hurt. His legs were numb from his hips downward. But they were not so deadened that he could not feel the heaviness pressing them down. All he could see through the helmet, which was covered with a very thin layer of white dust, was the tiled floor. A large crack in it was just below him. His nose was flattened against the front of his globed helmet. When he licked his lips, he tasted blood.

The room was silent except for a single muffled groan from somewhere. He called out. Silence answered him.

He tried to roll over, but his legs were pressed down against the floor. While struggling to pull himself free, he saw green boots sticking out from a pile of cement blocks mixed with fragments of various materials. They were lightly covered by the plaster dust covering everything in the room. But parts of the boots were not so veiled that he could not see that they were green. Ashatelon was the only one wearing green footwear.

When he lowered his head and turned it to his right, his vision was blocked by a metal ceiling beam an inch from his helmet. Torn loose from its wall support, the beam had probably struck one side of his curved helmet. The impact had hurled him to one side so that his shoulder had just missed being crushed by the beam.

He strove to drag himself forward to escape whatever it was that felt like a Titan's thumbs pressing down on his legs. Not until he was breathing very hard and was exhausted did he stop. At least, he had managed to move forward several inches. Or was that wishful thinking?

After lying still a few minutes, he began struggling again. He quit that when he suddenly saw the huge, dusty, light-blue boots of Manathu Vorcyon before him. Her voice filled his helmet.

"Lie still, Kickaha. I'll try to lift this beam from your legs."

The boots disappeared. Presently, after much grunting and many expletives, she said, panting, "I cannot do it. I will get my boat, if I can find it in this mess and use it to haul up the beam. There is a rope in the supply bag on the boat."

While she was gone, Wemathol came to Kickaha. He croaked when he spoke. "She told me to dig the debris from around the beam. Just lie still, Kickaha. You cannot do anything until she gets back."

"As if I didn't know that," Kickaha muttered. He longed for a tall glass of iced water.

He heard scraping sounds and a loud panting for some time. Then Wemathol said, "There is a chance your legs might not be crushed. They were buried in debris before the beam fell on top of the pile."

"I can feel something now," Kickaha said. "The numbness is going away."

The giantess came on an airboat. She had had to tear away a mass of debris before she could uproot it. It was not hers, but it was the only one she could find. She helped the clone dig out the debris on top of and around the massive beam. Then she got the rope through the space beneath it. Within a few minutes, it was lifted up far enough for Wemathol to drag Kickaha out from under it. She landed the boat and got off it to examine Kickaha.

His legs would not yet obey him. He sat, leaning against the pile of debris, while Manathu Vorcyon felt his legs through the cloth. She reported that they did not seem to be broken, but she would have to examine them after his clothes were off. Then she said, "Ashatelon is dead."

"I'm surprised he is. He seemed to be a survivor."

"Time makes sure that nobody is."

Kickaha looked up at what was left of the ceiling. Only its outer part was left, but the collapsed story above that had plugged up the hole. Parts of it looked as if they would soon fall through. Moreover, the broken wall of this room had spilled out into the hallway. While he was looking at the damage, the building shifted slightly, and the other walls became even more cracked. The far end of the ceiling collapsed with a roar and a cloud of white plaster dust, plunging into the room and forming a great mound that reached up through the gaping hole.

He said, "Maybe we should get out of here."

Before she could reply, Wemathol came into the room after exploring the hallway.

"We're not on Earth II!"

Kickaha and the giantess spoke as if they were one person. "What? How do you know?"

"I could see the sky through a small opening in a part of the hallway ceiling. A stone pillar must have fallen from the palace roof and pierced through all the floors of the rooms above. There is not much of the sky to see, but it is enough. It is green."

Kickaha said, "That means . . ."

"It means," the Great Mother said, "that Khruuz wrapped up the entire palace, perhaps some of the surrounding grounds, in a gate and transported it to this universe. That took great power. It would also take some time to be arranged. He must have set it up before he came to this room with Dingsteth. When the palace came through the gate, it was up in the air, by accident or design, and it fell. It could not have been very high above the surface or we would be dead."

"Just what I was going to say," Kickaha said. He looked around. "Where's Dingsteth?"

"It's either buried under a pile or it woke up before we did and walked off. It may have been in a daze. But I would assume that, if it did wander away, it will not get far because of its wounds."

"It was half flesh and half electronic circuits," Kickaha said. "Its recovery powers must be greater than ours. Is there a trail of blood leading out of the room?"

"No," she said. "But Dingsteth was next to you when the palace collapsed. It should have been hit by the same beam that came close to smashing you."

"Or it's seeking Khruuz so it can get revenge," Wemathol said.

"With its hands bound behind its back?" the giantess said.

Kickaha cried, "Anana!" He tried to get up, but his legs were still too weak. At least they were showing signs of getting their strength back.

The woman and the clone looked at each other but said nothing. They knew what Kickaha was envisioning: Anana in a suite of rooms inside the building but sealed off from the rest of it. The only access was through a gate. But the wall containing the gate activator could be buried under rubble.

Red Orc would be in a similar situation. Kickaha was not worried about him.

Manathu Vorcyon, however, was more concerned than he about the Thoan. She said, "It is possible that the collapse might not have buried them. It could have opened a way for Anana, and Red Orc, too, to get out of their rooms."

"Not very likely," Wemathol said.

"Anything is possible. But we cannot take a chance. We have to locate Khruuz and also determine if Red Orc did get away."

"Aren't you going to look for Anana?" Kickaha said.

"Later," Manathu Vorcyon said. "Wemathol, you come with me. I am sorry, Kickaha, but we cannot wait for you to recover. Khruuz would not have stayed inside the palace when he gated it to this place. He would have taken another gate to it after it was transported. He would not care to be in the palace when it was transmitted to here, wherever this is. It is certain that he'll be looking for us. I am surprised that he has not come back to this room by now."

"He's somewhere around here, waiting to ambush us," Wemathol said. He looked around nervously.

The Great Mother decided that they should remove their tanks, backpacks, helmets, and suits.

"They slow us down, and I doubt we have to guard against poison gas," she said. When she and the clone had stripped down, they put on their weapons belts. Then they removed Kickaha's suit and helped him strap on his belt. In addition to his weapons, the Horn of Shambarimen was attached to the belt.

Wemathol removed the radio sets, which were attached by suction discs to the interior of the globed helmets. The three stuck these on their wrists.

The air was dusty and getting hot. The palace must have landed in a tropical area, Kickaha thought.

He watched the two ride away on the boat, which had two seats in tandem and was a very thin and lightweight metal structure supporting a small motor, a small storage space, and two rotatable beamers. The Great Mother was at the controls. Wemathol sat behind her. Kickaha was to stay behind the pile but keep on guard. His gate detector was in a small pouch hanging from the belt. A canteen was by him, and his beamer was in his hand, ready to shoot if the scaly man or Red Orc appeared. Though the room did not seem to be accessible behind him, he looked there now and then. The large masses of rubble might conceal an opening into the room approachable from the other side of the wall.

All was silent except for the occasional creaks caused by the shifting parts of the ruins. Anybody in here with good sense should get out of the structure before all of it crashes, he thought. But anybody with good sense wouldn't be in this mess in the first place. And I still hurt very much.

It seemed improbable that Khruuz could be tuned in to their radio frequencies, but it was best not to chance it. They were to use the radios only if a situation absolutely required it.

He felt helpless. Though he usually was content to be alone, he would have been glad to hear a human voice. Also, that the entire building might collapse and bury him at any moment made time seem to stretch out like a glowing hot wire in a drawing machine. If it got too thin, it snapped. That would be when the debris suspended above him fell through the ceiling.

He was beginning to sweat a lot from the increasing heat. However, the numbness of his legs seemed to be completely gone. Though they still pained him, he stood up. He was shaky but getting stronger. He drank deeply from the canteen Manathu Vorcyon had given him. A few minutes later, he walked out of the room. No use staying here. Not when Khruuz was prowling around out there and armed with God only knew what.

The going was not so tough at first. Though what was left of the hallway was jammed halfway up to the open ceiling, he could scramble up, slipping sometimes, crawl through the space between the top of the mound and the ceiling, where there was ceiling, and slide down the other side of the mounds. A beam of pale light slanted from the opening Wemathol had mentioned. Kickaha looked up through it. No mistake. The sky was green.

Beyond the hallway was a room the size of two Imperial palace ballrooms. But it was shattered. He was confronted with numerous obstacles: hillocks and dales of plaster chunks, pieces of wood, stone slabs and blocks, broken and unbroken marble pillars, marble chunks, and greater-than-life-sized stone statues. Many of the slabs and pillars and statues were sticking up at a slant from the mounds like cannons from the ruins of a fort. Also protruding were jagged broken-off legs and backs of chairs and tables; dented metal and wooden cabinets; broken bottles, the odors of spilled beer and wine making the air pungent; twisted and broken chandeliers; and warped frames of large paintings, the cloth fragments hanging from them. Getting over or around these made him sweat. The perspiration mingled with the white dust, covered his body and hair, and ran down into his eyes, stinging them. He thought that he must look like a pale ghost with scary red eyes.

Now and then, he took the gate-detector out of a belt pouch and turned it on. The instrument lit up a dozen times. But he could not use the Horn now to open them. Khruuz might be within hearing range.

The Great Mother had said that she and Wemathol would go to the northeast corner of the palace. From there, they would separate for individual searches. Once the scaly man was taken care of, they would find each other by radio. Kickaha headed toward the northeast section of the palace, but he was forced to take a circuitous path. Despite his strenuous climbing, his legs were gaining, not losing, strength.

When he got to the tremendous heap of debris on the other side of the huge room, he seemed to have deviated from a straight path. Manathu Vorcyon and Wemathol had probably ascended through an opening to the second story and then to the third. But he could not even see entrances to the next room. Towering peaks of debris blocked his view.

He began going up the slope of rubble but slid back now and then. The sliding material made noises. Near the top of the mound was an opening to a tunnel of sorts. It seemed to go through the pile and into the wall, which was somehow still standing. He used a tiny flashlight to illuminate the interior of the tunnel, which had been formed by accident. Two huge marble columns coming in almost parallel angles to each other but slanting somewhat downward had punched through the wall and stopped side by side. The big hole they must have made in the wall had been plugged up by a mass of large fragments. Stone slabs had crashed down to make a roof over the pillars. The pillars were not so close to each other that there was no space for him to move forward, molelike, between them. Some debris half-blocked the passageway, which pointed upward at about ten degrees from the horizontal. But he had room enough to pass the stuff half-blocking the tunnel behind him. Beyond the dark tunnel was light, feeble but brighter than that in this cramped space. If he could get through it to the next room, he would be coming out in a place an enemy lurking there would not expect. He began worming his way through it.

Though he was making as little noise as possible, he was not quiet enough. For a second, he envisioned Khruuz standing to one side at the end of the tunnel, waiting for anyone who came through it. No. If the scaly man was there, he would shoot his beamer rays down its length when he heard noise in the tunnel and would slice his enemy. In any event, he, Kickaha, could not stop going forward. And why would the scaly man be there? He wouldn't know there was a tunnel there.

When he cautiously poked his head from the thirty-foot-long passageway, he saw that he was near the top of a mountain of debris. Most of the ceiling of this gigantic room had fallen through and, perhaps, some of the floor of the third story. He took his time looking at the ruins below him. If anyone was hiding down there, he would have to be behind a very large mound near the wall at the other side.

His beamer in one hand, he slid down on his back. He silently cursed the noise he could not help making. When he got to the bottom, scratched and bleeding from small gashes and smarting from plaster dust in the wounds, he waited a while for an attack. None came. He went over smaller piles and then found behind the second mountainous ruin a gaping hole in the wall. It was large enough for a Sherman tank to pass through. In fact, it looked as if a tank had made the hole. He did not know what kept the rest of the much-cracked wall from collapsing.

He stepped through the hole after sticking his head through it to scout the territory. Above him, all the stories had partly fallen through. Down here, the light was almost that of dusk. Up there, it was bright. He could see a much larger piece of the green sky than he had seen in the hallway.

The heavens around the World of Tiers were the same color. Could Khruuz have gated the palace to the planet shaped like the Tower of Babylon? If so, why did he choose it? Or . . . No use speculating.

A pile of timbers and stone stuck out several feet from a twenty-foot-high jumble to his left. He had just seen something stir in the darkness under the ledge. The shapeless mass, covered with white dust, could be a man. He looked closely at it and finally determined that it had its back to him. That might be a ruse. Whoever it was could have seen him, then turned away to make him think he saw a dead or badly injured person. When he heard Kickaha's footsteps, he would twist his body to face him and would shoot. Maybe.

Kickaha got into a sort of ready-made foxhole in the rubble and then fired a beam near the figure's head. That would startle anyone who didn't have absolute control of his nerves. But the man did not move. Kickaha got out of the hole with the least noise possible and walked slowly along a curve toward the ledge. When he got within twenty feet of it, he saw that the figure was neither Khruuz nor Red Orc. It was Dingsteth. But his hands were no longer tied behind his back.

The creature must have ceased bleeding. It certainly had left no trail. Kickaha still did not go directly to it. When he stopped by it, he was half-concealed by the pile. He leaned over and poked the back of its head with the end of his beamer. It groaned.

"Dingsteth!" Kickaha said.

It muttered something. He dragged it out from under the ledge and turned it over. Under the dust on its skin were many black spots. Burns? Unable to hear distinctly what it was saying, Kickaha glanced around, then got to his knees and put an ear close to Dingsteth's mouth. Though his position made him feel vulnerable, he kept it.

"It's me, Kickaha," he said softly.

It said, "Khruuz . . . not believe that . . ."

"What? I can't hear you."

"Kickaha! Khruuz . . . when I said . . . not have data . . . in my brain . . . tortured me . . . did not believe me . . . took me along . . . got away . . . Zazel . . . proud of me."

"I'll get help for you," Kickaha said. "It may take some time . . ."

He stopped. Dingsteth's eyes were open. His mouth, filled with the diamond teeth, was still.

He had to break radio silence. Manathu Vorcyon would want to know about this. He called her at once, and she replied at once. After he told her what had happened, she said, "I am still where I told you we were going. I sent Wemathol to look for you. If he does not find you at the end of ten minutes, he will return to me."

If Wemathol was going to take only ten minutes for the search, he would be in the airboat. After twelve minutes had passed, he used the radio to ask Wemathol to report. But the clone did not reply.

Manathu Vorcyon's voice came immediately. "Something may have happened to Wemathol! I will give him two more minutes to report."

Which is mostly up and down and around and along, he thought. Fifteen minutes later, he stopped to give his aching legs time to recharge. When he felt stronger, he got to his feet and plodded on. Shortly thereafter, he came to another large area. Parts of the roof had fallen down on it. The sun blazed down through the opening but was past its zenith. It shone near one end of the room where a winding staircase by the wall had somehow escaped being smashed. Its upper part, shorn of its banister, protruded from the peak of a very high mound. He climbed to its top, though not without slipping and sliding and making noise. The staircase, made of some hardwood, seemed to be stable. He went up it slowly, looking above and below him at every step.

But with only twenty steps to go, he had to get down and grab the edge of the rise. From somewhere nearby, something had crashed with a roar as if it were a Niagara of solid parts. The staircase shook so much that he thought it was going to break from the wall. Screeching, it separated from the landing above. It swayed outward, then swayed inward and slammed up against the wall. The stone blocks of the wall moved, and some were partly displaced. He expected the wall to fall apart and carry the staircase with him. If that did not happen, the swaying and banging of the staircase would snap it off and tumble it to the heap thirty feet below.

Though he gripped the edge of the rise, he was moved irresistibly sidewards toward the open side of the staircase. A few more such whipping movements would shoot him off the steps even if the structure did not fall. And he could now see for only a few feet around him. Thick dust raised by the newly fallen mass stung his eyes and clogged his nostrils.

Suddenly, it was over except for a shuddering of the stairs. When that ceased, Kickaha began climbing on hands and knees. The structure was leaning away from the wall, though not quite at the angle of the Tower of Pisa. Not yet, anyway. The higher he climbed, the more the structure bent at its apex and the louder it creaked and groaned.

By then, he had to lean to the right to compensate for the leftward slant of the steps. When his hands clung to the rise of the highest step, he slowly and awkwardly stood up, balancing himself precariously, his left leg straighter than his right. Before him was the floor of the second story, exposed like a doll house by the ripping away of its wall. It was bending in the middle, groaning under the weight of a gargantuan pile of debris. It could collapse at any moment. He had to leap through the eight feet of space between him and the floor. Do it at once.

Or he could go back down the staircase, though it might snap off before he got far.

He reholstered the beamer. He would need both hands to grip the edge of the exposed floor if he could not soar out and up to it. Under normal circumstances, he could have made such a jump easily and landed on the floor with his feet. After glancing around, he crouched down and propelled himself outward. The staircase gave way then, bending down under the force of his jump. It was too much for it. It snapped and the upper part fell down and struck the heap with a loud crash.

Although the recoil of the staircase made the leap longer than he had planned, he reached the floor. His belly was even with the edge of the floor just before he began to fall. His arms banged against the floor, and his chest struck the edge. He was supporting his body with the upper part of his arms while his legs dangled. He twisted and threw his right leg up over the edge and pulled himself entirely onto the floor.

He was panting, and he wanted to lie on his back for a minute to recover his strength. But the wood underneath was bending, and he could feel alarming vibrations running through it. Maybe the floor, overburdened by the immense pile in the middle of the room, had been close to the point of breaking before his weight was added to it.

He scrambled to his feet, drawing the beamer from its holster as he did so. As he sped toward the nearest door to the north, he heard a great cracking noise. The floor suddenly slanted down. He was almost caught by its shifting, but he leaped through the doorway just in time. For a few seconds, he came close to being borne backward with the avalanche. A pile of debris plugged all but a narrow opening in the upper part of the doorway. He landed on its slope and clawed away at the rubble to keep going as it spilled out onto a floor that was no longer there. Dust billowed out from behind him and blinded him.

He managed to get over the top of the pile in the doorway, though it was like running on a ground that was moving in the opposite direction. When he got to the bottom of the pile on the other side, he was suddenly face down on the floor of a room. Most of the heap was gone, having avalanched into the emptiness of the room he had just left. Even so, his legs were now dangling over the bottom of the doorway. And the floor of the room that was to be his refuge was moving downward.

He pulled himself away from the edge, got up, and sprinted up the increasingly slanting surface of this floor, which was attached to the wall on the other side but would not be for long. Leaping over small piles of debris sliding toward him, racing around the larger heaps also sliding toward him, he strove to get to the exit to the room beyond this one. He did not make it. He was deafened by another roar, and he fell through to the room below. Somehow, he landed on his feet and rolled down a mound and ended, his breath and his wits knocked out of him, upon the back of a huge divan. He had been fortunate not to have been buried.

Also, the edge of the riven floor had missed by a few inches slamming into him. It undoubtedly would have killed him. As it was, it had only half killed him.

It took him an undeterminable time to regain all of his senses. Then he was aware of how much he hurt and of how many places on him were painful. But he got up. His beamer was still clutched in his hand, and the bag containing the Horn had not been torn from his belt. While the dust was still settling, he walked slowly forward. Though he felt like coughing, he suppressed it. And then he heard a cough from somewhere ahead of him.

He stopped. A vague form was moving slowly in the dust toward him. It seemed to be in the air a few feet from the surface. Wemathol in his airboat? Instead of calling out, he dropped behind a small mound and pointed his beamer at the object. Never assume anything—even if he had broken that rule now and then.

More debris fell in the next room, the one from which the unknown had come into this room. More dust billowed out, enveloping the object. He squinted toward where it had been, his eyes stinging and wet. If that was not Wemathol, then it must be Manathu Vorcyon. Or, if Khruuz had somehow gotten hold of an airboat, he could be riding it out there.

He waited. A minute passed by. Then he was startled by another crashing sound. This was followed by four less-loud collapses. The dust thickened. He held his nose and breathed out through his mouth to avoid sneezing. But a sneeze was building up in him that he would not be able to control. And then, someone out in the dust went "Ah! Choo!" This was followed by a series of nose blasts.

Kickaha, despite heroic efforts not to do so, sneezed mightily.

Though it was hard to do while the nasal explosions racked his body, he reached out and felt what seemed to be a large piece of broken crockery. He tossed it as far as he could to his right. If it made a noise that the hidden person could hear, it wasn't audible to him. His own sneezing drowned it out. There was no reaction from the being. No ray beam cutting through the dust; no voice.

He could not wait until the dust settled. The rider might have heat detectors or be wearing night-vision goggles. Or he could be lifting the boat up high so that he could spot anyone in the room after the dust settled down.

He crawled away from behind the mound, trying to do it silently and keeping down close to the floor. The best thing for me to do, Kickaha thought, is to stand up and get out of this room swiftly. But, if he did that, he could not avoid making a lot of noise and stumbling into and over debris. Moreover, he did not know where the exits were.

When he felt a large pile in front of him, he went behind it. To hell with radio silence. He called. Manathu Vorcyon's voice, much softer than usual, came at once. "What do you want?"

Kickaha whispered, "You still in the same place? I ask because there's someone on an airboat very close to me. I can't see him because of the dust."

"It is not I. And Wemathol would have answered you if he were capable of doing so. Make sure, though, before you shoot, that it is not he."

"Off," he said.

Kickaha groped around until he felt several large chunks of plaster. He cast these into the dust before him. But the unknown did not fire at the source of the noise. Probably his boat was hovering high up and was making sure of his target before he attacked.

That person had to be Khruuz.

He stood up and began making his way toward the far wall. After a few steps, he jumped to one side. Something wet had fallen on his left shoulder. He felt the spot with his right hand. Though he had to bring his fingers close to his eyes, he saw a dark mass of dust and something liquid.

Was it raining blood?

He looked upward. The particles were beginning to settle down. It would not be long before he would be able to distinguish any dark object near where the ceiling had been. Especially since the light was brighter up there.

He started walking again, then stopped. He had heard a low moan. After listening carefully for a moment, he stepped forward. He jumped aside with a suppressed oath. Something heavy had struck the floor near him. He walked as slowly and as silently as possible toward the source of the thump. It could be a trick, but he doubted it. The impact had sounded like the body of a man striking the earth. Wood or stone would have made a different sound. There had been a hint of a splat in the sound, flesh giving way and bone broken against the unyielding stone floor.

At last, he saw the thing. It was indeed Khruuz. He was lying on his back, his eyes open. Blood had spread out from under his body as if Death had unrolled a scarlet carpet for him. Even that thick skull had caved in. Coming closer to the corpse, though still warily, Kickaha saw that a wide and thick bandage was wrapped around its left thigh. Blood had trickled from it down the side of the leg. Clifton must have shot the scaly man before he was killed by him. Khruuz had only taken time enough to bandage himself before he gated Dingsteth with him for the invasion of the palace. He must have been aflame with desire for revenge. He could not wait to get it; he had lauched his attack despite his injury. But the slow loss of blood had weakened him so much that he had fallen off his airboat.

Score one for Clifton.

He radioed Manathu Vorcyon the news. She said, "It is unfortunate that we did not take him alive; he was such a repository of knowledge and the last of his kind. But I am also much relieved that he is no longer a danger to us. By the way, I can see the landscape around the palace. Khruuz gated not only the building but the lawns and gardens around it. They're wrecked, but I believe that Khruuz gated himself and Dingsteth to a lawn or garden after the palace had been transmitted here. He would not have wanted to be inside the palace when it landed. Then he entered it to finish the killing."

Kickaha said, "Now we can look for Anana and Red Orc."

"I understand your wish to do that," she said. "But first, we have to find Wemathol."

They talked for a few minutes. She would proceed from the northeast corner of the palace and search. He would be looking for the clone while he headed for her. They would keep in radio contact and describe where they were every five minutes.

Kickaha signed off. The airboat was hovering about fifty feet above him. He had no way to get to it. He shrugged and started walking and climbing. Eventually, he found an archway that was not entirely jammed with debris. Halfway through the next room, he saw a man propped up in the semidarkness against the side of a fallen and broken marble pillar. He turned his flashlight beam on the figure. It was Wemathol, unmoving, his eyes shut. Dust did not conceal the crimson color of his boots and headband. His chest was smeared with blood mixed with dust. His beamer was not in sight, and his only weapon was a dagger in a scabbard.

Kickaha cried out, "Wemathol!"

His voice was bounced back to him from the vast walls. The clone did not stir.

Kickaha lifted the wrist radio to his lips, then decided to determine Wemathol's exact condition before reporting. He came close to him and, bending over, spoke his name.

Wemathol's right foot kicked the beamer from Kickaha's hand.

=== 22 ===

*T*hough locked up by surprise for one of the few times in his life, Kickaha unfroze in a sliver of a second. He hurled himself at the man, stabbing at the same time with his pen-sized flashlight.

The Thoan had snatched out his long dagger as he straightened up. Kickaha grabbed the wrist just above the hand holding the dagger. At the same time, his flashlight drove toward his attacker's left eye. It would have punched through to the brain if the Thoan had not turned his head slightly. It caught in the corner of his eye, gashed it, and slid on. Kickaha dropped the flashlight and twisted the Lord's left wrist. At the same time, he turned his body sideways to prevent the man from kneeing him in the testicles. Though Kickaha had rotated his antagonist's wrist with such force that it should have been broken, he was unable to do more than half turn it. The man was indeed powerful. But his dagger dropped to the ground.

Kickaha leaned back then and jerked the man forward, at the same time shifting his footing so that his sidewise stance would enable him to swing the man around. But the man did not resist. He allowed Kickaha to whirl him around and cast him away as if he were a throwing hammer. He spun for ten feet, fell, rolled several times on the ground, and bounded to his feet as if he were a leopard.

Kickaha had charged him even while he was rolling. The Lord dashed for the beamer, which was lying between two small piles. Kickaha changed direction to intercept him. The Lord bent down to scoop up the weapon on the run. Kickaha leaped and struck with both feet the buttocks presented to him. The man cried out as he toppled forward. But he did not let loose of the gun even as he slid on his face and chest.

Though Kickaha had fallen on his back with a thump, he stood up quickly. The Lord turned over, blood welling from deep scratches and shallow gashes on his face, chest, and belly. Then he bent his torso up off the ground, swinging the beamer upward. Just before he pulled the trigger, Kickaha's throwing knife sped like a dark barracuda in a half-lit sea. Its point drove about an inch into the man's left biceps, and he dropped the beamer. But he jerked the dagger out and gripped it in his right hand. Then he rose to his feet with astonishing swiftness. Bending over, he reached with his left hand for the beamer.

Roaring, Kickaha leaped, and his feet slammed into the man's chest just as he straightened up. The beamer shot once, its violet ray slicing the twilight. Kickaha's right wrist burned. The weapon skittered across the floor. The breath drove out of the Lord's chest as he went backward. The dagger fell from his hand as he flailed his arms to keep his balance. But he fell on his back.

Kickaha had managed to twist so that, instead of slamming onto the ground on his back after his kick, he landed on his feet in a crouch. But he did not take the time to pick up the dagger. Hoping to catch the man while he was still lying down or in a vulnerable position while rising, Kickaha ran toward him. The Lord sprang upright as if he had been lifted by an invisible hand. He was holding something; he hurled it at Kickaha.

For a moment, Kickaha was half-dazed. His brain and body seemed numb. The stone had come flying out of the duskiness, slammed into his forehead, and stopped his charge. A chunk of red, apple-sized marble lay bloodstained on the ground. That it had not killed him or knocked him completely unconscious showed that the Lord was weakened. Or had made a bad pitch.

His own condition was not up to par. And he was at a disadvantage because the Lord had picked up the dagger. But he was also wheezing for breath, and blood was flowing from the wound in his upper arm.

Kickaha wiped his own blood from his forehead and his eyelids. When his wind was back, he would attack again.

Between gasps, he said, "Red Orc! How'd you escape! What did you do to Wemathol before you took his boots, headband, and dagger?"

The Thoan managed to smile. He said, "I did fool you!"

"Not for long."

"Long enough! Before I tell you how I got away from my prison, tell me what happened here."

Red Orc wanted to put off renewing the combat until he regained his breath. That was all right with Kickaha. He needed time, too. Time, he suddenly realized, to call Manathu Vorcyon. She would come a-flying. If, that is, she could find him. When he started to raise his arm, he saw that the radio was no longer on it. Where it had been was a burn wound. Red Orc's one shot had cut through the suction disc holding the radio and taken some skin with it. He was lucky that the ray had not severed his wrist.

Losing the radio was no handicap. He did not need her help, and he would be very disappointed if she, not he, killed Red Orc.

His breathing was not so quick now. He said, "Khruuz gated the entire palace to another universe. The World of Tiers, I believe. The rest you can figure out easily. Now, what's your story?"

While he had been talking, he had looked around hoping to see the beamer. No luck.

"Ah!" Red Orc said. "So that is it! Is the Khringdiz still alive?"

"No. Did Anana escape with you?"

"I do not know. I was able to crawl out from my prison after it collapsed. I lost much skin getting through some very tight openings. And then I saw Wemathol riding his airboat. I jumped down on him from a pile and knocked him off the boat. Unfortunately, that kept on going. During the struggle with Wemathol, his beamer fell through a hole in the floor and I could not find it later. When I broke his neck, I put on his boots and headband and took his dagger. I deceived you long enough to get you into this situation. And now I am here to end the saga of Kickaha."

"I'll see about that. What makes you believe that you can defeat me? You're inferior to me, though you're a Lord and I'm a *leblabbiy*."

"How can you say that?" Red Orc said loudly.

"You had to use me to get into Zazel's World after you had failed during a search of many thousands of years. I was the one who deceived Dingsteth and talked it into releasing us. You didn't have the imagination to think of the ghost-of-Zazel idea. I had you at my mercy when I locked you up here. You'd still be there if Khruuz hadn't gated the palace. So, what makes you think you're a better man than I am?"

"You're a *leblabbiy*, a descendant of the artificial humans we Thoan made in our factories!" Red Orc howled. "You are inherently inferior because we made your ancestors inferior to us! You were made less intelligent than we! You were made less strong and less swift! Do you think that we would be stupid enough to make beings who were our equals?"

"That may have been the case when you first made them," Kickaha said. "But there is such a thing as evolution, you know. If I am indeed one of a lowly lesser breed, why is it I have killed so many Lords and gotten out of so many of their traps? Why do they call me the Trickster, the Slayer of Lords?"

"You have slain your last Lord!" Red Orc bellowed. "From now on, I will be known also as Kickaha's Killer."

"Old English saying: 'The proof is in the pudding.' Get ready to choke on what I'm going to feed you," Kickaha said.

Red Orc was getting into a terrible fury, and that would shape his judgment. Or was he just pretending to be overwhelmed with anger so that his enemy would be too confident?

"I'm pleased you have the dagger," Kickaha said. "It gives you an advantage you really need."

"*Leblabbiy!*" the Thoan screamed.

"Don't just stand there and call me names like some ten-year-old kid," Kickaha said. "Try me! Attack! Let's see what you got!"

Red Orc yelled and ran at Kickaha, who stooped and picked up the marble chunk that had struck him in the forehead. He wound up like a baseball pitcher, which he had been when in high school. He aimed the stone for the Thoan's chest. But Red Orc stabbed at it, and it struck the point of the dagger. This was knocked loose from his grasp. No doubt, it also paralyzed his hand for a moment. In that time, Kickaha, yelling a war cry, was on him. Red Orc tried to dodge him, but Kickaha slammed into him and squeezed his hands around the thick neck and forced him to stagger backward. The Thoan tried to box both Kickaha's ears; Kickaha ducked his head so that he was struck on its upper part. The blows made his head ring, but he pulled the Thoan close to him, banged his head against Red Orc's (it was a question who was more dazed by this), and then fastened his teeth on Red Orc's neck.

The Thoan fell backward, taking Kickaha with him. Red Orc came out the worse from the fall. His breath whoofed out, and he had to fight Kickaha at the same time that he was trying to get his wind back. Kickaha was now in his own rage. He saw red, though it might have been his own blood or the Thoan's. Despite the impact and his loss of breath, Red Orc managed to turn over, taking Kickaha with him, and they rolled until they were stopped by a debris heap. Kickaha had fastened his teeth on the Lord's jugular vein and was biting as deep as he could. He did not expect to cut through the vein. He was no sharp-fanged great ape, but he strove to shut off the flow of blood.

Kickaha's body was pressed against Red Orc's left arm so tightly that, for some seconds, Red Orc could not get it free. But he brought the other arm up and over, a finger hooked. It dug deeply into Kickaha's right eye, and then was yanked back toward Red Orc. Kickaha's eye popped out and hung by the optic nerve. He was not aware of his other pains; his fury overrode them. But this one pierced through the haze of red.

Nevertheless, he kept on biting the vein. Red Orc then began slamming the side of Kickaha's head with the edge of his hand. That hurt and dazed Kickaha so much that he unclamped his teeth and rolled away. He was only vaguely aware that the optic nerve had been torn loose. When he stopped rolling, the lost eye, flat, its fluid pressed out of it, stared up at him, a few inches from the other eye.

That sent a surge of energy through him. He got to his feet at the same time that Red Orc rose. He charged immediately. Red Orc turned to meet him. He was borne backward as Kickaha's head slammed into his belly. Kickaha fell, too, but reached out and squeezed the Thoan's testicles. While Red Orc writhed in agony, Kickaha got up and jumped on him with both feet. The Thoan screamed; the bones of his rib cage were fractured.

That should have been the end of the fight. But Red Orc was not the man to be stopped by mere crippling and high pain. His hand shot out and gripped Kickaha's ankle even as he writhed, and he yanked with a strength he should not have possessed. Kickaha fell backward, though he twisted enough to keep from falling completely on his back. His shoulder struck the floor. Red Orc had half turned, his grip still powerful. Kickaha sat up and pried one of the Thoan's finger loose and bent it back. The bone snapped; the Thoan screamed again and loosed his clutch.

Kickaha got onto his knees and slammed his fist against the

Thoan's nose. Its bridge snapped. Blood spurted from his nostrils. Nevertheless, in a wholly automatic reaction, he hit Kickaha's jaw with his fist. It was not the knockout blow it would have been if Red Orc had not been weakened. It did make Kickaha's head ring again. By the time his senses were wholly back, he saw that Red Orc was getting back onto his feet. And now he was swaying as he stood above Kickaha.

"You cannot defeat me," he croaked. "You are a *leblabbiy*. I am Red Orc."

"That's no big deal. I am Kickaha."

Kickaha's voice sounded feeble, but he rolled away while the Thoan staggered after him. Red Orc stopped when he saw the dagger on the ground, and he went to it and picked it up.

"I will cut off your testicles, just as I cut off my father's," he said, "and I will eat them raw, just as I ate my father's."

"Easier said than done," Kickaha said. He stood up. "What you did to so many people, especially what you did to Anana, will drive me on, no matter how you try to stop me."

"Let us get this over with, *leblabbiy*. It is no use for you to keep hoping you will overcome me. You will die."

"Sometime. Not now."

The Thoan waved the dagger. "You will not get by this."

Looking at the man's face, squeezed with agony, and at his bent-over posture, Kickaha thought that he might be able to dance around Red Orc until he collapsed. But the chances were fifty-fifty that he might crumble first.

His hand brushed against the deerskin pouch containing the Horn. In his fury, he had forgotten about it. He pulled it out from the pouch and gripped its end as if it were a club. Ancient Shambarimen had not made the instrument to be used as a bludgeon. But it would serve. He advanced slowly toward the Lord, saying, "It will be told that you had to use a knife to kill an unarmed man."

"You would like me to cast it aside. But no one will have seen this fight. Too bad, in a way. It should be celebrated in epic poetry. Perhaps it will be. But I will be the one who tells others of how it went."

"Always the cowardly liar," Kickaha said. "Use the dagger. I'll kill you anyway. You'll gain even more fame as the only man ever to be killed by the Horn."

Red Orc said nothing. He came at Kickaha with the knife. The Horn swung and struck the Thoan's wrist as he jabbed. But Red Orc did not drop the knife. Instead, he lunged again, and the blade entered Kickaha's chest. But it only made a shallow wound because Kickaha grabbed the man's wrist with one hand and banged Red Orc over the head with the Horn. Red Orc tore his wrist from the grasp, retreated for several seconds, breathing heavily, then attacked again.

This time, he used one arm as a shield against the bludgeoning while he thrust with his right hand. His dagger sliced across Kickaha's lower arm, but Kickaha brought the Horn down and then up and slammed its flaring end into Red Orc's chin. Though the Thoan must have been dazed by the blow, he managed to rake the edge of the blade across Kickaha's shoulder and then gash the hand holding the Horn. Kickaha dropped it; it clanged on the ground.

Red Orc stepped swiftly forward. Kickaha retreated.

"You can run now," the Thoan said hoarsely. "That is the only way you can escape me. For a while, anyway. I will track you down and kill you."

"You have a lot of confidence for a beaten man," Kickaha said.

He stooped to pick up the bloody marble chunk. For a few seconds after he had straightened up, he was dizzy. Too much blood lost; too many blows on the head. But Red Orc was in as bad a condition. Who won might depend upon who passed out first.

He wiped the blood from the marble chunk on his short trousers, and he held it up for Red Orc to see.

"It's been used twice, once by you, once by me. Let's see what the third time does. I doubt you'll be able to bat it again."

Red Orc, wincing, crouched, his knife held out.

"When I was a youth on Earth," Kickaha said, "I could throw a baseball as if it were a meteorite hurtling through space. And I could throw a curve ball, too. A scout once told me I was a natural for the big league. But I had other plans. They didn't work out because I came to the World of Tiers and from there to other universes of the Lords. Let's see now how an Earthly sport is good for something besides striking out a batter."

He wound up, knowing that he was out of practice and that the irregularly shaped chunk was no lightweight ball. Also, he did not have much strength left. But he could summon it. And he was only ten feet from Red Orc.

The chunk flew spinning from his hand. Just as it did, the Thoan dropped to his knees and leaned to one side. But the stone, far from going into its target, the chest, veered off the path Kickaha had intended for it. It thudded against Red Orc's head just above his hairline. The Thoan fell over on his side, dropping the dagger. His eyes and mouth were open; he did not move.

Kickaha picked up the dagger while keeping his one eye on the Thoan. Then he slammed his boot into the man's side. The body moved, but only because it had been kicked.

Kickaha knelt down and ripped off the man's shorts. He held up the testicles and prepared to cut them off. He might eat them raw. He did not know if he was up to it. But, despite his exhaustion, he was still raging. This Thoan must suffer what he had intended to inflict upon his enemy.

Manathu Vorcyon's voice came to him. "Kickaha! You cannot do that! You are better than he! You are not the savage he is!"

Kickaha looked up at the Great Mother with his good eye. She was sitting on her airboat. But both were blurred. The good eye was not so good.

"The hell I'm not!" he said. His own voice seemed far away. "Watch me!"

He did it with one swipe. And then everything rushed away from him, and the darkness of nothing rushed in to fill the space.

23

Kickaha's wounds were healed, and a new eye had grown in the socket. The latter process had taken forty days, during part of which time his eye had been a nauseating jellylike mass. But he was as fit and as whole as ever.

He sat near the edge of the monolith on which was the palace Wolff had once occupied as Lord of this world. Now and then, Kickaha sipped a purplish liquor from a cut-quartz goblet. He looked up at the green sky and yellowish sun and then at the vast panorama below him, unique among the many universes.

The palace was on top of a massive and soaring stone pillar, the highest point of this Tower of Babylon—shaped planet. It soared from the center of a circular continent, the Atlantis tier. This, in turn, was on top of a larger monolith, the Dracheland tier. Below this tier was the still larger tier that Kickaha called the Amerind, his favorite stomping grounds. Below this was the Okeanos level. A person on its edge would see nothing but space, empty except for the air filling it. If you jumped over the edge, you fell for a very long time. Where you ended up, Kickaha did not know.

Theoretically, if you had a very powerful telescope and the humidity was very low, you could see to the lowest tier, the outer part of it, anyway. He was content with the view he had.

Anana had survived the collapse of her prison suite, but when she was carried out of the room five days after Khruuz had gated the palace, she was severely injured and much dehydrated. Kickaha had stayed with her until she had recovered. Despite his nursing, she still had hated him.

Red Orc's wounds had healed themselves. Though not imprisoned, he was closely watched. Red Orc was no longer his name; it was now just Orc. He had not been given a choice of lifelong incarceration or having his memory shorn to the age of five. The Great Mother had worked with the Thoan's computer until she had found the access code that opened up all the files. She was probably the only one in the many universes who could have done it, and that took her a long time.

After the machine had been built, the Thoan was placed in a chair and subjected to the memory-stripping process. Now, he was only five years old in mind. Those raising him, volunteer native house servants, would give him the love and attention every child required. Kickaha was not glad that he had not killed the man who had robbed him of the Anana Kickaha had known. But he could not hate the man who was no longer Red Orc. However, it would be a long time, if ever, before he would like him.

One problem with Anana had been solved. The machine had been used to strip her memory of the events immediately after Orc had taken away her memory.

The ethics of doing this without her consent had bothered Kickaha. But not very much. She was no longer in love with Orc because she did not remember him. And, now, she did not hate Kickaha. Never mind that she did not love him either. He had already started his campaign to win her back. How could he not succeed? Modesty aside, what other man in all the universes could compare with him?

The Great Mother had returned to her own world, but she and Kickaha would visit each other now and then.

He looked again at the view. Unsurpassed in beauty, in mystery, in promised adventure!

He would never again leave this world, the land area of which was larger than Earth's. To roam in it forever with Anana by his side would be to live in Heaven. Though it would be unlike Heaven in that it had a streak of Hell and he could be killed . . . Ah! that gave it its savor.

"My world!" he shouted. And while those words soared out over the planet, they were followed by a roar like a lion notifying everybody that this was his territory.

"Kickaha's World!"